THE
GENERAL
& THE
LADY

A TRUE STORY OF CIVIL LOVE AND WAR

J. PAUL HICKEY

PAGE PUBLISHING, INC.
Conneaut Lake, PA

First originally published by Page Publishing 2020

Cover Artwork, "The Last Promise" by Dale Gallon
www.gallon.com

ISBN 978-1-64701-537-4 (pbk)
ISBN 978-1-64701-538-1 (digital)

Printed in the United States of America

Praise for J. Paul Hickey's *The General & The Lady*

"Between the flashing brilliance of Hickey's description of battle and the delicacy with which he treats the story of a forbidden love, The General & the Lady proves that Hickey is worthy to stand in the company of such masters of the modern Civil War novel as Michael and Jeff Shaara. The battle scenes, from Mexico to Virginia to Pennsylvania, are brought to vivid life as is the delicate dance of two gentle hearts in this gallant period. I would recommend this without qualm to any fan of military or historical fiction-the details are real and true while the heart's gladness and terrible sorrow are enough to bring tears to the most 'manly eyes.' It's a great book."
—Terry Irving
4-time Emmy-Winning Journalist.
Bestselling Author of Courier
and Warrior and Editor of On the
Frontlines of the Television War.

* * *

"J. Paul Hickey's The General and the Lady offers a powerful work of historical fiction that reminds us of the remarkable treasure trove of stories that live in the past. A master storyteller, Hickey delivers a veritable page-turner in The General and the Lady, an unforgettable novel that will leave you pondering the characters and their exploits long after you've finished this delightful book."
—Kenneth Womack, author
of I Am Lemonade Lucy

Among those who were eminent in the late war for martial ability, General Reynolds stands in the first rank. His life had been devoted to the profession of arms from his youth, and when the noise of battle sounded in his ears, his soul, instinct with warlike custom, was aroused to the deed of heroism.

—Samuel P. Bates, *Martial Deeds of Pennsylvania*

* * *

She spent the latter half of her life...in view of the Hudson River, the same river that ran along West Point where John Reynolds had received the education that had brought him to the Army and, ultimately to her and then his death. Kate Hewitt could never escape, it seems, any part of her past.

—Marian Latimer, *Is She Kate? The Woman Major General John Fulton Reynolds Left Behind*

PREFACE

The story you are about to read is true. To further paraphrase the old TV crime show *Dragnet*, some of the dialogue has been altered or imagined, as have some of the events, to protect the integrity of the story.

This is a work of fiction, based on historical fact. The characters are, or were, real. Major General John Fulton Reynolds truly was a highly admired officer of the Union Army before and during the Civil War. Catherine Mary Hewitt truly was referred to as Kate. They truly fell in love. They met either in San Francisco or while traveling to the East Coast via steamship from the City by the Bay. Historical documents differ on that part of the story. In our imagination, they met onboard the boat.

General Reynolds was killed during the Battle of Gettysburg in 1863. No spoiler alert needed here. Volumes have been written about him and his exploits. He occupies a notable place in Civil War history.

Less is known and, therefore, less has been written about Kate Hewitt. As Marian Latimer writes in her book *Is She Kate? The Woman Major General John Fulton Reynolds Left Behind*, "To find Kate Hewitt it becomes necessary to work backwards and ignore the commonly accepted 'facts.'"

We do know that Kate had a difficult childhood. We do know that she traveled from New York to California as a young woman.

We do know, raised as a Baptist, she converted to Catholicism. We do know that she fell madly in love with John Reynolds.

Countless historical tomes have been written about Reynolds. Those are his true stories. The little that has been written about Kate Hewitt is also historical and factual to the extent possible. Those are her stories.

This novel is their story as it truly happened, and as we imagine it happened. For example, did they really have long conversations about what it takes to be a soldier in the nineteenth century? It is easy to believe they did. We know they had serious and intimate conversations about other aspects of their relationship. What we imagine they might have said to each other shows up on the pages to follow.

In addition, John Reynolds was a prolific letter writer, often sending long descriptions of his experiences, feelings, and opinions to members of his family. Much of his writing has been preserved. Franklin and Marshall College in Lancaster, Pennsylvania, Reynolds's hometown, keeps many of those letters on file. Furthermore, excerpts from some of the letters have been included in historical documentation of his life.

Letters come from thoughts. Thoughts can become words. So, it is in this novel that some of the general's thoughts written on paper become words he speaks. In those cases, the source of those word-thoughts is referenced.

This is a story of two Americans who loved each other during a time when other Americans were doing their best to kill each other. It is love and war hand in hand, but still in mutual competition where victory is hard-won, if won at all.

PROLOGUE

Gettysburg, Pennsylvania
July 1, 1863

Major General John Fulton Reynolds sits high in the saddle, "like a Centaur," as described by one of his subordinates, "tall, straight and graceful" astride his horse Fancy, a powerful, black stallion.[1] The day is hot and very humid. The moisture in the air is thick. He can see in the distance soft, wispy clouds, fog-like and hanging low over the tree-covered verdant forests of the foothills surrounding Gettysburg, Pennsylvania. The clouds are so low, they are massaging the tops of the trees. They remind Reynolds of cotton balls, suspended in mid-air. Far off to the southeast he can see dark, ominous storm clouds over Washington, DC, a portent, he thinks, of the dangerous political firestorm besieging his country.

As he surveys the scene in front of him, the Union officer is not happy. He can see, through a forest of trees known as Herbst Woods, a large brigade of Confederate soldiers advancing on the position held by the unit he commands.

He is about a mile northwest of Gettysburg. The seventy-five-thousand-strong Confederate Army, under the leadership of General Robert E. Lee, is making a move to invade Pennsylvania on multiple fronts.[2] Gettysburg is one of Lee's key targets. Over the next three days, this is fated to be one of the most decisive battles of the Civil War.

Reynolds has command of the left wing of the Army of the Potomac meant to defend Gettysburg. He has, under his command, three corps of Union soldiers. The general has been awake on this hot first day of July since four in the morning. He had spent the night near Emmitsburg, Maryland, just over the border from Pennsylvania. Reynolds had been ordered to move his men north toward Gettysburg to relieve the First Cavalry Division led by fellow West Point graduate, General John Buford.

All during his move north on the Emmitsburg Road toward Gettysburg, Reynolds had done his best to determine the strength and exact whereabouts of the Confederate enemy. It was difficult because this area of Pennsylvania is marked by ridges and valleys and areas of heavily forested land, giving the invading Southern soldiers plenty of cover.

But, now that he finally sees the gray uniforms of the Confederacy advancing through the trees of Herbst Woods, Reynolds moves quickly to fortify his position. Reynolds knows Robert E. Lee, another West Pointer, well enough that he suspects what the wily Confederate general is up to. The enemy soldiers Reynolds sees are only the tip of the spear. He knows Lee always keeps large numbers of troops in reserve. *This is going to be a very big problem*, he thinks, nodding to himself.

Looking around, he can see a Union infantry brigade off in the distance about a mile away. He orders messengers to ride out and tell the unit to hurry forward. Reynolds, himself, then rides off in another direction where he finds the Second Wisconsin Brigade.

"Forward, forward, men!" he shouts. "Drive those fellows out of that woods!"

General Reynolds is frantic with urgency.

"Forward! For God's sake, forward!" he shouts again.[3]

The brigade surges forward with Reynolds in the vanguard. Massive musket fire bursts forth from the trees as the Confederates take aim at the advancing Northerners. The scene is all smoke and noise from the rifle and artillery fire mixed with men yelling as they charge forward, others screaming in pain as they fall, wounded and killed by Confederate minié balls and bullets striking them down.

Knowing that his men are vastly outnumbered, General Reynolds looks around to see if he can find other reinforcements. Among the Confederate riflemen is one who had taken up a position in a nearby tree. He has a clear view of the Union general, sitting high atop that black stallion. The Southern soldier takes aim and fires. As Reynolds turns his head, searching for more troops, the round fired by the Confederate soldier smashes into the back of his neck behind the right ear.[4]

The black stallion bolts in panic. Reynolds falls hard to the ground. His right foot is caught in a stirrup, and he is dragged about ten yards as his horse flees. Then his foot lets loose. He lies still on his left side. His orderly, Sergeant Charles Veil, sees him fall. He jumps from his horse and runs to help his commander. Veil has great admiration for his boss. He would later say that "wherever the fight raged the fiercest, there the General was sure to be found, his undaunted courage always inspired the men with more energy and courage."[5]

With rebels shooting at them from less than a hundred paces away, Veil quickly grabs the stricken general's body by its arms and, with help of two officers, drags it from the line of fire. As they do, Reynolds lets out what seems like a deep sigh and breathes no more. He is dead.[6]

As the men struggle with the lifeless body, Confederates yell at them from the tree line.

"Drop him! Drop him!"[7]

They ignore the taunts and continue to move their commander to a safer spot.

Later, as his aides are examining the general's body, they discover a Catholic medallion hung around his neck. That is strange to them because they know he was not Catholic. Why was he wearing it? They also see a gold ring hanging from another chain. It is inscribed with the words *Dear Kate*. They had never heard him mention anyone named Kate. Stranger still, they notice that his West Point ring is missing. West Point officers traditionally never remove those rings. Where could it be, they wonder?

The answers to those questions would lead to one of the best-kept secrets of the Civil War.

CHAPTER ONE

San Francisco
July 1860

The Army officer stood at the railing of a steamship as it sailed out of San Francisco Bay. Major John Reynolds gazed at the ocean in front of him, idly smoking a cigar while contemplating what might be coming next in his military career. He was heading home, to Lancaster, Pennsylvania, after spending long years at distant outposts in such states as Louisiana, Texas, and Oregon, in the territories of Utah and Washington. He had fought Mexicans. He had fought Indians. He had even gone up against the Mormons, for God's sake. Mormons, he grumbled to himself. He had a problem with Mormons.

At forty years old, Reynolds was feeling restless. That was not unusual for him. It was a behavioral quirk of his that he always felt as though he had to be on the move. Tall and ruggedly handsome, John Fulton Reynolds could come across as stern and aloof. He was a man of high principles. Yet, at times, he seemed almost petty when matters didn't go his way. Still, he was highly respected by the men he served under and by the men who served under him.

The sense of disquiet he was feeling now was born out of disappointment and more than a little anger at the way he'd been treated by his superiors. He had proven himself on the battlefield. He knew he certainly had during the Mexican-American War more than a decade ago. He had citations to prove that. Major Reynolds had also served with distinction in a peacetime military during the years since, proving his organizational skills as well.

Nevertheless, his requests for specific assignments had fallen on deaf ears. The position of commissary of subsistence had become available. Reynolds believed he was well suited for the job. As commissary, he would have had authority over hundreds of millions of dollars of supplies for the Army, a huge responsibility. He thought there was "a good chance," as he wrote in a letter to his family,[8] that he would get the appointment. Now that six years had passed the major still harbored ill will toward Secretary of War Jefferson Davis who had denied the request and gave the position to someone else.

By now, the sun had set on the Pacific horizon and the steamship had reached the open ocean as twilight fell over the water. Reynolds took a long, deep draw on his cigar and let out a large cloud of smoke as he thought about what he believed was the second affront against him.

Five years ago, he had learned of a vacancy for a commander of a light battery of the Third Artillery Regiment. The unit was fully equipped with guns and horses. He had hunted and ridden horses all his life growing up in Pennsylvania. A light battery is designed to be highly mobile and flexible, just the thing for his restless spirit. In another letter home, Reynolds had written, "A Light Battery, the very thing of all others that I wish for. By my services in that arm and, I trust, my reputation in the Army, I have every claim to this particular company."[9]

Still stinging from the failure to land the commissary position, he had even asked his brother Jim, who had become politically connected, to speak with Jefferson Davis. "Remind him," Reynolds had written to Jim, "how last year he did me a great injustice when in the face of every military recommendation he overlooked my application and services when he appointed my junior, Captain Kilburn, to the Commissary Department." Then, in an obvious fit of pique, Reynolds had written, "I shall be very much tempted to resign if I am treated unjustly this time."[10]

A few months later, Reynolds had written his brother another letter asking Jim to redouble his efforts on the matter. This time his bitterness had come through loud and clear.

"I am satisfied of one thing now," he had written to Jim. "In the Army, merit is no recommendation and political influence is everything. I have given it a fair trial and give it up." Then he added, "I may say that I have never been so fully disgusted with the Army as within the last twelve months."[11]

Disgusted as he may have been, Major Reynolds continued to follow orders and perform as a dedicated officer of the United States Army. In the summer of 1856, he found himself in the far west at Fort Orford in Oregon where he commanded troops who fought the Indians in and around the Rogue River. There had been skirmishes between the Indians and white settlers in the area. The fighting was relatively brief, and when it was over, Reynolds had once again returned to his obsession, getting command of a light battery.

"I have the strongest claim to it of any Captain in the Regiment," he had written in yet another letter. "Should Mr. Davis give it to anyone else I do not see there is any chance of ever getting justice in the Army and shall think it is almost time to think of leaving it."[12]

He finally got the command for which he had lobbied so hard, but it was something of a hollow victory. By the time he had taken over Battery C of the Third Regiment, the Army was modernizing weapons, developing long-range guns to replace light artillery. Furthermore, the battery had been stripped of its most appealing features. The guns were fixed, no longer so highly portable. To make matters worse for Reynolds, the unit had no horses.

Standing the deck of the ship now, he was still feeling irritable about those turns of events. Leaning on the railing, watching the setting sun, he recognized he was being a little cranky and more than a little petulant but, *By God*, he thought, *I'm justified.*

He wasn't even sure he was all that enthused about his next assignment. He was headed back east to become the commandant of cadets at the US Army Military Academy at West Point. There was a time when he would have been eager to return to the Point. He had told his sister back in 1847 that "I should be very glad if I could be ordered to West Point in any capacity."[13] He had graduated from West Point in 1841, and returning there should be a pleasing homecoming. In his unhappy mood now though, he groused that the posting would be very different from commanding men in the field. His feeling was that "the position to be filled is no sinecure for any man."[14]

His dark thoughts were interrupted by the presence of another person who had approached the railing twenty or so feet away from Reynolds. He glanced over and could see that it was a young woman. Even in the dimming light, he could see that she was very attractive. No, the lady was more than that. She was beautiful, with blonde hair and blue eyes. She was small of stature, and he could see she had large round eyes, full lips, and a lovely Greek nose.

The young woman could feel his eyes on her. With his six-foot height, dark hair, thick black beard, and penetrating eyes, the major presented an imposing profile. One of his soldiers much later wrote that "his look and manner denoted uncommon coolness, and he spoke not unpleasantly. His countenance was not likely to encourage familiarity."[15] Another soldier, a fellow officer and friend, General George Meade described Reynolds as "a man of very few words."[16]

Nevertheless, the woman turned her head demurely and nodded slightly at Reynolds in a way of greeting. Caught slightly off guard, the major quickly tipped his hat and said politely in a deep voice, "Good evening, ma'am. I hope I haven't offended you by staring."

"Why, not at all, sir, and a good evening to you," she replied. "I take no offense."

"I was just surprised to see someone else out here on deck, is all," he said.

"It is such a lovely evening," she said. "I just love the smell of the sea and the beauty of San Francisco there off in the distance. See how the lanterns on the streets create such a warm glow to the city? And this breeze! How wonderful it is!" She shook her head briskly to allow her long blonde hair to wave and flow in the light wind.

Reynolds was intrigued. He smiled, bright white teeth showing through the dark facial hair.

"Yes, ma'am. It is a delightful evening" was all the man of few words said.

"I see you are in the military," she said, looking pointedly at his uniform.

"Yes, ma'am. The Army."

"Are you an officer? Yes, I think you are," she said, her eyes twinkling in the subdued lights of the steamboat. "At least, I think that's what your shoulder boards tell me. Am I right?"

"Yes, ma'am. You are exactly right. I hold the rank of major."

"A major? My, my! That's pretty high up, isn't it? You must be very important!"

The young woman smiled broadly, boldly flirting with Reynolds now. He blushed beneath his dark beard.

"Oh, no, ma'am," he chuckled. "Not very important at all. There are a lot of men who outrank me. I'm only partway up the totem pole, so to speak."

Growing serious, she frowned and looked up at the man. She walked closer to him and tilted her head to ask another question.

"Is it, um, hard being in the Army these days? I mean, isn't it dangerous with all this talk about bad feelings between abolitionists and slave owners, and that awful raid at Harper's Ferry last year by that man, um…" She put her fingers to her chin, trying to remember the name. "John, um…"

"Brown?" John said.

"Yes. Brown. John Brown. That was horrible! Seven people killed. Awful. Just awful! I hear folks are really mad about what happened."

"Yes, ma'am. I reckon so," Reynolds replied. "Things are a little worrisome right now. But you needn't fret. The Army and the decision makers in Washington, you know, the politicians, have everything under control."

Reynolds had stronger opinions about the Harper's Ferry massacre than he let on. Although a Northerner, he was not necessarily antislavery. He seemed almost ambivalent about the subject. But he had no truck with abolitionists. While still on duty in the West, he had written a letter to his sisters in which he said, "I think if they could hang along with old Brown…and few more of the abolition stripe, it would eventually stop this agitation for a time, at least."[17]

But with this young lady, he kept all that to himself. "This will all work out, I'm sure" was all he said.

"Well, I hope so," the woman said. "I've even heard some folks say…" She lowered her voice to a whisper, as if to keep anyone from overhearing her, although they were the only two people on the deck right then. "Some folks say we might be headed for war. Is that even possible. A war? Right here?"

"Uh, I'm not at all sure it will come to that," the major said, trying to sound sure. Truth be told, he was not sure at all. On the contrary, from a military strategic point of view he thought war was a real possibility given all the heated rhetoric he'd heard about in Washington and elsewhere after the Harper's Ferry incident.

"Well, I hope you're right, Major…Major…say, what is your name, if I may ask?" the woman asked, playful once again.

"Reynolds, ma'am. Major John Reynolds."

"I am so pleased to meet you, Mr. Major John Reynolds!" She smiled and thrust out her right hand. "My name is Catherine Hewitt. My friends call me Kate."

Reynolds reached out to shake her hand.

"Very pleased to make your acquaintance, Miss Hewitt."

"Oh, please. Call me Kate!"

"Does that mean we're friends?" He laughed. "I mean, we've just met and all."

"Well, this is going to be a very long voyage, and I think, by the end of it, we will be friends. We certainly won't be enemies, I believe. So, let's be friends right now!" She smiled.

It was, indeed going to be a long voyage. Their steamship out of San Francisco was bound for Panama. Once there, the passengers would disembark and ride a train across the isthmus to the Atlantic side of the country. There they would board another steamship to sail up the eastern seaboard to New York. All in all, the trek would take more than a month, depending on the weather. Catherine Hewitt and John Reynolds would have plenty of time to get to know each other.

"Well," she said finally. "I think it is about time that I retire. Perhaps I will see you in the morning, Major Reynolds?"

"It would be my pleasure," he responded with a smile.

"Well then. Good night, sir."

"Good night, Miss Hewitt…I mean, Kate! Sleep well."

With a little wave, Kate turned and headed down the deck to find her cabin. John watched her go. His sour mood had disappeared. *This isn't going to be such a bad trip, after all*, he thought.

* * *

The next morning, Major Reynolds sat at a breakfast table in the dining area of the steamship. He kept an eager eye out for the woman he had met on the deck the night before. She had delighted him with her easy laugh and twinkling eyes, and he was looking forward to a further conversation with her. He knew there was a word to describe her. What is that word? He furrowed his brow in thought trying to come up with it. Fetching! Yes, that's it. She's fetching. Very much so, indeed!

He looked up to see Kate Hewitt entering the dining room. He stood up quickly to catch her attention. She saw him and headed in his direction, a young girl following in her wake.

"Why, good morning, Major Reynolds. I trust you had a good sleep," she said, smiling brightly.

"That I did, ma'am. Thank you for asking. And you?" he asked.

"I had a lovely sleep, thank you," she said. "I just love the sound of the water on the side of the boat, don't you? And that gentle rocking during the night was so peaceful. I certainly hope it stays that way for the rest of the voyage."

"So do I, ma'am. So do I," the major replied, nodding his head. He looked at the young girl.

"And who do we have here?" he asked, pleasantly.

"Major Reynolds, may I have the pleasure of introducing you to Miss Catherine Dunn? Yes, she has the same first name as I."

Kate looked at the girl.

"Catherine, please meet Major John Reynolds of the United States Army."

John bowed slightly and said, "It is my pleasure to make your acquaintance, ma'am."

Catherine giggled softly.

"It is nice to meet you, too, sir," she said.

"Um, Miss Hewitt and Miss Dunn." John motioned toward the table. "Would you care to join me for breakfast? Perhaps some biscuits and sausage? Perhaps some tea?"

"Why, I believe we would like that, Major," Kate said. "Thank you so much for asking. That's very kind of you, sir. How is it the French say it? C'est tres bien, or something like that."

She and Catherine giggled again as Reynolds stepped around the table to pull out a chair for Kate and signaled a waiter to bring another one for Catherine.

"My, you are indeed an officer and a gentleman!" Kate smiled as she sat down. Reynolds gently pushed her chair in closer to the table as she got comfortable. "Thank you, kind sir," she said.

He did the same for Catherine when the waiter arrived with an extra chair. As Reynolds regained his chair, the waiter addressed the three of them.

"Good morning, everyone. May I get you something to drink to start your breakfast?"

"What would you like, Miss Hewitt," the Major asked.

"Oh, please do call me Kate, Major. Remember? We agreed last night. We're friends!" She smiled brightly once more.

"All right, then," he responded with a smile of his own. "What would you like…Kate?"

She looked at the waiter.

"I believe I would like a cup of tea," she said. "And perhaps a little juice, please. Would that be all right?"

"Yes. ma'am. That would be fine," the waiter said. "And you, ma'am," he said to Catherine.

"I'll have tea, too, please," she said, shyly.

"And the gentleman?" the waiter said, looking at Reynolds.

"Just coffee for me, please. Make it strong, if you would. I like my coffee strong."

"Yes, sir. Strong it is."

The waiter turned and headed for the galley.

"Major Reynolds, Catherine is an orphan I met in San Francisco. She is ten and is under my care now, traveling with me to Philadelphia. I plan to enroll her in a good school there. She is very bright," Kate said, turning to smile at her charge.

John thought it slightly odd that a ten-year-old girl would be traveling all the way across the country escorted by a woman to whom she was not related and without the protective accompaniment of a gentleman. However, he kept his counsel and said nothing about that.

Kate looked through the porthole next to the table. The Pacific Ocean stretched out before her, radiant blue, with no land in sight. The water was relatively calm, and the morning sun was shining brightly as the steamship plowed south on its way to Panama.

"It is so beautiful out here on the water, don't you think, Major?"

He paused for a moment, then said, "I think three things, Kate. First, I think I'd like it if you called me John. Or, even Josh, if you'd like. That's what some of my friends at West Point called me. Josh. And, as you say, we are friends now, right?" John tilted his head and smiled.

Kate laughed. "Yes, sir, John. Josh. We are. First-name basis!" She reached out to shake his hand. He returned the favor, his large weathered hand enveloping her small delicate fingers. They shook hands briefly and let go.

"And while we are at it," the major said, looking at the young girl, "do you mind if I call you Catherine?"

The little girl giggled again and said softly, "Yes. That would be okay."

"Good. That's the second thing settled. Now, the third thing," John continued. "I agree with you, Kate. It is certainly beautiful out there. I understand now why my brother decided to join the Navy."

Kate looked at him with wide-eyed interest.

"Oh," she said. "You have a brother?"

At that moment, the waiter returned carrying a tray, which held a pot of tea, a pot of coffee with steam drifting out the top, a plate containing biscuits, small containers of cream and sugar, some jam and butter, three linen napkins and silverware. He placed everything on the table in front of Kate and John.

"May I get you anything else?" the waiter asked.

John and Kate looked at each other. Each nodded no. So did Catherine.

"No, I don't think so," the major said to the waiter. "Not right now. Thank you very much."

"Yes, sir," the waiter said. "Ladies," he said to Kate and Catherine as he turned and walked over to another table where other passengers were ready to order their breakfasts.

"So, you have a brother," Kate repeated as she reached out to pick up a biscuit and lifted a knife to dip into some butter and jam.

"Actually, I have three brothers. One of whom, William…I call him Will…is in the Navy. Right now, he is on sick leave in Hawaii treating a leg tumor. I think it's pretty serious."

He stopped talking to put some sugar in his coffee.

"I'm so sorry to hear that," Kate said solemnly. "I hope he will be all right."

John just nodded. Then he continued.

"One of my other brothers, Sam, is also in the Army, and brother Jim is a lawyer. Or at least he was. He retired a few years ago and now is active in Pennsylvania politics."

"So, you have three brothers," Kate continued. "Any sisters?"

"Oh, yes." He laughed. "Five of them. Let's see, there's Lydia and Catherine."

He looked at Catherine Hewitt with raised eyebrows and a grin. She laughed merrily.

"Catherine seems to be a highly popular name around here," John said, looking at young Catherine. They all laughed.

"Then there is Harriet. We call her Hal. And Eleanor and Jane."

"My goodness!" Kate exclaimed "That's quite a family."

"Yes, you could say it got plenty noisy around the Reynolds home when I was growing up. There would have been even more, but four others, two boys and two girls, died while they were just infants."

"Oh dear," was all Kate could say. "I am so sorry."

"Thank you, but they passed away a long time ago. I never really knew them."

Kate looked at him with sympathetic eyes. Then she smiled kindly.

"What was it like for you growing up, John? Where are you from? Tell me more about yourself." She grinned. "Just who is this dashing man with whom I am sharing a breakfast table? What's his story?"

Major Reynolds chuckled and took another sip of coffee while Kate took a bite of her biscuit.

"Well, let's see," John said. "I grew up in Lancaster, Pennsylvania, which is about seventy or so miles west of Philadelphia. As I indicated, we had a large family. It was a happy family, really. My father was a newspaper man. He ran the *Lancaster Journal* for a while, then moved to Cornwall, Pennsylvania, because he had been offered a job managing a big ironworks factory there."

John picked up a butter knife and slipped it into the jam to slather it on one of the biscuits. All the while, he continued to talk.

"My brothers and I hunted and fished a lot when we were kids. It was great hunting territory. We got to be fairly decent shots. We hunted so much. We'd bring game and fish home so often, our ma said the family would never go hungry."

The major, warming to the subject, continued to describe his childhood with enthusiastic eloquence. For a man of few words, he had a lot to say, regaling Kate with anecdote after anecdote about his youth. She was fascinated and listened to him with rapt attention. His ability to paint word pictures made her feel as though she were there, in Lancaster, reliving the life and times of Major John Reynolds.

CHAPTER TWO

Lancaster, Pennsylvania
August 1831

The two young boys moved stealthily through the briars and thick turkey grass lining the Big Swamp near their Lancaster, Pennsylvania home. They both were armed with long unwieldy shotguns on this hot August morning.

"Slow down," the youngest of the two hissed at his older brother. "You're gonna scare the quail!"

"Aww, pipe down yourself," the older boy growled in reply. "It's your clamoring that gonna spook the birds. We'll never get close enough if you don't shut your trap!"

Young John, he was called Johnny then, and Will Reynolds were fairly experienced hunters for how young they were. William was sixteen years old. Johnny was just eleven. But the two of them had been introduced to rifles and shotguns early in their short lifetimes. Lancaster had long been an important center for the manufacturing of firearms that were adapted to frontier life. Some of the earliest models of American long rifles were made in southeastern Pennsylvania by German gunsmiths who had immigrated and settled there in the 1700s. The boys often went hunting for wild turkeys, rabbits, and woodcock, as well as for quail, in the woods and fields lining Long Rifle Road and other sections of Lancaster.

As they rounded a copse of oak trees, the brothers spotted a covey of quail about thirty yards ahead, feeding in a shallow ravine. Without a word, Will and Johnny each silently took a knee and lifted their shotguns, aiming at the quarry in front of them. The movement, slight as it was, must have frightened the birds because they suddenly took flight with a frantic beating of wings and wild squawking. The boys drew a bead on the panicked fowl and pulled their triggers almost simultaneously. Two thunderous explosions rang out through the countryside as clouds of smoke poured out of the shotguns. A pair of the quail began to tumble clumsily through the air, spinning and turning as their flight arched into a rapid descent. They hit the ground and moved no more.

"We got 'em!" Johnny shouted in triumph.

"You bet we did!" Will cried out, laughing. "There's gonna be good eatin' tonight, I'll tell ya!"

"I bet we are as good a shot as any soldier you ever saw!" Johnny said with the exuberance of his youthful eleven years.

"Well, I don't know about that," his brother replied. "But, yeah, we're pretty damn good!"

They both laughed as they walked over to pick up their catch and carefully put the lifeless birds into a burlap sack that they had carried with them. They turned and began the long walk home.

* * *

Home for the Reynolds boys, as John had told Kate, was a happy place for the most part. He was right when he said it was also a noisy place. John's father, the newspaper man after whom he was named, had installed printing presses in the house. Located on the main floor, they seemed to be running almost nonstop, clunking and clanking loudly, printing out issue after issue of the *Lancaster Journal*. People coming and going with news copy and news articles had to negotiate around and through the multiple Reynolds children, playing, working, or studying throughout the house. Other daily visitors added to the cacophony, arguing and debating the politics of the day.

The Reynoldses were a prominent, if not wealthy, family in Lancaster, a community of about eight thousand people. The senior John Reynolds had represented the area for two years in the Pennsylvania legislature when Johnny was just a toddler. Founded in the early 1700s, the town was one of the oldest in the country. It was a bustling place with the manufacturing of the famous Conestoga wagons, railroad cars, hardware, and the firearms.

For young Johnny, life was fairly carefree with swimming holes to cool off in during hot summers and the nearby Conestoga River in which to fish. Of course, there was the hunting of the abundant fowl and game scattered throughout the Pennsylvania countryside that the youngster so enjoyed.

"Hey, Pa!" Johnny shouted as he slammed through the front door of their large three-story house at 42 West King Street. He held the burlap sack up high as he ran through the entrance. "Look at what me and Will got!" Will came through the door behind him.

"Johnny, no shouting, please," his mother, Lydia Moore Reynolds, admonished from the kitchen where she was preparing lunch for her family. "And, grammar, please! It's 'Will and I,' not 'me and Will.'"

"Oh, sorry, Ma. Look at what Will and I got!"

He ran into the kitchen, opening the gunnysack to show his mother the contents.

"See, Ma? Two quail! Me and Will, oh, I mean Will and I, each shot one. Bang! Bang! You should have seen it!"

"Well," his mother said, smiling. "I guess I know what we're having for dinner tonight."

"Yeah," Johnny said excitedly. "That's what I was thinking. Where's Pa?"

"I believe he's in the study," she said.

Johnny turned and ran toward his father's study on the other side of the house, gripping the bag tightly in his hand. "Pa!" he shouted. "Look!"

"Johnny!" his mother called out, sternly.

"Oh, sorry again." Johnny took a breath. "Pa, look," he repeated in a quieter voice as he entered the room. He saw his father sitting at a desk, focused intently on something he was reading.

"Pa?" Johnny said, crossing over to the desk.

His father did not respond. He continued to read with a serious frown on his face.

"Pa?" Johnny repeated hesitantly. "Pa? Will and I got two quail this morning. See? Look."

He held out the burlap bag with the top open. Again, the elder Reynolds ignored the young boy.

"Pa?" Johnny said, very quietly. "What's the matter, Pa? Is something wrong?"

That got his father's attention. He turned to his son, still frowning. Realizing his behavior bordered on rudeness, he replaced his frown with a broad smile.

"What do you have there, son?" he asked kindly.

"Like I told you, Pa. Will and I shot two quail this morning. Look. They're here in the bag."

Johnny held the bag wide open so his father could peer inside. As he did, the older man nodded his head approvingly. He looked up and reached out to tousle Johnny's hair.

"That's some mighty fine shooting, son. Mighty fine!"

Johnny smiled proudly. Then, a small frown crossed his own face.

"Is something the matter, Pa? You didn't look happy when I came in the room."

John Reynolds leaned back his in chair and sighed deeply. He picked up the paper he had been reading.

"There's been some trouble over in Virginia," he told his young son. "This news arrived by messenger this morning. I'm getting ready to publish it in the newspaper."

"What trouble, Pa? What happened?"

"Well, it appears a slave…umm, what's his name?" John peered at the paper. "Here it is. Turner. Nat Turner. Looks like this Turner fellow up and killed a bunch of white folks."

Nat Turner was a thirty-one-year-old slave who, in 1831, led a bloody rebellion near Southampton, Virginia. Believing that he was a prophet, "intended for some great purpose" by God, Turner claimed to hear voices and see visions instructing him to take action to end the enslavement of his people. Early in the morning of August 21, Turner and a few other slaves killed the entire family of John Travis, who was his owner at the time. They continued their rampage, gathering more slaves and moving on to other plantations, slaughtering up to sixty white men, women, and children.

Turner and some of his coconspirators were captured several weeks later. He and 55 other slaves were executed. Local militias hunted down and killed about 120 other black people in retaliation. The entire episode spread fear and anger throughout the South.

"My God!" John Reynolds whispered in horror as he continued reading the report. "Children! They slaughtered innocent children!"

Johnny just stood there, taking in the news. Finally, he spoke.

"That's not right, Pa. Not right at all. Why? Why'd they do it?"

"I don't rightly know, son. Not the details, anyway. But I suspect they got tired of the way they were being treated. You know that for many white folks, slaves are considered property, no better than farm animals, and that's the way they treat them, with whippings and beatings and such."

"That's still no reason to go around killing folks," Johnny said with passion. "Did they catch the slaves who did it?"

His father pointed to the paper he was reading. "Says here there's a big manhunt underway."

Well, I hope they catch them and hang them. They deserve what's coming to them, I say!"

"A lot of other folks will say the same, I expect," his father observed. Then, he looked at his son with a serious expression. "One thing you need to understand, boy. This slavery question is very complicated. It's a might dangerous, too."

"What do you mean, Pa?"

Before he answered, John Reynolds reached into a desk drawer, pulled out a brown pipe and a silver tin of tobacco. He filled the bowl of the pipe, struck a match, lit the tobacco, sucked on the stem and inhaled deeply. He leaned back in his chair and let out a large blue cloud of tobacco smoke. Its pungent odor filled the room. All the while he was thinking about what he should say to his young son. Finally, he turned to him.

"The slavery issue is a hot one, Johnny, very controversial. People have had slaves since this country was founded, even long before that. Now, some folks say slavery is an abomination. Others say it is God's will. You'll find some people, especially in the Southern states, who say without slavery they would be destitute, dirt poor, even worse. They'll tell you they must have slave workers to farm their fields, pick their cotton, take care of their cattle, and so on. Without slaves, the farmers say they'd be lost."

"It's not just the South, though, Pa. Right?" Johnny said, pulling up a chair to sit down. "People in the North have slaves, too."

"Yes, they do. Not just as many in the South. There are a lot of reasons for that. But to put it very simply, it's like the North and the South are almost two different countries. Look around our town. What do you see? Lots of industry, that's what. We have factories that make Conestoga wagons. We have companies that make nails and all kinds of other hardware. We have the railroad. It's like an industrial revolution, and you see it all over the North. Machines, Johnny. Machines do the work, so there is less of a need for manual labor."

"But in the South...," Johnny started to say.

"But in the South," his father repeated. "It's much different. This industrial revolution hasn't quite reached them yet, and most folks depend on manual labor to make a living. They rely on slavery to support their families, to put food on the table. Industry in the North, Johnny. Agriculture in the South. That's the big difference."

The man took another deep draw on his pipe.

"But you're right, son. Up here we still have some farms and farmers, and they need farmhands, to be sure. And some of them do own slaves."

He waited for his son to respond. But Johnny just sat there, thinking hard.

"A lot of people around here think that's wrong," his father continued. "That's why the Pennsylvania legislature passed its Emancipation Act back in 1780."

"Yeah, we learned about that in school, Pa. That law made slavery illegal in this state, right?"

"Well, not exactly, son. Here, I'll show you."

John Reynolds got up from his chair, walked over to a shelf of books, and pulled one from its place. He thumbed through the pages until he found what he wanted.

"Here, Johnny, take a look."

He handed the book to his son and sat down. Johnny saw that it was a compendium of Pennsylvania commonwealth laws. His father pointed to the page.

"Read that paragraph out loud, please. Will you, son?"

Johnny began to recite what he was reading. "Be it enacted, and it is hereby enacted, that all persons as well Negroes and Mulattoes as others, who shall be born within this state from and after the passing of this act..." He took a big breath and continued, "Shall not be deemed and considered as servants for life, or slaves; and that all servi...servi..." Johnny struggled with the pronunciation. "Servitude, that's it!" he said. "Servitude for life, or slavery of children, in consequence of the slavery of their mothers..." Another breath. "In the case of all children born within this state from and after the passing of this act as aforesaid, shall be, and hereby is, utterly taken away, extinguished, and forever abolished."[18]

Johnny stared at the paragraph for a few more moments. Then he looked at his father.

"That's a lot of words just to say you can't own slaves," he said.

His father chuckled a little.

"Well, it means that in Pennsylvania any Negro or colored person born in 1780 or later cannot become a slave. But folks here who own slaves born before that year can keep them. This being the year 1831 means that the youngest legal slave in Pennsylvania is now fifty-two. In not too many more years, those folks will start dying out, and soon there will be no more slaves around here at all."

Johnny frowned as he thought about that.

"I don't understand," he said. "Why didn't they just say, 'No more slavery allowed,' and be done with it?"

"Well, you see, son, it's a compromise. Call it an effort to keep everyone happy."

"So, is slavery right or wrong?"

"Well, now, again that's the big, hot question, isn't it?" his father replied. "The answer is different depending on who's doing the answering. Some say it is a moral disgrace, treating human beings no better than chattel. Others insist that by owning slaves, they are giving Africans and other Negroes a better life, teaching them Christianity and moral values."

"Can't the government do something about it?" Johnny asked.

"Pennsylvania has," his father replied. "I just told you."

"No, not the Pennsylvania legislature. The federal government. You know, Washington."

The elder Reynolds pursed his lips before answering.

"Well, they've tried. The year you were born, 1820, they passed something that was another compromise. In fact, that's what they called it. The Missouri Compromise."

"What's that?" Johnny asked.

"The Missouri Compromise," his father replied, "was one of the earliest efforts to solve the slavery problem to everyone's satisfaction." The elder Reynolds shook his head in disgust. "In reality, it satisfied practically no one."

The Missouri Compromise was an attempt to reach a political as well as a moral solution for the slavery issue. Missouri wanted to join the Union as a slave state. Antislavery forces in Washington were unmoving in their opposition to that happening. Moral considerations aside, if Missouri came on board as a slave state, that would have given proslavery factions a majority in Congress. Opponents of slavery just would not have that.

"The answer was to admit Missouri into the Union as a slave state and Maine was admitted as a slave-free state. That kept a balance in Congress, which also created an imaginary line along the thirty-six-degree, thirty-minute parallel. The line divided the remaining incorporated western territories creating a slave-free North and slaveholding South."

Johnny frowned again.

"But, Pa," he protested. "That really didn't solve anything, did it? I mean, people still argue over slavery and even get into fights about it, don't they? Isn't it still a big problem for everybody?"

John smiled at the boy, proud of his son's insight and perceptiveness.

"Yes, you are absolutely right, son. Even Thomas Jefferson would agree with you. He called the Missouri Compromise just a reprieve and not a final sentence about slavery."

John reached over and pulled a file from one of his desk drawers.

"Shortly after the Missouri Compromise was approved, Jefferson sent a letter to Massachusetts congressman John Holmes, who was an author of the legislation. I published it in the *Lancaster Journal* at the time and saved a copy."

He looked at the file.

"This is what Jefferson wrote about that imaginary line. 'A geographical line, coinciding with a marked principle, moral and political, once conceived and held up to the angry passions of men, will never be obliterated and every new irritation will mark it deeper and deeper.'"[19]

John looked at his son.

"With this Missouri Compromise, Jefferson said that the country had the 'wolf by the ear,' when it comes to slavery. You can't hold it, nor can you safely let it go."[20]

"You said Jefferson used the words 'angry passions.' Are people angry enough to go to war over slavery?"

"Son, I hope not, I truly do. But to be honest, I can't say for sure."

"Well, if there is war, I, for one, want to go to sea to fight it!" said a new voice in the room.

Both John and Johnny Reynolds turned, startled by sound. It belonged to William, who had been standing silently in the doorway, listening to the conversation.

"How long have you been standing there, son?" John asked.

"Long enough to hear you say there might be war over the slavery question, Pa."

"Now, I didn't say that. I said I couldn't say there would, but that I hope that there wouldn't."

"Well, whether there is or isn't a war, I still want to be a sailor, and that's my plan."

"Me, too! Maybe." Johnny said. Then he thought about it. "Now that I think about it, I think I'd rather be in the Army, maybe the cavalry or light artillery. You get to ride horses in the Army, and I love horses! Yes, the Army's for me."

Johnny had military blood in him. His grandfather on his mother's side, Samuel Moore, had been a captain in the Continental Army and fought the British at Brandywine and Germantown, Pennsylvania, two great battles.

John turned and looked at this older son.

"Well, William," he said. "Since you have raised the subject, I have news for you, too."

He reached out and picked up another letter from the pile on his desk.

"What is it, Pa?" Will asked as he approached the desk.

"This arrived today. It's from Congressman Buchanan."

James Buchanan was a Reynolds family friend for whom John often conducted business affairs. John had reached out to him asking Buchanan to use his influence to get William an appointment to the US Navy. John handed the letter his older son.

William took it and read it, his eyes growing wide as he did.

"Holy cow. I'm in, Pa! I'm in the Navy. Wow! Wow! I'm in!"

"Lemme see!" Johnny exclaimed, reaching out for the piece of paper. "Lemme see!"

"It says I'm supposed to report to the USS *Boxer* in Boston next November," Will exclaimed, handing the letter to Johnny. "That's a new vessel, Pa! I've been reading about it. It's a ten-gun schooner, but it hasn't even been launched yet. That's scheduled for November 22nd. I'm gonna be on a brand-new ship! Hallelujah!"

"Wow! That's really neat, Will. Congratulations! Hooray!" Johnny cried out as he handed the letter back to his brother.

"I gotta go tell Ma!" Will said as he turned and ran out of the room. "Ma! Ma!" he called. "I'm gonna be in the Navy!"

Johnny watched his brother leave the room and got very quiet, deep in thought.

"You know, Pa," he finally said. "If there is war, I think it will be really bad. I mean, any war is bad, of course, with people dying and all. But if there is a war over slavery, that means it would be a war of states against states, of Americans against other Americans. And what happens if family members disagree about the question of slavery?"

He paused, thinking about Will.

"That means it could be a war of brother against brother," Johnny said. "That could tear this country apart."

John put his hand on his young son's shoulder and said solemnly, "You have no idea how right you are, boy." He paused and looked at Johnny with renewed respect. "But, then again, maybe you do."

CHAPTER THREE

Pacific Ocean
July 1860

Kate sat at the steamship's breakfast table, still as can be, hands in her lap, listening to John tell his story. He had paused to butter another biscuit.

"Those are some pretty serious things for an eleven-year-old boy to be thinking about," she said.

"I suppose," John replied. "But Pa being a newspaperman and all, the whole family was always pretty aware of current events. And with reporters and others, you know, politicians, people with news items and just plain gossip always coming and going, we heard a lot about a lot of things." He grinned, a little slyly. "Some of it not fit for discussion in polite company, if you know what I mean."

Kate's cheeks reddened slightly. She picked up her napkin and patted her lips. Her eyes blinked as she said mischievously, "Well, I do declare, I have no earthly idea what you are talking about, Mr. Major John Reynolds."

They both laughed.

"Anyway," he continued, "there was always a lot of discussion about worldly matters in our family. Both my Pa and Ma made sure all of us children were educated. Both the boys and the girls. They didn't hide much from us."

At that point, Catherine interrupted their conversation.

"I've finished my breakfast," she said to Kate. "I'd like to walk around the boat, explore it a little. Would that be okay?"

"Why, yes, Catherine that would be fine. Just be careful, okay?"

"Okay, thanks." She slipped out of her chair and skipped away.

"See you in a little while," Catherine called over her shoulder.

Kate watched her go, then turned back to John.

"So, you were talking about growing up. Where did you go to school?" she asked.

"Well, now I'd be happy to tell you all about that," John replied, smiling. "But first, Miss Catherine Hewitt, how about you telling me a little about yourself? Just who is this fetching young woman with whom I am sharing a breakfast table?"

Kate blushed again and said, "Oh, my, there is really not much to tell."

"I am sure that is not true," John said, lightly. "Where were you born and raised? What was your childhood like?"

He thought he could detect her face clouding a little at that, but the impression was gone as quickly as it came.

"Well, let's see," she said. "I was born in Stillwater, New York, in 1836."

John blinked at that news, realizing that she was sixteen years his junior. He was surprised because she had the grace and poise of a more mature woman. He was beginning to really like this twenty-four-year-old lady.

"My mother died when I was quite young," Kate continued matter-of-factly. "I was raised by my grandmother, my father, and an uncle."

"What does your father do?" John asked.

Again, a cloud passed over her face. This time it remained as Kate frowned and busied herself with reaching for a biscuit, putting cream in her tea, and stirring it for a long time as she stared out the porthole to the open ocean. John remained silent. He sensed that he had broached a sensitive subject. He waited patiently.

Finally, Kate took a deep breath and turned to him. She looked at John, with some sadness, he thought, but perhaps with some anger, too.

"I am an orphan," she said, tersely.

John's thick black eyebrows shot up.

"An orphan?" he stammered.

She looked out the porthole again and didn't respond for another long moment. Eventually, she closed her eyes and sighed, as if coming to a difficult decision. She turned her head toward John again and opened her eyes, looking straight at him. She was not smiling.

"As far as I am concerned, I am an orphan. My father is still alive, but yes, I am an orphan."

John looked at her quizzically. "I'm afraid I don't understand, Kate," he said.

She wiped her mouth with the linen napkin before she spoke.

"Well, quite frankly, my father is a rapscallion, you know, a...a...scalawag. Oh, let me just say it. A cheat."

"What did he do, if I may ask?"

"It's not so much what he did, John. It's what he didn't do. He never really had a decent job. Our family is traditionally of the Baptist faith. But the year I was born, my father was ostracized by the First Baptist Church of Stillwater. As the church put it, "the hand of fellowship" was withdrawn.[21] I never really found out why."

She took a sip of tea and continued.

"Then, in 1852, just before I turned sixteen, my father got in trouble with the law, and a court ordered a sheriff sale of his property. He lost everything. Not that we had much, anyway. I was humiliated and embarrassed. He was never much of a father to me. My grandmother was seventy years old when my mother died. Plus, Grandma couldn't read. She was illiterate. My uncle wasn't much of a help. I pretty much raised myself. So, yes, I consider myself an orphan. I have disowned my father."

It was obvious to John that Kate was still bitter about those events in her life. She had covered her bitterness well, until now. He waited a moment or two before gently asking, "Do you have any brothers and sisters?"

"I have two. A sister, Sarah, and a half brother, Morey. I did have another brother, but he died, too, the same year my mother passed away. Sarah and Morey moved out of the house when they were old enough to do that. I haven't spoken to either of them for a long time."

"I'm sorry you've had a difficult time in your life. But I must say, you seem to be handling things well. You seem happy. You seem to be at peace," John observed.

"Well, I guess I owe a lot of that to my faith, my religion," she said.

"The Baptist Church?"

"Oh, no. I am no longer a Baptist. In fact, I'm no longer a Protestant. I'm Catholic now."

"You are?"

It was another unexpected revelation. John decided that this delightful young lady was full of surprises.

"How did that come about?"

"It's because of the children," she said.

"Children?"

"Yes. You see, I left Stillwater four years ago and traveled by steamboat to California. It was a long ride, but it was quite an adventure, I must say!" she said, the twinkle in her eyes returning.

"There is this family who my family knows back in Stillwater. They have relatives in San Francisco who needed a governess. Woodworth is their name. I had to get away from my father and all that was going on at home, so I jumped at the chance. The Woodworths are quite wealthy. Their business is importing pianos as well as dealing in metallurgy. When I got to San Francisco, I discovered they live in a very large home that has five servants. I was the governess for the Woodworth children. They provided a little place for me to live just a couple of doors away from their home."[22]

Kate paused long enough to take another sip of tea.

"By and by, I was able to secure employment at an orphanage in San Francisco run by the Catholic Church. Actually, it is run by an order called the Daughters of Charity. The orphanage is called the Roman Catholic Orphan Asylum. I became a teacher at the school that is part of the orphanage.[23] It was because of my experience there with the Daughters of Charity that I converted to Catholicism. Those sisters are wonderful. They made me feel whole again. It was just what I needed after all that, well, you know, happened back home."

She glanced down the deck to where Catherine had gone. Turning back, she took a sip of her tea, then continued.

"That's part of the reason I have Catherine with me. The first ten years of her life have been horrible. Her mother died in childbirth, and her father died of cholera when she was only three. She was moved from foster home to foster home and finally ended up at the orphanage where I taught. She is so bright and personable. I wanted to see that she got a better chance at life."

"So, you adopted her?" John asked.

"Not really adopted. I'm her guardian. The sisters arranged for that. They also arranged for their Daughters of Charity chapter in Philadelphia to help Catherine get enrolled in school, and they are going to help me finish my religious conversion. I am so grateful to them. I could spend all my life with the Daughters of Charity, if it came to that."

John smiled, delighted by Kate's enthusiasm, but also thinking about the implications of what she had just said about becoming a devout Catholic. He wondered about the ramifications since he was raised, and still was, a God-fearing Protestant.

Kate interrupted his thoughts.

"So, John, speaking of school and getting back to you, I believe that's where we left off your story. Would you tell me about your schooling?"

"Well, let's see," John said, rubbing his chin. "I was educated in a few different places. Let's start with the Lititz Academy for Boys."

CHAPTER FOUR

Lititz, Pennsylvania
October 1833

"And so, my dear students, probity, purity, and perseverance are three of the most important qualities young men must possess if you desire to conduct yourselves without awkwardness in society."

Thirteen-year-old John Reynolds, listened raptly as his teacher lectured enthusiastically about virtues and good character in the modern-day nineteenth century.

"Above all," his teacher continued, "gentlemen must have virtues, which include religion, humility, mercy, charity, truth, and cheerfulness if you are to be considered to be of good character. At all costs, avoid the evils of anger, revenge and avarice.[24] They will do you no good in whatever endeavor you pursue. They are the devil's playthings!"

John found himself nodding solemnly at the teacher's words, which fell comfortably on his ears. In fact, he felt very comfortable at this school, known as the Lititz Academy for Boys. His older brother, William, now a midshipman in the US Navy, had attended the school before him. John's younger brother, James, was also a student with him at the academy. It was founded by a man named John Beck, whose ancestors included Swiss educators. It was Beck who now stood at the front of the class giving his young charges lessons in civility.

Beck was a kindly man with an easy smile and friendly features. Lititz town fathers had asked him to take over the little village school, noting his fondness for children. Under his direction, the academy had grown in size and reputation and now included students from as far away as the Carolinas and Louisiana. Some of John's classmates and new friends were young boys who, in later years, would be opposite him in a great upheaval that would threaten to destroy their country.

Lititz Academy was a boarding school, and although the town and the academy were only twelve miles from Lancaster, that was far enough away that John, like most of the more than seventy other students, were housed in apartment-like facilities. John and James were very happy with their situation, and John told his father so. One night in late autumn, while in his room, he wrote one of his many letters home.

"We are in the care of very kind people," he wrote. "And we have a very fine school. The school is very large at present, and there are more than 74 boys here. We have three teachers. The boys are divided into three apartments."

Later in that same letter, John was even more effusive about his state of affairs.

"I think I have never passed the evenings happier and more to my advantage than I have since the first of November," he wrote.[25]

There were many things at the academy that John loved, especially the horseback riding. Headmaster Beck had purchased two ponies and had built a riding course.

"C'mon, Robert!" John said one day to his friend Robert Coleman. "Let's go riding."

"Aw, I'd like to, John," Robert replied. "But I gotta study."

"Yeah, well, so do I. And we will. C'mon, it's a beautiful day, and we can take the ponies for just an hour or two."

The two boys were in their living quarters and could see through the windows that it was indeed a bright fall day. John put his hand on his hips and leaned forward slightly, a bright twinkle in his eyes.

"Besides," he said, "if I'm gonna be a soldier, I'll have to learn how to ride really well, right? This will be great practice! C'mon, Robert. Let's go!"

"Oh, all right!"

They both ran out of the building and toward the stable, laughing all the way.

Not that John wasn't a serious student. He was very serious and recognized what opportunities had opened up for him. With a little awkwardness in composition, he told his father, "I think I have improved very much since I am here, and I think every boy ought to improve here every opportunity for us to do so is given us."[26]

Young John especially enjoyed studying science.

"Mr. Beck has been lecturing on Pneumatics, which was very interesting to me," he wrote.[27]

Pneumatics is the study of gases and pressurized air and how they act on mechanical devices, including boilers and steam engines. He was especially impressed by the power of forced air. He told his father that Mr. Beck "showed us how the boilers on steam-boats burst."

Other practical applications of scientific principles also got his full attention. One evening, Professor Beck gathered his students in the lab where he had set up several electrical devices.

"Today, gentlemen," Beck said. "We are going to experiment with electricity a little to discover how this relatively new power source works."

An excited murmur rippled through the group of boys.

"But we must be careful," the teacher warned. "If you don't pay attention, electricity can cause a painful shock."

"Shocking!" one smart aleck in the back of the group piped up.

"Exactly," Beck replied.

Everyone laughed.

Their teacher had placed a small wooden stand on the worktable. A horseshoe-shaped magnet was affixed horizontally to the top of a small eight-inch pole attached to the stand. A copper disk was suspended vertically on a second small stand. The outer edge of the disk was placed between the two arms of the magnet, while a crank was attached to the center of the disk.

"This is called a Faraday disk," the headmaster explained. "It's a brand-new development created by the English scientist Michael Faraday. When the copper disk is turned rapidly, using this crank, the interaction between it and the magnet will create what is called an electromagnetic force. In other words, sparks should fly."

"Wow," several of the boys said simultaneously.

"Now, who wants to go first?" Beck asked.

John's hand shot into the air ahead of his classmates.

"I do!" he shouted.

"All right, Mr. Reynolds. Stand over here," Beck commanded. "Now, when I say go, you turn that crank as fast as you can. Remember, though, you will be creating a form of electricity, and if you feel any pain, like a hard pinch, let go immediately!"

John stared, wide-eyed, at his teacher for a moment.

"Yes sir," he said, bravely.

He took hold of the handle on the crank.

"Go!" Beck said.

John turned the crank, and the copper disk began to spin between the arms, or poles, of the magnet. But nothing else happened.

"Faster," Beck said. "Turn the crank faster."

John doubled his effort. The disk spun faster and faster.

All of a sudden, his entire body jerked. He let go of the crank and yelled.

"Ow! Ow! That hurt!"

He shook his hand violently, then felt it throbbing as he held it against his chest with the other hand.

"Congratulations, Mr. Reynolds," Beck said. "You just got an electric shock."

All the other boys started laughing.

John scowled at them. "It's not funny!" he said.

"No, it is not," said the teacher. "As a scientific experiment, you can say this one failed. The idea is to create electricity, but not get harmed by it."

"But I did what you told me," John complained.

"Yes, you did," Beck said. "But, surprise, I didn't tell you everything. For that I apologize, but I needed to show you what electricity can do." He grinned. "Call it a teaching moment."

John just looked at him with dark eyes, still rubbing his stinging hand.

"The reason you got a slight shock—"

"Slight?" John spit out. "I wouldn't call that slight!"

Beck smiled.

"The reason you got that shock is because you are standing on the ground, which acts a sort of conduit for electricity. You completed what is called a circuit."

"Hey, Johnny," one of the other boys said, laughing, "teacher just called you a circus!"

"Circuit, you dolt!" John shot back. "He said circuit."

"That's enough, gentlemen," Beck admonished, giving them all a stern look. Then, he continued. "What we need is something to insulate you from the electrical charge." The headmaster walked to the other side of the lab, picked up a squat black wooden box. Its top was covered with a rubber mat.

Carrying the box back to the students, Beck explained. "The rubber acts as an insulator to protect us from the electrical charge. You may still feel some vibration whilst standing on the rubber mat if the charge is strong enough when you turn the crank. But this time, it should not be painful. Care to try it again, Mr. Reynolds?"

John swallowed deeply and stared at the box for a moment.

"Su...sure," he said, finally.

He stepped up on the box, planting his feet firmly on the rubber mat. Then he bent over and began to turn the crank with some force, causing the copper disk to again spin rapidly between the prongs of the magnet. Within seconds, sparks started flying out from the disk in all directions.

"Woo, that kind of tickles." John laughed as he turned the crank harder and faster. A shower of sparks poured forth from the contraption. All the other boys started clapping. "Hooray, John! Hooray!" a few of them shouted. "You're making electricity, John!" his friend, Robert Coleman, cried.

John stopped cranking and hopped down off the stool. His classmates crowded around him, slapping him on the back.

"Way to go, John," one of them said. "You're a real, for sure, scientist now!"

John laughed at that.

"Now, let's try some other experiments," Headmaster Beck said as he began to set up more electrical paraphernalia.

John wrote to his father the next day, telling him all about the experience and the headmaster's science lesson. "Yesterday evening he lectured on electricity, but the atmosphere was not favorable," John explained. "Many experiments failed, but we all got several shocks and stood on the insulating box and electric fire then discharged from every part of our body."[28]

* * *

By the time 1834 rolled around, John Reynolds was growing into the strapping six-foot-tall man he would become. At fourteen years old, his thoughts focused more frequently on whether he would join the Army. During his second year at Lititz Academy he found that discussion among the students reflected the growing tensions in the country. Conversations centering on politics often erupted into heated arguments between Southern boys from states like Georgia and Louisiana, and boys from the Northern states such as New York and Pennsylvania.

"Well, it just weren't fair. That's all there is to it!" A freckle-faced teenager from Charleston, South Carolina, was turning red in anger as, over lunch, he and John discussed recent events in Washington.

"That damned tariff law, or act, or legislation or whatever y'all wanna call it, was wrong. Just plain wrong, I tell ya! That's why South Carolina had to do something about it!" The young man took a furious bite of his sandwich.

Six years earlier, Congress had passed the Tariff of 1828, the latest in a series of laws ostensibly designed to protect American industry from being undercut by artificially low prices of products imported from other countries. The tariff imposed stiff new taxes on foreign goods brought into the United States. New England textile manufacturers who accused Great Britain of dumping cheap clothing on US shores were especially eager for the new legislation.

But, many in the South were incensed. They called it the Tariff of Abominations, claiming it would cost them their livelihood. Great Britain had threatened to find other markets to replace Southern cotton because the cost of the crop had become so expensive. Southern legislators also protested because the loss of cotton income was coupled with an increase in prices for goods and materials the South had to buy.

In a failed effort to appease the South, Congress passed another tariff act in 1832 which reduced many of the tariffs imposed in 1828. The South, especially South Carolina, where cotton was truly king, was still outraged. Later that year, South Carolina passed the Ordinance of Nullification, which declared tariffs imposed by the federal government unconstitutional and were null and void in the Palmetto State. The issue was so tense, Vice President John Calhoun, a South Carolinian, quit his post to defend nullification.

Congress then upped the ante by giving President Andrew Jackson the power to use the military against South Carolina, if it became necessary. That action was avoided only when agreement on tariffs was finally reached that satisfied South Carolina, which withdrew its nullification ordinance in March of 1833.

For many, however, the precarious relationship between the North and South had not been settled. For some, including John Reynolds, it was a grave harbinger of what might yet come. In his youthful innocence, John had a vague and uncomfortable feeling that leaders of his country were leading the nation down a dangerous path.

"I understand your point," John said to his angry South Carolina classmate. "But it seems to me politicians in your state really barked up the wrong tree. We are, after all, the United States of America. The important word is united! We are a union, joined together to make life better for everybody. I mean, that's why my grandfather and your grandfather fought the War of Independence, to get Great

Britain off our backs. You can argue the tariffs were sort of meant to do the same thing."

"Well, hell, John, what kind of union is it when one part of it does things that hurt the other part?" his friend replied. "My daddy is a cotton farmer, you know that, right? He says those tariffs were hurting him so much in the pocketbook, he was afraid he'd have to sell some of his land and some of his slaves just to make do! Tell me that ain't fair! He says his cotton sales dropped by more than half after that 1828 abomination was passed. Plus, he had to start paying a lot more for supplies he bought from you Northerners when you started raising prices. That was happening to most everybody in South Carolina. Hell, the entire South was headed to the poor house. That's why South Carolina passed the nullification declaration, and I'm proud we did. That took guts, I'll tell you!"

"Guts, but no brains, that's for sure," John snickered. His friend doubled his fists and turned red again.

"Take that back, you bastard!" he snarled.

"All right. All right. Calm down," John said. "I take it back. But still, I gotta say, that was a pretty stupid thing to do. It went against everything the country and, well, the US Constitution stand for. Remember what we learned the preamble says? We, the people of the United States, in order to form a more perfect union and so on? A more perfect union! That's what it's all about. When South Carolina joined the Union, it agreed, just like all the other states, to allow the national government to make rules and laws that everybody would have to follow. Individual states don't have the right to willy-nilly ignore the laws they don't like. It would be like if we formed a club here at school and everybody joined and voted on certain rules. And then, say, you or me or some other guys decided they didn't like some of the rules and went against them. Well, that wouldn't be much of a club, would it? The same is true with the national government. If more states acted like South Carolina, we would no longer have much of a country, would we? It's gotta be one for all and all for one, that's for sure."

"Ha!" the Carolina boy blurted out. "All for one, except when it comes to kicking South Carolina in the rear, you mean! What is the union but a collection of...a, umm, what's the word...aggregation, yeah, that's it...an aggregation of states and people? You even just said it. We the people of the United States. We are the ones who are supposed to be making the decisions, not some highfalutin scalawags in Washington who probably have never even been in the South! Look, even Thomas Jefferson said so. I looked it up and wrote it down."

The young man opened his notebook, which was sitting on the table beside his lunch plate.

"Here it is." He looked up at John to make sure he was listening. "This is part of his argument for what they called the Kentucky Resolution written by Jefferson himself, back in 1798. This is what he says about the Constitution."

Putting his finger on the quote he had found, he began to read.

"Where powers are assumed which have not been delegated, a nullification of the act is the rightful remedy: that every State has a natural right in cases not within the compact, to nullify of their own authority all assumptions of power by others within their limits: that without this right, they would be under the dominion, absolute and unlimited, of whosoever might exercise this right of judgment for them."[29]

The boy slammed his notebook closed.

"See? South Carolina had the absolute right to nullify the tariffs. He uses the word twice! James Madison said just about the same thing in the so-called Virginia Resolution also in 1798. It was an assumption of power by those know-nothings in Washington. Worse, it was an assumption of power that favored the north over the south. You, yourself, made the same case a minute ago when you mentioned the War of Independence. Our grandfathers fought against the same thing, assumption of powers by the king of England that hurt the New World colonies, meaning us! Likewise, South Carolina simply exercised the right of states to act in their own best interests. States' rights, that's what it's called!"

"You have a point," John replied. "But there were, and are, better ways to solve the problem than just up and turning your back on the rule of law. Obviously, they figured it out, you know, with another compromise. It's a good thing South Carolina cancelled that nullification stuff last March. I'll tell you, my friend, that was a lot of trouble for a lot of nothing, if you ask me."

John's South Carolina friend took a deep breath, trying to keep his temper in check.

"It wasn't for a lot of nothing, John! This was serious! I heard my mama crying some nights when I visited back home because she was so worried about losing the plantation. That made me mad. Real mad! Sure, I'm glad now that some kind of agreement was reached, but I'll tell you this. Folks in the South still don't trust you folks in the North. They're not gonna let this sort of thing ever happen again. And now, John, now you've got, what do you call them? Abolitionists! Yeah, Northern abolitionists who are trying to tell us we can't have slaves anymore. The North had better be real careful from now on. If this keeps up, some people down South are talking about succeeding. No, that's not the right word. Umm, secession. That's it. They are talking about seceding from the Union, you know, quitting the US, becoming an independent republic. I've even heard tell that some are willing to go war over all this. They are already forming militias to fight what some people say will be a War of Northern Aggression someday."

"Oh, it'll never come to that," John said dismissively. "Never in a million years."

"Don't be too sure, John. Don't be too sure."

"Hey, what are you guys talking about?"

The two boys turned to see John's younger brother, James, joining them at the lunch table, setting his tray of food down and hopping over the bench seat."

"Oh, our Southern friend here thinks we are nothing but a bunch of scalawags," John said, grinning.

"Who? Us?" James said with surprise. "How can that be? We're kindly folk. Nice as you please!"

"Not us as a family," John replied. "Us as Yankees. Northerners. He thinks we're gonna march right in and take over the South, you know, make 'em do things our way!" He laughed aloud and elbowed his brother in the ribs. "You know what I mean. They'll have to learn how to do things the right way!" Now James started laughing at John's sarcastic humor.

"Hey, that's not funny, John!" their friend said angrily, and started turning red again. James's laughter suddenly developed into a hacking cough.

"Are you all right, James?" John asked, patting his brother on the back. "Did something go down the wrong way?"

James coughed a few more times, then managed to catch his voice.

"I'm okay," he squawked. "I've just got a sore throat, is all. Started coming on last night." One more cough.

"You have to be careful with your health, brother. Real careful. You know what Mr. Beck always says about the importance of staying healthy."

Along with his lengthy and often repeated life lectures about good manners, the Lititz headmaster was also fanatical about wellness and physical fitness. He was well-known and well respected for the strict health regimens he had set up for his students. There was good cause for that. Two years earlier, in 1832, a serious wave of cholera swept through the Eastern Seaboard. More than 3,500 people in New York City alone died. Beck was always on guard for any sign of illness within the walls of Lititz.

As a result, John developed a well-honed sense of good hygiene and good health. He became acutely aware of other students who became ill. His friend, Robert Coleman, was laid low with a very bad cold, Robert's brother came down with the mumps, and John became extremely concerned when his own brother, James, fell ill with a sore throat and other symptoms. John dutifully reported these illnesses in the letters he wrote home.

This heightened sense of physical, mental, and social well-being would serve John well as a military officer in later years. But, as would become evident in the still distant future, no amount of physical fitness or healthy routines would stop a well-aimed bullet.

CHAPTER FIVE

San Francisco to New York
July 1860

For John Reynolds and Kate Hewitt, the voyage to New York had a strange bipolar quality to it. On the one hand, it was a slow trip. The steamship chugged along at a rather sedate eight knots per hour.

Other the other hand, time for them seemed to fly by. They spent nearly every waking hour together, often talking long into the night. They were often accompanied by young Catherine, but sometimes they found time to be alone, enthralled with each other's company. John had come to realize Kate had, as one of his sisters would years later describe, "a delicate, refined mind" and "a superior personality."[30]

They had reached Panama without incident. Now it was time to take the train that would transport them to the Atlantic side of the narrow country, a distance of about forty-five miles. They had arrived in Panama City in the evening, and the train didn't depart until the next morning. So, they each booked a room for the night in a local hotel, a single for John, a double for Kate and young Catherine.

"If you ladies do not have other plans, I'd like you to be my guests at dinner this evening," John said as they all stood in the lobby of the small hotel. "Perhaps we can order some delicious Panamanian carne guisada, along with platanos maduros or corn tortillas."

"Oh, John, that would be lovely!" Kate said. "What do you think, Catherine?" she said, turning to the girl. "Shall we dine with the major tonight?"

Catherine stood next them, shyly looking down at her shoes. She nervously scraped her right foot back and forth across the floor. After a moment, she mumbled something so softly neither Kate nor John could hear it.

Kate squatted down so she could be eye to eye with her young friend.

"Is something wrong, Catherine?" she asked with concern. "Are you all right?"

The girl looked at her tentatively. She glanced up at Major Reynolds who stood towering above her with his six-foot plus height. She then whispered to Kate.

"I don't know what those things are," she said. "What's carney kesaday? And that other thing, plant something or other?"

Despite her whisper, John could hear what the young girl had said, and he burst out in a hearty laugh. Kate was smiling, too.

"Oh, I think you are going to love the food, Catherine. It is a lot like Mexican food, and I learned a lot about it while I was there a few years ago."

The major squatted down so he, too, could be eye to eye with Catherine.

"Carne guisada is delicious!" he exclaimed. "It is beef and pota-toes cooked to perfection in a special sauce. Tender as can be. And platanos maduros are plantains, which sort of look like bananas. They are cooked in butter, vanilla, and cinnamon. They're very sweet and very, very good!"

Catherine had stopped fidgeting, and her eyes had gotten very wide. "Ooh, that sounds really good!" she said.

Kate and John stood up.

"Now, you don't have to have those dishes," Kate said. "You could order something else. Right, John?"

"Absolutely. The restaurant a few doors down has lots of things we can order."

"Yay! Let's go," Catherine cried out, forgetting her shyness.

"Okay!" John replied. "Let's go to our rooms and freshen up. I'll meet you ladies down here at seven o'clock."

* * *

During dinner that evening, Catherine discovered that she really did like carne guisada and ate her portion with gusto. John discovered that he was growing very fond of Kate Hewitt.

The three of them engaged in small talk during the meal. John was fascinated by Kate's wit and charm. Despite the tragedies in her life, she was ebullient and good-natured, he thought. He loved her laugh and the way her eyes sparkled. Her independent spirit was, for John, immensely appealing.

Kate, likewise, was becoming infatuated with this dashing officer seated across the table from her. She had discovered, once she got past the stern visage, dark eyes, and thick beard, Major John Reynolds was a warm, caring, and dare she say, passionate man. That thought raised a question in her mind. It was something she wanted to ask him but wasn't sure it was proper to do so. Well, Kate thought to herself, nothing ventured, nothing gained.

"John," she said, halfway through their dinner. "May I ask you a personal question?"

He was focused on cutting a piece of the Panamanian beef, and the query caused him to pause in mid slice. He looked at her questioningly.

"Of course," he said. "Ask anything you'd like."

"Well, I…umm…I was wondering…oh, my, this is a bit embarrassing."

"Please, Kate, ask away. It's all right."

Her face blushed a little.

"I'm not sure it is proper, you know. It's probably not becoming to ask a gentleman this."

He put his fork and knife down on the table.

"Oh. Well, you really have my attention now. Come, Kate. Don't be priggish," he said with a gleam in his eye.

"All right. Here goes. How is it that a handsome, charming, and clever man such as you aren't married?"

Suddenly she put her hand to her mouth and grimaced. Her face turned bright red.

"Oh dear," she blurted out, then lowered her voice to just above a whisper.

"You aren't married, are you?"

The major stared at her for a few moments. Meanwhile, Catherine sat very quietly in her chair watching the conversation. She sensed something was going on but wasn't quite sure what. Suddenly John burst out laughing.

"No!" he said between laughs. "I am not married and never have been."

Kate was still flustered over what she was convinced was her serious faux pas, but deep inside she was greatly relieved by his answer. She took a deep breath and tried to breathe normally.

"Please forgive me for being presumptuous. I really shouldn't have asked."

But, then, she couldn't help herself. "Why not? Why haven't you been married?" Kate blurted out. "A man like you would be quite a catch!"

It was John's turn to blush beneath his heavy black beard. He cleared his throat.

"Well, the Army has kept me pretty busy. They keep me on the move a lot from this fort to that fort. I guess I really haven't had much time for, you know, romance. I don't think I've really thought about it."

That wasn't quite true. Back in 1847, the then Lieutenant John Reynolds was in Mexico, cooling his heels after tough battles in the Mexican-American War. He had been stuck there for more than a year and a half with little to do. By the time 1848 had rolled around, he seemed to have reached the end of his rope. He wrote a letter to one of his sisters asking her to keep an eye out for any marriage proposals that might be proffered from any eligible women back in their hometown of Lancaster. He advised her that any of the candidates "must be good-looking, amiable, and have a small portion of what is usually termed common sense."[31]

"So, no lady friends at all?" Kate pressed on.

"Oh, yes," he said. "I have enjoyed the companionship of some very fine ladies."

Suddenly, he realized how that must have sounded. "But nothing scandalous, you understand. Those relationships were all very proper and perfectly in keeping with all social expectations," he added, stiffly.

Kate giggled.

"Oh, I am sure they were," she said, kindly. "Relax, John. I am positive your decorum was of the highest degree."

He took a deep breath, then a deep drink from his glass of wine. He looked at her, and they both laughed again.

"Tell me more about your life, John." Kate grinned mischievously. "And if you dare, maybe you can tell me a little about your social life."

Still holding his glass of wine, John stared off into the middle distance, remembering adventures of his youth.

CHAPTER SIX

Lancaster, Pennsylvania
April 1836

While the infant Kate Hewitt was drawing her first breaths of life in New York, sixteen-year-old John Reynolds was beginning to feel teenage pubescent urges three hundred miles away in Pennsylvania.

"My, Miss Isabel, don't you look lovely this fine spring morning?" John said as he and Isabel Coleman strolled through a field filled with yellow daffodils and purple lavender.

"Why, Mr. Reynolds, you say the kindest things," Isabel replied overly sweetly. "You make a girl just want to blush!"

She giggled. John just smiled. He carried a picnic basket containing bread, cheese, a couple of glasses, a jar of cold tea, and a small blanket as the two of them headed for the shade of a large oak tree on the outskirts of Lancaster. John and Isabel Coleman had known each other for years. She was the sister of his schoolmate and chum, Robert.

Although they were old friends, the innocent flirting between John and Isabel was a recent development. Now slightly more than six feet tall and handsome, John was considered a desirable catch among several of the teenage girls in town. If there was anything about John they might have thought was amiss, it was that he was too serious much of the time and could have had a little better sense of humor. Yet, John always remained fond of his friends including young neighbor girls named Mary Elizabeth and Annie as well as Robert's other sister, Sarah.

He had also developed close friendships with other boys in town. While he could be warm and engaging and certainly had a young man's sense of adventure, his friends always felt a vague sense of distance from John. Perhaps it was because of what they had discerned was his seriousness of purpose and a streak of independence that would serve him so well in the war that lay ahead. Still, in later years he would have pleasant memories of his "soirees" with his friends.

His independent nature got away with him during an opportunity to strike out on his own, riding a rented horse alone all the way to Philadelphia, seventy miles distant. For a sixteen-year-old teenager, this had all the promise of an exciting adventure. In spite of his usual conscientious behavior, he gave the horse its head on a very long stretch of road during the second day of the trip.

"C'mon, boy! Let's go!" he shouted, loosening the reins, allowing the big animal to leap ahead at full speed. On he ran, mile after mile. John was exhilarated, whooping and hollering all along the way. The wind whipped his hair. Trees sped by in a blur. John had become an expert horseman, despite his young age, and he was able to nicely control the steed, even at top speed. He spurred the horse on, encouraging him to run and run at full gallop. *This*, he thought, *this is what I am meant to do. Lord, I love horses!*

After a long while, he finally gently pulled on the reins. The horse responded, gradually slowing down to a comfortable walk, but breathing heavily and covered in a sheen of perspiration. John noticed there was something a little different in the animal's gait. It wasn't quite as rhythmic as it was before.

When he arrived at the appointed Philadelphia barn owned by a Mr. Durkee, the stable hand immediately noticed something wrong. The animal had gone lame. This was a serious problem because the rented horse was fine when he had left the Durkee Lancaster stable. The stable hand gave John a sour look.

"Rode this boy pretty hard, did ya?" the stable hand asked, accusingly.

John looked nervously from the stable hand to the horse and back again.

"Umm...well...umm," he stammered. "Not that hard, I should think." That was all he could say.

John fretted about it all day. Staying in Philadelphia for a few more days, he penned a note to his father about the incident. The horse's owner had yet to confront the teenage boy about the problem.

"Mr. Durkee has not yet come," John wrote in his note. "I do not think he will come but keep the horse and say no more about it."[32]

This was uncharacteristically impetuous behavior for a young man whose reputation was one of responsibility and having a sense of duty.

* * *

During the afternoon picnic under the old oak tree, John and Isabel relaxed on the blanket, listened to the chirping of nearby birds, munched on bread and cheese, and sipped tea. Isabel wrinkled her forehead, deep in thought, while she gazed at a couple of hawks circling lazily high overhead.

"John," Isabel finally said. "We're all going to miss you when your family moves to Cornwall. Why do you all have to move?"

Cornwall, Pennsylvania, was small town about twenty miles north of Lancaster. John's father had accepted a job as the manager of the Coleman Iron Furnace in that town. John's school friend was the grandson of the foundry's proprietor, whose name was also Robert and who owned other ironworks as well. He had become a leading producer of iron and was Pennsylvania's first millionaire.

Although moving to Cornwall was something of a sea change for most of the Reynolds family, it had no real impact on John nor on his brother, James. After two years at the Lititz Academy, both boys had transferred to another school near Baltimore. Then they had returned to Lancaster for one more year of study.

"Well, I won't be gone all the time," John said to Isabel as he cut two pieces of cheese for each of them. "In fact, I'm not really moving at all. James and I are going to stay with our Aunt Lydia over on Orange Street so we can finish our last year of school right here in Lancaster."

"Oh, good!" Isabel squealed with delight. "That means we'll still get to see a lot of each other. I'm so happy! Aren't you?"

"Mm-hmm," John murmured absently as he took a sip of tea.

If Isabel had any dreams or schemes involving young John Reynolds, he didn't share in them. His plans would take him on a path that would not include real romance. Not, at least, for another twenty-four years.

* * *

John's plans began to crystalize in March of 1837 when his father wrote a letter to the US secretary of war.

"I have given the Secretary my full and free assent[33] for you to be appointed as a cadet at West Point," the elder Reynolds told his son. "If you want to sign the papers, I will endorse them for you."

"What does Senator Buchanan say?" John asked his father.

"He says that this time there should be no problem. He's promised to follow through and make sure you get the appointment."

Buchanan had tried once before to secure a West Point position for young John Reynolds. That was the year before, when John was not quite yet sixteen, the required age for a West Point recruit, and not yet eligible. Buchanan told the senior Reynolds that he was "mortified" to have forgotten the age requirement.[34]

In a little more than twenty years, Buchanan, as president of the United States, would have a lot more to worry about than age regulations. He would preside over the beginnings of the biggest challenge to ever face the nation. He would see states secede from the Union. He would see the country split over taxes, tariffs, slavery, and states' rights. He would leave office mere weeks before the Civil War began, leaving for Abraham Lincoln a vicious and violent confrontation that would eventually cost more than seven hundred thousand American lives. It was into this world that Buchanan was ushering young John

Reynolds. Although the signs of the impending trouble were there, neither of them saw the signals clearly.

John was truly excited at the prospect of joining the Army. In early March, he wrote his own letter to the secretary of war, confirming that he had "the honor" of receiving a notice of conditional appointment "as a Cadet in the service of the United States."

"I, therefore, hasten to assure you," John continued, "that with great pleasure I thankfully accept the appointment and shall report myself to the Superintendent of the Military Academy at West Point within the time specified."[35]

CHAPTER SEVEN

Panama
August 1860

The next morning, John, Kate, and Catherine boarded the steamship to begin the third leg of their long voyage to New York. Somewhere in the Caribbean Sea, between Honduras and Cuba, John realized that, at forty years old and for the first time in his life, he was falling in love.

He was thunderstruck at the notion, but he couldn't deny it. He was smitten with Catherine Mary Hewitt. The woman was beautiful, charming, and beguiling. He was coming to realize they were kindred spirits. He admired and was attracted to her streak of independence. It matched his own. He was even beginning to think that he might even want to marry her! My God! Was that possible? Never mind that he was sixteen years older than her. People with great differences in ages got married all the time, didn't they?

All he knew was that he wanted to spend the rest of his life with Kate Hewitt. Of course, he didn't know it at the time, but that wouldn't be very long. He would be dead inside of three years. He did realize, of course, that the life expectancy of a career military man could have its limitations. With the once faint beating of civil war drums growing louder every day, those limitations would take on a more certain probability.

But, at the moment, he wasn't thinking about any negatives that might surface with their union. People in love rarely do. He wasn't thinking about the odds of cheating death during wartime. He was falling in love, and that was all that mattered.

For Kate Hewitt, all that mattered was that for the first time in her life she was happy. Truly happy. This man, this Army officer, was the answer to her prayers. He had all the attributes that she had demanded in a man. He was good-looking, amiable, and had more than his share of common sense. But beyond that, Kate thought, he was strong and exuded power. She could put her trust in him. He was also, Kate had fantasized, affectionate.

If she was troubled by the Catholic-Protestant complication, she put it in the back of her mind. It was an issue she could deal with later. And besides, she thought, she was getting well ahead of herself. They had not even kissed. Not yet.

One evening, as the steamboat chugged steadily across the Caribbean, they stood together at their favorite spot, next to the railing on the deck of the boat. Catherine had gone to bed early. The whole of the sea laid out before them. The sun was disappearing over the western horizon. The first visible stars were just blinking into view. A warm breeze blew past them. It was a beautiful, clear night.

They stood there quietly, hands at their sides, taking in the view, each alone with their thoughts. After a few moments, she felt John's hand take hers and hold it gently. Kate did not resist. Instead, she clasped John's hand more snugly. They stood that way, not speaking, hardly breathing for a few more moments. Then, they turned to each other. He looked into her eyes. She looked into his. They both smiled. Then John leaned his six-foot frame down, and now they kissed, longingly and lovingly.

* * *

A little later that evening found John and Kate strolling, hand in hand, around the deck of the steamship. They found two deck chairs and sat down to further enjoy the night air, the moon, and stars.

"When do you report to West Point?" Kate asked eventually.

John had told her he would be heading home in Lancaster for a few weeks' leave and then would travel up to West Point to report in as the commandant of cadets.

"I'll have to be there during the first week in September," he replied.

Kate thought about that for a while. Then she spoke again.

"You know, John, Stillwater is not that far from West Point."

He grinned at her. He knew what she was getting at. He also smiled at how forthright she was.

"Kate," he said, affecting a false tone of mild reproach. "It is at least 130 miles!"

Stillwater sits sedately along the shore of the Hudson River, which flows nearly straight south, passing West Point and emptying into New York Harbor and eventually the Atlantic Ocean. Once the territory of Iroquois and Mohican Indians, Stillwater was settled by the Dutch and played a significant role in the Revolutionary War. Part of the famous Battle of Saratoga was fought in town, which gave the colonialists a major victory over the British.

Kate looked at the major innocently.

"It is? One hundred and thirty miles? My, my. Well, that's not too, too far, is it? An Army sometimes has gone that distance, right? Surely that's not too far if you want to be with someone you…you… well, you know."

Despite herself, Kate blushed, which caused John to explode with laughter.

"No, Kate," he said. "I reckon you're right. That's not too far to go." He paused for effect. "If a person has a good-enough reason to travel that distance," he added with just a touch of sarcasm.

She feigned outrage and lightly slapped his arm.

"Why, John Reynolds, you scoundrel! How dare you insult a lady like that!"

They both engaged in a fit of laughter.

"Well, I suppose I could get away to Philadelphia, too," he said when they had recovered. "You are going to be there for a while, aren't you?"

"Yes, I am," Kate replied. "I plan to be there long enough to get Catherine situated in school. Plus, I want to introduce myself to the Daughters of Charity and deliver the greetings to them I'm carrying from the Daughters in San Francisco. They are going to help me in my full conversion to Catholicism, as well."

Then the twinkle in her eye that John found so charming returned.

"But, Major," she continued. "Philadelphia is at least as far from West Point in one direction as Stillwater is in the other. Are you sure you want to trouble yourself to travel that far just to see little old me?" Now, she was clearly teasing.

He looked straight into her eyes, trying to be serious.

"Kate, I'd travel to the ends of the earth just to see little old you."

She stared at him for moment, then laughed softly. Kate put her hand to her mouth.

"Oh, John. I'm so sorry! That was a happy laugh. That's so sweet. So corny, but so sweet."

She leaned over and kissed him on the cheek. They both leaned back comfortably in their deck chairs. John had never felt so content. Kate had never felt so safe.

"This will be your second trip to West Point, won't it, John?" Kate asked.

"Yep," John replied. "I went there back in 1837."

"You were a plube, right? Isn't that what new cadets are called?"

"Plebe. They are called plebes. But that's after a summer of basic training. The really new cadets, the ones who first arrive at the Point are called just that, new cadets, or cadet candidates."

"Tell me more about that, John. I'm interested. Was it fun? Was it a good time?"

"Well, fun is not a word I would use about the Point. A good time? Let's just say it was a good adventure."

He began to tell Kate more of his tale.

CHAPTER EIGHT

West Point Military Academy
Early Summer 1837

"Hurry up! Hurry up! We haven't got all day! Come on! Move it! Move it, New Cadet!"

It was R-Day, Reception Day, at the West Point Military Academy in New York. Upper-class cadets in their junior and senior years were doing their best to harass and intimidate new cadets on their very first day at the academy. Seniors, or at West Point, first-class cadets, were nicknamed firsties. Juniors, or second-class cadets, were known as cows.

"What is your name, New Cadet!" one firstie shouted at John Reynolds, who stood stiffly at attention. The first-class cadet was dressed in a West Point uniform adorned with striped shoulder boards indicating he had a rank of a student officer. He stood nose to nose with John, shouting directly into his face.

"Reynolds! John Fulton Reynolds!" John shouted back, trying to match the other boy's volume.

"John Fulton Reynolds, sir!" the older student hollered. "You will address me and all other upper-class cadets as sir! Do you understand, New Cadet!"

"Yes, sir!" John shouted.

"Now, New Cadet, pick up your gear and get moving to your barracks! Quickly, New Cadet! Quickly! Move it! Move it! Do you hear me, New Cadet!"

"Yes, sir!" John shouted again. He leaned over to pick up a canvas bag containing clothes, toiletries, and other supplies. Throwing the bag over his shoulder, hanging on to it with one hand, John trotted off to join a line of other cadet candidates heading into one of the academy's ornate buildings, the firstie yelling at him all the while.

For some new cadets, R-Day at West Point was a rude awakening. It is the first day of a rigorous six-week basic training course. The day began calmly enough with a reception for all the newcomers and their families. John and the other civilians were welcomed with a warm, gracious, and patriotic greeting by the West Point commandant. Then the cadet candidates were given sixty seconds to say goodbye to their loved ones. Just sixty seconds. At that moment, life for John and his fellow newcomers changed instantly and dramatically.

For them, R-Day became a blur of orders, getting haircuts, getting fitted for uniforms, collecting gear, finding their quarters, answering demands of firsties and cows, being yelled at some more, falling in for forced marching here and there around campus, learning how to march, how to stand at attention, how to salute, or in other words, how to lose every vestige of civilian life in a single day.

There was a purpose to the hazing and harassment. Among other things, it quickly exposed young civilian men to the concept of the chain of command and how crucial it is in the military to obey orders. It was also the beginning of constant evaluations of the young men on several levels that would last throughout their West Point experience, even throughout their entire military careers. If any of the cadet candidates could not stand up to the stress and pressures of R-Day, they did not belong at West Point. In addition, R-Day gave firsties and cows an opportunity to exhibit leadership qualities under the watchful eyes of the West Point faculty.

At the end of the exhausting day, the candidates gathered in formation, dressed in academy uniforms, to take an oath of allegiance. For John, this was a moment of great pride. He stood straight and tall at attention, his new uniform immaculate, and raised his right hand, ready to repeat the hallowed words.

"I, John Reynolds," he said aloud in unison with a few hundred other cadet candidates, "do solemnly swear that I will support and defend the Constitution of the United States against all enemies, foreign and domestic; that I will bear true faith and allegiance to the same; that I take this obligation freely, without any mental reservation or purpose of evasion; and that I will well and faithfully execute the duties of the office on which I am about to enter, so help me God."

John was a little taken aback by how he felt. He was bursting with pride. *I'm in the Army now*, he thought. *Yes*, he reflected, *this is what I am meant to do! I can feel it!*

He was, indeed, in the United States Army, but just barely. He was still just a cadet candidate with six weeks of tough physical training ahead him. It wouldn't be until after then that he, and any of the other candidates who survived the summerlong test, would be fully accepted in the West Point corps of cadets. Even then, as a freshman, or fourth-year cadet, he would still be known as a plebe, as in the days of ancient Rome, the lowest of the low.

* * *

"Nice shooting, New Cadet. I gotta say, that was some darn nice shooting."

Cadet Candidate John Reynolds smiled at a rare compliment from the West Point instructor. They were on the rifle range, and John had just hit several targets in quick successions with impressive accuracy. It was mid-August, and the new cadets were just a few weeks from wrapping up what was called Beast Barracks, initial military training that is so intense, more than 2 percent of the trainees drop out nearly every year.

Throughout the summer, the young men were pushed harder and faced more difficult challenges than they had ever known. They were always on the move in the summer heat, rain or shine, from one field exercise to the next. It was a grueling time for them. It was a physically and mentally demanding experience, designed to weed out all but the truly committed and to instill confidence and self-assurance in those who succeeded and made it to the end.

John Reynolds loved almost every minute of it. The years as a youngster hunting with his older brother back in Lancaster had paid off. He was a crack shot at West Point. His love of horses paid off as well. In later years at the academy he showed a talent for riding and maneuvering during mock battles and other drills, always sitting tall and straight in the saddle, a posture for which he would become known as he rose through the ranks in his lifelong Army career.

John also was drawing the attention of academy instructors and ranking officers for his leadership skills, showing an innate ability to develop effective strategies during battle drills. In addition, John was making an impression with his military bearing, courtesy, seriousness of purpose, and quiet respect for those who outranked him. Young John Reynolds was turning into the type of officer the Army needed especially with the faint, but unmistakable, rumblings of war that were beginning to grow louder.

What John didn't love was the boredom of the repetitive drilling and training during those hot summer months. A fast learner, he was ready to move on and begin life as a full West Point cadet with advanced training in weaponry, tactics, and other academic classes. Sleeping in tents, cooking over open fires, and trying to stay clean day after day in the field began to grow old for him as well. Toward the end of August, he found some time to write to his brother, William.

"Our life in the tented field is nearly at an end for this year," he wrote. "I begin to tire of living in Camp and wish we were in Barracks." Despite his complaint, however, Reynolds was happy overall.

"I am very much pleased with my life here," he told his brother. "I think I shall continue to like it."

As he was still a cadet candidate, John remarked that he didn't know "any persons at the Point." That would soon change. He was about to meet several people who would in the years ahead have a great impact on his life, for good and for ill.

Finally, the big day came when he would no longer be called cadet candidate or new cadet. At the Point, it is called Acceptance Day. The arduous basic training period was, at last, over. Once again, John and all the other cadet candidates formed up in their immaculate uniforms to march out onto the Plain, the large academy parade ground, to become official West Point cadets.

Standing at stiff attention, they waited for the much-anticipated order from the reviewing stand. A hush fell over the crowd of families and visitors as the West Point band finished the last stanzas of martial music, its echoes fading out over the Hudson River. Finally, the commandant called out in a loud voice.

"New cadets! Join your company!"

Applause erupted from the visitors as the new cadets marched in formation to join the various military companies to which they had been assigned, and with which they would live, work, eat, sleep, and train for the next four years. That was the moment of transition. That was the moment they became fourth-year cadets. Plebes. They would be called plebes.

Once the companies had formed up, they marched in review past the commandant and his staff. The plebes snapped their eyes right and saluted as they paraded by the reviewing platform. As John's right hand came smartly up to the brim of his new West Point hat, his sisters in the visitors' section let out a squeal of delight. His father and mother applauded proudly, smiling big, broad smiles. John could see them out of the corner of his eye, but he did not break his military bearing as he marched past the reviewing stand.

Cadet John Reynolds was happy that his family was there for this memorable event. He was disappointed that his brother Will couldn't attend. But he understood why. Will was in line for a promotion to lieutenant in the US Navy and was preparing to join an important naval expedition exploring the antarctic in a few months. He was very proud of his brother. The assignment was a real feather in Will's cap because it was designed to be of major significance to the new science of oceanography.

At the conclusion of the Acceptance Day ceremony, John joined his family to get hugs and kisses from his mother and sisters, plus a hearty handshake, a hug, and a couple of thumps on his back from his father. He would have the rest of the weekend to relax with the family. Then, come Monday morning, the work, the real work of becoming an officer in the United States Army would begin.

* * *

For the next four years, Cadet John Reynolds performed admirably at West Point, on his way to becoming a highly regarded and competent commissioned officer in the United States Army. Fellow cadets and instructors often commented on his "clear and independent thinking, even temperament and courtesy."[36]

Several of his newfound friends, other cadets, at the Point would go on to occupy notable places in history. It is a remarkable fact that many of the general officers, on both sides in the Civil War, were alumni of the West Point Military Academy. Many, on both sides, knew one another well. Many had been friends.

Nathaniel Lyon would be the first Union general to be killed in the Civil War during the Battle of Wilson's Creek in Missouri.

Cousins Richard and Robert Garnett served as generals for the Confederacy.

A mapmaker, Amiel Whipple would conduct a reconnaissance of Confederate lines from a hot-air balloon at Bull Run early in the Civil War.

All those men were in the same 1841 graduating class as Reynolds. In the class ahead of them was a cadet who became one of John's close friends. Known as "Cump," he would go on to become one of the Civil War's most famous and controversial generals, William Tecumseh Sherman.

In the year behind Reynolds, James Longstreet came into John's field of view. Something of a loose cannon at West Point, earning many demerits, Longstreet would move on to become a formidable general on the Confederate side of the war. He would be an important member of General Robert E. Lee's staff.

Reynolds would also meet Abner Doubleday who would become second-in-command of Union forces at Fort Sumter when the South Carolina militia fired cannons at the facility early in the morning of April 12, 1861, marking the beginning of the Civil War. Doubleday would later be erroneously credited with inventing the game of baseball.

Another Reynolds acquaintance was Daniel Harvey Hill. Like the Garnett cousins and Longstreet, D. H. Hill became a Confederate general during the war. It would be Hill who would offer John comfort and kind words when Reynolds would be captured by Confederate forces in 1862.

Henry Kendrick graduated from West Point in 1835. He rose to the rank of colonel in the Union Army and eventually returned to teach at the Point while John was a cadet. Kendrick enjoyed a reputation as one of the academy's finest instructors. He remembered being impressed by the young Pennsylvanian, Reynolds. Kendrick was especially taken with John's clearheaded thinking.

The low rumble of national discord continued in the background of John's training to become an Army officer. It would still be nearly twenty-five years before actual civil war exploded early one April morning. But the pot was brewing.

The 1831 Nat Turner slave rebellion was already history. In 1837, when John entered West Point, abolitionist Elijah Lovejoy was murdered by proslavery forces in Illinois. The year John was a cow, or second-class student, 1839, another slave rebellion broke out. This one was aboard the ship *Amistad* en route to the United States from Cuba.

Those and other incidents sparked lively conversations among cadets during precious free periods. States' rights, slavery, abolition, North versus South, sedition, politics, taxes, tariffs, the meaning of freedom, and possibilities of war were all on the agenda over time. The conversations, now and then, would become heated as cadets from the South and cadets from the North clashed over ideology.

Few, except perhaps the most insightful of them, would guess that one day many of these classmates, these proud warriors-in-training, these friends, would be leading forces eager to kill each other in the most divisive, earth-shattering and wrenching epoch the nation had ever faced. Even John Reynolds, with his clearheaded thinking, never imagined such a thing. At the time, he and all the other cadets were just trying to get through a demanding time of their own.

West Point life, for any cadet, no matter what year they were in, was difficult in many respects. One night, exhausted from day-long strenuous activities, John took a moment to write a letter to one of his sisters.

"From 5 o'clock in the morning," he wrote, "or speaking 'a la militate,' from Reveille until 10 o'clock at night we have only two hours to ourselves. Besides our military duties, such as Guard, Drill, Parade, all the rest of the time we are obliged to be in our rooms studying Calculus, French, Ethics, etc. Cannot even visit our neighbors without getting 5 demerits."[37]

His complaining notwithstanding, John managed to make it through the tough West Point years without many demerits. Things got, if not easier, more pleasurable at least, in his third year. That's when West Point brought out the horses so cadets could learn to ride and care for them properly. John was in seventh heaven. Of course, because of his childhood, he already knew how to ride, and his cavalry-like abilities were noticed. Plus, he continued to impress staff and fellow cadets alike with his leadership capabilities. He seemed to have a knack for military modus vivendi, the way things are done in uniform. He was comfortable with the lifestyle.

While excelling in practical military matters, John's performance academically was another matter. For example, in such subjects as field artillery, which involved horses, Reynolds finished close to the top ten in his class. In other areas, such as philosophy, he fell as low as thirty-six. In the end, he graduated from the Point literally as an average student. He was twenty-sixth overall in a class of fifty-two, exactly in the middle.[38]

John's reputation for stoicism and as a "man of few words" was belied in a very long, maudlin letter he wrote to his sister Jane as he was nearing graduation. He clearly was going to miss West Point and the friendships he had made. In language of extreme sentimentality, he waxed philosophically, as many twenty-one-year-old adults do, about the next phase of his life.

"Will you not leave the halls of your 'alma mater," and the friends and classmates you have acquired here?" he opined. "Yes! But it is a case of necessity!"[39]

He goes on to lament the "contract" by which all cadets must live, a contract which requires them to leave the institution for an uncertain future.

"We leave scenes endeared to us by a thousand pleasing memories," he wrote to Jane. He hoped that visiting family and old friends back home would "sweeten the bitter tear of separation and sad farewell, perhaps forever, for we do not know how long."[40]

For John Reynolds, it would not be forever. He would be back.

CHAPTER NINE

Gulf of Mexico
August 1860

John, Kate, and Catherine were finishing lunch on the upper-aft deck of the steamship as it plowed through the waters of the Gulf of Mexico where it connects with the Atlantic Ocean. They were making good progress. The vessel was now north of Havana headed toward Florida's eastern coast. The sun was bright, and the sea was placid. They were close enough to the Cuban island that seagulls followed the boat, cawing and wailing, swooping and diving to catch bait fish that were being churned up by the passing steamer. They, too, were having lunch.

"Mmm, that was good," Kate said as she dabbed her mouth with a napkin.

"Yes, I thought so, too," John responded. "The fish was delicious. How about you, Catherine? Did you enjoy lunch?"

"Yum!" The little girl enthused. "I liked the pudding the best!"

John and Kate laughed.

"No surprise there," John said.

Now that lunch was over, Catherine was fidgeting in her seat, clearly bored with the conversation the two adults were having.

"Catherine, would you like to go back to our cabin to read or draw or something?" Kate asked.

"Yes. May I?"

"Of course. Come on. I'll go with you to let you in."

Kate looked at John.

"I'll be right back. Please don't go anywhere."

John looked around the deck with a bemused look.

"I'm not sure where I could go. Not many places to hide around here," he smirked.

"Don't be smart!" Kate laughed as she and Catherine got up from the table. Then she quickly grew serious and bent down as if to kiss him on the cheek. Instead, she whispered in his ear.

"John, there is something we need to talk about some more when I get back."

She looked at him meaningfully and leaned closer. This time she did kiss him, stood up, and headed toward the passenger quarters with Catherine in tow.

The Major's gaze was drawn toward the seagulls frantically competing for the little fish that were tossing and turning in the steamship's wake. He sat there alone, feeling mostly content. He was comfortable with his deepening relationship with Kate, and he had a good guess at what was on her mind. It had been on his as well. Religion. He was Protestant. She was Catholic, and that could mean trouble.

John picked up his cup of coffee and took a sip as he thought about the differences in their two religions. That wasn't so much of an issue for him as it was for Kate. She had brought the subject up the other day, worried that if they continued to see each other after they arrived in Philadelphia, people would talk. It wouldn't be friendly talk either, she had said. John had to admit that his own family might find it peculiar that he was seeing a woman of the Catholic faith. He was confident, however, that they wouldn't object. For all his life, his parents, brothers, and sisters had been pretty open-minded about all sorts of social issues. If any of them did object, well, to hell with them, he grunted to himself.

John knew, however, the religion issue ran much deeper than mere family matters. It had become political. Anti-Catholic senti-ment was running deep through much of the country. Protestant children were often taught to distrust people of the Catholic religion.

So-called popery was considered a menace. Much of that prejudicial attitude was created by resentment of German and Irish Catholic immigrants who had fled Europe to find religious liberty in the colonies. One Boston clergyman railed against them as allies of tyranny. In the years leading up to 1860, more than one half the population of Ireland arrived on US shores. In those same years, seven and a half million immigrants came to the United States, more than the entire US population in 1810.[41]

Voting at some election polling places turned violent. New anti-Catholic political movements sprang out of fear and anger. One became known as the Know Nothing party because when its members were asked about the organization, their stock answer was that they knew nothing about it.

But John knew plenty. Not about that political organization, but how emotions can soar out of control when people are seized with fear and mistrust. He had seen it happen repeatedly in battles he had fought since joining the Army.

In the middle of his ruminating, Kate returned to the table and sat down.

"Well, I'm relieved to see you are still here." She grinned at John.

"Huh," he sniffed. "I did try to jump overboard, but one of the deckhands stopped me," he said, looking at her with owl eyes.

"Oh, stop, you scoundrel." She laughed. He smiled broadly, then grew serious.

"I've been thinking about what you said the other day," he said, seriously.

"About our religious faiths?"

"Yes, about that."

"That's what I wanted to talk to you about," Kate said.

"Who cares about what religion we are?" he said defiantly, but he knew better.

"A lot of folks will, you know that, John," she said with emotion. "My family and the stuffed shirts back in Stillwater certainly will. I've told you, sweetheart, I come from a long line of very conservative Protestants. My family has never been very forgiving. They can be really mean about matters with which they don't agree, especially when it comes to faith. We never really got along, like most families do. That's why I decided to leave the Baptist Church and become Catholic."

John had stopped listening. He didn't hear anything she had said after the word *sweetheart*.

"Sweetheart?" he said quietly.

She immediately went into full blush mode.

"Oh, John, I'm sorry! That just came out of my mouth. I didn't mean to be so forward! Oh dear, I'm so embarrassed!"

"No, no, please, don't be," he said, gently. "You do me a great honor. I love that you feel comfortable enough with me to call me that."

He paused for a moment, biting his lip. Then John continued.

"Kate, I not only love you calling me that…"

He looked directly in her eyes and reached across the table to hold her hands.

"And, sweetheart, I love…you."

Kate's eyes welled up with tears as she whispered.

"Oh, John, I love you, too. I really do!"

John moved around to her side of the table. He pulled close to Kate the chair Catherine had occupied during lunch. He sat down and leaned over. The two of them held each other in their arms. Then they kissed with great passion.

Soon, he realized she was weeping silently.

"Kate, what's the matter?" asked.

She sighed.

"You know what the matter is, John. How can this relationship possibly last? Besides having trouble with my family, and maybe, yours, I'm afraid our being together might hurt your military career. I know how anti-Catholic prejudices can ruin lives. I hate that. But that's the reality we have to recognize. It's just the way it is!"

"I don't agree," John said with equal passion. "We are free to be with, and love, anyone we wish, no matter religious differences. Isn't that what our grandparents and their parents fought…and died for? Independence? Freedom of religion along with all the other things?"

"Yes, they did, John. Yes, they did. But you know as well as I that ideas and beliefs that appear on paper don't always translate to reality. People will believe what they believe. Traditions, like superstitions, are hard to overcome. I just don't what you to be penalized by the Army for some silly bias about religion."

John thought for a moment.

"I won't be penalized if they don't know about it."

"What do you mean?"

"What if we kept it secret? Not tell anyone about us."

Kate frowned.

"How can we keep our relationship secret?"

"We just can. Right now, no one knows about us, except for Catherine. Can she keep a secret?"

"I...I don't know. I guess she can."

"No one else on this boat knows who we are. And when we get to port, we can be careful in public. I'm headed for Lancaster to see my family before going up to West Point. You are going to Philadelphia. We'll just go our separate ways, as much as I will hate that. But I will write you private letters. Hopefully, you will write to me—"

"Of course, I will," Kate interjected.

"And I will quietly visit Philadelphia whenever I can. One of my sisters lives there, and I can explain to anyone who asks that I am visiting her. While I'm doing that, I can easily slip away to be with you."

John smiled, his eyes bright.

"You know, now that I say that out loud, this all sounds very clandestine and adventurous. You know, like spies or something."

Kate frowned deeply.

"I don't know, John. I'm much rather be open about us. Go out in public, attend concerts together, go to restaurants, take long walks in parks, tell our families. I'd want to be seen with you!"

"Likewise," John said. "But it would be a risk, as you just said. I hate that society is like that in this day and age. But you are right. It is the reality we must recognize. There will come a day when religious differences won't matter, I hope and pray."

Now, John sighed.

"But for now, that's just the way things are."

Kate stayed quiet for a long moment. Then she spoke.

"Okay. We'll keep us a secret. Our secret."

John smiled. He leaned over and kissed her again.

* * *

Later in the day, John and Kate were sitting in deck chairs, relaxing in the sun, and reading. Catherine was playing quietly with a doll she had brought along on the journey. After a while, Kate put down her magazine and looked over at John.

"What is that you are reading, John?" she asked.

John looked up from the book he held in his hands.

"Oh, it's a new military manual," he said.

He turned it over to peer at the cover.

"It's called *Rifles and Rifle Practice*. It was published...let's see..."

He flipped to the fly leaf.

"Just last year, 1859."[42]

"Is that something you are reading to get ready for West Point?" Kate asked.

"Yes," he answered. "It has all the latest and most modern techniques for firing and maintaining military rifles. New cadets at the Point will have to know everything in this book backwards and forwards, and as their commandant, so will I."

"What else will you be teaching them?"

"Well, I won't necessarily be teaching them all the subjects, but as commandant of cadets I will have to oversee what they must learn. That includes tactics for artillery, cavalry, and infantry. There is also military strategy, grand tactics, and army administration. If those young men want to be officers, they have to be well-rounded. One subject I'm really looking forward to is equitation, you know, horsemanship.[43] I may teach that one myself. Any chance I can be around horses, I'll grab!" He laughed.

"Are you looking forward to going back to West Point?" Kate asked.

He sighed.

"I suppose so," John said. "I mean, it will be enjoyable to be at the Point again. But, to be candid, I am somewhat disenchanted with the military."

"I was under the impression you loved being a soldier," Kate said.

"A soldier, yes!" John replied, sounding infuriated. "As long as the damn politicians, pardon my language, let us do the soldiering! I have seen so many decisions about battle tactics made by men who have never even seen a battlefield, it makes my brain boil. They sit up there in Washington, second-guessing Army generals and other highly trained officers, risking the lives of good and brave men in the ranks. I have seen it over and over again, out west and in Florida in the Indian wars and down in Mexico during that fight over Texas."

Kate remained silent for several moments, thinking about what John had just said. Pursing her lips, she looked at him.

"Begging your pardon, my love," she began gently. "Is it political inference in military matters that you are so angry about? Or, is it really that you're are upset at being passed over for those commands you told me about?"

He turned sharply to look at her. Kate could see she had provoked him, but she stood her ground, looking unblinkingly into his dark flashing eyes. After a moment, he relaxed. The tension left his body.

Shaking his head and with a rueful smile, he said, "We've known each other for just a few weeks, and already you know me so well."

Kate smiled, covering her nervous relief that he apparently accepted her critical observation with equanimity.

"I guess it's a little of both," he admitted and smiled again. "You have some pretty good insight, you know."

He leaned over to give her a kiss on her cheek. He leaned back and continued talking.

"There is something else I've only recently decided about West Point commandant duty, which is all about teaching and training young, inexperienced boys to become soldiers. The task is a most exacting one to the patience, industry, and temper of any person."

After a pause, he added, "And, of course, very different from commanding men."[44]

"What's that like?" she asked. "I mean, commanding men, sending them into battle, knowing that they could get hurt? Or worse."

Major Reynolds thought about that for a few moments.

"Well, I guess you could say it is a learned process," he said. "And it is something you learn to accept as a military officer. We all have to expect death as a possibility, even probability, in war. If the cause is right and just, well then, death is a comprehensible outcome."

"My goodness," Kate said. "How can you be so cavalier about it?"

"Oh, I'm not cavalier at all," he replied. "I certainly do not wish to die. It is just the way it is. Not all the time, of course. In fact, the first few years after I graduated from the Point, things were pretty boring."

"Boring?" Kate replied with surprise.

"Yes. In those days, the Army was actually getting smaller. With the war against the Seminole Indians in Florida winding down, there wasn't as much need for officers. Promotions were slow. I think something like 117 officers actually resigned their commissions the year I graduated. Obviously, I didn't, though. My first assignment was at Fort McHenry in Baltimore. Actually, it wasn't too bad there. Our sleeping quarters were excellent. Each officer had sleeping quarters to themselves. That was a lot better than the barracks or the tents at West Point, I can say. There was an elegantly furnished parlor, too."[45]

"What did you do there?" Kate asked.

"It's called garrison duty. Not very exciting. Lots of drilling, marching around. I was assigned to supervise repairs to the road leading from Baltimore to the fort. That meant being on a horse a good bit of the time. But even that was boring. Not much riding involved. Mostly it meant sitting in the saddle for hours and hours, making sure the work was getting done. I just remember my rear end getting very sore."[46]

They both heard Catherine giggling at that last comment. She was obviously eavesdropping while playing with her doll.

"Well," Kate said, playfully. "With all that terribly boring duty, you must have had time for...how should I put this...socializing?

There must be plenty of pretty ladies in Baltimore who would be attracted to a handsome fellow in uniform, hmm?"

John laughed. He knew she was baiting him.

"Well, none nearly so pretty as yourself, ma'am," he said, cutting her joking sarcasm off at the knees.

Kate blushed.

"Well played, Major. Well played," she said with a laugh. "And, thank you, sir. Very kind of you to say."

"Truth be told," John went on. "Despite evidence to the contrary, I really didn't have time for, umm, socializing, as you put it. Besides, I wasn't at McHenry all that long. A few months later, in the summer of 1842, I was transferred to St. Augustine, Florida."

"St. Augustine? That's the oldest city in the country, right?"

"Oldest city in the continental US, sure. It was founded in 1565 by Spanish explorers. Yes, it is really old and really, really hot! So, hot that in July, for the first time in my life, I got seriously ill."

"Oh my goodness, John! What happened?"

"I came down with a case of bilious fever. It is sometimes caused by malaria, or what some folks call marsh fever. Not to be indelicate, but I lost a lot of bodily fluids by means I care not to describe."

"John, that's horrible! I'm so sorry!" Kate said.

"Well, I got plenty of rest and recovered, thanks to my company commander, Captain Braxton Bragg. I tell you, Kate, he is one tough bird. Very strict on discipline and a stickler for the rules. There are even claims that at one of his postings, out in the west somewhere, he was a company commander and served as quartermaster as well. The rumor is he submitted a requisition for suppliers as company commander and then turned down the request as quartermaster! He allegedly turned down the request a second time. I heard the post commandant was so exasperated, he said something like 'My God, Mr. Bragg, you have quarreled with every officer in the army, and now you are quarreling with yourself!'"[47]

"Goodness gracious!" Kate exclaimed. "That's pure folly. Ridiculous! Is he barmy?"

John laughed heartily.

"Well, he is unusual. But he treated me all right when I was ill. That fever was unusual, too. I've always been of good mind and body, I believe. Never sick, really, a day in my life. That bilious business was worrisome, confound it."

"I must say you look healthy now, John." She looked at him with coquettish eyes. "Very healthy."

"Why, Miss Hewitt, how you do go on!" he said in jest.

"What was it like, there in St Augustine?" Kate asked, changing the subject. "I've never been to Florida."

"Oh, I'll tell you, Kate, it was the dullest of dull places.[48] I was bored to tears, especially during my convalescence. Couldn't wait to get out of there. Fortunately, I wasn't there all that long. By early the next spring, our regiment was transferred to Fort Moultrie in Charleston, South Carolina. It was a surprise, but we know not what changes a week of time make in this unsettled life of a soldier.[49]

"The places you have been, and my, the things you have seen. You make being a soldier sound so romantic."

John looked into the middle distance, thinking about that for a moment.

"Not romantic, not really," he said, thoughtfully. "Necessary, I should think. Necessary to help preserve and protect the freedoms for which our grandparents fought…and died. This is serious business, soldiering. You asked me a moment ago what it is like commanding men. I believe good and effective commanding means you must lead men, not direct them. I will always be in the battle with them. At the front. A commander must prove to his men that he cares about them. If he must lead them into harm's way, he does so only after careful and exacting consideration of the situation at hand and determine, to the extent possible, whatever decisions he makes will affect future events. I will always be loyal to the men I lead."

He paused a moment, reflecting further on the subject and warming to it.

"That does not mean I am their best friend," he continued. "Discipline is key. It is, in my view, one of the most effective elements in maintaining an effective command."

He chuckled slightly.

"That may be one of the reasons Captain Bragg and I got on so well. At least at the beginning. His dictatorial manner and temper, however, became tiresome. But, as I said before, despite his strange behavior at times, he was rabid about discipline within the ranks. And he was right about that. There have been times when I was compelled to order my men to take dangerous, life-threatening actions, especially in Texas and Mexico. There will be times in the future, I'm sure, when I will be called upon to do the same again. In those cases, there must be no hesitation on the part of the troops. That takes discipline. An enemy will not care if my men waver or falter. In fact, an enemy will prefer it. I am not saying my men should never be afraid. No, not at all. Fighting battles is often very frightening. I will admit, there have been times when I was quite afraid. But fear can be controlled and put to use, keeping one sharp and acutely aware. That takes discipline."

"It appears a good commander must be really tough," Kate observed.

"Not tough," John said. "Strict. But, also, fair. Discipline must be fairly observed. Discipline must be consistent as well. The men must know that infractions will be punished. At the same time, they must realize that punishment will not be administered just for punishment's sake. Once that is well understood, when ordered to take on difficult, dangerous missions, they will respond. On the other hand, and, perhaps, just as important, a commander must show that he supports his men to the last degree. He must also praise and be generous to them when they complete missions successfully, however small. Strict, caring, brave, thoughtful, fair, supportive, principled, consistent...those are the marks of an effective commander."

John looked at Kate and grinned.

"None of that sounds very romantic to me."

Kate laughed lightly.

"Well, I think, you are very romantic, if I can be so bold to say. And I'd follow you anywhere, Major John Reynolds."

She gave him a loving look.

"Anywhere," she repeated.

* * *

The next afternoon, Major Reynolds strolled up to the wheel-house of the steamship to introduce himself to the ship's captain. He knocked on the door, which was opened by the vessel's first mate.

"Good afternoon," John said, politely. "My name is Major John Reynolds, United States Army. I'm on my way to Philadelphia and wanted to pass along my greetings to the captain and relay to him what a fine voyage this has been so far."

"Come in! Come in, Major!" the skipper called from inside the wheelhouse. He was sitting in his chair, which was bolted to a slightly raised platform above and behind the helm.

"Steady as she goes, helmsman," the captain said.

"Aye, aye, sir," responded the young helmsman standing at the wheel.

The captain stood and greeted Reynolds with a handshake.

"I'm Captain Stevens," he said in a gruff voice. "Pleased to be makin' yer acquaintance, sir."

"Likewise," said John. "As I said, this has been a pleasant voyage so far. I thank you for your excellent seamanship."

"Well, we've been blessed with fair weather and followin' seas. It don't get much better'n that. We've been lucky, so far, thank God."

John looked down at a chart table positioned next to the captain's chair. He could see markings indicating the ship's course and heading.

"If I am reading this right," John said, pointing to the chart, "it appears we are about abreast of Charleston Harbor, is that correct?"

"Exactly right, sir," the captain replied. "We're about 140 miles due east of the harbor. We oughta make Philadelphia in the next few days, I reckon. Are ya familiar with Charleston, Major?"

"Indeed, I am, sir. I spent some time there back in '43."

"Ya musta had a mighty good time there," the captain said with a snicker. "I hear the Charleston woman are good-lookin' and some of them are, how should I say, very accomodatin', if ya catch my drift."

Her gave John an exaggerated and salacious grin.

"Hmm, I…ah…don't know about that," John replied, diplomatically. "But, yes, the social life in Charleston is quite active, and the citizens there, woman and men, are very hospitable."

Captain Stevens snickered again.

"I bet," he said.

"Now, that's not what I—" Reynolds started to protest.

"Aw, I'm just pullin' yer leg, Major. Relax. Just havin' a little fun, that's all."

"Yes. Well, I see."

John was beginning to wish he hadn't come up to the wheelhouse.

"So, where else have ya been, Major?"

"Well, I've crisscrossed the country a couple of times. After Moultrie, I was given some time off and then sent to Texas for that Mexican fight. That was in '45."

John's time off had lasted for three months while he attended family matters back in Lancaster. His mother had died while he was at Fort Moultrie, but he was unable to attend her funeral because, as he had told Kate during one of their talks, "Lieutenant Bragg was away and I was in command of my company." It wasn't until March of 1845 that he could return home and properly mourn his mother's death.[50]

It was also while posted at Fort Moultrie that Reynolds came to the aid of his friend, William Tecumseh "Cump" Sherman who, like John, was then a young lieutenant. One of the pleasures of being posted at Fort Moultrie was the opportunity to spend off time up-country, in the vacation homes of Charlestonians who appreciated the presence of the federal soldiers, a sentiment that would radically change in the decades to come.

During one such winter visit to a plantation on the Cooper River, Sherman and Reynolds were hunting deer with the owner's son. Soon a deer appeared near a swamp where the hunters were hidden and waiting. The son fired a shot and wounded the animal who took off past the swamp, through pinewoods, to escape. Reynolds watched as Sherman mounted his horse and took off after the prey at full gallop. Suddenly the horse tripped and fell violently to the ground, taking Sherman down with him, painfully dislocating the lieutenant's shoulder.

Tangled up in broken bridle and saddle, with his horse struggling, Sherman called out.

"Reynolds! Need your help here! Come quick!"

John rushed over, mended the gear, got the horse standing again, and got Sherman back up in the saddle. His shoulder and arm were so painful, he had to be taken back to the plantation.[51]

A few months after that incident, Reynolds went on his extended leave to Lancaster and then on to Texas and Mexico.

"Mexico, eh?" the captain said. "I hear that was a helluva fight."

Reynolds had to agree. It certainly was a hell of a fight. It was also during the American war with Mexico that he had been promoted for gallant action. Twice.

CHAPTER TEN

Matamoros, Mexico
1845–1846

He had been training for this moment for eight long years, perhaps for all his life, he thought, if you considered all the hunting and horseback riding during his youth. He knew this day would come someday. Now that it had, Lieutenant John Reynolds was distressingly impressed by the violence of it all. It was the first time in his young life of twenty-five years that John had come under serious hostile fire. When it was over, he had written to his sister Jane, telling her, "I can never again, I don't think, be placed in a more uncomfortable situation than the one we just got out of."[52]

The uncomfortable situation was in being outnumbered three to one by enemy soldiers at what was known, for the moment, as Fort Texas across the Rio Grande River from the Mexican town of Matamoros. By this time, Second Lieutenant Reynolds had received a relatively minor promotion to first lieutenant, only the first of many of his steps up the chain of command.

John and his unit had arrived in Corpus Christi, Texas, in August of 1845 as territorial disputes between the United States and Mexico were heating up. His company of men had been reorganized for light artillery duty. Thus, horses were required and most of his troops had to be taught how to ride properly. Between his demand for excellence, and given his equine expertise, this task frustrated him to no end.

"I have been so much employed for the last two or three weeks in imparting my knowledge of horsemanship to twenty of thirty stupid Germans, Irishmen and so on",[53] he complained.

The following spring, with the US-Mexican dispute over the annexation of Texas growing more tense, American general Zachery Taylor moved his Army from Corpus Christi about 160 miles south to take up positions near the Rio Grande. His soldiers were put to work building an earthen fortress. They formed it in the shape of a six-sided star with each side nine feet high and fifteen feet high. The soldiers dug an eight-foot-deep moat around the entire facility. It was hot, hard work digging trenches, erecting embankments, building durable, protective bombproofs, and creating gun emplacements.

At the end of April 1846, Mexican forces were on the move along the disputed border. General Taylor marched most of the units out of the new Fort Texas to confront them. A relatively small contingent of five hundred US troops was left behind. They included Lieutenant Reynolds and his company. Major Jacob Brown, an officer who had come up through the enlisted ranks, was put in command of the fort.

Mexican soldiers attacked the stripped-down Fort Texas garrison on the third day of May. Mortar shells and artillery rounds rained down on the garrison for nearly a week. The Americans gamely fired back. It was a slugfest. A reporter, who happened to be present inside the fort, said, "It will ever be a matter of surprise that so little damage was done to [the fort] and its inmates by this severe and continued bombardment."[54]

Finally, General Taylor, out in the field hunting down other enemy combatants, turned back to relieve the fort. Eventually, the Mexican units were turned away, but not before the Americans suffered more than a dozen casualties, including the death of Major Brown. Subsequently, the fort was renamed in his honor. John Reynolds later said, "I rather be on ten battlefields than take another week's bombardment such as we had in Fort Brown."[55]

It was after this battle that young Lieutenant Reynolds first saw the horrors of war, close up. If he was stunned by the ferocity of the Mexican shelling, he was equally shocked by what he witnessed in the Matamoros hospital, which he visited with a few of his fellow junior officers.

"My God," John exclaimed, as they walked among the wounded and miserable Mexican soldiers, suffering under little or no medical care. "These poor wretched souls!"

Blood was everywhere, on the floor, staining the bedsheets, drawing big, fat, ugly flies. The stench was overpowering. Several of the wounded, lying on their soiled beds, conscious and able to talk through their pain, begged John for money.

"Por favor, señor," one man cried out pitifully, trying to grab John's arm as he passed by. "Dinero, por favor, dinero, señor."

John reached into his pocket, pulled out a few dollars, and gave it to the man. He turned to the other American officers.

"Who, I say, could look upon all this and not thank God most devoutly and exclaim, I am not a Mexican!" he said.

Looking around at the deplorable and odious scene, John shook his head.

"How different would have been our fate if fortune had picked on the Mexican banner in these battles. The few who served to fall in their hands would have been the most unfortunate."[56]

His sympathy for the wounded enemy soldiers, however, did not lessen his resolve, whatsoever, to remain victorious in the battles that were yet to come. It would be that drive and determination for which he would be remembered by family, friends, colleagues, and history. It would also be those attributes, and others, that would make him so appealing to the enamored Kate Hewitt in another fourteen years.

* * *

"There are too damn any of them!" General Zachery Taylor complained.

"Yes, sir," Lieutenant Reynolds replied. "And, still they come."

John and his commander were discussing the influx of American volunteer fighters arriving by the thousands for the war with Mexico.

Lieutenant John Reynolds found that most of the new citizen soldiers were like the "stupid" men who had so frustrated him during horsemanship training earlier. It infuriated him that so many were ill trained and undisciplined. He agreed with a general who accused the volunteers of being "perfectly ignorant of discipline and most restive under restraint."[57]

The problem John, and other regular Army officers, faced is that the volunteers tended to act as a force unto themselves. They came from farms, cities, and towns, formed up in units by local officials whose decisions and appointments were often politically motivated. Many of the volunteers elected their own officers who commonly were friends, neighbors, or relatives from back home.

"They are, in consequence, a most disorderly mass who will give us, I fear, more trouble than the enemy,"[58] said the same general who found them so ignorant of discipline.

John's worry was not so much that they wouldn't fight well when the time came. He even believed they had courage. What bothered him was that they likely could not withstand the harsh conditions soldiers often face in a state of war. He discussed it one night sitting around a campfire with fellow officers.

"I have no doubt they will fight well enough when it comes to that, but that is not half of what we have to undergo in the field," he said.

The other officers shook their heads in agreement as John continued.

"It is not the fighting they object to," he said. "It is the hot weather and marching that has disgusted them, and this lying idle in camp subjected to the strictest discipline that has disheartened so many of them."[59]

John's assessment was proven accurate as the weeks and months passed. Spring became summer, and temperatures soared well above one hundred degrees. Dust and insects were constant and irritating companions. In August, General Taylor marched fifteen thousand of his men about one hundred miles northwest across Mexico to the town of Camargo. He planned to resupply his army, then head south to Monterrey.

The trek overland, however, was so debilitating with the stifling heat, attacks by insects, along with other ailments, many of the troops fell ill. Hundreds of the citizen soldiers were hospitalized when they reached Camargo. Many of them died from their illnesses. Many others were sent home.

By the time he set out for Monterrey, General Taylor only had a little more than a third of the men with whom he began the mission, divided about equally between regular soldiers and volunteers.

John Reynolds, on the other hand, was undaunted by the hardships and the extreme elements. Ever the outdoorsman, he reveled in Mexico's stark landscape.

"We are entering into very beautiful country up here," he wrote to his sister Jane. "It is quite broken and, in some places, quite picturesque. This is so different from any country we have yet seen that we are all anxious to move forward."[60]

Move forward they did, finally arriving in mid-September on the outskirts of Monterrey. Captain Braxton Bragg, the same man who had nursed Reynolds back to health in Florida, immediately put his battery of men through a series of training exercises. Here in Monterrey, Reynolds again was one of Bragg's junior officers.

"All right, men!" John bellowed to his men gathered at attention in formation. "We are called light artillery for a reason! We move fast, aim sharp, fire quick, reload, and fire again. That's what we must do. That's why we train again and again. Let's show Captain Bragg how good we are! Are you with me!"

A loud hurrah emanated from the battery of men in front of him.

"The drill this morning went fairly well," the lieutenant said as he paced in front of them. Then he stopped and glared at them. "But, not well enough! Not by a long chalk! You can do better. You must do better! You must be faster, more accurate, more precise in your movements and in your shooting. I'm giving you a second chance this afternoon, but by God, the enemy won't! On my order, load the guns!"

The battery of soldiers leaped into action, running to their six-pounders, artillery pieces that fired six-pound projectiles great distances. They spun the gun carriages around, pointing them toward an imaginary enemy, and stood by, waiting for the order to load and fire.

Reynolds shook his head.

"Fall in!" he shouted.

The battery quickly reformed at attention. They had moved smartly with hardly any wasted motion. But Lieutenant Reynolds took on an air of impatience.

"Sloppy. Just sloppy. You all know your jobs. So do them! And do them right! When we are called to provide fire support, we cannot, must not, hesitate. So, let's do it again. And again, if we have to, until we get it perfectly right! Do you understand!" he roared.

"Yes, sir!" the men hollered back.

"All right, then. The enemy is behind you now. Get to those guns and turn them around and aim, ready for firing. Go!"

An officer passing by observed the training and was impressed with the performance.

"The horses, as well as the men," he said, "seemed to understand their business perfectly and being of fine bone and blood, they whirled their caissons over the plain with wonderful rapidity and ease."[61]

Among the soldiers handling the horses, of course, were the same men of whom John had been so disparaging earlier. He had whipped them into shape, and his efforts would not go unnoticed.

Reynolds also drew attention from higher-ranking officers for his actions during the rugged Battle of Monterrey, which he described as "a regular street fight." Mexican forces outnumbered the Americans by about one thousand men.[62] General Taylor decided to attack the city from two fronts, from the west to cut Mexican supply lines, and from the east as a diversionary tactic. The company led by Reynolds was part of the feint in the east.

September 21, 1846, the day the attack began, was John's twenty-sixth birthday. His "celebration" was hardly a festive occasion. His artillery battery was ordered into the city to support a column of infantrymen who had gotten into trouble in the narrow streets and high stone walls. They were not accustomed to this kind of urban fighting. In the confusion, they were being attacked by Mexican rifle-men on rooftops and hiding in the maze of buildings.

John plunged into the city with his battery of four guns, four caissons, and six horses. But the cramped latticework of lanes con-stricted their movement and rendered the artillery guns all but use-less. He saw that only one gun had any chance of firing at all, but the others were exposed to enemy fire.[63]

"Turn around!" he ordered his men as enemy bullets whizzed past them. "Let's get those guns and horses out of here. They're no use to us in these damned alleyways!"

That was not easy. The streets were much too narrow to simply turn around. John's troops needed help from the infantrymen they had come to rescue.

"Lift men, lift!" John shouted, as they struggled to lift the heavy gun carriage up against a wall, making some room for the pivot. Enemy musket fire continued to slam into the streets and nearby walls with chips of brick, adobe, and shrapnel pinging all around them as they scrambled their way back out of the city.

While they were repositioning, the lieutenant's section was ordered to the north end of town. Here, out in the open prairie, his guns were much more effective. They drew a bead on a couple of hundred Mexican horse-mounted lancers from what was called the Black Fort, attempting an end run around the American infantry units.

Standing tall and stern just to the rear of his artillery pieces, John ordered in a loud voice, "Load!" His gunners at each piece quickly loaded bags of gunpowder, called cartridges, down the muz-zles of the guns. They then sighted the guns downrange and stepped back. A second group of soldiers stepped up to load the cannonballs. Once satisfied the guns were properly loaded, they also stepped back.

"Ready!" the lieutenant ordered.

Other soldiers took hold of the lanyards attached to the friction primers on the guns.

"Fire!"

The soldiers sharply pulled the lanyards simultaneously. All four guns roared like the devil's own thunder. The cannonballs screamed out of the muzzles, amid clouds of smoke and flame, flying toward the enemy. Lieutenant Reynolds had trained his men well. The shots were deadly accurate, falling among the advancing Mexicans several hundred yards away. They scattered and turned tail, spurring their horses back to the Mexican lines.

The men in Reynolds's battery began to cheer at their victory. He let them blow off steam for a few minutes, then called them to order.

"You did a good job, men," he said. "Well done. But do not get cocky. We may have won that skirmish, but the battle, indeed the war, is far from over. Stay alert and maybe we will all stay alive!"

It was as if John had had a premonition, for shortly thereafter his and another battery were ordered back into town. Things quickly went from bad to worse. Two horses pulling one of the caissons were shot. Reynolds and another lieutenant struggled, along with their men, to move the dead animals from where they fell to ditches on the side of the street. More horses were hit by gunfire as the battle wore on. It was a catastrophic mess with the narrow streets again adding to the muddle and disorientation.

John found himself awash in blood and foam from the gasping, dying horses. The grounded guns became slippery from the equine body fluid as his men scrambled to remove the tangled harnesses from the dead and wounded animals to refit other horses in reserve, all the while taking heavy fire from Mexican marksmen.

Miraculously, the batteries were finally able to vacate the area. Later, John told other officers what had happened.

"I was amidst a continuous shower of grape and musketry," he said. "I escaped without a touch, although I had my horse twice hit with a musket ball. How we all escaped I am unable to imagine. Not an officer in the battery was wounded. But our battery suffered considerably."[64]

Still, John's day was not over. That afternoon he and Captain Bragg teamed up with two-gun teams to drive off another attack by

Mexican lancers. After two more days of fierce fighting through the city, the Mexican forces finally surrendered.

On the last day, September 23, Lieutenant Reynolds and his troops were called into crucial fire support again. His men moved quickly and fired accurately, but John was frustrated all the same. He discovered the Mexican adobe houses were strong enough to withstand significant damage from his light six-pounder rounds. Worse, the cannonballs just kicked up dust and debris, making it difficult to find proper targets while still taking shots by sharpshooters from shelters perched on the roofs of houses around them. By the time the Mexicans surrendered, John had counted the loss of fourteen men and twenty-two horses in the artillery units.

Despite the losses and the questionable effectiveness of the light artillery guns, John and his unit were highly praised for their efforts. General David Twiggs, in command of the division which contained Reynolds's unit, said the lieutenant and a few other officers he mentioned by name deserved "the highest praise for their skill and conduct."[65]

It was the kind of official commendation young career officers dream of being included in their personnel files. It is the stuff of which promotions are granted, something Lieutenant John Fulton Reynolds would soon find out.

* * *

John stomped his feet and blew on his fingers in a futile effort to keep warm. He was shivering.

"I will say, I do not like this devilish cold," he said to his friend and fellow officer Lieutenant Samuel French.

Sam looked at him with a bemused smile.

"If it were devilish," he chided cheerfully, "wouldn't it be hot? Or at least warm?"

John shot him a sour look. Reynolds was not in a good mood, and it wasn't just because of the cold. After the searing heat during the Battle of Monterrey the previous August, Reynolds, French, and the rest of General Taylor's men had gotten several months of respite because of a lull in the fighting. It was a welcome rest.

But, by December they were on the move again, and the summer's blistering hot weather had turned uncomfortably cold. John's battery and others marched more than three hundred miles, first to the town of Victoria and then to the Mexican Gulf Coast town of Tampico. The task force was made up mostly of the citizen soldiers, the volunteers. The bulk of the regular soldiers in the division had remained behind. It was little more than an exploratory expedition, and before long, John and his men were back in Monterrey.

Lieutenant Reynolds thought the march was useless. Back in camp, he said as much to his fellow officers.

"I will tell you," he groused, "we had anything but a pleasant time of it."[66]

That was not entirely true. As strict a disciplinarian as he was becoming, twenty-six-year-old John Reynolds was not afraid of a little mischief. The unit's round-trip march had encompassed New Year's Day of 1847. He and French wanted to celebrate the holiday properly, with proper eggnog. They had procured some eggs from a local farmer along the way. But they still needed liquor. So, they had asked the company doctor to join them in their quarters.

"Doc, we need some liquor," John had said.

"What for?" the doctor had replied.

"Eggnog. We want to make eggnog, you know, to celebrate the new year," Lieutenant French had told him.

"Right," Reynolds had said. "You have some in your medical supplies, don't you?"

"Well, yes, I do. But I can't authorize it for that purpose. It's medical supplies."

Reynolds and French had looked at each other and nodded.

"Well, then," Reynolds had said, turning back to the doctor. "We'll just have to put you under arrest."

"What?" the doc had cried. "Arrest? You can't be serious!"

"Oh, but we are," French had said with a smile. "Dead serious."

"Preposterous," the doctor had sputtered. "Not allowed. Not at all."

"Well," Reynolds had said calmly, "consider yourself under arrest until further notice."

French had stood up to stand guard by the front flap of the tent to prevent the doctor from leaving.

"Well, I never…" the doctor had said, trailing off, unbelieving what was happening to him.

"Look, Doc," Reynolds had said. "All we want to do is make a little bit of eggnog. Can't you let us have just a little rum or brandy, or a little of both?"

John had paused and looked at the doc with a grin.

"We'll even share the eggnog with you. We can all celebrate 1847 together!"

The doctor had stared at Reynolds, turned to look at French, then had turned back to John with a grin beginning to form on his face.

"Well, I guess I can spare a bottle or two," he had said finally.

Lieutenant French had returned to his seat while the doctor left to go fetch the liquor. When he had returned, the three of them worked together to make the spiked concoction and pour it into mugs.

"Happy new year, Sam. Happy new year, Doc," Reynolds had said, raising his mug in a toast.

"And a happy new year to you, Lieutenant," French and the doctor had said simultaneously. Then all three drank to the holiday.[67]

That had been the only bright spot on the march, and now John's current foul mood was not helped by a surprise that greeted General Taylor and his officers upon their return. It was as unpleasant as the turn in the weather. Most of the regulars were gone. They had been taken by American general Winfield Scott as he built up his army for a major invasion of Mexico. He needed experienced and well-trained soldiers, so he used his authority to attach General Taylor's regulars to his invasion force. What's more, he did it while Taylor was out of town.

Although only a young lieutenant, far down the ranks, Reynolds was apoplectic about it. Throwing down his gear in a tent he shared with a fellow officer, he vented about the injustice of Scott's action.

"General Taylor had no idea of this plan!" he said angrily. He directed some of the blame at Army officials in Washington.

"If Washington would have informed General Taylor what was going to happen beforehand, it would have saved that futile march toward Tampico!"

Furthermore, John had learned that dispatches describing the transfer of troops had been apparently intercepted by Mexican spies. That infuriated him ever more.

"If they aren't very careful in Washington," he spit, "they will get the Army whipped yet! Some of their ideas are so absurd that they really are laughable."[68]

Of course, he said these things only in the privacy of his quarters and in letters he sent home. Airing opinions like that in public or in front of his superiors would likely damage his hopes for promotion. But young John Reynolds was maturing, growing older and bolder. This was the beginning of his mistrust of political interference in military matters. He was deeply offended by rumors circulating from Washington indicating it was General Taylor who had initiated the idea that General Scott would take over plans to launch a major invasion.

He sat down to explain his feelings in a letter to his brother with language that was laced with indignation.

"True," he wrote, "General Taylor did inform the (Army) Department that he did not wish to be in the way of General Scott, or interfere in any way of his being sent to take command of the Army then, but with the distinct understanding that he would be permitted to serve under him in the active movements then contemplated. He certainly never expected the treatment he has now received at their hands, withdrawing all the regular troops and the greater part of the volunteers to go upon a distant and dangerous expedition and leave him behind with a small force scarcely sufficient to hold the country he has conquered."

John wrote the next sentence with a special degree of anger.

"This, however, is not the first instance of ingratitude they have been guilty of!"[69]

Now, John found himself shivering in Saltillo, a town about fifty miles west by southwest of Monterrey, through Encantado Valley, bordered on both sides by mountains. They made camp in a wide-open barren plain with little protection from the wind. It was bleak. Wrapping a blanket around him, John sat close by a campfire discussing the weather with other soldiers.

"I don't know when I have suffered more from the cold in many years than I have since we left Monterrey to march for Victoria. It was exceptionality cold during the whole march and since we have been here we have had ice every night and last night it tried hard at snowing!"[70]

"But, Lieutenant," one of his troops piped up. "You are from Pennsylvania, aren't you? Aren't the winters really cold there? I'd think you'd be used it."

John wrapped the blanket tighter around him, scooted closer to the fire, and let out a soft growl.

"Yes, soldier. But we are far south of Pennsylvania. And it is supposed to be warm in the south. Isn't that why Mexicans sing and play such lively music and eat so well? Because it is usually warm, that's why! The way it should be! Not this infernal, godforsaken cold!"

The soldiers around the campfire, all volunteers, laughed. It was funny to see a regular Army officer so miserable. John's sleeping arrangements added to his misery, in a tent, on the ground, covered by four blankets. Rations from the mess tent were meager. He drank nothing but "pure water," called the Mexican liquor "villainous," and told his brother he has seen "little or nothing at all of the Señoritas."[71]

Lieutenant John Reynolds had been in Mexico for nearly a year now. He was growing weary of this country. He, like many Americans, was also growing more impatient with religious influence on this war. A sense was emerging north of the border, and through the ranks as well, that the strong Roman Catholicism in Mexico threatened to pose as much a threat to fundamental American religious ideals as did any political considerations. Manifest Destiny was under attack, many believed. America's rightful growth in the west, that divine mission, was being undermined by the evils of popery, they cried.[72]

Thus, John's restless spirit was calling him. But he had one more test south of the border ahead of him. It would be an important one.

* * *

A few miles south of Saltillo sat a hacienda with the elegant name of Buena Vista. It was positioned along a road that divided a barren landscape that was beautiful in its starkness. To the east stood the tall Zapalinamé Mountains. To the west were deep gullies and ravines. In the middle, just a little farther south along the road, the mountain-ravine divide narrowed into what was called the Angostura Pass. It was in that squeeze point, in February of 1847, that perhaps the most dramatic battle of the Mexican-American War took place. It was here that Lieutenant John Reynolds and his artillery battery faced their toughest test.

It was another bitter cold night. John slept on the frigid, hard ground covered only with his overcoat. Nevertheless, the next morning he professed he "never went into action in better spirits"[73] in his life. He knew his artillery troops would prove crucial before the battle was finished.

Mexican general Antonio López de Santa Anna, upon learning that much of the American force had been diverted from General Taylor's army, was determined to take advantage. He headed toward Buena Vista from the south with an army that outnumbered the Americans by about five to one. What Santa Anna hadn't counted on was the precision and dexterity of his enemy's artillery, led by men, including John Reynolds, equally as determined to emerge victorious.

Throughout the battle, the lieutenant's deft repositioning of his battery gave life to the definition of light artillery. They moved from one skirmish to another and back again with speed and agility. John's first challenge came on the second day of the battle when his battery was called to the front to counter an assault by a long line of Mexican troops.

It was a sight to behold. The Mexican Army relished its colorful uniforms and military displays. As one historian put it, "All the colors of the rainbow—red, green, yellow, crimson, sky-blue, turkey-blue—clothed the troops. Even the horses appeared to be in uniform, for those of a corps were alike in color. Silken banners and plumes of many bright hues floated on the breeze."[74]

As he looked out over a plateau, John was moved as only a soldier can be by the sight of enemy forces maneuvering with precision.

"I never in my life beheld a more beautiful sight," he said. "Their gay uniforms, numberless pennants, standards and colors streaming in the sun shone out in all their pride and pomp."[75]

Indiana and Illinois volunteers were engaged in a pitched battle with an overwhelming number of Mexican units when Reynolds's two-gun section arrived to provide support.

"Those volunteers are fighting for their lives!" John called out to his artillerymen. "Let's get in there, give them a hand, on the double!"

The battle was raging. The citizen-soldiers gave as much as they got, first advancing, then retreating, then advancing again. John was precisely right in his earlier prediction that volunteer soldiers would be up to a fight when truly faced with one. John noted that "now giving way and advancing, they maintained their ground against fearful odds for an hour or two."[76]

But trouble was brewing behind them, back near the Buena Vista hacienda. Reynolds was ordered to head north to the ranch to help protect a supply train which was being threatened by other Mexican forces. John and his men quickly hitched up their two artillery pieces, saddled up, and headed for the hacienda at full gallop. The Mexican cavalry was already beginning to flee by the time the Reynolds team arrived, but the artillerymen were still able to get off some shots and caught the enemy in mid retreat.[77]

"Sam!" John shouted to Lieutenant French as they dismounted. "You direct the fire! I will help the men to prepare the fuses. We can fire faster that way!"

They kept firing, forcing the retreating Mexicans out of range.

"All right, men! Limber up!" John shouted, ordering his team to ready the artillery pieces for moving to another location. "Follow me!"

The lieutenant repositioned his men to just east of the hacienda where more enemy forces were getting away from, other American units. Quickly setting up and aiming the guns, his team opened fire on the fleeing enemy with precision and speed. Watching the enemy making a break for it, one cavalry officer said, "Although distant, they were not out of reach of Lieutenant Reynolds' guns. He had brought his section into battery just below the hacienda…and continued to play upon them with astonishing accuracy and great execution."[78]

John was transfixed watching his unit's projectiles fall like meteors exploding among the throng of the fleeing enemy. Bodies, and parts of bodies, arms and legs, flew through the air, mingled with orange flames, blue smoke, brown dust, and red blood. John knew victory was at hand, yet with the sight he beheld, his heart was heavy.

In the midst of all this mayhem, John's favorite commander, General Zachery Taylor, appeared on the battlefield in support of his troops. He was escorted by units of the Mississippi Rifles commanded by Colonel Jefferson Davis, the same Jeff Davis who later would become a major figure in American history as president of the breakaway Confederate States during the Civil War. In the coming hours, Reynolds did everything possible to support Davis. In the coming years, he would despise the man.

The Mississippi Rifles, along with other volunteer militias, had taken up positions to counter another enemy attack on a plateau near the narrow pass. Along with an Indiana unit, they formed a large inverted V with the opening toward the approaching enemy. As they waited, the scene became surreal. Army captain James Carleton, the same man who had been so impressed with the performance of Reynolds's battery, described what he saw.

"The enemy was formed in a close column of squadrons and came down the slope at an easy-hand gallop. His ranks were well closed, his troopers riding knee to knee, and dressing handsomely on their guides." Carleton declared the entire assemble as "most admirable" that moved "with the ease and regularity of the best drilled troops on a field-day." The Mexican force, he observed, "had a sort of air about it; an easy, nonchalant manner of going into the work."

"Opposed to them," Carleton continued, "were our men on foot, a mere handful in comparison and having about them none of the pomp and circumstance, the glitter and gold and feathers and tassels of their antagonists."[79]

Other soldiers remarked on how quiet the battlefield seemed to have gotten, as if it was a harbinger of some awful, catastrophic event, waiting to be unleashed.

"It was a sublime, a terrible sight," Carleton agreed. "The troops on both sides were so cool and determined, that all knew the struggle must be sanguinary and desperate in the extreme. Not a word was spoken; the din of the surrounding battle seemed for a moment hushed."[80]

The Mexican force, numbering in the thousands, slowly closed in on the American position.

"Hold fast," Colonel Davis ordered the American troops. "Do not engage the enemy. Not yet."

The Americans' open V formation, reminiscent of a deadly Venus flytrap flower, waited patiently for their adversaries to advance closer and closer. Mexican officers became confused, expecting they would draw the fire of the Americans.

"But finding, on the contrary that not a piece was discharged, nor a man moving," Captain Carleton said, "the whole brigade began instinctively to diminish its gait."[81]

That was a huge and fatal mistake. As the Mexican column slowed to a halt, they were neatly in the crosshairs of two lines of fire.

"Now!" shouted Colonel Davis. "Open fire! Fire at will!"

The order was instantly repeated by other officers up and down the two lines of US troops in that V formation. Rifle after rifle after musket opened fire in a thunderous roar. Flame and smoke and death poured forth from the weapons. Bullets and minié balls tore into Mexican flesh and bone.

Carlton called it appalling.

"The whole head of the column was prostrated, and riderless horses, a multitude, and crimson with blood, scattered from it in every direction."[82]

Suddenly, Reynolds and his battery burst onto the scene, having ridden hard and fast from the hacienda. They jumped into action, joining other artillery batteries, and poured devastating fire into the melee. The combined American force was able to drive more than five thousand Mexican troops off the plateau. The ground they left behind was covered with their dead.

Santa Anna was down, but not out, however. Not yet. In one more desperate foray, he threw twelve thousand troops against the Americans aligned on and around the plateau. It was another slug-fest. American volunteer soldiers from Illinois, Kentucky, Texas, and Mississippi pulled together to repel the dogged advance of Santa Anna's troops. In the end, it was the artillerymen that took the day. Reynolds and his team joined with several other batteries to hammer the Mexican forces over and over again. Seventeen guns mowed them down with repeated grapeshot and canister rounds, metal cylinders packed with lead balls, ammunition designed to act like oversize shotgun shells. When darkness fell, so did Santa Anna's grand plan.

John believed this was the greatest battle he had been in yet.

"I thought that at Monterrey I had been in a pretty tight place," he said to other officers later. "But it was nothing to this. For eight hours incessantly we were in the hottest places and only one officer touched."[83] He meant wounded, and that officer was his friend and fellow lieutenant Sam French who had been shot in the leg. Others in John's company had also been wounded, including a sergeant, a couple of corporals, and six privates, some of whose wounds were fatal. At least a dozen horses were either killed or wounded as well.

At the end of the day, Reynolds was exhausted. Back at camp, he stumbled into his tent and dropped to the floor. Covering up with a few blankets, he closed his eyes, hoping to get some shut-eye. Reynolds was not quite asleep when suddenly the tent flap flew open and Lieutenant French hobbled in with the aid of two crutches.

"Hey ho, Johnny boy!" French hollered. "Up and at 'em, son! You can't lie around all day! Whattaya think this is? The Navy?"

John peered at his friend with one opened eye.

"Go to Hades, you scalawag," he grumbled. "You better never let my brother, Will, hear you talking like that," John mumbled, rolling over, pulling the blankets over his head.

French laughed and awkwardly sat down, favoring his wounded leg.

"We sure gave them a licking, didn't we, John," he said more seriously.

Reynolds lay still for a few moments. Then he rolled over, sat up, and looked at French.

"We sure did, Sam. We sure did. But those guys fought back hard, those Mexican troops. I have to hand it to them. We are pretty well used up, both men and horses,"[84] he said.

He looked down at Sam's heavily bandaged leg.

"Are you okay?" he said.

"Yeah, I'll be all right." He grinned. "A minié ball caught me in the calf. It bled like a son of a gun but didn't hit any arteries. The doc says I should be good as new in a few weeks."

French was one more of the 450 US soldiers wounded in that battle. More than 260 were killed.

"I'll tell you what, Sam, General Taylor is one hell of a commander."

"Yes, I suppose he is, John, despite all the criticism from Washington and those other generals for going too easy on the Mexicans after Monterrey."

"Yeah, well, let them do now what they will, General Taylor will be the next president, in spite of everything. Just wait and see."

"President? You are really high on him, aren't you?"

"I never saw him so perfectly cool and determined in my life before. He was in a good humor the whole fight and appeared perfectly certain of winning the day."[85]

"Well, I guess he's pretty high on you, too."

"What do you mean, Sam?"

"While I was being treated over in the hospital tent, I overheard a couple of his staff officers talking about Taylor's battle report they were helping to prepare. According to them, Taylor is giving the artillery lots of credit for the victory. He's apparently even commending you by name, along with some other officers."

Even before the battle, Reynolds had been in the general's good graces. A Taylor staff officer had written to one of John's instructors telling him that "your young friend has the general's high regard and is the idol of his men."[86]

General Taylor was not the only senior officer impressed with John's performance. Another general reported that "without our artillery, we could not have maintained our position for a single hour…A section of artillery, admirably served by Lieutenant Reynolds played an important part in checking and dispersing the enemy in the rear of our left."[87]

One senior officer gave John his "warmest thanks for the gallant and bold maneuver in which he rendered the most important and effective service."[88]

Whether he appreciated it or not, Lieutenant Reynolds clearly was on track for higher callings. At the moment, though, he was too exhausted to think about any of that. Too exhausted, and too depressed by the toll the war had taken on his enemy.

"Those Mexicans, did you see them, Sam?" he asked. "They were miserable beings. Half starved, ragged, and tattered. I'm told they haven't eaten for two days."

He shook his head in disgust, visualizing the wretchedly wounded Mexicans he had seen in Matamoros.

"This business," he continued. "This business of waging war is sometimes necessary, I know. But it is a nasty business, Sam. Nasty. Killing for killing's sake is not right. Do not misunderstand me. If we fight, we fight to win. We must. But I cannot hate the enemy. We must always have a logical reason to kill him. Just for the purpose of killing him is not enough."

CHAPTER ELEVEN

Off Chincoteague Island
August 1860

"So, is that when you were promoted to major? In Mexico?" Kate asked.

"Well, yes and no," John replied. "I was awarded what's called brevet promotions. Twice actually. First, I was made a brevet captain by virtue of my performance, or rather, my battery's performance at Monterrey. Then I was upgraded to a brevet major after the battle at Buena Vista."

"Oh, John! That's wonderful. Congratulations!" she gushed.

John smirked and scratched behind his ear.

"Truth be told," he said. "They don't mean all that much. I mean they are not real ranks. As far as the Army paymaster was concerned, I was still a lieutenant. A brevet is an honorary promotion for a job well done or for gallant fighting and such. The only real difference is that I could write brevet major below my signature on official documents. Frankly, I am perfectly indifferent to it and care not whether I am included amongst those so distinguished or not. The system is a complete humbug, and until it changes, I believe it is to be rather more of a distinction to be passed over than to be breveted."[89]

Kate cocked her head and frowned him.

"But you are a real major now, are you not?"

"Yes, I am. But that official promotion came later."

John and Kate were nearing the end of their voyage. The steamship was opposite Chincoteague Island, Virginia, headed north in the Atlantic Ocean toward the mouth of Delaware Bay. From there it would proceed to Philadelphia up the Delaware River. John, Kate, Catherine and some other passengers would disembark there. The vessel would then retrace its track and proceed north to its final destination, New York.

John planned to travel overland to home in Lancaster for a couple of weeks, then head to West Point to assume his position as commandant of cadets.

A heavy thunderstorm had blown in over the ocean with brilliant flashes of lightning and long, loud, rolling thunder. High winds rocked the steamship from side to side in the darkness of the evening. The passengers and crew were in no real danger. This was a sturdy vessel. But the ride had become uncomfortable. Nevertheless, John and Kate gamely sat in the ship's dimly lit parlor, trying their best to enjoy a couple of glasses of wine. Catherine had felt woozy from all the motion and had gone to bed early.

"Are you feeling all right?" John asked Kate as the steamship once again tilted from side to side.

"I'm fine," Kate said. "This rocking really doesn't bother me. How about you?"

"Oh, I'm okay, too," John said. "This is kind of like riding an unruly horse. No problem."

Kate smiled as, sitting in soft and plush leather armchairs, they both watched with amusement the wine sloshing back and forth in their glasses. The red walls of the parlor were lined with books neatly stacked in shelves seven feet high. The crimson in the pattern of the carpet matched the color of the walls. This could have been a quiet reading room in some land-based club by the way it showed off its decor.

John and Kate had picked up the discussion about his adventures in Mexico John had begun with the steamship's captain.

"Was that the end of that war? The Battle of Buena Vista, I mean?" Kate asked him, picking up her glass for a sip of the Merlot.

"It was for me. The fighting went on for about another year and a half, but my unit had nothing more to do with it. We were not needed and were not called to the front as other forces invaded Mexico. I must say, Kate, sitting around, twiddling our thumbs for twenty months was maddening! I could not wait to get out of that place."

Kate smiled, bemused by what she had come to learn and appreciate was John's restless spirit.

"What did you do in the meantime?"

"Kept up the training with my battery, wrote a lot of letters, went chumpy, you know, bonkers from boredom. For a while I was appointed as sort of a judge advocate for the courts-martial of soldiers who got into trouble, most likely from sheer tedium of doing nothing, I would say. That also meant volumes of reports to write and write and write. After a while, that grew tiresome."

He paused while both he and Kate took another sip from their wineglasses. As he put his back on the table, John continued his tale.

"That was what, twelve, thirteen years ago? Even back then I wanted to go back to West Point as an instructor or assistant of some sort. It was not imperative, though. I was just sick of Mexico and everything in it and just wanted out!"[90]

Suddenly a bolt of lightning lit up the sky and filled the rocking parlor with a blinding flash of light, followed instantly by a tremendous crash of thunder. Kate shrieked and grabbed John, holding on to him tightly. They both sat together in the close embrace for several moments, listening to the storm rage outside the boat.

"I think you are safe now, ma'am," John finally said in a deep voice, playing up the role of a gallant knight for all its worth. But his arms remained tightly wrapped around Kate. She didn't move either. Then she looked up at his face and fluttered her eyelids.

"Oh, my handsome prince," she said sweetly, in a high-pitched voice. "You have saved me!"

They stared at each other for about three seconds, then both broke out in howls of laughter. As they regained their composure, John released his hold on Kate and put his hands softly on both sides of her face. He drew her nearer to him. They pressed their lips together, kissing lovingly and with longing.

Without a further word, both rose from their seats and walked out of the parlor to the passageway, leaving their half-finished glasses of wine behind. They kept their balance in the rolling ship by holding on to each other. They headed toward their cabins. When they came to hers, Kate and John looked at each other. Kate smiled but didn't stop. Neither did John. They strolled past her cabin. They headed for his.

* * *

The next morning, at breakfast, John felt completely at peace. He was more content than he had ever been in his life. His normally stern visage had softened; the lines and wrinkles in his face were not as deep. He was surprised to realize that he was smiling. He was smiling at nothing, except for the goodness of his feelings.

He saw Kate, across the breakfast table, looking at him with a Mona Lisa-like smile on her face. She reached her hand out to him, resting it on the table with her palm up. He nodded slightly and reached out to put his hand in hers. They sat utterly still like that for several moments, gazing into each other's eyes.

Catherine, eating a bowl of porridge, looked at Kate, then at John, and back at Kate again. She sensed something was different between them, but her ten-year-old mind couldn't comprehend what. Finally, she blurted it out.

"Are you two boyfriend and girlfriend?"

John's eyes grew very wide. His eyebrows shot up. Kate blushed a deep crimson. Boyfriend and girlfriend were relatively new terms in the mid-1800s. Neither one of them had ever been called that.

"Well," John said finally, "I guess you can say that. Tell me, Catherine, if you would, please. If I like someone, a woman, very, very much, does that make me her boyfriend?"

Catherine frowned a little, thinking and took a bite of her toast. Then she nodded her head.

"Yes," she said gaily. "I think it does!"

"Well then, it is settled," John said and looked at Kate. "I am definitely Kate's boyfriend, because—"

"Because you like her very, very much," Catherine interrupted with enthusiasm.

"Yes, I do, very, very, very much," John said, still looking at Kate and emphasizing the last *very*.

"Wait a minute," Catherine said, a little puzzled by this new atmosphere between the two adults. "I don't think you can be Kate's boyfriend unless she asks you to be."

Kate, just taking a sip of coffee, guffawed and nearly spit her drink out on the table. John blinked twice at this thoroughly modern concept emanating from the mouth of the precocious young girl.

"Catherine," Kate said. "You are so wonderfully smart! I think you are going to be a big success at your new school in Philadelphia. And, you are absolutely correct. John can't be my boyfriend unless I ask him to be."

She paused and looked at John teasingly. After a few moments of silence, Catherine couldn't stand it any longer.

"Well, will you!" she said impatiently.

"Will I what?" Kate responded, enjoying her little game immensely.

Catherine let out a loud, agitated sigh.

"Will you ask him to be your boyfriend!" she said, thrusting her head forward in exasperation.

"Well, let me think," Kate said, looking at John with an impish smile. "Okay," she continued after a moment. She took a deep breath.

"Major John Reynolds, will you be my boyfriend?" she said with warmth.

"Miss Catherine Hewitt, it would be my honor to be your boyfriend," John replied with equal solemnity.

"Hooray!" Catherine shouted out. "Okay, John. It is your turn. Now, you have to ask Kate to be your girlfriend. Come on. Ask her!"

John smiled and held Kate's hand tighter.

"Miss Hewitt, would you grant me the favor of being my girlfriend?"

"Why, Major Reynolds, I thought you would never ask. I would be delighted to be your girlfriend," she said with a big smile.

"Hooray!" Catherine shouted again, drawing the attention of people at other nearby breakfast tables. "Now it's official. You are officially boyfriend and girlfriend!"

Catherine settled back in her chair, satisfied that she had solved the little mystery of Kate and John. Then her attention quickly focused on other matters, as only the mind of a ten-year-old can.

"May I be excused?" she asked Kate. "I want to go back to our cabin and finish reading my book."

"Of course," Kate said. "We will see you later."

Catherine hopped down from her chair.

"Bye, John. Bye, Kate. See you later."

The adults watched Catherine as she skipped away. John turned to look at Kate.

"Boyfriend and girlfriend, huh?" he said with a smile.

"I think there is another word that covers it," she said, grinning.

John looked puzzled.

"Word? What word?"

Kate leaned forward in her seat and looked around to make sure no one could overhear. She lowered her voice.

"Lovers," she said quietly. "Especially after last night."

"Yes," he said, serenely. "That's a good word. A very good word."

They both sat quietly for a while, drinking their coffee and thinking.

"John," Kate said after several moments. "We will be in Philadelphia tomorrow. I know we have discussed this briefly, but what are we going to do after we arrive?"

"Do about what?"

"About us. About our relationship. We agreed to keep it secret, but how are we going to do that?"

John took another bite from a biscuit while he thought about that.

"Your first order of business will be to get Catherine enrolled in a school, is that not correct?"

"Yes," Kate replied. "The Daughters of Charity will help me do that."

"What are your plans after that?" he asked.

"I hope myself to enroll at the boarding school in Philadelphia called Eden Hall. It is part of the Sacred Heart Academy there. Perhaps that is where Catherine will be, as well."

"Eden Hall? That is a Catholic School, is it not?" John asked.

"Yes, it is. I want to complete my conversion to Catholicism by engaging the sacraments of the church," she looked at John, waiting for him to react. When he said nothing, she continued.

"Also," she said, somewhat shyly. "I understand Eden Hall also acts of sort of a finishing school for cultured ladies. I wish to learn how to be more proper in polite society."

Since meeting Major John Reynolds, Kate had developed fantasies of being on the arm of a dashing, high-ranking military officer at public events and important receptions. She wanted to be up to the task.[91]

John nodded in understanding.

"I am going home to Lancaster to visit my family for a short visit, then report to West Point for duty as commandant of cadets. I think I shall travel to the Point by way of Philadelphia so we can see each other. How does that sound to you?"

"Oh, John, I would love that!" Kate responded.

"I will say nothing about us to my family. Of course, while in Philadelphia I must visit my sister. But I will make some excuse to get away to be with you."

For the next several minutes, they discussed details of their planned rendezvous, what date John would return to the City of Brotherly Love and where they would meet. John told Kate of discreet lodging he knew about. She would make arrangements for them so they could spend the night together before he left for West Point.

"John," she said. "This is so exciting and so...so...scandalous!" She giggled.

"Yes," he laughed. "This is deliciously dangerous, I believe. Even more risky than any battle I have ever been in, I assure you," he said, with a twinkle in his eyes and a broad grin on his face.

"Speaking of that," she said, still smiling. "Speaking of battles, I mean, you haven't told me what you did after Mexico. I apologize for asking so many questions, but, John, I really want to know all there is to know about you."

"Oh, my love, no apology is needed. Well, let's see. I finally got out of Mexico at the end of '48 and went home on leave for a short time. That was the first leave I'd had in about three years. I was there only for a very short time because in January of 1849 I was assigned to Fort Preble. That's up in Maine."[92]

"Maine!" Kate exclaimed. "That must have been quite a shock for you."

John laughed lightly.

"Yes, it was a bit of jolt. The winters were harsh, and, I must say, the work was terribly boring. It was a lot of paperwork for the company I was in. It was a far cry from the Mexican adventures, that is for certain. Still, all in all, Preble was pretty good duty. I liked the commander, Major Robert Anderson. He is smart and very capable."[93]

Reynolds, of course, didn't know it then, but Major Anderson would go on to become an important part of American history. Anderson was the commander in charge of northern troops at Fort Sumter when the South Carolina militia attacked it in 1861. That was opening salvo of the Civil War, in which Reynolds would soon find himself so deeply entangled.

"Three years later, I was reassigned to Fort Adams in Newport, Rhode Island. Let me think. Yes, that would be back in 1852. From there it was to New Orleans less than a year later. I was reunited with General David Twiggs at that post. Remember, he was one of my commanders in Monterrey? New Orleans is a lively city, but it was tough when I was there in 1853, because that's when the yellow fever epidemic hit the city. More than 7,800 people died."[94]

"Yes, I remember hearing about that," Kate said. "I was seventeen years old then. That epidemic was horrible. All those poor people who suffered and died."

"You are right. It was pretty bad. I came down with the fever, too. But I was lucky and recovered fairly quickly."

"Let us thank God for that," Kate said.

"Yes. Let's," John agreed. He stared out the window of the boat, watching the water and thinking for a few moments. He turned back to Kate.

"That was when I was really hoping to be appointed to be the commissary of subsistence for the Army. That's like being in charge of all the supplies. I thought I had a good chance. My friend Cump Sherman held the job at the time, but he was taking extended leave. Even he thought I should have succeeded him. But Jefferson Davis, the secretary of war at the time, had other ideas.[95] Blast it all! I should have had that job!"

There was something else Reynolds didn't know talking to Kate. Jefferson Davis would again disappoint and greatly anger him in the next few years about something much bigger and much more important than a job assignment.

"My father died that spring, the spring of '53. I went home to mourn with the family. After that, it seems I was always traveling. In 1854, right after the first of the year, it was back north again, this time to Fort Lafayette in New York Harbor."

He smiled lovingly at Kate.

"I wish I would have known you then," he said. "Fort Lafayette was a lonely place. There were times when I was the solitary soul there, alone for a week at a time without seeing a soul I could talk to.[96] I sure could have used your company then."

Kate smiled, but said nothing, so John continued.

"By the end of March, our command headed west, to the far west. Our destination was California. I must admit, Kate, that was a very difficult overland venture. When we arrived at Fort Leavenworth, in Kansas, we joined more units, ending up with a very long wagon train of at least three hundred men, several hundred horses, four hundred mules, and eighty baggage wagons. The roads were rutted and muddy. The horses repeatedly tried to stampede. Some of them came down with distemper. We even had to deal with bouts of cholera along the trail."

"My goodness," Kate exclaimed. "It's a wonder you got anywhere at all!"

"So true," he said. "Well, by mid-July we finally made it to Fort Laramie in Wyoming. It was there that I dealt with Indians for the first time. A delegation from the Sioux tribe came to the fort to show us they were friendly."[97]

"Were they?" she asked.

"Reasonably so," he replied. "At least they were a good sight friendlier than the Mormons we ran into along the way."

"Why, what do you mean, John?"

"After Laramie, we had a rough trek over the Wahsatch Mountains, but eventually made our way to Salt Lake City. There, we became acquainted with the Church of Jesus Christ of Latter-day Saints. You know, Mormons. It pains me to say it, but I found them to be the most disagreeable people I had ever met, and that includes the Mexicans I had to fight."

"John!" Kate said with surprise. "That is not very Christian of you to say."

"Perhaps not. But I speak the truth. Oh, they invited us to receptions and such. But their politeness was only skin-deep."

"I truly do not understand," Kate said.

"For example, at one party, given by Governor Brigham Young, we met several families and a number of young women. But do you think those folks would invite us into their homes? Not for a moment! I could see that they are jealous of all gentiles and, of course, discouraged any intimacy among their young people with us. This did not amount to much, however, as there are very few people among them of any pretensions to respectability at all. Therefore, it was not much of a deprivation,"[98] John said snidely.

"John Reynolds," Kate said in a scolding tone. "That is not a very kind thing to say. Not at all!"

Reynolds rubbed his beard in irritation.

"You would not say that, Kate, had you been there. The Mormons' idea of justice is pathetic. I was put in command of a group of soldiers to ride more than a hundred miles down to Fillmore City to round up five Indians who were accused of murdering Captain John Gunnison and several of his men. They had been on a mission to survey the area for a possible railroad line. When we brought the Indians back to Salt Lake City, they were put on trial by the Mormons. I swear to God that the Mormon jury was influenced by Governor Young. As a result, I believe it was justice denied! May God have mercy upon them because they would hang two Indians for killing two Mormon boys when there was scarcely any proof at all. Hang them! But, when a gentile is murdered, why, the verdict was only manslaughter."[99]

He slammed his hand on the table.

"It was as if the lives of brave American soldiers mattered not a whit to those despicable Mormons."

In relating the story for Kate six years after the event, John clearly was still incensed about it. When he paused, he was breathing heavily, and his face was flushed. He took a drink of water and several long breaths to calm down. Kate was becoming alarmed.

"Are you all right, John?" she asked.

After a moment or two, he answered her.

"Yes, I am fine. And I apologize for my display of temper. I know it is unseemly in the presence of a lady. It is just that the Mormon community has snubbed its nose at the rule of law and has insulted the United States government time and again. It's not only that trial I speak of."

Despite John's effort at remaining calm, Kate could see he was beginning to get wound up again.

"All through the latter part of the 1850s, the Mormons continued to cause trouble. Three federal judges said Mormons had run them out of the territory. An Army unit led by General Albert Johnson was sent out there in 1857 to maintain law and order. Local officials had the audacity to say they were soldiers of a foreign power! Soldiers of the United States of America? A foreign power? The Mormons even attacked General Johnson's supply chain, drove off the horses, burned the Army's grazing lands, and burned the buildings at a fort where Johnson and his men planned to spend the difficult Utah winter. Hundreds of mules, oxen, and horses were lost!"[100]

John paused for a moment to collect his thoughts.

"I was sent back to the territory just two years ago, in 1858. The so-called Mormon War was pretty much over by the time I got there. The territory had a new governor, and an agreement had been reached with the church. I tell you this, Kate. The Utah troubles may have been settled, but I put no faith in anything of the kind and will not believe it until the Mormons are out of our territory!"[101]

If Kate was troubled by this show of prejudicial anger and temper from her lover, she did not show it.

"God says we should forgive, John" was all she said.

"Well, I'd wager that God never met a Mormon," he replied.

Kate chuckled, in spite of herself, which caused John to join in.

"There was some good news during that time, however, I am happy to say," John went on.

"Oh? And what was that, pray tell?" Kate said.

"I got a promotion. A real one this time. In March of 1855, I got word that I had been promoted to captain. A real, honest-to-goodness captain!"

Kate clapped her hands lightly a couple of times.

"Hooray," she said. "I must say, it was about time. Let's see, in 1855 you had been in the Army for, what, eighteen years, counting your time as a cadet at West Point?"

"Yes, I suppose it was about time," he agreed. "With the promotion to regular Army captain came an increase in pay, which was a good thing, of course. But because of the earlier brevet ranking, I was still addressed as major."

"And you still are," she observed. "Right, Major darling!"

That remark caused John to laugh loudly.

"Ah, right! But no one, I say no one, in the military calls me darling, if they know what is good for them," he said, between laughs.

Kate leaned over and kissed him on his cheek and whispered in his ear.

"Only I get to call you that, right, darling?"

He smiled broadly.

"Right, sweetheart."

Now, he kissed Kate on her cheek. Then, he sat back in his chair.

"So, to continue the story, after spending the winter of '55 in Salt Lake City, we were off to California in May when the melting snow made mountain passes negotiable again. After many months, we finally got to Fort Orford in what was then Oregon Territory. It is a state now. I must say, Kate, it was quite an adventure getting there. I boarded a steamship, called the *California*, in San Francisco, heading up the coast to Oregon when the boilers on the boat burst! It made me think back to my school days at Lititz in Pennsylvania and old Professor Beck teaching us about how boilers on boats can rupture. The explosion set the ship on fire. It started drifting out of control, heading for the bar where it could have run aground in the shallows, maybe strike rocks in the process. Fortunately, we put the fire out and got a secondary boiler running to build up a head of steam. Then, by God, we were hit with a gale and one of the vessel's steam pipes burst! It took us sixty hours to limp back to San Francisco. The whole business was terrifying.[102] I am not ashamed to admit it! You know, it makes me wonder how and why my brother, Will, in the Navy, loves the sea so much. Give me good old terra firma any day!"

"When did you say this all happened?" Kate asked.

"That voyage from hell was in the fall of 1855. For one reason or another, it wasn't until after the new year of 1856 that we could depart San Francisco for another try at sailing up the coast."

Reynolds went on to explain how he became involved in the so-called Rogue River Wars after he arrived at Fort Orford on the Oregon Coast just north of the California line. Hostilities had erupted between white settlers and Native Americans in the region. He had spent three months leading an artillery unit over mountainous, treacherous terrain to subdue the Indians. For the newly appointed Captain Reynolds, it was hardly a war, more like a series of skirmishes. Still, local citizens had awarded him a gold watch for protecting them during their "defenseless condition."[103]

"From there, I was again back and forth across the country for the next few years. I spent some time at home, at Fort Monroe in Virginia, then it was back west again to Camp Floyd, about fifty miles south of Salt Lake City and those vexing Mormons, then on to California again and finally, just last year, to Fort Vancouver on the Washington-Oregon line. I will tell you, Kate, I had become quite the wanderer and..."

He realized Kate was no longer paying attention.

"Kate? Hello, Kate? Is something wrong?"

She was looking out through one of the windows of the boat.

"Well, I'll be…," Kate said, almost to herself, her voice trailing off.

"You'll be…what?" John asked her, puzzled.

She looked at him with a bemused smile.

"John, do you realize that you and I may have been in San Francisco at the same time four years ago! 1856 is when I arrived there to work as a governess for that family I told you about."

"Huh, I did not realize that," John said. "What a pleasure it would have been to make your acquaintance then, my lady. I only wish that I had."

"Why, Major Reynolds. You are too kind, sir. The pleasure would have been all mine," Kate replied, smiling at him.

"Oh, I surmise you would have been too busy holding off all the would-be San Francisco suitors wanting to court you to notice someone like me," he said, artfully.

"Sir, you flatter me!" Kate replied with a laugh. "I am afraid it was nothing like that, I assure you. Do not mistake me. There were plenty of fine-looking, cultivated gentlemen in that city. But, quite frankly, I was far too busy taking care of children, first as a governess, then as a teacher in that Catholic school, I believe I told you about."

"Yes, you did. A little. I am still curious, though, why you converted to Catholicism. Not that, as a Protestant, I am offended. I most certainly am not, but I do find it somewhat peculiar that a person would do such a thing."

Kate took a deep breath and sighed.

"Oh, John, there were a lot of reasons, I suppose. During all those troubles with my father when I was young, the church, our Baptist church, did not provide much comfort. When I left home… oh, let me be frank. When I ran away from home and went to California, I guess I was trying to get away from Protestant influence as much as I wanted to get away from my father. After beginning work as a governess, I still needed more income, so I applied to be a teacher at the Roman Catholic Orphan Asylum in San Francisco."

She paused to pull out a small handkerchief from her pocket-book to wipe her eyes, which were beginning to get misty. She sniffed daintily.

"It was there, John, that I found what I was looking for. The nuns, they are called sisters there, were so comforting and support-ive. They spoke to me. Their prayers spoke to me. I was where I belonged. I could feel it! Can you understand that, John?"

He nodded silently.

"And the children, the young women in the school, all of them were amazing. Brilliant and thoughtful and devout. But it was Catherine who had the greatest influence on me. Despite being an orphan who experienced such terrible things in her life, she is strong, John, and confident and smart. Oh, so smart. Also, her belief, her faith in God is unshakeable. How ironic. Here I was, the teacher, and I wanted to be like her, a child! It was the Catholic influence, John, plus the teachings and support of the sisters that convinced me to convert. So I did. I am. That's why I'm going to Philadelphia. As devoted as the sisters in San Francisco are, I know Catherine can get an even better education in Philadelphia with all the resources that city has at its disposal. Furthermore, I can still be near Catherine and complete my religious conversion with the Daughters of Charity at the same time. Who knows? Maybe someday I'll even take the vows of the order."

Kate looked at John fondly.

"Unless, that is," she said quietly, "some fine gentleman comes along and sweeps me off my feet."

Major John Reynolds, an officer of the United States Army, a veteran of wars, a leader of men, just sat there, speechless. The "man of few words" had no words.

CHAPTER TWELVE

West Point
September 1860

Captain John Reynolds stood on the Plain, the sweeping parade ground of the United States Army Military Academy at West Point, New York. He gazed at the powerful Hudson River, flowing north to south, about four hundred yards away. It had been nineteen years since he last stood on these grounds as a brand-new Army cadet. He had left West Point as a young, inexperienced, wet-behind-the-ears lieutenant and had returned as a tough, battle-tested veteran of bloody skirmishes and a major war.

Still, he was somewhat uncertain of his role here. He was the new commandant of cadets, having complete authority over the present-day cadre of would-be Army officers. He thought back to his days as a cadet and the then commandant, Charles F. Smith. Young Reynolds had decided the man was a complete tyrant. *Would that be how today's young men will think of me?* John wondered. *I have not been on duty yet a week trying to persuade myself that I shall like it.*[104]

He expressed his doubts in a letter to one of his sisters. "I shall try for a week or so longer the duties, which I find so disagreeable to me," he wrote. "So different from anything I have ever had before, and so confining, annoying and various that I have hardly yet time to test them fully. Then I can make up my mind as to whether I will remain or not."[105]

John's nettlesome uncertainty stemmed from the belief that he was a leader of men, not a teacher of them. However, his duties as commandant included instructing cadets in the arts of artillery, cavalry, and infantry tactics as well as outpost duty, army organization and administration. That all meant being confined to a desk and managing piles of paperwork, something Reynolds basically abhorred. He was also responsible for organizing military ceremonies and reviews by the cadets.

His impatience was also triggered by his absence from Kate. He knew it would be days, if not weeks, before they could be together again. He thought about the last day he had seen her. After visiting his family in Lancaster following the sea voyage, he traveled to West Point by way of Philadelphia, as he had promised he would do. Their time together in the city was magical. Their conversations were easy and loving. They experienced great comfort in each other's presence. They even risked scandal by spending a couple of nights together in the lodging Kate had found on John's recommendation.

"Kate, my darling, I am so in love with you," he had said softly as she lay in his arms.

"And I with you, my love," she had whispered back. "I do love you so."

"My time away from you at West Point will be abominable," he had said. "I do not know if I will be able to stand it."

She had put a finger gently on his lips.

"Shush, my love," she had said. "The time will pass quickly, I am certain. I will be right here waiting for you."

John smiled now, remembering that conversation. He also decided, right then, that the next time he went to Philadelphia, he would ask her to marry him.

A knock on his office door interrupted John's reverie.

"Come in," he called gruffly.

A young cadet entered the room, came to attention, and saluted Captain Reynolds smartly.

"Brigade Commander O'Rorke reporting, sir!" the young man said.

Reynolds saluted back.

"At ease, Cadet. Take your seat."

O'Rorke was the highest-ranking cadet at West Point, a position traditionally known as first captain. He was a first-class cadet, meaning he would graduate as a commissioned officer at the end of the current academic year in 1861.[106]

As the new commandant of cadets, John wanted to foster an appropriately close relationship with the first captain, as he would be the eyes and ears of the cadet brigade. John waited until O'Rorke sat down and got comfortable.

"So, how are things going, First Captain?" Reynolds asked.

"Fine, sir. It looks like we have a good group of plebes this year," the first captain said, referring to the crop of freshman students.

"Any problems?"

"Not…not really," the first captain said hesitantly.

"Cadet, in my experience, when someone says, 'not really,' they actually mean…really. What do you have?"

"Well, there is this one first-class cadet, sir."

"What about him?"

"He doesn't seem to care about the, umm, etiquette, sir, in our daily routines."

"Meaning?"

"Among other things, his bed, sir."

"His bed?"

"Yes, sir. He refuses to make it properly in the mornings. Sometimes he doesn't even fold the blanket back properly. He knows better. Sets a very bad example, sir."

Reynolds leaned back in his chair and sighed heavily. As commandant, he was also responsible for discipline at the academy. This was another task, like the paperwork, that he knew would annoy him.

West Point always had very strict behavior requirements. It was part of the training to become an effective and honorable officer. The Cadet Code, which is meant to be solemn and inviolate, says simply, "A cadet will not lie, cheat, steal or tolerate those who do."[107] The code covers a multiple of major sins.

The Point also has a demerit system for lesser, but much larger multiplicity of infractions. The system is connected to everything a cadet does, from the time he wakes up until the time he falls asleep, and even then, if need be. The system can be applied for not making a bed properly, for example, or for not shaving close enough. One study "determined that there were eighteen thousand different opportunities for a cadet to earn a demerit in his four years at West Point."[108] Enforcing such Lilliputian rules was not what John Reynolds cherished.

Rubbing the back of his head, John looked up at the first captain and grimaced.

"And just who is this offender?" he asked.

"Cadet Custer, sir," the first captain replied.

"Custer?"

"Yes, sir. George Armstrong Custer."

Reynolds closed his eyes and rubbed his forehead as if he had suddenly developed a massive migraine headache.

Custer, he thought. Damn it to hell. George Custer had become one of the most troublesome cadets at West Point. He was on track to finish dead last for scholarship and conduct in the class of 1861. He had amassed so many demerits during his four years at the Point, he was close to expulsion. He had gotten demerits for snowball fighting, for leaving piles of rubbish outside his tents, marking up walls with a pencil, and for being late to just about everything, classes and formations included.[109] He appeared to care little or nothing of West Point's rules. There is no telling, John thought, what kind of officer this brash and reckless young man would become, if he even made it that far. Reynolds made a mental note to keep an eye on Custer.

"Anything else?" John asked, tiredly.

"No, sir. That's all," replied the first captain.

"Very well," Reynolds said. "You are dismissed."

"Yes, sir!"

The first captain stood up at attention and saluted his commandant, who returned the gesture. The young man then executed a smart about-face and marched out of the office. Would that they all could be like that cadet, John mused to himself.

CHAPTER THIRTEEN

Philadelphia
December 1860

Snow fell lightly as John and Kate walked hand in hand across Independence Mall in Philadelphia. It was a few days before Christmas. Reynolds had taken a two-week leave from West Point for the holiday. He had briefly visited his sisters, now living in the city, but told them he had business to attend to and would secretly spend long days with his love, Kate.

As they strolled through the mall, leaving footprints in the snow behind him, Kate looked at John with a worried expression.

"Are not you afraid that someone, perhaps your sisters or acquaintances of theirs, will see us?" she asked.

John smiled.

"Oh, it is a risk, I suppose. But my sisters live some distance from this spot, and I am wearing civilian clothes, making it less likely someone would notice me than if I were in uniform. Besides, does not this beard hide my looks?"

He grinned and added, "And does it not make me look dashing?"

Kate giggled and put her arm around his. John realized his rare attempt at humor was much out of his character as a serious, no-nonsense career military man. But he smiled to himself. *I guess that's what love will do for you.*

His seriousness of purpose returned when the couple approached Independence Hall to gaze at the Liberty Bell on display inside. Climbing the steps to the hall's entrance, John thought about how the popular meaning of the famed bell had changed. It had been acquired from a London foundry in the mid-1700s and placed in the Pennsylvania State House, which is what Independence Hall was first called. The founding fathers had called it the State House Bell. It rang to call the state assemblymen to their meetings.

The name Liberty Bell had come into use because of an issue that was now tearing the country apart. Slavery. The inscription on the bell reads, "Proclaim Liberty Throughout All the Land Unto All the Inhabitants thereof." Abolitionists began calling it the Liberty Bell, co-opting the inscription for their antislavery movement, in 1835 when John was just fifteen years old.[110] He feared that the slavery issue, along with protests over states' rights and taxation, was threatening to drive the country into civil war. In fact, he had learned that just a few days ago, December 20, South Carolina had seceded from the union of states over those issues, declaring itself a sovereign, independent republic. Several other Southern states were on the verge of following South Carolina's lead.

"Are you all right, my love?" Kate asked as they stood at the bell, its well-known crack clearly visible. "You seem troubled."

"I have worries, my dear," John replied. "Our country is perched on a precipice. War is in the wind."

He shook his head.

"It's unfathomable to me. Americans will be pitted against Americans. Killing each other."

They walked over to a nearby bench and sat down, talking quietly.

"It is difficult," he admitted. "I am vexed by what is happening. I can understand why South Carolina is so angry about efforts to abolish slavery. I also get that slavery is morally questionable."

Kate responded with a start.

"Just questionable?" she said sharply.

He looked at her.

"Okay, objectionable. Reprehensible, even. But you must realize, Kate, slavery is the foundation of South Carolina's economic system. And it's not just South Carolina. It is the same for several Southern states. I recall having this very same conversation with my father when I was a youngster."

Kate was getting uncomfortable.

"Do you mean to say that slavery is excusable? Justified?" she asked with slight indignation.

"No, that's not my point, sweetheart. Economically, in this day and age, it is understandable. Up here, in the North, we have new machines being invented practically every week to do the work, and to do it faster, better, and more efficiently. We have become an industrial nation, except for the South. There, in the agricultural South, manual labor is needed to get the job done. This sort of industrial revolution has not gotten there yet. Without manual labor, muscle power...yes, slavery...South Carolina and the other Southern states believe they would perish. I am afraid I cannot disagree. Morally, slavery is arguably wrong. Economically, it is a different question."

John sat up straighter and turned to face Kate.

"But what I cannot countenance, what I cannot tolerate, is a debasement of our great union as country over any issue. States' rights does not mean individual states may strike out on their own willy-nilly, no matter what the matter may be! Our grandfathers spilled blood to truly form a more perfect union, as the Constitution puts it. The states which joined that union vowed to work in concert with other states for the good of the entire nation. They cannot be allowed to dissolve that union simply because they have disagreements, or they oppose who has been elected president! My God, Abraham Lincoln wasn't even on the South Carolina ballot and he was still elected. South Carolina, or any other state, cannot be allowed to threaten the Union just because they don't like who is in the White House. Those states signed a solemn oath! The future of our democracy depends on that oath. They must remain committed! I will do everything in my power to help ensure that they do, even if it means risking my life."

* * *

Later in the day, after John had calmed down, he and Kate rented a horse and buggy for a ride in the country. The snow had stopped falling, and while it was a chilly December day, the sun was shining and, wrapped in warm blankets, the lovers were comfortable. The new fallen snow glistened in the sunshine, creating a beautiful crystalline landscape as they rode through the countryside.

They headed for Chadd's Ford, a small village just southwest of Philadelphia. It was the site of the Battle of Brandywine Creek where John's maternal grandfather had been wounded in the Revolutionary War.

John had chosen the spot because he had something very important to do. He pulled on the reins, coaxing the horse to stop in a clearing beside the babbling creek. Its current was strong enough to prevent it from freezing over. John tied the reins off and reached out to take Kate's hands.

"My darling," he said. "I am madly in love with you. So much so that I wish to spend the rest of my days with you."

Kate sat still, biting her lip, her eyes wide, as John took a very deep breath and let it out all at once.

"Catherine Mary Hewitt, will you do the honor of being my bride? Will you marry me?"

Kate stared at John for only a moment, but for him it seemed like an eternity. Finally, she answered.

"Oh, yes, my love, I will! I will marry you! You are my life, my love! My everything!"

John smiled broadly, his eyes glistening. They wrapped their arms around each other and kissed for a very long time. The horse even seemed to sense the importance of the moment as he pawed one hoof lightly on the ground.

Eventually, they sat back, his arm around her shoulders. Kate leaned comfortably into him, wrapping the gray blankets more tightly around them. They stayed like that for a while, saying nothing, basking in the glow of their love for each other. Finally, Kate spoke.

"When should we marry?" she asked quietly.

"Hmm, well," he said, "I guess I don't know. Perhaps soon? Right away, maybe? That would suit me fine."

Kate sat up straighter and turned to look at John with a serious expression. She reached up to gently stroke his thick dark beard.

"Perhaps, my darling, perhaps we should wait."

"Wait? Why wait?" he asked with puzzlement.

"Because of something you said this morning."

"What did I say?"

"It was about how you would fight to defend the country, you know, the Union, even if it means giving up your life."

John thought for a moment.

"I, umm, do not believe I put it quite like that," he said gently.

"Well, you did say you would be willing to risk your life. Isn't that the same thing," she replied.

John nodded.

"Yes, I suppose it is. I am sorry if that upset you."

"Oh no, my love."

She leaned over to kiss him quickly.

"I am not upset at all. In fact, I think you are very brave and quite noble. I love you for that. You make me so proud to be with you."

Kate paused and looked around at the gurgling creek and brilliantly white snow lining its banks. She thought carefully about what she would say next. She turned back to look at John again.

"I do so much want to marry you, my darling. I'd be happy to do it today. But…but if…if there is a war coming, you know, like you say, perhaps we should wait until it is over."

John frowned.

"What would be the point of that?"

Kate sighed.

"War…if there is a war, will be terrible," she said. "You would be in danger every day…every hour of every day. It would be awful if you had to worry about me, your wife, being home while you are off somewhere engaged in battles. I wouldn't want you to be distracted by that, to lose your focus by that. It would be better for you to concentrate on winning the war, to not have your attention diverted."

She paused again, then continued, very softly.

"To stay alive."

John put his arms around her again and pulled Kate close.

"Oh, sweetheart, you are an angel. But won't what you say be the same even if we aren't married."

"I guess so. But I think it is different between a man and his wife than it is between a man and his…you know…lover," she said with sadness in her voice.

Kate sat up again and spoke more firmly.

"John, it would be horrible if you were wounded…or worse, killed…because your thoughts about marriage responsibilities and all that somehow contributed to…oh Lord, I hate to say it…to your demise!"

Then she grinned a little and a small twinkle returned to her eye.

"Besides, wouldn't my sitting home waiting for you to return to get married be more of an incentive for you to remain alive?"

John smiled.

"Yes, ma'am, I guess it would," he said, chuckling. "Well, I suppose you are right. Let's wait, first, to see if there is a war. And if so, we can wait to marry until it's over. Besides, that shouldn't be too long. My bet is any war would last only a few weeks, a few months at the most."

John held up his right hand and looked at his West Point ring on his third finger. He reached with his left and pulled the ring off.

"Kate, this is proof of my love for you," he said, handing the ring to her. "I want you to have it and keep it as a token of our engagement."

Kate stared at the ornate gold ring, engraved with the words *West Point* and the date, 1841, the year John graduated from the military academy. An onyx stone was set in the crown with a small diamond embedded in the center. She reached reverently and took the ring from him.

"Oh, John," she breathed. "This is absolutely lovely. But, my darling, I thought you West Pointers never, ever, took off your rings. How can I ever accept this?"

"We rarely do take them off, you are correct, only for very special reasons. I can think of no reason more special than this."

Tears slid down Kate's cheeks as she leaned over and gave John a passionate kiss.

"Thank you, my darling," she then said. "I shall cherish this with all my heart and soul."

The ring was big enough to slip over her dainty thumb, which she did. Then she unbuttoned the top of her bodice and removed two small chains from around her neck. A Catholic medallion hung on one of the chains. A gold ring shaped as a pair of clasped hands was suspended from the other.

"My darling," she said, handing the chains to John, "this is a token of my love for you and of our engagement, as well. I will pray that they will keep you safe from harm."

John carefully took the chains and looked at the medallion and ring closely.

"I shall have the ring engraved with the words *Dear Kate*. Would that be all right?"

"Yes," Kate said. "That would be wonderful."

He unbuttoned the top of his coat and slipped the chains over his head and around his neck.

"I shall never take these off," he said. "I promise you that."

He smiled kindly and seriously.

"And as a Protestant, I will wear this Catholic medallion with honor and with pride."

Almost as an afterthought, they simultaneously said, "And it will be our big secret!"

Their laughter echoed across the low snow-covered hills surrounding Brandywine Creek.

CHAPTER FOURTEEN

West Point
April 1861

The war Major John Reynolds was so uncertain would occur became an even darker looming shadow when he returned to West Point after the holidays. Following South Carolina's secession from the Union five days before Christmas of 1860, six more states quickly followed suit in January and February of 1861. Together, South Carolina, Mississippi, Florida, Alabama, Georgia, Louisiana, and Texas formed the Confederate States of America. They chose Jefferson Davis as their president.

That choice was particularly repugnant for the commandant of cadets. Reynolds was dismayed that a fellow West Pointer, with whom he had fought in Mexico so many years before, would betray the United States of America by accepting the position. John had long felt animosity toward Davis for how, as secretary of war, he had blocked John's entreaties for advancement within the Army.

Now, Davis was the leader of rebel states. John was outraged, even more so when he learned that Davis was attempting to sway West Point cadets to join the Confederacy. Before secession became a reality, Davis had headed up a US Senate committee investigating West Point with the aim of reorganizing the institution. The committee's report was nearly complete when Reynolds first took over as commandant of cadets. Nevertheless, in a letter to his sister

Ellie, John angrily accused Davis of filling the academy "with the poisonous seeds of secession." John further despaired that Davis had "systematic plans for disorganizing the whole country." He wrote of Davis with a blistering pen, "The depth of his treachery has not been plumbed yet, but it will be."[111]

The growing tension in the halls of Congress and throughout the country also were causing problems at West Point. Arguments and confrontations erupted among cadets from the North and cadets from the South. A strict disciplinarian to begin with, John found himself handing out demerits and other punishments by the bushelful.

"This will not stand!" he berated two cadets one afternoon. One of them was from South Carolina, the other from Pennsylvania. Their argument over slavery, secession, and states' rights had exploded into a bloody fistfight. They now stood, bruised and battered and at rigid attention in front of their very angry commandant.

"You two are a disgrace to the military uniform! Your behavior is totally inexcusable! If we were not on a war footing, I would toss you out of the academy right now. Unfortunately, the time is coming soon when officers will be needed in the field. If this is the kind of leadership you will be showing your men, well, God help them. You will remain here at West Point and finish your training. But I am giving each of you fifteen demerits. You may consider yourselves fortunate that I don't court-martial you. I am also ordering you both to stand guard duty every night, all night, for the next two weeks. Do you understand!" John shouted.

"Yes, sir!" they both responded.

"You are dismissed. Get out of my sight," the commandant said with disgust.

Those tensions were exacerbated when the South Carolina militia opened fire on Fort Sumter in Charleston Harbor early in the morning of April 12. John knew that Robert Anderson, his commander at Fort Preble more than a decade ago, and his 85 men had held out for 34 hours of an intense bombardment by the Southern forces before they were forced to give up. Surrounded on all sides around Charleston Harbor by Southern militia fighters, Anderson had been plainly outmanned and outgunned. More than 3,300 canon and mortar rounds had been fired at Sumter.[112] Running desperately low on ammunition, food, water, and other supplies, he had given up the fight to avoid needless bloodshed. It was astonishing that in the near day and a half of the merciless bombardment, no one was killed. That battle was over, but, as history now knows, the Civil War had only just begun. John was appalled that the commander of the South Carolina militia in that battle was General Pierre G. T. Beauregard, who had been the superintendent at West Point just months before.

When word arrived at the academy that South Carolina militiamen had won the Fort Sumter battle, Southern cadets were jubilant, much to the chagrin and anger of their Northern academy mates. Maintaining order in the ranks was becoming increasingly difficult. Reynolds had to clamp down even more on discipline to prevent disorder among the cadet ranks from breaking out. Peace was restored somewhat when orders came down last month to immediately hold an early graduation ceremony for Southern first-class cadets, most of whom then departed to join the Confederate Army.[113]

As elated as they were over the turn of events, many were disappointed because when Southern troops captured Fort Sumter, they thought the war was over. They believed they had missed the chance to get in on the fight. But, never mind! The South had won, they cheered. The Yankees had been defeated! That was a common belief throughout the country, North and South. Very few people at the time had any concept of the terrible years of killing and horror that lie ahead. Those people included John Reynolds.

* * *

Lifting a billiard cue and taking aim at a red ball, John sharply struck his white cue ball. It rolled rapidly across the table, smacked into the waiting red and caromed off it to strike another red ball. "Point!" John said, triumphantly.

"Nice shot, Major," another officer said.

"Thank you, Captain. That was mostly luck." John laughed.

The four-ball billiard table in the officers' quarters was about the only relaxing recreation Major Reynolds could enjoy. He had taken a couple of hours away from his office to shoot a few games with fellow officer Captain Benjamin Fytche.

"How is it going with that troublesome cadet, Major? What's his name? Custer, isn't it?" Fytche asked.

"Yes, Custer. George Armstrong," Reynolds replied, with disdain. "I have confined him to his quarters as a result of his latest escapade. He will be court-martialed."

It was late June. Senior cadets, the firsties, had graduated. Most had departed West Point for leave and then their first regular Army assignments. Custer was still at the Point and was officer of the day for a new crop of recruits who had arrived for summer camp. When two of them got into a fight, Custer blocked others who tried to intercede. He was arrested for failing to stop the altercation.

"What in the blazes were you thinking?" Reynolds had scolded Custer.

Standing at rigid attention, Custer still was able to give his commandant a flip answer.

"The instincts of a boy," he had said, "prevailed over the obligations of an officer of the guard."

Exasperated, Reynolds had confined him to quarters until the court-martial. But, until his luck would run out in the Great Sioux War of 1876, Custer seemed to be blessed with good fortune. He only received a reprimand in the court-martial and, with his brashness and derring-do, would go on to distinguish himself in the Civil War.[114]

Distractions such as Custer and other disciplinary or administrative matters greatly frustrated Reynolds. He was anxious to join the North-South fight, which, to his surprise, had intensified since the fall of Fort Sumter to the South Carolina militia.

As he took aim at another billiard ball, Reynolds said to Fytche, "I tell you, Ben, this war is passing me by. I shouldn't be here. I should be in the fight. I would serve in any position the government may call me to, with all the energy and power I possess."[115]

He struck at the white ball with such force, it flew off the table. Fytche laughed as he retrieved the ball off the floor.

"I'll say this, Major," he said. "If you fight the rebels the way you play billiards, this war will be over in a week!"

John tried to laugh, but he wasn't in much of a jovial mood. Aside from his annoyance at being stuck at West Point, he was also sorely disappointed by the failure of Washington to prevent the Union from breaking up as more states seceded. He saved his deepest resentment for President Buchanan, the family friend who had helped him start his military career. John agreed with Buchanan's critics who accused the president of being complicit in the Southern rebellion. Those critics complained that "members of the President's cabinet were among the boldest of the southern conspirators." They condemned those accused, many who were slave holders, as being "unscrupulous and dictatorial," involving Buchanan in "a policy, which he knew was disastrous to the nation, he had no power to change."[116]

Leaning on his billiard cue, John sighed deeply.

"A more disgraceful plot, on the part of our friend Buchanan's cabinet and the leading politicians of the south, to break up our government without cause has never blackened the pages of history in any nation's record!"[117] he said with sadness.

Every day John waited anxiously for a wartime reassignment. Just this morning, he had written one of his long loving letters to Kate, telling her he was uncertain about how much longer he would be at the Point. He brooded about the tumultuous events overtaking the country.

"One can hardly realize this great nation is in the agonies of dissolution,"[118] he said.

So anxious was he to join the fight, he had already turned down an offer to be the aide-de-camp for Winfield Scott, the commander in chief of the Army, despite his intention to "serve in any position." It was an offer from Scott himself.

Finishing his game of billiards, putting his cue away, he turned to Captain Fytche.

"I don't know about you, Fytche, but my place is on the battle-field, not behind some desk."

* * *

Two weeks after the summer graduation ceremonies, John heard a knock at his office door.

"Enter!" he called out.

One of his staff officers entered the room.

"A message for you, sir," the young officer said. "From Washington."

"Thank you, Lieutenant. You are dismissed," John said, as he took the sealed envelope from him.

Sitting at his desk, he tore open the envelope and saw that it contained the orders for which he had been waiting. The message, however, held two surprises. The first was that he had been promoted to lieutenant colonel. The second was that his new assignment was not the one he had expected. Instead of being sent to some war front, he was ordered to report to Fort Trumbull, near New London, Connecticut, to organize a new infantry regiment.

"Well, I would have preferred an artillery unit," he said to himself. "And I would rather be at the front, but this will do. It will have to."

He got up from his desk to go deliver the news to his boss, Major Alexander Bowman, the West Point superintendent. Reynolds was bemused by yet another irony he was discovering as he moved up through the ranks. Major Bowman was one of the lead engineers in building Fort Sumter down in South Carolina, the same fort that was recently blasted by Southern soldiers.

"I have new orders, Major," Reynolds announced after he arrived at Bowman's office. They were both sitting in chairs, sipping coffee, in a little reception area off to the side of the superintendent's desk, overlooking the Plain down below.

"I also now outrank you," Reynolds continued with a friendly smile.

"How's that?" Bowman asked.

"Well," John said, holding up the message he had received, "it appears I am a lieutenant colonel now."

"My, my," the superintendent said, with a grin. "It looks like Washington will promote anyone these days. Well, that's what war will do for you."

Both men laughed.

"Seriously," Bowman continued. "Congratulations, John. Or should I say Lieutenant Colonel, sir?"

John chuckled.

"John will do."

"So, where are you headed?" Bowman asked, taking a drink of his coffee.

"New London. Fort Trumbull. Seems I'm to organize a regiment. That is what war will really do for you," John said. "I'll leave in a few days."

"Well, you have done a fine job here as commandant, the way you kept cadets in line and taught them discipline," Bowman said. "You will be missed."

John smiled a little crooked smile.

"That may be the case among officers and professors here, I suppose. But what will be more flattering is the likelihood of great rejoicing among the cadets at their being relieved of me."[119]

Both men laughed again.

CHAPTER FIFTEEN

Philadelphia
April 1861

Catherine Hewitt knelt on the red velvet-covered bench of a prayer pew in the chapel of the Sacred Heart Academy in Philadelphia. She rested her elbows on the flat top of the pew, folded her hands, bowed her head, and closed her eyes. Kate then began to intone a soft prayer.

"Our Father, who art in heaven," she whispered. "I beseech you to watch over your servant, my beloved, and keep him safe from harm in the conflict which is about to descend upon our nation. Dear Lord, please hold him in your arms and protect him in this time of tribulation. My loving God, you are my savior, and I pray to become a beacon in your righteousness and goodness. I am a sinner, and I confess all my sins to you, knowing, with joy, your forgiveness and love. In the name of your son, Jesus Christ, Amen."

Kate remained motionless for several minutes in silent meditation. Finally, she slowly stood up and turned to leave the chapel. She was startled to see another woman sitting in a nearby pew. She had not heard anyone enter.

"It is comforting to see you in prayer," the woman said quietly.

It had been nearly seven months since Kate had enrolled at Eden Hall, a boarding school established by the Philadelphia Order of the Sacred Heart. She had worked diligently to complete her conversion to Catholicism while, at the same time, studying the finer points of being a cultured, "proper" lady. She knew she needed this "finishing" process, fantasizing being wedded to a ranking officer and a gentleman, socializing in the circles of high society after the war. It was a breathtaking dream she could have never realized growing up in the strict and broken Baptist home of her youth. More than that, however, she so loved John Reynolds, she was distraught at the thought of ever being a disappointment or embarrassment to him with her simple ways.

She realized, deep in her soul, their religious differences could present difficulties in the future, especially with the anti-Catholic sentiment running through the country. But she hoped and prayed, especially prayed, that they would overcome those difficulties. She believed they could. She believed in him. She was working hard to believe in herself.

"Madam Superior," Kate said. "I did not hear you come in."

"I did not intend to intrude on your conversation with God." The woman smiled.

"Oh no, madam. There was no intrusion at all. It also gives me comfort to pray to our Lord."

The madam superior nodded encouragingly. Madam Superior Thompson was the current senior sister at Sacred Heart. Many people called it a convent, but that was not really correct. The sisters lived in "communities" where they worked. Its inhabitants were not called nuns. They were sisters of the Sacred Heart. Their philanthropic arm was called the Daughters of Charity.

"I am greatly pleased by the progress of your conversion, Catherine," Madam Superior Thompson said. "It is rather remarkable given the fact that before you started this journey you had never really been aware of the Catholic religion. I can see that you desire to know the truth, and that is good."

She patted the pew seat beside her.

"Please, come sit with me," she said.

As Kate sat down, the madam superior continued.

"I see strong character in you, Catherine. Impetuous, maybe." She grinned. "But, strong nevertheless."

"Thank you, Madam Superior," Kate said, blushing.

"I am especially impressed by your abjuration, your confessions of sins. You have done so with a furor that penetrates all hearts. I can see you have given yourself over totally to our Lord."[120]

Kate bowed her head at that, thinking, yes, she had come to love the Lord, but it was John to whom she planned to totally give herself. That thought, however, would remain unexpressed in this conversation, she told herself. Madam Superior Thompson had not noticed or preferred to ignore the slight change of Kate's expression.

"You are about ready for your first communion," Madam Superior Thompson continued. "Your feelings of faith and the recognition of the Lord our God are truly admirable."[121]

"Thank you, madam. I believe I have truly found my calling."

"Be with God, child."

The madam superior stood up and left the chapel.

Kate remained seated for a long time, thinking about the conversation. *Yes*, she thought, *I truly have found joy. For the first time, my life has meaning.* She believed the Catholic Church gave her the serenity and peace of which she had been deprived in her Protestant upbringing. The sisters at Sacred Heart had become the family she never really had. Under their tutelage, Jesus had become her rock; God, her foundation. She now knew the meaning of being blessed.

She thought about the Bible and the lessons she had learned. She smiled, recalling the words of Psalm 23:6, "Surely goodness and mercy shall follow me all the days of my life, and I will dwell in the house of the Lord forever." Kate nodded her head. *Goodness and mercy have, indeed, come into my life*, she thought.

"Thank God," she said aloud, softly. "Thank you, God, for bringing John into my life."

She thought about the letters she had written to John over the past months, and about the letters she planned to write. She wanted him to know how she believed faith and providence were shaping not only their future together, but also the war itself. In thinking this way, Kate joined countless other women who used their devotion to support their men, their husbands, brothers, and sons in far-off places fighting battles. Kate hoped John would read scriptures to give him solace and comfort.[122]

She also firmly had faith now that God's will would prevail in the months and years ahead. If he determines that John must be called to his heavenly home in the forthcoming conflict, then she must submit to his power and authority. Although she would continue to pray that would not happen, Kate was determined to recognize the incomprehensible omniscience of the Lord.

As she stood and slowly walked out of the chapel deep in thought, Kate wondered what would become of her if John, God forbid, were to die in the war. Perhaps, she thought, if that were to happen, I should really commit to the Lord and join a convent, or a community.

Back in her small room at Eden Hall, Kate opened the linen curtain at the window to let in more light. She sat at a modest desk, pulled out several pieces of paper from the drawer, lifted a pen, and began to write.

"My Dearest John..."

CHAPTER SIXTEEN

New London, Connecticut
June 1861

"...join a convent. All my love, my darling. I am thinking of you every waking moment. Kate."

John stared at the latest letter from Kate for several moments. Convent? He was stunned by her suggestion that, should he die, she would join a religious order. No, he decided, it was not so much a suggestion, but a vow.

He was struck by an overwhelming feeling of love and devotion knowing that Kate had become so faithful a companion that without him she would rather commit her life to celibacy and prayer. He longed, more than ever, to be with her now, at this very moment.

But, as appealing as that might be, the Army had more urgent matters for him. Suddenly, John found himself in the vortex of orders, counterorders, and quarrels over his command functions as headquarters in Washington toiled frantically to create an effective fighting force.

He had been at Fort Trumbull in Connecticut only about a month getting accustomed to his new shoulder bars as a regular Army lieutenant colonel when orders came down promoting him again, this time to brigadier general of volunteers.

John was sitting in his makeshift office, going over recruitment documents for the new regiment when, as at West Point, he heard a knock at the door.

"Enter!" he called.

This time it was a sergeant who walked in and saluted.

"A message, sir," the sergeant said, handing over a large envelope. "From HQ, in DC."

"Thank you, Sergeant. You can stand at ease, and you are dismissed."

"Yes, sir." The sergeant threw a perfunctory salute at Reynolds, spun around, and marched out the office, closing the door behind him a little too hard.

Ever the disciplinarian, John gazed at the closed door for a moment, then shook his head at the indolence of the man.

"Volunteers," he snorted to no one.

Opening the envelope, John saw the order promoting him to brigadier general. He also saw a message from Major General John McClellan who was scrambling to organize the thousands of Northern volunteers signing up for the Army of the Potomac to fight Johnny Reb in the South. McClellan's message to Reynolds was short and to the point.

"Do you accept your appointment as brig. general and, if so, when will you be here—answer."[123]

Now, John realized he was finally getting closer to the action, and he readily accepted the order. But three days later, another message arrived, ordering him to report to Hatteras Inlet, which was under the command of General John Wool whom John knew from the Mexican-American War. Wool was delighted that the high command was sending him "such an able and experienced officer."

McClellan, however, was not delighted at all. He complained to an even higher command, the secretary of war, that he needed Reynolds, and that was that. Subsequently, Reynolds received yet another set of orders sending him to Washington, DC, the headquarters of the Army of the Potomac.[124]

By now, John was totally exasperated. This was the type of dillydallying and meddlesome interference that he so despised in the military. But, he dutifully reported to McClellan who assigned the new Brigadier General Reynolds to command the First Brigade of the Pennsylvania Reserves.

* * *

"Governor Curtin certainly seems to have the ear of President Lincoln, doesn't he?" John asked his friend and fellow general George Meade.

Reynolds and Meade were standing on the ramparts of Fort Reno in a section of the nation's capital known as Tenallytown. The fort was one of several built around Washington to defend the city against attack. Reno was considered a prime location because it sat on the highest natural elevation in the area. From where they were standing, the two generals could see the Capitol dome and the White House off in the distance.

Meade chuckled at John's remark.

"Well, Curtin, you might say, approaches most everything he does with a certain amount of zeal."

They were discussing the recently elected Pennsylvania governor Andrew Gregg Curtin. He was a staunch supporter of Abraham Lincoln and, as Meade indicated, zealous in his patriotism. He was also the reason Reynolds and Meade were standing where they were.

Curtin had pestered the president to the point of annoyance about the urgency of forming a regiment of Pennsylvania volunteers. Lincoln finally gave the go-ahead to form fourteen regiments in the Keystone State, but Curtin said he could convince the Pennsylvania legislature to provide twenty-five or more, so eager was he to gear up for war.

By September, the volunteers had been organized into three reserve brigades with Reynolds and Meade leading the first two and another general commanding the third. The three brigades formed a division under the leadership of General George McCall.[125]

As much as he disdained volunteer soldiers, Reynolds was greatly pleased by the way matters were developing. He was in the field. He had a brigade. He was getting ready to fight, all the things he wanted.

Furthermore, he knew McCall and Meade well. All three men were Pennsylvanians, and all three had experienced similar action in the Mexican-American War. Reynolds was also pleased that a unit called the Lancaster Guards from his hometown had been included in the reserves.[126]

Reynolds was settling down in camp to begin training his new brigade of men when he received yet another message that was not quite so pleasing. It came while he was writing a series of instructions for his subordinate regimental commanders. Opening the envelope handed to him by a member of his staff, Reynolds read the message and frowned.

"Damn it!" he cursed under this breath.

The message came in the form of Special Order Number 71 issued by the Army of the Potomac. It directed that "a Military Board to consist of the officers herein named will assemble at Washington D.C. at ten o'clock on Monday the twenty-third to examine into the capacity, qualifications, propriety of conduct and efficiency of all commissioned officers of volunteers who may be ordered before it."

The name at the top of the list of "officers herein named" was Brigadier John Fulton Reynolds.[127]

Once again, John was being pulled away from what he really wanted to do, and where he really wanted to be, in the field with his men, even if they were volunteers. In that regard, he was in the same league as other commanders who did not trust volunteer soldiers. That's why he and a few other Army regulars had been ordered to screen officers in the volunteer ranks. Too many were just not fit for the job.

"I need you, John," the Army of the Potomac commander, General McClellan, said when they met at his headquarters. "I need you to vet these volunteers. Most of them don't know the first damn thing about leading men, let alone fight a war. We can't have a bunch of citizen soldiers stumbling around the battlefield like a bunch of idiots. I need you to pick the right men for the right job!"

"With all due respect, sir," John replied. "My job is in the field training the troops, teaching them how fight and then fighting with them. I do not belong behind a desk going though personnel records like some glorified clerk! Surely you must have others who can do that, others who wouldn't mind spending the war pushing papers."

McClellan looked hard at Reynolds, not sure if he appreciated John's tone.

"Look at it this way, John," he said. "We cannot win this war without qualified officers to lead the men in battle. It all starts with that. This is important. Furthermore, as you do this, if you want to develop some sort of instruction manual, you know, some sort of guide for training the volunteer troops, well, I encourage you to do that. Get rid of the rejects for me, John, and teach the bright ones how to wage war! Teach them discipline. God knows that with the thousands of men wanting to volunteer, there must be some among them who have good heads on their shoulders. There must be some who will make competent officers. Find them for me, John."

Reynolds looked at McClellan for a moment. Then he sighed.

"Yes, sir," he said, finally. "I will find a few good men for you."

"I hope more than a few," McClellan replied. "Besides, General, this part of your assignment is not a career. As soon as you finish the task, I'll send you right back to your brigade. How's that?"

"That will be fine, sir. Thank you."

True to his word, McClellan sent Reynolds back to his unit a few weeks later. John's animus toward volunteers was not alleviated neither by his temporary assignment nor by the actions of men in his unit later in the fall. He was angered by the behavior of the soldiers in the ranks during a reconnaissance mission near Dranesville, Virginia.

"In coming over here, they proceeded at once to plunder and destroy everything in the houses left by the people," he complained in a long letter to his sisters. "I almost despair from what I have seen of them."[128]

Letters he wrote to Kate were usually full of gentle thoughts, love, and longing for his intended bride. But his rant about the volunteers even bled onto the pages he sent to her.

"Those volunteers plundered and marauded most outrageously and disgracefully," he wrote one day.[129]

John expressed similar disgust in conversations with General Meade. The actions of the volunteers deeply offended his sense of honor and discipline, which John believed are the hallmarks of a military soldier. His friend did not disagree.

"They do not, any of them, officers or men," Meade said, "seem to have the least idea of the solemn duty they have imposed upon themselves in becoming soldiers. Soldiers, they are not, in any sense of the word."[130]

Reynolds and Meade were sitting in the officers' quarters, smoking cigars, and sipping brandy. Even those pleasantries did nothing to lighten John's mood.

"I have an officer and three men in arrest for their plundering at Dranesville," he said, angrily. "I hope to have them hanged if I can."[131]

Meade looked at John and raised his eyebrows at his friend's angry outburst. John saw the glance, put his glass down on the table, and leaned forward to make his point.

"Look, George," he said, "we soldiers have a sacred duty to protect and defend our homes, our country. By the same token, we have a sacred duty to honor the homes and families with whom we come in contact. We are gentlemen, not savages. We must act like gentlemen. We must be bold, to be sure. But we must also be honorable and respect our adversaries, yes, our enemy. Our mission is to destroy his army. His army, George! Not his home. Not his stores. To violate his private property, to vandalize his hearth and home, why, that makes us little more than wretched scoundrels. That will not stand! Not in my units, at any rate."

The volunteers felt John's wrath in the following weeks. He trained them hard and put them again and again through their paces, punishing the slightest of infractions. He was determined to whip them into an effective and honorable fighting force. General Reynolds did not yell or shout at his troops, however. He didn't need to. His look and demeanor were enough to instill respect, if not fear, in his men.

"Did you see the general this morning?" one volunteer said to a buddy during a brief break in the training. "I do believe those dark, piercing eyes of his could burn right through a man."

"That's the truth," said the buddy. "He uses few words, but his look could crush a man, I think."[132]

John's dark and piercing eyes, if anything, grew darker and more piercing as time went on. In December, brigades under his and Meade's command were called in to support another unit involved in a skirmish with Confederates near Dranesville again. John had been itching to get into battle, and this was a good opportunity for that. But, alas, his men had not gotten there when they were needed. The battle was over by the time they had arrived. Reynolds was livid despite the official report of the action commending John for his leadership.

"I must not forget the prompt manner in which General Reynolds came up from Difficult Creek, some four miles off, as soon as he heard the cannonading," the commanding officer of the other brigade wrote. "He arrived too late, it is true, to take part in the affair, but the certainty that he would come with his brigade insured a victory and stimulated our men to earn it."[133]

All John could see in those words was "he arrived too late." Back at camp, he vented his anger to fellow officers. Indiscreet, perhaps, but he had to let off steam.

"The officers in my regiments suffer from the want of knowledge," John said scornfully. "Would that I could transfer away from these despicable volunteers and command a regular unit."

That would not happen for some time, just as he would not see real action for some time, frustrating him even more.

CHAPTER SEVENTEEN

Washington, DC
January 1862

"My Dearest Kate, Words cannot describe how deeply I miss you. I dream constantly of your beautiful face, charming features and pleasant countenance. This new year brings me hope that this war will end soon, and we can be together again in wedded wonderment. It will be good for the country, of course, if this conflict does end presently, which I suspect it might. However, I have yet to see any real battle. Perhaps that is for the best. Still, I wonder how a proper soldier can be such without having done any proper soldiering. I must simply put my faith in Providence and trust that all will turn out as it should.

"By now, you no doubt will have noticed a photograph of yours truly comes with this letter. It is a print from a new daguerreotype I had made here in camp. I hope you like the cut of my beard. It is quite a bit shorter now. I must say, in all modesty, this picture is the best I ever have had taken, I think. Please forgive my self-praise.

"I have news! I bought another horse. Now I have three. My rank of Brigadier allows me to have four of these fine animals, but three will do for now. This one is an impressive black stallion. I think I shall name him Fancy, because that describes him perfectly."[134]

John included more pleasantries and news about his camp life in the letter to Kate and sent it to her in January before he took some time to visit his brother William and his wife, Rebecca, who had arrived in Washington. William had received orders to command a Navy ship at Port Royal, South Carolina, participating in the Union blockade of Confederate vessels as part of the South Atlantic Blockading Squadron. He had come to Washington to be briefed about the mission.

John was overjoyed to see his brother again. It had been years since they had been together. Over dinner and glasses of brandy, they reminisced about their days growing up in Lancaster, regaling Will's wife, Becky, with tales of their hunting, fishing, and other boyhood adventures. During the course of their conversations, John became increasingly worried about Will. The lines in his face were deep. He looked drawn and, John thought, a little pale.

Two of their sisters, Eleanor and Catherine, traveled down from Philadelphia also to visit Will and Becky. It was a risky time to visit the nation's capital, and not just because of the war. Smallpox and typhoid fever had spread through the city. John advised his sisters not to come, but they did anyway, and the gathering turned into a family reunion.

"I'm very worried about Will," John said to them as they sat in the parlor, drinking coffee. "He does not look well. His trips to government offices here leave him exhausted and in great discomfort. I fear for his health."

Despite John's concerns, Will continued to serve in the Navy with distinction, eventually becoming a rear admiral. Finally, in 1877, he retired due to failing health. He died two years later.

The family reunion was also taxing on John. He spent what time he could with his relatives, but that meant commuting from Fort Reno to downtown DC on horseback after fulfilling his duties in camp. Finally, on January 17, he sent them a note of apology.

"I intended coming this evening," he wrote. "But, having been out most of the day, I returned so much covered in mud that I am loath to make another trial of it today, as it involves cleaning up only to muddied over again. So, I will come tomorrow morning to have breakfast with you."[135]

He loved seeing his brother and sisters again, but it was wearing him out. So was waiting around for some action against the Confederate Army. The Army of the Potomac had grown to almost 180,000 men. But still, for the most part, it just sat. The Army commander, General George McClellan, was reluctant to act and repeatedly delayed making any aggressive moves. Even President Lincoln was growing impatient. He wasn't the only one.

"When are we going to do something?" John's friend General George Meade complained, as the two them sat astride their horses watching their men train on a rifle range. "The condition of quiescence is ruining the country! This Army is gaining nothing by inaction!"[136]

John couldn't agree more. He was disgusted that he was reduced to reading of victories by Union forces elsewhere. He tried to put a good face on it, though. When he heard about Union advances in the south and west, he called it "glorious news!"[137]

He did receive word that actually made him happy. It was about his brother's command in the Navy, which was achieving success with the blockades along the Carolina Coast.

"One good effect the gallant work of our Navy has accomplished," he said to Meade, "will be to show England that the spirit and pluck that lowered her proud banner so often in the War of 1812 has not diminished in the last 50 years."[138]

* * *

At long last, in March, Brigadier General Reynolds saw an opportunity for which he had so long been hoping. General McClellan decided, finally, to move the Army of the Potomac south to engage the enemy. In the middle of the month, John called the officers of his regiments to a meeting.

"Gentlemen," Reynolds said. "We are, at last, going to war. Make your units ready to move out in the next forty-eight hours. We are headed to Alexandria to await further orders."

The men of the Pennsylvania Reserves were just as bored as he was, and these orders buoyed their spirits to new levels. Enlivened by the prospect of military action, the men prepared to march in record time. Even a driving rain and sloshing along muddy roads for two days did not dampen their spirits.

"We're finally gonna git them rebels, ain't we, General?" one volunteer called to Reynolds as he trotted on his horse past the column of men.

"You bet, soldier!" he called back. "We are going to show them just what kind of fighting men we Pennsylvanians are!"

A great cheer went up from the long line of Union soldiers slugging through the muck and mire as rain continued to fall.

Arriving in Alexandria with the rest of the First Corps, Reynolds discovered one of the three other corps had already boarded ships and sailed down the Potomac River to Chesapeake Bay. The others would follow suit, as the Army moved into position to engage Southern forces in and around Richmond, the capital of the Confederacy. The entire Army of the Potomac was gathering at the lower peninsula of Virginia to prepare for what would be a major engagement. The entire Army, except for the First Corps, that is, and unknown to Reynolds, that exception included him and his Pennsylvania Reserves.

A knock at General Reynolds's door disturbed his focus on making travel and bivouac plans for his troops.

"Yes. What is it?" he snapped.

A staff officer stepped into his office.

"A message, sir, from General McDowell," the officer said, handing Reynolds and envelope.

Major General Irvin McDowell was the commander of the First Corps and, as such, was John's immediate superior. McDowell was politically connected, but not a talented commander. He was promoted to major general primarily through his contacts with the secretary of the treasury. Before the Civil War, he had never commanded troops in combat. During the first Battle of Bull Run in 1861, under political pressure, he ordered an attack against Confederates and was soundly defeated. McDowell also was not popular with his troops.[139]

So, when President Lincoln expressed his displeasure that Washington was being left unprotected with the Army of the Potomac leaving, McDowell was ordered to stay away from the war front, remaining with his First Corps, to shield the nation's capital. This meant it would be yet another time John was missing the action. It was just the kind of political interference in military affairs that he despised.

"Hell's bells!" he cursed, reading the message from McDowell. His Pennsylvania Reserves were ordered to guard the Orange and Alexandria railroad south of the capital. Adding insult to injury, he was ordered to repair track that had been destroyed by Confederates. All this occurring, of course, while what he believed would be the biggest battle of the war was about to take place out of sight and out of reach.[140]

In April, the weather turned foul. Bitter cold snowstorms plagued the troops. If that weren't bad enough, Reynolds was confronted with another personnel issue. A surgeon in his volunteer brigade desecrated a grave on the site of the Battle of Bull Run. He had the surgeon brought in for a dressing down.

"Just what in the blazes were you thinking, Captain?" Reynolds demanded, glaring at the officer. "Did you really dig up that grave?"

"Yes, sir," the captain said. "It was in the interest of science."

"Science?" The general was incredulous.

"Yes, sir. I wanted to study the bones. Besides, sir, what difference does it make? It was only a rebel corpse."

John was apoplectic. He had to keep himself from leaping at the surgeon.

"Captain, you have dishonored the memory of that brave soldier. It does not matter a whit whether he was rebel or Union. He was a warrior and, in death, must be respected with dignity! Furthermore, I do not believe for a second that you had some fool scientific experiment in mind. There is no good reason for doing what you did! You are a disgrace to your uniform and a disgrace to the medical profession!"

Reynolds continued to be appalled by the behavior of volunteers.

"I do not know what these men will do in action under their officers," he said to one of his aides. "They appear to have no control over their troops under the most ordinary circumstances. I have done all I can to correct these evils but must say without being able to effect much change for the better."[141]

Yet again, he threatened to resign his commission as commander of volunteers and return to regular Army duty, even though that would mean a reduction in his rank to lieutenant colonel.

Before he could act on his threat, or even take it seriously, Reynolds was given new responsibility. General McDowell's region of command grew beyond Washington southward to include Fredericksburg, Virginia, and the Rappahannock River area. In May, the First Corps began a march over rutted, muddy roads made difficult to traverse by a spring thaw. They eventually took up positions around the town of Falmouth, across the Rappahannock from Fredericksburg. Through a sequence of events, Reynolds later found himself the military governor of Fredericksburg, a rebel stronghold.

Late in the month, two of McDowell's divisions were ordered into the Shenandoah Valley to take on General Stonewall Jackson who was conducting a vigorous Confederate offensive against Union forces. That left one Northern division, which included John's brigade, to keep an eye on Fredericksburg. Because Confederate troops had left the town when the large contingent of federal troops had moved into the area, a rare opportunity had presented itself.

"John, I want you to take your brigade across the river and occupy Fredericksburg," his division commander, General McCall, told him. "This is a moment when we can control key Confederate resources. It is enemy territory, but I suspect resistance will be minimal since most of the Southern troops have left. Once you have taken the town, you will act as the military governor there."

Fredericksburg was a town of about five thousand inhabitants, and John saw this as an ideal situation to put his philosophy of warfare to work; wage war on the enemy military, not on its people.

"Yes, sir," John said to his commander. "We will move out right away."

Reynolds wasted no time in setting up martial law in the town after his troops crossed the river. He called his brigade staff together for a mission briefing.

"Gentlemen," he said. "Under no circumstance will you or your men interfere with or cause any harm to the citizens of Fredericksburg. We will impose a strict curfew, issue passes the people must possess to cross the river, and take every step we must to stop the smuggling of medical and other supplies in and out town. We will also impose restrictions on the consumption of liquor. My adjutant will work with you to set up a schedule of patrols throughout the town, day and night, around the clock. We must make sure the citizens understand who is in charge now."

He paused to take a breath and looked hard at the officers sitting in front of him.

"But make no mistake, you will not prevent the people from going about their daily business. They are not to be molested in anyway. Understood?"

"Yes, sir," they responded as a group.

"A question, sir?" said a voice from the back.

"Yes, Major, what is it?"

"The curfew, sir. Does that apply to the troops as well?"

"Absolutely!" Reynolds replied quickly. "Except for the soldiers on patrol, or on guard duty, the curfew will be applied to everyone, soldiers, townsfolk, and traders alike. We will maintain order by force, if necessary, but I prefer we accomplish the mission by example."

He paused, then continued, almost as an afterthought.

"And that restriction on the consumption of liquor? That goes for the men, as well. I don't want any of the troops thinking, in a state of inebriation, that they can somehow end the war, right here, right now. Punishment for drunkenness will be harsh."

John's velvet glove approach to martial law appeased most of the townsfolk, but on June 4, some of the more impassioned secessionists tried to make trouble. Heavy rains brought a violent surge of water down the Rappahannock, washing bridges away, leaving Reynolds and his men cut off from the main body of the division on the opposite shore.

When the Southern townsfolk realized that the troops imposing martial law on them were isolated, they gathered at the river to celebrate, cheering and wildly waving handkerchiefs and other pieces of cloth. Some of the daring began planning more serious action.[142] Several men huddled together under a tree a few yards from the bank of the river.

"We can take 'em!" one of them said.

"You're right!" said another. "There are enough of us here in town to fight 'em."

"Yes," agreed a third. "And they have no place to run. I have guns hidden in my barn!"

Others joined in the excitement, ready to grab whatever they could to use as weapons to chase "those damned Yankees" out of Fredericksburg. A more level-headed citizen of the town overheard what the plotters were planning. He knew their plan would only lead to disaster. The Union Army was simply too powerful, he thought. The man quietly left the celebration to go inform on them to Reynolds and his staff.

A short time later, General Reynolds, astride his imposing black stallion and accompanied by several well-armed soldiers, appeared on the scene, calmly riding among the crowd in a clearly nonthreatening manner. He stopped to address the townsfolk.

"Good citizens of Fredericksburg," he intoned, smiling. "It appears Mother Nature has given us a little problem to solve. But never fear. As soon as the river water settles down, my men will begin to repair and replace the bridges that have been damaged. We will reconnect with the other side of the Rappahannock as soon as we can."

Then John's smile disappeared, and his dark eyes flashed with warning.

"Now, if anyone believes this is an opportunity to cause mischief or try to do my men harm in any way, I assure you, such belief is folly. I will not allow any attempt to disrupt the order we have established in this fine town. In the event anyone needs more evidence, I direct your attention to the relatively short distance across the river. There, the artillery of General McCall's division remains aimed at the town, and there will be no hesitation to open fire in full force if any demonstrations against my troops here are attempted."

Reynolds paused and gazed, unsmiling, at the now silent crowd. No one moved for several moments. Then John's smile came back, white teeth showing through his dark beard.

"Thank you for your attention," he said amiably. "And for your cooperation. Let's go, men."

Although Reynolds thought the rabid secessionists in town were "secesh of the first water" he got along with most of them. He wrote to his sister that the townsfolk "were distant, but the ladies especially, they behaved with…dignity and propriety."[143]

Reynolds gently turned his horse and slowly ambled away. His men followed, keeping an eye on the gathered townsfolk as they departed. There was no more open talk of trouble after that.

With the town sufficiently chastised, Reynolds and his men spent a relatively quiet and comfortable summer along the banks of the pleasant Rappahannock. But for John, this was no way to fight a war. Once more, he felt he was excluded from the real business at hand. He knew many of his colleagues were benefiting from promotions and other advancements as a result of battles they fought. The war was passing him by.

* * *

Reynolds finally caught up with the war thanks to Confederate general J. E. B. Stuart, whose actions resulted in a military chain of events. Stuart, a flamboyant and daring officer, led his 1,200 cavalry soldiers to circumvent Union forces who were in a position to threaten Richmond, Virginia, the Confederate capital. As a result, Stuart was able to report back to the Confederate commander, General Robert E. Lee, the approximate size and location of the Army of the Potomac. Based on Stuart's intelligence, Lee devised a bold plan also not only protect Richmond, but to also cause havoc and inflict massive casualties on Union forces by attacking from two directions, north and south. That's when Reynolds got the orders that would take him to the war for which he so yearned.

"A message for you, sir, from Army HQ."

A corporal had arrived at Reynolds's tent with a satchel in hand.

"Thank you, Corporal. You are dismissed."

John opened the satchel to find sheets of paper marked "Confidential. Eyes Only." After reading the message he turned to his adjutant, sitting on a nearby cot.

"Captain," he said, "it looks like we have some real work to do."

Holding up the sheets of paper, he added with a smile, "Finally!" John was being relieved of his short stint as military governor of Fredericksburg, and that was just fine with him.

"Captain, I want you—"

"To call the regimental commanders together for a briefing," the adjutant said, finishing John's sentence for him. "Yes, sir. Right away, sir."

John grinned as his aide stood up and left the tent to summon the officers. Unrolling a map on a small worktable, John began to plan his new mission. Several moments later, his aide returned, followed by the commanders of John's three regiments.

"At ease, gentlemen," John said. "Please, take a seat."

The four men sat, two of them sharing a cot, the other two sitting in folding chairs.

"We are moving out, gentlemen. We are going to leave the good folks of this delightful little town in the hands of some other victim...I mean...official."

The officers all snickered at his little sarcasm.

"We have been ordered to head toward White House, Virginia. We board the steamer *Cannonius*, sail down the Rappahannock to Chesapeake Bay, then around to and up the York River to the West Point, where we will overnight. Then it's up the Pamunkey River to join the rest of the Army closing on Richmond. It appears General Lee is planning some big push to defend the city, so make sure your men are well rested and ready to fight."

Five days later, Reynolds and his troops arrived at West Point Landing, directly east of Richmond, and immediately were pressed into service. Along with their evasion of and spying on Union troops, a few of J. E. B. Stuart's men had attacked an important Union supply depot along a main rail line. They surprised a small squad of guards, took them prisoner, tore down telegraph lines, burned supply

159

wagons, and fired on an approaching Union supply train, killing two civilian men.[144]

Reynolds was ordered to render assistance. He moved his brigade to the depot as quickly as he could, eagerly anticipating a showdown with one of the South's most aggressive warriors. Arriving at the remote location around midnight, he stealthily positioned his three regiments, placing one on a nearby hill, which had a commanding view of the area. At the same time, he quietly concealed another regiment in a wooded area and moved with the third to confront the Confederate soldiers.[145] But when he approached, all he saw was the carnage left behind by Stuart's cavalry troops who had fled the area.

"Damn," John cursed, when he surveyed the scene. He later reported that he "found a car loaded with corn on a sidetrack on fire, the telegraph poles on the cross-road down and the wires severed, the bridge beyond the depot on fire. Both fires were at once extinguished. One dead body on the track near the depot run over by the train. Another body afterward found in the woods with a gunshot wound in the head."[146]

The entire incident failed to give Reynolds the fight he was looking for. A rebel spy, however, would. Late in June, Union forces captured a man who falsely claimed to be a soldier in the North's First Maryland Regiment. Under intense interrogation, the man revealed that he was spy for the Confederates and had been ordered to find out the strength and location of Union troops and to ascertain the best roads over which General Lee's units could attack.[147]

"Gentlemen, we now have a fairly good idea where Lee plans to concentrate his forces."

John was in the headquarters tent of General Fitz John Porter, commander of the Fifth Corps. Reynolds had returned from the rail depot less than a week earlier and had taken his brigade further west, toward Mechanicsville, bringing him closer to Richmond, and closer to the real war. He and other officers, including Third Brigade commander Truman Seymour, were getting their marching orders.

"General Reynolds, General Seymour," Porter said, "I need you to take your brigades to the east side of Beaver Dam Creek. Entrench your men and stay well concealed. We want to give Lee a surprise he won't quickly forget. You will protect our right flank. General Reynolds, I want you to organize the divisional line there."

Beaver Dam Creek was little more than a small meandering stream which flowed into the Chickahominy River less than a mile south and east of Mechanicsville. John had a good eye for how to use terrain strategically. It was a skill learned from all those years of tracking and hunting game as a youngster around Lancaster.

The brigades commanded by Reynolds and Seymour were joining the Army of the Potomac confronting Richmond with a total of more than 150,000 men. Confederate General Lee was believed to be advancing with 180,000 soldiers.[148] Beaver Dam Creek was looking to be ground zero for this battle.

In laying out his defenses, Reynolds saw the creek was heavily wooded and provided good cover for the two brigades of 5,000 men. The creek was also lined by a rise along its east bank, providing an even greater advantage for the Pennsylvania Volunteer Reserves. From their elevated, dug-in, and hidden positions, the troops had controlling views of the approaches to Mechanicsville from the north, west, and south.

Reynolds moved with purpose all along the rise, ordering, extolling, and encouraging his men for the coming fight. His instinct told him that his position, the right flank of the Fifth Corps, is where Lee would focus his attack. He surmised that by the lay of the land, the fields of fire, the access roads, and it was how he would conduct an assault.

He got confirmation of his suspicions when he came across a young soldier of the Sixth Pennsylvania Cavalry, which was attached to Reynolds's division. The young man was encamped in the woods, tending to his horse.

"How are you doing, son?" Reynolds asked as he approached the soldier.

The soldier, caught by surprise, snapped to attention and, with a flourish, gave the general a salute.

"Fine, sir! I'm just doin' just fine!" he said.

Reynolds grinned.

"Relax, son. Stand at ease. What's your name?"

"Smith, sir. Corporal Thomas Smith."

Reynolds pointed to a tall loblolly pine tree a few yards away.

"See that tree, Corporal Smith? Think you could climb it?" he asked.

"Climb it, sir?"

"Yes, climb it. I'd like to know if the rebels can be seen from up there. You know, try to get an idea where exactly where they are, especially how close they are. Think you can do that for me?"

"Yes, sir. I, for sure, can do that!"

The soldier tethered his horse and went over to the tree. Grabbing hold of a few lower branches, he shinnied up quickly. In a few moments, he was all but hidden in the pine branches high overhead.

"What do you see, Smith?" Reynolds called to him.

"Well, sir," the soldier called down. "I can see smoke from their fires just beyond the ridge over there, just across the river. Hang on, sir. I got a glass with me."

Since horse soldiers of the cavalry were often sent on reconnaissance missions to scout out the enemy, many were supplied with a monocular, referred to as field or spyglasses.

"Sir, I can see some of their batteries over there. It looks like their pickets are only about three-quarters of a mile away from here. They're pretty close, sir. And over there, I can see some of them rebs digging a ditch, like a trench or something."[149]

"That's good information, Corporal," the general called up to him. "Come on down, now. Be careful."

"Yes, sir."

Knowing how close the Confederates really were spurred John on to redouble his efforts to lay down an effective defense line.

"Dig in deep, men!" he commanded, walking along the rise. "Stay hidden! Don't give those rebels any chance of seeing you. We are going to give Johnny Reb a licking!"

He stopped at one point where a trio of soldiers was resting under the cover of a thick longleaf pine tree.

"You men, there!" he called to them. "What are you doing?"

"Waitin' for Johnny Reb, sir," one of them called back.

"Well, he's going to see you a mile away if you don't make cover."

"We have, sir. Look! And we got this tree to give us more cover."

Reynolds jumped down into the shallow hole the soldiers had made under the tree.

"This dugout isn't near deep enough," he said. "Come on, men, put your backs into it. Dig deeper or the enemy will blast you to kingdom come. Count on it. Get off your asses, you lazy pokes!"

"Yes, sir!" they shouted. The men jumped up, grabbed their shovels, and resumed digging as if their life depended on it. As far as John was concerned, it did.

His attention to detail encompassed big picture issues as well as such minutia as the depth of foxholes. He sent patrols to scout north of Mechanicsville, keeping an eye out for Confederate general Stonewall Jackson who was believed to be advancing from his victories in the Shenandoah Valley. If his force of nearly nineteen thousand men joined this fight, Reynolds and the rest of the Army of the Potomac could be caught in their middle, Jackson to the north of Mechanicsville, Lee to the south.

Reynolds also sent troops to occupy the town and posted guards at local bridges crossing nearby rivers. Finally, he issued specific orders to his regimental commanders holding troops in reserve.

"You are to break camp at the first sound of battle," he told them. "Send all your supply wagons to the rear and move your men to your assigned positions.[150] There shall be no hesitation."

John had identified several locations along his defense line that might need reinforcing when the battle was met. He wanted to plug those holes before they became openings for the enemy. With a practiced eye, he placed five batteries of artillery along the east bank of Beaver Dam Creek, aimed north, toward Mechanicsville and beyond to counter any possible attack by Jackson from that direction.[151] It was an enemy that John believed he felt in his veins now. They were that close. He knew an engagement was at hand. It would be the beginning of what came to be known as the Seven Days Battles.

Early in the morning of June 26, General Porter arrived to inspect Reynolds's preparations. He was more than pleased.

"I have the best reasons not only to be contented," he told Reynolds. "I am thoroughly gratified with your admirable accomplishments. I am also encouraged by your cheerful confidence and that of your assistants, whom I must say are able and gallant. You are an accomplished officer."[152]

Reynolds noticed that General Porter clearly enjoyed a flourish in his language. Nevertheless, John was impressed that Porter recognized he was leaving nothing to chance, even though, John knew, in war that is next to impossible.

CHAPTER EIGHTEEN

Philadelphia
June 1862

The weather in Philadelphia was wet and nasty. Major flooding from record-setting rainfall sent water from the Delaware River[153] cascading over Penn's Landing and into the main streets of the city. The river's water level was more than fifteen feet above normal. The muck and mire of the rain-clogged dirt roads made travel difficult and treacherous.

"Fiddlesticks!" Kate exclaimed as she stepped up to her calf into a puddle of water. She was immediately embarrassed and looked around nervously to see if anyone had heard. Fortunately, there were few other people who had dared to venture outside in the driving downpour. Those who had were too focused on avoiding Kate's fate than to take notice of her mild cursing.

She was on her way to visit young Catherine Dunn, who was now twelve and doing well at her boarding school. Kate was pleased by how easily Catherine had settled into her new life. The girl was proving to be a quick learner with an active mind and appeared to be making friends easily. Arriving dripping wet at Catherine's boarding school quarters, Kate knocked on the door.

"Oh my goodness!" Catherine said when she opened the door. "Kate, you are drenched! Please, come in! Quickly!"

Kate, wet and cold, shivered as she entered the small room.

"Give me your shawl," Catherine said. "Take off your jacket, too. Here. Take this."

Catherine picked up a wool blanket from her bed and wrapped it around Kate, taking her shawl and jacket, hanging them over a wood chair to dry.

"May I take off my shoes, too?" Kate asked.

"Of course! Here. Let me help."

Catherine knelt down to unlace Kate's soaked high button shoes. Kate slipped her feet out of the soggy leather. She reached down to take off her wet stockings and draped them over the chair. Looking around, Kate walked over to the only other chair in the room and slumped down in it, wrapping the blanket tightly around her. Catherine grabbed a towel from a tiny closet and rubbed it vigorously on Kate's head, attempting to dry her long blonde sodden hair.

"Oh, thanks, Catherine. That feels good," Kate said. "My, what a miserable day it is today. Here, I can finish that. Thank you."

Kate reached up to take over the hair-drying operation.

"Would you like some tea?" Catherine asked. "We have a shared kitchen down the hall. I can quickly make you a cup or two."

"That would be nice. Thank you."

Catherine hurried out the door to go make the tea while Kate tried to relax. The wool blanket around her was helping.

The young girl returned a short while later carrying a tray with two cups, a pot of tea, and a few biscuits.

"Here you are, Kate," she said, handing the older woman a cup and pouring tea into it. "The house mother made these biscuits this morning. They are usually delicious."

Kate took the cup and a biscuit. She bit into the baked sweet and swallowed a sip of tea.

"Mmm," she said. "That is good! Thanks, Catherine. I'm beginning to feel much better. I now know what is meant by a drowned rat!"

They both laughed.

"That's silly," the young girl said.

Kate eyed Catherine maternally. She was not the girl's mother, of course. They were not even related. But Kate felt responsible for her and cared for her as much as any mother would.

"You look well, Catherine. I assume you are still enjoying the school?"

Kate knew very well that Catherine was delighted with her school, the teacher-nuns, and her classmates. Kate visited Catherine at least once a week, sometimes more often. But inquiring about her state of mind was something mothers do.

"Oh, yes! I love it here! I am so glad I came with you from California. The Daughters of Charity are wonderful."

Based on the recommendation and introduction from the Daughters of Charity in San Francisco, where Kate had taught, the Philadelphia chapter of the order not only accepted Catherine's enrollment in the Catholic school, but also they were generously allowing Kate to board there at no cost to her or Kate.

"Yes, they are wonderful," Kate agreed. "They certainly have turned my life around."

"Mine, too," Catherine said. "I am learning so much about the religion from them. Oh, I'm learning a bunch of other stuff, too. We started on algebra this week. It seems kind of hard, but I'm working at it."

"I have no doubts." Kate smiled.

"We sometimes get news about the war, too. There is not much detail, though, and it is hard to tell who is winning. But there is lots of talk among the other girls about this North-South fight. Some of them have brothers who are fighting on different sides of this war. Brothers from the same families, shooting at each other! It's hard to believe!"

"Yes," Kate said, sadly. "It is hard to believe. What a terrible thing war is. And this one is even more terrible because it is American versus American, neighbor against neighbor, and, as you say, brother against brother. Such a shame."

"They should call it the Brothers War," Catherine said.

"Maybe someday, someone will," Kate replied.

Catherine looked at Kate with concern.

"Have you heard from General Reynolds…I mean, John?" she asked "Do you know where he is?"

"Yes, I have gotten a few letters from him. According to the last one I got, he is doing all right, so far. I believe he is up in Virginia somewhere. I'm not sure where, exactly. He doesn't get really specific in his letters. Military secrets and all that, I suppose."

"Has he gotten any more promotions?"

"Not that I know of. He is still a brigadier general."

"That's really high up, isn't it? He was just a major when we all met on that boat. I thought that was pretty high up then!"

"Yes," Kate said. "He is doing well for himself. He seems to like the military, and it looks like the military likes him, too."

"Do you miss him?" Catherine asked, quietly.

"Terribly," Kate said. "I think about him all time." She said nothing more, taking a sip of her tea.

"Are you worried about him?" Catherine asked after a moment.

Kate sighed.

"Yes. Of course. I worry about him because he is such a good, dedicated soldier. Sometimes, I think, maybe too dedicated. He has told me what he thinks it takes to be a good leader. He says a real leader must be in the thick of things with his men. When there is a battle, he says, leaders don't sit back behind the lines. They are right up there where the action is, where the shooting is. His feeling is you cannot effectively drive men to fight. You have to lead them to fight."

She took another sip of her tea before continuing.

"I worry because that attitude may be bold and loyal, it is also very dangerous. It could get him hurt. Or worse."

"When is he coming to visit next?"

"I don't know. It all depends on the war, I suppose. But soon, I hope," Kate said without smiling.

She was troubled. Kate had a nagging feeling that John was in real danger. It was nothing she could put her finger on, but she had a sense of foreboding that would not go away. It was the first time since they had met that she had such a strong premonition of peril. Catherine interrupted her unquiet thoughts.

"Are you still planning your wedding for next year?" Catherine said, eagerly.

Kate had told Catherine about her engagement to John. The girl knew all about their exchanges of the Catholic medallion and rings. Kate had revealed everything to her during the visits but had sworn Catherine to secrecy. She was the only one who knew about their relationship.

"Well, we have talked about it. We are sort of planning for next July. That's July of 1863. But, again, it all depends on the war. John thinks it will most likely be over by then, but I am not so sure. We shall see."

Catherine reached over to pick up a biscuit and took a small bite. After chewing for a moment and swallowing, she took a long look at Kate.

"Are you really serious about joining a convent if…if…Lord, I hate to even say it…if something bad happens to John in the war," she asked, finally.

"You mean if he is killed?"

Catherine swallowed hard and blinked. This was a difficult subject for a twelve-year-old girl.

"Ye…yes," she stammered. "I guess that is what I mean."

Kate nodded her head solemnly.

"Yes. I am very serious. There is not another man in the world I would want to be with if John is not here. He is irreplaceable. Furthermore, the next man in my life is already in it, Catherine. That man is Jesus. The Lord. I will devote the rest of my life to him if John does not survive this war. And I will trust in the Lord to care for and love John until the time I will join him in heaven, if it comes to that. I pray, of course, that it does not. But I believe God has a plan for us all and I serenely submit to God's will. This is what the Catholic Church has taught me, Catherine."

"Okay," the girl said. "I guess I understand that. What I don't understand, though, is why you and John want to keep everything so secret. Don't you want to shout your love for him to the heavens? Don't you want people to be happy with you?"

"Sure! Of course, we do. But these are difficult times, Catherine. This country is plagued, not only by war, but also by political and social differences. We have religious intolerance, as well. Being Catholic can be risky in this climate. Many people are intolerant of the Catholic religion. You know what intolerant means, right?"

Catherine nodded in a way that said "Of course."

"Well, not everyone is intolerant," Kate continued. "But can you imagine our country ever having a Catholic president? I sure can't. Not the way things are today, at any rate. A lot of Protestant families would never countenance a Catholic-Protestant marriage either. I know. Remember, I was raised as a Protestant, a Baptist. My family, such as it is, would recoil at such an idea. There would be such a fuss! That's why we want to keep our engagement secret, Catherine. I know how my family would react. God only knows how John's Protestant family would take the news. So, please, I beg of you, Catherine, say nothing to anyone about us! Please protect our secret."

"You have no need to worry, Kate. Your secret is safe with me. My lips are sealed!"

Just then an earsplitting crack of thunder shattered the air outside. The pouring rain suddenly became a torrent. Kate's sense of foreboding returned even more strongly.

CHAPTER NINETEEN

Mechanicsville, Virginia
June 1862

Brigadier General John Reynolds could have used some of the rain that was pouring down on Kate in Philadelphia. The morning of June 26 was uncomfortably hot and humid in the forests around Mechanicsville. There was no breeze to alleviate the heat. John had awakened before dawn. He saddled his horse and rode out to make an inspection of the pickets and sentries he had placed all along his defensive line. He also made sure that all his units, his regiments, companies, and squads were ready for the coming battle. Reynolds had done all he could to prepare for it. *Now, let them come*, he thought to himself as he returned to his headquarters.

Late in the morning, a messenger burst into his tent.

"Begging your pardon, sir," the corporal said, out of breath and giving the general a quick salute. "I'm here to inform you that the cavalry pickets north of here are being pressed hard by rebels. They're pulling back, sir, but still fighting."

Reynolds knew those Confederate troops had to be part of Stonewall Jackson's force. Setting down the cup of coffee he was drinking, John quickly stood up and strode out of the tent to his horse.

"Corporal," he said, climbing into the saddle. "Ride over to the Third Brigade and ask General Seymour to meet me forthwith down by the creek where it meets the pike. And make it quick!"

"Yes, sir!" replied the messenger, who jumped on his horse and galloped away.

Less than a half an hour later, Reynolds waited for Seymour where Beaver Dam Creek intersected with Mechanicsville Pike. He could hear the multiple cracks of rifle fire and see the smoke in the short distance as his cavalry units fought to stop the Confederate advance on the town. John was scanning the scene across the creek through his glass when General Seymour rode up at a full gallop.

"It looks like the pickets are in some trouble," Reynolds said without a greeting to Seymour. "We need to tell them to withdraw gradually as they feel the pressure from the rebs. Hopefully, they will entice Jackson's troops to close in on our main defensive line."

John's meticulous preparations for just such a situation included placing eight regiments along the creek, well hidden under timber and brush.[154] These were troops from his, Seymour's, and General George Meade's brigades. It was also the reason Reynolds had placed the artillery batteries where he had. The plan was to draw the enemy into a trap of hellfire. Several other brigades were close enough to call in for support should that become necessary. Seymour agreed with Reynolds's assessment, and they rode off in different directions to deliver the orders to their regimental commanders.

As attentive as John was to this initial assault, he learned that these were only skirmishes. The main southern attack began full force in midafternoon. As the vanguard of Stonewall Jackson's force continued to apply pressure from the north, Confederate general Robert E. Lee's troops began to advance from the west and south, all rebel forces closing in on the Army of the Potomac with overwhelming numbers.

"The enemy appeared in force about three o'clock in the afternoon," John later said. "He opened up with his batteries from the high ground surrounding Mechanicsville, impetuously assailing with superior force and sat the same time the right and left of our position by the roads leading from that place."[155]

This was the battle John had been waiting for since the war had begun. Under fire, in the midst of exploding artillery shells and rifle fire, John moved among his men, encouraging, cajoling, supporting them. He was all over the place, as usual for him, in the face of danger.

Lee's forces had to cross Beaver Dam Creek to reach Union positions. The creek was waist-deep. Its banks were steep and bordered by a muddy swamp, making traversing the stream difficult.[156] John could see that rebel troops caught in the swamp were sitting ducks, or as he put it, more like trapped insects.

"Look at them, boys!" he cried out to his men. "In the swamp there! They as thick as flies on gingerbread! Fire low! Fire low!"[157]

Bucked up by their commander, the Pennsylvania volunteers fought with grit and resolve, firing again and again, to stop an enemy that kept coming at them.

The enemy "was repulsed in every effort to turn our position," he said, "as well as in an attempt to the right by the ford and old dam where he was handsomely checked by the Second Regiment."[158]

These were the men with whom John had been so disappointed and about whom he had been so critical. This time, they proved themselves so worthy, his opinion of them changed dramatically.

"The conduct of the troops, most of them for the first time under fire was all that could be desired," he said proudly. He called them a credit "to their state and their country."[159]

The battle raged on throughout the scorching hot afternoon and into the evening, with the rebel yells, the answering Northern curses, the painful screams of the wounded, the rattle of musketry, the reports of rifle fire, and the booms of cannons intensifying and growing louder by the hour. Gun smoke clogged the air. It became difficult to see the enemy. The water of the creek began to turn red with blood. Men lost arms and legs. Faces were shot away. Confederate dead littered the creek bed. Union dead lay motionless among the brush and briar along the banks. It was becoming a slaughter, which continued until about nine o'clock that night. One Confederate unit alone lost about as many men as the entire Union force in this fight.[160]

John was congratulated for the effectiveness of his defenses at Beaver Dam Creek. His corps commander, General Fitz John Porter, lavished his praise on both Reynolds and fellow general Truman Seymour of the Third Brigade.

"I desire specially to commend the admirable dispositions made by Brigadier Generals Reynolds and Seymour, owing to which, with the skillful management of their men, the losses were few," he reported.[161]

Seymour, for his part, graciously commended John, saying that "much of the credit of this day belongs justly to him, his study of the ground, and ample preparation, even to the smallest detail, justify his high reputation as a soldier and his conduct of the right wing is worthy of all praise."[162]

Even the supreme commander of the Army of the Potomac, General George McClellan, alluded to the effectiveness of John's strategy.

The enemy's "repeated efforts were constantly repulsed, with but little loss on our side, but with great slaughter on the part of the enemy,"[163] McClellan wrote in his report.

The Confederates suffered about 1,600 casualties in the fight. Only about 80 Union soldiers were lost, and about 63 were wounded.[164] Yet, the Southern forces pushed on, their seemingly endless numbers giving them a two-to-one advantage over the North. Finally, well after dark, Reynolds and the other commanders in the Fifth Corps were ordered to pull back to a new defensive line about four miles east and south near Gaines Mill.

* * *

"We need to protect this withdrawal," Reynolds said to his fellow generals Truman Seymour and George Meade. "The enemy is too close to merely cut and run."

It was after midnight. The pitiful moans and cries of the dying men still lying wounded along the creek echoed mournfully in the dark. The three brigade commanders and their aides were huddled under a large tree just behind the defensive line John had organized.

Although their troops had performed bravely and admirably, being vastly outnumbered by the Confederates made a strategic withdrawal of Union soldiers the wisest move at this point.

"I will hold the road on the right to Cold Harbor with the sharpshooters and other riflemen," Reynolds continued as he poured over a map illuminated by a dim light. Cold Harbor was a set of crossroads just up the road from Gaines Mill.

"Truman, I suggest you do the same on the lower road. George, if you agree, let's get the heavy weapons batteries moving now so they are out of enemy range by daylight."[165]

The two other officers agreed with the plan, and all three moved quickly to put it in motion. By dawn, the batteries had cleared the road and were safely on their way east to the crossroads area. As John had expected, the Confederates renewed their advance at dawn. Wary of the fierce resistance by Union soldiers the day before, the Southern units moved with caution across the Beaver Dam Creek and up the opposite bank held earlier by the Pennsylvania volunteers.[166] Reaching the tree line and heavy underbrush that had hidden John's units so effectively, rebel fighters opened up with what Reynolds called "spirited rifle fire"[167] as the Fifth Corps commenced its major withdrawal at daylight.

"Slow those rebels down!" John ordered his troops remaining in the rear to protect the departing units. "Let's make good the withdrawal! Make careful aim! Fire! Fire!"

The Northern sharpshooters went to work with pinpoint accuracy. John's light artillery units shelled the woods, which were filling with Confederate soldiers. Once again, the Pennsylvania volunteers rose to the occasion.

Their performance "in covering the withdrawal of the troops cannot be too highly extolled," John reported. "They maintained their advanced positions alone for more than an hour in the face of greatly superior numbers and with a firmness and boldness that that would have done credit to experienced veteran troops."[168]

Finally, all the Union troops were withdrawn from Beaver Creek Dam to take up their new defensive positions in and around Gaines Mill. By the description of several after-action reports, it almost appears as if the first day of the Seven Days Battles was a Union victory. One historian of the Fifth Corps was effusive in his praise of Reynolds and fellow commanders.

"The retirement from under fire and in the face of such largely superior forces was effected in a manner that elicited, even from the enemy, the warmest acknowledgments of the skill evinced by Generals McCall, Reynolds, Meade, and Seymour," he wrote.[169]

It was no Union victory, by any stretch, but neither was it a rout. The controlled withdrawal allowed the Fifth Corps to regroup for another confrontation. This time, John's brigades were held in reserve, behind the new defensive line. This gave them a few hours' rest to have something to eat and drink, to reload their ammunition packs, and maybe get an hour or two of shut-eye. By noon, things had quieted down. Most of the shooting had stopped, but the scorching heat was still making life miserable for both sides all over the battlefields. John sat in the shade of a large oak tree. He pulled out a pencil and a piece of paper to write a letter.

"My Dearest Kate," he wrote. "Well, we have had a fine battle. I am unharmed and our losses are light, but we have been forced to pull back due to the overwhelming numbers of our enemy. I must say, I am very proud of my Pennsylvania Volunteers. They have exhibited themselves in a most professional and brave manner. My opinion of these volunteers has, thus, changed dramatically. They are good soldiers now. You would not believe, my love, the scene here. It is surreal. We are in a lull of the battle and we can rest a little. Still, preparations are being made by some of the troops to prepare for the next confrontation. But amidst all that military activity, and with the enemy almost within hailing distance, mail has arrived from the north and it is being distributed among the troops. There are even newsboys wandering among the troops selling newspapers from New York and Philadelphia.[170] One would think that war is over by those sights. If only God would grant that were so. I miss you, my Darling and…I am so sorry, my Dear, I must end this letter quickly. The shooting has resumed, and we are being called to front. I love you and God grant that I see you soon. John."

Reynolds stuffed the letter into an envelope, hastily addressed it, and gave it to a messenger.

"See that this gets in the next mail going out, Private," he said.

The shooting had indeed resumed in earnest. Reports reaching Reynolds indicated that Stonewall Jackson's force of fifty thousand men had joined with other Confederate units and were "advancing with the determination to crush the Army of the Potomac." Looking to the west, back toward Richmond, John could see the dust rising from the columns of Southern troops on the march miles away.[171] His brigades were ordered out of reserve and into the action.

"What's the news, soldier?" John said to the messenger who had brought the order to him.

"The rebels, sir, they're everywhere, covering our entire front. There's thousands of 'em, sir."

The messenger spurred his horse and galloped on to deliver more orders. John called his regimental commanders together.

"It appears we are going to have a busy afternoon, gentlemen," he said. "It looks like our day off is over. Those units on the front line are going to need help. I want you all to stay loose and ready to move. Be flexible. Be smart. And be quick!"

John's evaluation of the battlefield was exactly right. General Robert E. Lee was driving his forces forward with nearly unstoppable resolve. The Union's defensive front line was beginning to fragment. The thunder of cannon and the din of rifle shot resumed, drowning out orders shouted out by officers to the men. Fog drifted over the lowlands and mixed with smoke from the thousands of weapons being fired. Visibility was severely reduced. Units became disorganized. Situational awareness became nearly impossible. Stumbling around in the muck and swamp water, troops became lost and confused.[172] According to one report of the battle, the Union "loss under the tremendous fire of such greatly superior numbers was very severe."[173]

"Major, take your regiment down there to the front line and plug that hole," Reynolds ordered to the commander of his first regiment.

He saw that Confederates were beginning to make advances through swamp-infested woods to his left. He sent his Second Brigade down into the mire to hold those rebels off.

"You men take your regiments to the other end of the line. The troops down there are being pressed hard by the enemy. Move! Move! Move!"

His regimental unit known as the Bucktails ran in double time, along with his fifth regiment, to where he had indicated and were quickly pinned down by Confederate artillery just five hundred yards away. Casualties were mounting up. The fighting continued, hour after hour. Reynolds and the other brigade commanders rode back and forth, up and down the line, moving troops, squads, companies, whole regiments around to choke off the Confederates who never seemed to run out of men. Despite John's best efforts, his troops were being worn away by the enemy. To make matters worse, his men were running out of ammunition.[174] The same was true with other elements of the Fifth Corps.

As the sun was beginning to set, Reynolds's brigades were scattered all over the battlefront. They were exhausted. So was he, but John continued trying to desperately find troops to shore up the disintegrating defense line.

"What are you doing, soldier?" he shouted to a man on horseback who was turning in circles at a clearing in the woods.

"I'm lost, sir," the young soldier shouted back. "I can't find my way!"

"Where are you supposed to be headed?" John said, riding up next to the soldier to calm his nervous horse, which was whinnying and stomping about.

"I got orders for General Seymour, sir. But I don't know where to find him."

Just then the messenger's horse reared up on his hind legs and neighed in fear as an artillery shell exploded a few yards away, throwing dirt and debris all over them.

"Holy Jesus!" the young soldier cried as he hung tightly on to his saddle horn.

"Steady. Steady," John said to the man as much to the horse.

"We're gonna git killed!" the messenger cried in panic.

"Calm yourself, soldier," John said, sternly.

The man looked around nervously but said nothing further.

"All right, son," John said. "General Seymour is off to the south a little ways. That's in that direction."

Reynolds pointed to a path leading to the trees.

"Take that path and stay under the cover of the tree line. You should be okay. Now move along. Get going!"

"Ye...yes, sir," the soldier replied. He kicked his horse in its side and rode away at a fast clip, just as another artillery shell landed with a loud explosion, throwing more dirt and debris over Reynolds and his horse.

"Holy Jesus, is right," John muttered softly.

By nightfall, John was still patrolling the lines, playing a massive real-life military chess game, moving men and weapons around to counter the moves by the other side. Along the way, his horse was wounded and needed rest. Heading across ground he thought was safe, the general discovered that Confederate troops now blocked the way. Taking a detour, Reynolds and his adjutant, who had been with him all afternoon, got bogged down in Boatswain's Swamp. His horse could move no further.[175]

"We'll have to stay here until daylight," John said to his adjutant. "Make yourself as comfortable as you can."

By now, Reynolds was beyond exhausted. The day had left him mentally and physically spent. After getting his horse settled as best he could, John found a relatively dry spot to hunker down and wait out the night. Taking the saddle from his horse, he used it as sort of a hard pillow, sat down on the ground, and leaned back on it. Within moments, his eyes had closed, and he drifted off to a restless sleep.[176]

What seemed like mere seconds later, he felt someone kicking at his foot. He tried to blink his eyes open but had to squint because of bright morning sunlight. He turned his head and found he was staring square into the barrel of a rifle pointed at his face.

"Well, well, well," he heard someone say in a heavy Southern drawl. "Lookee here. I got myself a Yankee prisoner. A officer, no less!"

CHAPTER TWENTY

Philadelphia
July 4, 1862

Kate reread the last line of the letter yet again.

"...I must end this letter quickly. The shooting has resumed, and we are being called to front. I love you and God grant that I see you soon."

The letter had arrived yesterday, and since then she had read it over at least a dozen times. The sense of foreboding that had been hanging over her head for the past several weeks was now a real, tangible, sinister thing. Something has happened to John; she knew without a doubt. Something terrible.

A loud explosion of fireworks outside of her window brought Kate out of her reverie. In the streets below her boarding room, people were celebrating another Independence Day holiday. The picnics, the parades, the gaiety, the fireworks were all doubly meaningful for many who believed this irritating war of the states would soon be over. It had to be, they said. It has already gone on for more than a year. It was time to bring it to an end, they said.

Kate decided to go outside and join the celebrations. Maybe they would ease her troubled mind. She grabbed a light shawl from a hook and left her room. Reaching the sidewalk, she watched as a parade passed by. She saw a band playing a robust version of "The

Battle Hymn of the Republic." It was a relatively new version, with new lyrics, of a fighting man's song called "John Brown's Body."

Behind the band, a formation of Union soldiers marched smartly down the street to the cheers of bystanders waving small American flags. The men at the head of each of the four columns of troops carried larger flags, which were flapping in the breeze. They were emblazoned with red and white stripes, plus thirty-four stars, representing the states of the union. Kate frowned. Eleven of the states represented on the flags had seceded and were in rebellion.

Next came a wagon dressed up like a hangman's gallows. Swinging from a rope was an effigy of Jefferson Davis, the president of the Confederate States of America. Kate scowled at the sight. Though she had no sympathy for the South, she believed such a display was obscene.

This is a celebration of our nation's independence, she thought. But, instead of real joy, we have anger and despicable displays, such as the outrage in front of her. Families all across the country are in mourning over the loss of husbands and sons. Blood flows freely in the hills and valleys, north and south. And for what? A civil war that has no civility at all! *This parade is a sham*, she thought with a shake of her head. It is madness. It is a mockery in this time of a terrible division in our land.

Kate's mind was not eased in the slightest by the gaiety around her. Finding she was not in a celebratory mood of any kind, she returned to her room, terribly unsettled. Upset by the parade, yes, but other distressing thoughts tugged at her brain, especially her worries about John. However, a small part of her had to admit that was not the entire cause of her restlessness. Their different religious beliefs continued to make her extremely anxious. Furthermore, converting to Catholicism, she admitted privately, was hard. Rejecting long-standing Protestant beliefs, learned since early childhood, took more work than she had ever imagined.

Unable to relax, Kate paced around her room. She paused to look at herself in the mirror atop her dresser.

"Do you really have what it takes, Catherine Hewitt?" she said aloud to the mirror. "Do you have the true faith and discipline to become a God-fearing Catholic? Are you certain this is the right path for you?"

She shook her head and frowned at the notion. She resumed pacing. *Of course, I do*, she thought. *What a silly thing to say. I do have what it takes, don't I? Well, if I do, why am I so troubled?*

Another thought came to mind that stopped her short. John. *What if the doubts I am having about religion are really about him?* The idea nearly took her breath away. She sat down heavily on the bed to steady herself.

Am I asking too much of him? she wondered. Here he was, risking his life to save his country with all the heavy responsibilities demanded of him as an officer. Wasn't it preposterous for her to hope he would think of marriage in the midst of a war? Wasn't it unfair of her to expect him to focus on their future when he had the lives of thousands of men in his hands, many of whom would never even have a future? When this war is over, she thought next, many wives will have become widows. Is a fear that fate could happen to her a fair burden to place on such a man as John?

Kate stood up and started pacing again. Thinking about the possibility that John might not survive the war led her to consider something else. *I made a vow*, she thought. *A solemn promise. It was a pledge to give my life to Christ if John failed to come out of this war alive. I promised to commit myself to a life of celibacy, join an order of nuns and, as the scriptures say, sanctify the Lord in my heart. I say I am willing, but am I really able to make the sacrifice?*

She stopped in front of the mirror again. All this was too much!

"Stop it, Kate!" she said aloud to the image looking back at her. "You are working yourself up into a lather. You are only making matters worse."

She realized her stress and strange feeling that John was in danger were causing her to spiral out of control.

"John's not dead!" she said to the mirrored image. "Believe me! He is not dead! He is fine. He will come home to me, safe. And sound!"

She turned sharply away from the mirror.

"Leave me alone!" she shouted. She slumped down in a chair, breathing heavily, her chest heaving.

Kate so wanted John in her arms right then. Gazing around the room, her vision settled on the bed. She wanted him there, lying next to her.

Her hands flew to her face, flushed red with embarrassment. She was both ashamed and aroused by such carnal thoughts.

CHAPTER TWENTY-ONE

Richmond, Virginia
July 1862

Brigadier General John Reynolds awoke feeling well rested for the first time in days. He had slept in a soft bed in a well-appointed room of the Spotswood House, a fine Richmond hotel. It was where he had been taken after his capture by Confederate soldiers.

Although now a POW, a prisoner of war, John was benefiting from the amenities of his private room. He'd had his first real bath in weeks and had trimmed his bushy beard.

He may be benefitting from his condition, but he was not comfortable nor happy with it. He was mortified by his ignominious capture. A Confederate guard stood outside the door because as a prisoner John was confined to this room, alone with his thoughts.

Sitting on his bed, he thought back to that awful moment when he had opened his eyes to find a rifle pointing just inches away at his face. He had been less frightened than he was embarrassed.

He had been taken to rebel headquarters in Richmond where he encountered several Confederate officers, including General D. H. Hill, an old classmate from West Point. They had been friends at the Point and had even shared a tent for a while.

John had been told to sit in a chair and wait to be interrogated. He sat there for a long while, distraught, his face in his hands. After a while, General Hill had approached him.

"Hello, John," Hill said quietly.

Reynolds slowly looked up and stared at his old friend for several long moments.

"Hill, we ought not to be enemies," he said at last.

"There is no bad feeling on my part, John," Hill had replied gently. "You ought not fret at the fortunes of war, which are notoriously fickle.[177] I am sure you know that."

"Yes, I do know that." John shook his head in disgust. "But what I really ought not be...is caught!"

Hill grinned at his fellow general's attempt at humor. John had responded with a small grin of resignation.

* * *

A few days after Reynolds had been captured and confined to his plush hotel room, he heard a commotion outside the door. It sounded to him like the shuffling of feet, and he detected a tense conversation among three or four men. Suddenly, the door flew open. Two Confederate officers entered the room, frog-marching a Union officer whom John recognized right away. It was Brigadier General George McCall, his division commander. The manager of the Spotswood House remained at the open door, his eyes wide and his mouth agape, but he said nothing.

Releasing McCall from their grasp, the two Confederate soldiers, dressed immaculately in their gray uniforms, turned toward the door. One of them motioned to the hotel manager, who quickly backed into the hall. The soldiers left the room, closed the door, and locked it from the outside, leaving Reynolds and McCall staring at each other.

"Welcome to the Spotswood House, General," Reynolds said with a grin.

"Why, thank you, General," McCall responded. "This is quite a prison cell you have here."

The two men shook hands heartily and slapped each other on their shoulders.

"So, the rebs got you, too, eh, George?" John said.

"Yup. 'Fraid so. I walked right into them. It's not like they had to work very hard," McCall replied.

They both sat down on the one sofa in the room.

"What happened?" John asked.

"We were engaged in a hell of a fight at the New Market Crossroads southeast of Richmond. I'll tell you, John, I couldn't be prouder of our Pennsylvania volunteers. The contest was severe and put the steadiness of these regiments to the test.[178] A determined and furious artillery duel gave way to a violent hand-to-hand combat. It was one of the fiercest bayonet fights that perhaps ever occurred on this continent. Bayonets were crossed and locked in the struggle. Bayonet wounds were freely given and received. I saw the desperate thrusts and parries of a life-and-death encounter, proving, indeed, John, that Greek had met Greek when the Alabama boys fell upon the sons of Pennsylvania."[179]

McCall leaned back in the sofa and crossed his legs. He let out a long sigh.

"Unfortunately, we lost a lot of good men," he said, "including several of my staff."

John shook his head in sadness.

"How did your capture occur?" he asked, quietly.

"The sun had gone down. It was so dark. It was difficult to see. The firing of rifles and artillery, by then, had ceased. I had positioned one of my companies as an advance guard about a hundred yards to the front. I rode forward with two soldiers to locate them and, in the darkness, ran smack into a small enemy unit resting under a tree. They were, in fact, from the Forty-Seventh Virginia. Before I could determine who they were, they took us prisoner, and here I am."[180]

"Well," John said, ruefully. "At least you weren't asleep when they captured you."

McCall looked at John with surprise.

"You mean…you…?"

"Yes, sir," John said, with a grimace. "Dead asleep."

McCall stared at his friend for a moment, then burst out laughing.

"It isn't that funny, George!"

"Yes, it is, John. Oh, yes, it is!"

* * *

Very early one morning in July, Reynolds was awakened by loud talking and the sound of heavy boots crossing the floor outside his Spotswood House room. Without warning, John's door burst open. A high-ranking Confederate officer strode in and stood in the middle of the room.

"It's reveille time, General," the officer said curtly. "Time to rise and shine. We are moving you to new quarters."

John stared at the officer for a moment, then turned to look at the door. He saw three Confederate soldiers standing just outside in the hall, armed with pistols and each holding a rifle.

"Yes, sir," John said genially. He got out of bed, got dressed in a pair of his uniform trousers, a shirt, and his Union Army jacket, complete with his general's epaulets. After donning his regulation Union Army cap, he turned to the Southern officer.

"Ready when you are, sir."

Escorted down the hall by the three Confederate soldiers, John saw George McCall ahead of him, also being escorted out of his room. When they reached the front doors of the hotel, John saw a horse-drawn wagon filled with Union officers, with more climbing on board.

"Where are we going, if I may be so bold to ask?" John said to the high-ranking Confederate.

"Why, we are taking you to a brand-new prison, General. We call it Libby Prison. It is much larger than this hotel. You'll have lots more room," the officer said, barely covering the smirk on his face. John knew this was not welcome news.

So many Union soldiers became prisoners during the Seven Days Battles that an old tobacco warehouse on the James River was pressed into service as a prison. In 1854, the warehouse had been leased to L. Libby & Sons who used it to sell shipping supplies and groceries.[181] It thus became known as Libby Prison when the Confederate Army took it over.

The prison was located in an isolated part of Richmond. It was a complex of three buildings, each containing three stories. It was here that the Confederates decided to hold captured Union officers. It also became a processing center for all Union prisoners.[182]

The conditions at Libby Prison were a far cry from the lavish quarters John enjoyed during his short stay at the Spotswood House. "Lots more room," he now realized, was just cruel sarcasm. Union officers were confined to the upper two floors, several to a room with few blankets, no beds, and only a few chairs for sitting.

Entering one of the rooms, John was dismayed to discover the one tiny window was covered with bars, but open to the elements. In the July heat, the room was sweltering.[183] He could only imagine what it would be like during the winter months.

As more and more Northern soldiers were captured, Libby Prison quickly became overcrowded. The facility soon became infamous for its wretched conditions. Sometimes more than a hundred men were crammed into each of just six rooms.[184] As the war wore on, circumstances inside Libby became dire. Prisoners suffered from dysentery and other diseases.

Reynolds was surprised, and pleased, to learn that he and George McCall would be confined to the same room. He was not pleased to see how filthy the place was. Several other Union officers of various ranks were imprisoned with them. Everyone slept, bathed, and ate meager prison rations in the same fetid, confined quarters.

"If I ever get out of here," Reynolds said to McCall as the two talked quietly in one corner of the room, "I will make it my business to make sure the rebels learn what mistakes they are making by having us here. These conditions are an affront to the dignity of any soldier, no matter whose side they are on!"

Outside Libby Prison, forces were at work on Reynolds's behalf. Back behind Union lines, one of his aides had opened a package that arrived for his general after he had been captured. It contained a half dozen pairs of cotton socks and two soft woolen undershirts. Through guile, clever negotiation, and a little bribery, the aide managed to get the package delivered through enemy lines to Libby Prison.[185]

The door to the room occupied by John and about a dozen other officers flew open. A Confederate guard, a sergeant, walked in carrying a box. He stepped over to where John was gazing out the small window.

"I sure don't know how y'all managed this, General," the guard drawled. "But this here package is for you. Don't think we didn't check for weapons and such, because we sure did!"

The guard handed John the box, turned on his heel, and left the room. All the other prisoners stared at Reynolds, dumbfounded by what they had just seen happen. John sat on the floor and opened the box. He found the socks and undershirts inside. He also found a folded piece of paper. He opened it and read the note written there.

"Waiting for you to come home, my Darling. All my love, Kate."

John could feel the tears welling up in his eyes. It was a foreign feeling for him. He couldn't remember the last time he had cried. John cleared his throat and quickly averted his head from the wide-eyed gazes of the other prisoners.

More than ever now, he was determined to return to battle, help end this cursed war, and go home to the only woman he had ever loved.

* * *

As resolute as he was to get out of this Southern hellhole, John had promised he would not try to escape. It was his word of honor. As far as he was concerned, honor was to be valued equally as high as any other measure, especially for a soldier.

A few of the other younger officers did not hold the same value system. They believed it was their duty to attempt an escape. So, they tried, unsuccessfully, to break out. As punishment, their Confederate captors forced those men, and every other incarcerated officer, including John, to march through the streets of Richmond in something of a parade of shame.[186] For Reynolds, a proud warrior, this was indignity piled on top of indignity.

"This is not how war is fought!" he said angrily. "This is not the old Army. This is not honor!"

There were, however, some Confederates who understood John's definition of honor. Given his current state of mind, he would have been astounded. They were the Southern citizens of Fredericksburg, the same folks over whom John had been the military governor, the same folks he had described as "secesh of the first water." Upon learning of his capture and imprisonment, townsfolk created a petition to appeal for his release.

In their entreaty to the Confederate secretary of war, the people of Fredericksburg proclaimed that "we do feel that inasmuch as when we were prisoners in the hands of General Reynolds we received from him a treatment distinguished by a marked and considerate respect for our opinions and feelings, it becomes us to use our feeble influence in invoking for him, now a prisoner of our Government, a treatment as kind and considerate as was extended by him to us. We would therefore hope that he might be placed on parole."[187]

Whether the appeal had any direct impact, no one ever said. However, on August 13, the same high-ranking Confederate officer who had imprisoned John at Libby came to him in the crowded room.

"General Reynolds, I ask that you come with me," the officer said. He turned to address McCall. "You as well, General. Please come with me."

The Confederate officer called several other prisoners together, and they all trooped down to the main floor.

"Gentlemen, you are free to go," he said. "We are exchanging prisoners with your command. That wagon outside will take you to Union headquarters at Harrison's Landing. May we never meet again under these same circumstances. Go with God."

When Reynolds and McCall reached Harrison's Landing, several miles southeast of Richmond, they were greeted with cheers and shouts by the Pennsylvania Reserves who had been waiting for them. Even a band was on hand to welcome them with rousing music. John's military aide walked up, saluted, then shook his hand warmly.

"This whole brigade is decidedly attached to you," the aide told him. "And, if I may say, sir, it is obvious that your respect and regard for the brigade is equally evident."

John nodded and replied.

"It is with great relief and appreciation that I am back under the old flag again."

He paused and then spoke again with firm determination.

"I will never again be subjected to rebel tyranny."[188]

CHAPTER TWENTY-TWO

Harrison's Landing, Virginia
August 1862

The two generals, Reynolds and McCall, sat eating an evening meal in the officers' mess at Harrison's Landing. They had been back at camp for a day.

"It is a joy to be back on this side of the line, wouldn't you agree, George?" John asked.

"It is indeed," McCall replied. "The food is sure a damn sight better."

Reynolds chuckled in agreement.

"How has the division held up in your absence, General?" John asked.

"I must say," McCall replied, "Truman did a pretty fine job at holding things together."

McCall's Third Brigade commander, General Truman Seymour, was put temporarily in charge of the Pennsylvania Reserve Division when McCall was taken prisoner.

"I would wager," John said, "that you are eager to resume command."

McCall looked at Reynolds thoughtfully, slowly chewing his ration of meat. He reached for his cup of coffee and took a drink to wash the food down. Setting the cup back on his table, McCall shook his head.

"I'm afraid my battle days are over, John."

"What do you mean?"

"I am not well, John. Libby Prison took its toll on me and made my health matters worse. I am just past sixty years old now. It's time to hang up my sword," McCall said sadly.

"You are leaving?" John asked incredulously.

"Yes. I am going home, back to my farm. I will get medical treatment there, but I don't believe I will be back. Most likely I will resign sometime after the first of the year."[189]

Reynolds sat unmoving. He was stunned.

"Who will take command of the division? Who will replace you?" he said finally.

McCall, with his soft jowls, bushy black handlebar mustache, and deep-set eyes punctuated by dark half circles beneath them, looked at John sternly.

"Well, there is Seymour, I suppose. He already had them under his command while I was…well, otherwise occupied."

With that little joke, McCall's gaze softened a little. The corners of his mustache turned upward ever so slightly.

"But from what I hear, you, my young friend, are in the running."

"Is that so?" John said. "What, pray tell, have you heard?"

"Apparently there is a movement afoot in your brigade to have you promoted to division commander. I heard tell one junior officer said you were the leading spirit of the day in the battles we've been in. I also hear you are in the good graces of General Porter and that even General McClellan has said positive things about you. It is quite an accomplishment to have the Fifth Corps commander and the Army commander in your pocket."

"Well now," John protested. "That's a little over-the-top, George. I don't have anyone in my pocket."

Now, the tips of McCall's mustache rose even higher as his white teeth were exposed by a growing smile. His eyes, however, remained as piercing as ever.

"Perhaps not, but I must confess, John, I am more than a little envious of all these accolades you are getting from bottom to the top of the command."

Reynolds was not totally surprised by this news. He was an ambitious officer and made it a practice to keep his ear to the ground. He knew his reputation in the Army was growing. Although he was sympathetic about the health problems of his friend across the table, he also knew this was a perfect opportunity for him to advance.

As John was mulling this development over, a young corporal walked up to the table, stood at attention, and saluted the two general officers.

"At ease, soldier," McCall said.

"Yes, sir," the soldier replied. "I have a message for General Reynolds. You are wanted over at corps headquarters, sir. I will be happy to escort you there."

John looked at George who said nothing but gave Reynolds a broad smile.

* * *

The Fifth Corps commander, Major General Fitz John Porter, was pouring over battle maps when Brigadier General John Fulton Reynolds walked into the corps headquarters tent.

"General Reynolds reporting as ordered, sir," John said as he rendered a salute to his commander.

"Oh, relax, General," Porter said as he returned a desultory salute. "It was not so much an order as a request. Have a seat, John."

"Yes, sir," John said as he pulled up a chair to the map table and sat down across from Porter.

"I'll get right to it, John," Porter said. "It appears we have a vacancy to fill in our Third Division, the Pennsylvania Reserves. I have no doubt you have heard that General McCall is headed home for medical treatment."

"Yes, sir, he just spoke to me about it."

"Did he tell you who his replacement might be?"

194

Reynolds paused for just a moment. He wanted to be careful with his answer.

"Well, sir, he did mention it might be General Seymour who, after all, was the acting commander while he…um…we were held captive by the rebels. He speculated that Seymour could be made permanent in that position."

Porter smiled at Reynolds. The general appreciated John's careful, but diplomatic reply. He noticed that John did not endorse McCall's conjecture.

"Well, it is true that we did consider Seymour. But, John, you are my man. And, you are a Pennsylvanian. I know the volunteers respect and admire you. I want you to command the Third Division, taking effect immediately."

John could have acted surprised, but that would have been a phony gesture.

"I would be honored, sir. I appreciate your trust in me," was all he said.

Porter turned to an aide who was sitting behind him.

"Colonel, push the paperwork through. As of this moment, General John Reynolds is the commander of the Pennsylvania Reserve Division."

"Yes, sir. Right away, sir," the aide responded.

Porter reached into a side desk drawer and pulled out two glasses and a bottle of whiskey.

"This deserves a toast, don't you think, Commander Reynolds?"

"Yes, sir. Absolutely, sir."

Porter poured two fingers of the liquor into each glass and handed one to John.

"To the Pennsylvania Reserves, your command, and to the Union!" Porter declared.

"To the Union!" John repeated.

The clinked glasses and downed the sharp-tasting liquid in one swallow.

"Okay, down to business," Porter said. "Come around to this side of the table and take a look at the map, John."

John got up from his chair and joined Porter at his side. The corps commander pointed at lines and symbols on the table-sized chart in front of him.

"Look here, John. Our scouts tell us Confederate general Lee is making a run at the recently designated Army of Virginia in the Shenandoah Valley."

President Abraham Lincoln, impatient and dissatisfied with the performance of General George McClellan and his Army of the Potomac near Richmond during the Seven Days Battles, had ordered the formation of a new Army of Virginia. Its main mission was to "protect Northern Virginia and the national capital from danger or insult."[190] The new army was also tasked with attacking rebel forces where and whenever possible. Lastly, it would try to capture Richmond.

Unhappy with his current crop of generals along the eastern front, the president ordered General Henry Halleck to Washington from St. Louis and appointed him the general-in-chief of the armies. General John Pope, who had success against the Confederates in Mississippi, was brought in as the commander of the Army of Virginia.

Lincoln was displeased with McClellan because the general, who had command of the largest army America ever created, had retreated from Richmond and was stalling in taking any further action. McClellan, for his part, believed that taking the Confederate capital should still be the top Union priority, but at the right time with the right strength of soldiers. He would not be rushed.

All of these changes in units and command structure had been ordered and directed by political forces in Washington, from the president on down. It was the type of political interference in military matters that Reynolds abhorred. So did many of the troops in the ranks. One of them called McClellan "the most able general we have had." The soldier observed that the general "has many enemies...snarling politicians...at home. Whenever you find an enemy of General McClellan, you will find an inveterate civilian. No brave soldier will ever turn his tongue against 'Little Mac.'"[191]

For Reynolds, the new strategy opened the Union armies to dangerous weaknesses that could be easily exploited by the enemy. John was further annoyed that General Halleck was a desk-bound officer in Washington making decisions about the fate of his men in the field miles away.

John closely examined the little symbols on the map indicating the location and commands of the Union and Confederate armies. He didn't like what he saw.

"I have been ordered to send our corps north to support General Pope. Your division will board barges and muster at Acquia Creek. You must make preparations immediately," Porter told him. "From there you will road march and rendezvous with Pope at Rappahannock Station. At that time, place your division temporarily under his command. I will take the rest of the corps to provide additional support for the Army of Virginia. We are to avoid Richmond, at this time."

John looked at Porter and frowned. Who did the ordering, he wondered. Just who is in command here?

"Permission to speak freely, sir?" John asked.

"Of course, General."

"From a strategic point of view, I do not think this is a wise decision. I do not approve of the operation of leaving the line of the James River.[192] I don't have to tell you, sir, the importance of keeping this position here secure. Taking Richmond, the capital of the Confederacy is, in my view, the key to ending this war. It may have not worked the first time around, but I am confident the Army of the Potomac can do it, eventually. But that will be impossible if we abandon this position. Furthermore, as you well know, sir, the James River is a major waterway to Richmond, and we must not give the Confederates any opportunity to control it."

General Porter stared at the map, nodding his head slightly, his hands clasped behind his back. Then he turned to Reynolds.

"I agree with you, John. And so does General McClellan."

Porter looked closely at him.

"I tell you this in the strictest confidence, John. A few of the corps commanders have urged General McClellan to ignore these orders and march on Richmond in force. At least we could hold the

Confederates in check and prevent them from moving north and threatening the capital. McClellan even sent a letter to the high command in Washington to that effect.[193] But he was overruled by the new general-in-chief Halleck. And, I suspect, Halleck's orders came from the White House."

Reynolds remained silent for several moments. It was his turn to stare at the big battle map.

"Well, begging your pardon, sir," he said finally and turning to look his commander directly into his eyes, "I believe it is an insult to you having decisions about the movement of your units managed from Washington. No one can conduct a campaign at a distance from the field or without being in the actual presence of the operating armies. Our situation is very critical, sir. I think the whole movement from the peninsula is wrong. I am afraid there will be nothing but failures."[194]

If Porter was put off by John's bluntness, he didn't show it.

"I know, John," he said quietly. "I know."

Reynolds reached up to rub his thick beard.

"I suppose, though, political considerations will, as they have heretofore, overrule all military ones,"[195] he said grimly.

Porter continued to look at Reynolds through tired eyes. He sighed.

"Nevertheless, General, those are our orders."

"Yes, sir. I understand. I will do my best to complete them successfully."

* * *

After ten days of preparation, the Fifth Corps was ready to move. It took the better part of another week for Reynolds's Third Division to ride the barges down the James River to Chesapeake Bay, then to Acquia Creek, a small tributary off the Potomac River southwest of Washington, DC. The August heat in 1862 was unbearable. The Pennsylvania Reserves bore it the best they could. The barge trip was manageable, but the twenty-five-mile march from Acquia Creek to Rappahannock Station was truly grueling. All along the way, Reynolds rode back and forth among the columns of men, encouraging, coaxing, and supporting them.

"All right, men!" he called out to them astride his horse. "Only ten more miles to go! You have proven yourself time and again in battle! Be proud! You there! Standard bearer! Carry that Pennsylvania flag high! We are a brave, fierce fighting machine! Keep it up! That's it! That's it!"

Over and over he urged the troops to persevere, never letting on for a moment what folly he believed this mission to be. When they finally arrived near General Pope's headquarters at Rappahannock Station in Remington, Virginia, the troops were exhausted. But these volunteers were battle-tested and a much tougher force than when Reynolds first commanded them all those months ago.

"The Pennsylvania Reserves have arrived," one of General Pope's senior aides informed him in his headquarters tent.

"Make sure General Reynolds understands that his division will be attached to General McDowell's Third Corps of our Army of Virginia," Pope instructed.

"Yes, sir."

"How do they look?" Pope inquired.

"They've been in a fight, sure enough," the aide said. "Their faces are bronzed, their colors are pierced and torn by bullets, and their ranks have thinned. They've lost quite a few men. But, General, you should have seen it. There was great cheering when they marched in.[196] I heard loud huzzahs from the troops in our units as well as from those reserves. General Reynolds, it appears, has done an impressive job, keeping their morale up. I believe, with a few days' rest, they will be more than ready to go."

They didn't have a few days. The spent and drained troops didn't even have twenty-four hours. The day after the Pennsylvania corps arrived, General Pope moved his entire operation north to Warrenton because a massive contingent of Confederate soldiers were encroaching from the south.

Pope then received intelligence that Confederates had attacked the railroad depot at Manassas Junction. So, on August 28, he, Reynolds, and the rest of the Army of Virginia were off again.

Although it was only a little more than a fifteen-mile march, the road to Manassas Junction became clogged and congested with thousands of soldiers, wagons, and artillery limbers. The disorganized march slowed to a crawl under a blazing sun. Overheated horses and men faltered. Soon, some of the animals refused to move in the overwhelming heat. Many troops fell out of formation to take refuge in the shade of trees along the way, ignoring the shouts of sergeants and lieutenants to get back in line. Water supplies quickly fell to dangerous levels.

Suddenly, a loud boom echoed across the fields.

"What the hell was that?" one soldier shouted.

"Cannon fire!" another one cried. "We're under attack!"

A shell flew over their heads and exploded in a ball of smoke and dust in the field off to the right. The men dived for cover in the ditches alongside the road. More shells rained down all around them. One exploded in the middle of a company formation, instantly killing three soldiers and wounding five others.[197] General Reynolds, on his horse, suddenly appeared among the chaos, seemingly oblivious to the incoming cannon fire.

"Lieutenant," he shouted to a young artillery officer. "Get your battery into position and return fire!"

"Yes, sir," shouted the lieutenant, who sprang into action.

John turned to the troops taking cover in the ditches.

"You men! Get up and form a line of battle! Now! Quickly!"

He spurred his horse and galloped several dozen yards away to repeat the order, sending an aide to do the same in the other direction. All up and down the road, the Pennsylvania volunteers of John's division scrambled out of the ditches, loaded their rifles, and took up a long line, prepared to assault the enemy off in the distance.

As his men were getting organized, John could see the silhouettes of rebel infantry about a mile to the front left of his position. He turned to the company commander who was at his side.

"There they are, Captain! See them? Looks like we are in for a battle!"

Just then a colonel whom John did not know rode up to him at full gallop. He violently pulled on the reins and his horse came to a sudden, if bouncing, stop. He saluted, but in a way John could see it was merely a formality.

"What are you doing, General?" the colonel asked imperiously.

Reynolds cocked his head and looked at the officer through squinted eyes.

"Do you mean, 'May I ask what you are doing, sir?'" he replied.

The colonel was not at all chastened by John's tone, but he took the hint.

"Yes, sir, that's what I'm asking."

"Well, Colonel, you can no doubt notice that we are under attack and I am preparing to do battle."

"No, sir."

John looked at the man incredulously.

"I beg your pardon?"

"Sir, I am the adjutant for General McDowell, Third Corps commander in the Army of—"

"I know who he is," Reynolds interrupted curtly.

"Well then, sir. General McDowell has ordered that you keep moving. Do not engage the enemy here. You are to keep marching toward Manassas Junction."

"His orders?"

"Yes, sir. General McDowell, sir."

"All right, Colonel. You are dismissed."

The impertinent adjutant looked at Reynolds with something akin to contempt but held his tongue.

"Yes, sir" was all he said. The officer flipped Reynolds a quick salute, turned his horse, and galloped away at full speed.

Reynolds watched him ride away for a moment, shaking his head at the man's gall. But John had his orders, and orders were meant to be followed. He turned to the men in the battle line near him who had been watching the entire encounter. The cannon fire from the distance had ceased.

"Okay, men!" he shouted. "Back in formation. We are to leave the rebs alone for now. We're going to Manassas Junction. All you officers, get your men back in line and forward march!"

John watched for a few minutes to see that his orders were being carried out. Then he dug his heels into the sides of his horse.

"C'mon, boy, let's go," he said to the stallion.

He headed toward the front of the long column to join General McDowell. He had some questions for the corps commander. By the comments he could overhear as his horse sauntered forward, so did the men in the ranks.

"What the Sam Hill was that all about?" said one soldier.

"Man, we had Johnny Reb dead to rights!" said another. "We coulda taken them!"

"I just don't get it," said a third. "We had 'em trapped!"

Astonished, amazed, chagrined, disappointed[198] were just some of the less profane words John could hear as his troops shouldered their weapons, crossed the road, headed up a hill into an acre or two of woods, away from the enemy.

What they didn't know was that a much larger enemy force was waiting for them in the distance ahead. Nor did John fully appreciate the extent of the danger that lay ahead for him.

CHAPTER TWENTY-THREE

Philadelphia
August 1862

"Mmm. This is really good!" Catherine Dunn exclaimed as she dipped her spoon into a cup of ice cream.

"Yes, it is. It's delicious." Kate replied, putting a spoonful of the sweet-tasting dessert into her own mouth.

The two of them were attending an ice cream social in the garden behind Eden Hall, the boarding school Kate attended. Ice cream socials in America dated back to the mid-1700s, when Maryland's governor had them at dinner parties.[199] Since then, they had become popular events in Philadelphia society. The nuns at Eden Hall always held at least three of them during the summer months.

One of the nuns approached Kate and Catherine where they sat at a wrought-iron table in the shade beneath a large chestnut tree. It was a warm but beautiful August day. A gentle breeze blew across the deep-green lawn. The sun was bright. The flowers in the garden were in full bloom with red, purple, yellow, and pink blossoms everywhere. Their fragrance was tantalizing. Birds chirped noisily in the tree branches above their heads.

"How are you two ladies doing?" the nun asked.

"We are doing very well, Sister," Kate replied. "Thank you. And thank you, as well, for this wonderful ice cream social!"

"It is certainly our pleasure," the nun said. "We are so happy you are here!"

She turned to look at Catherine.

"How do you like your ice cream, young lady?" she asked kindly.

"Oh, it's really, really, good, Sister. Thank you," Catherine responded.

"I am so happy to hear that." The nun smiled. "If there is anything you need, please, just ask. God bless you both."

"Thank you, Sister. And God bless you as well," Kate said.

The nun turned, walking to another table to greet other visitors.

"She seems really nice," Catherine mumbled through a mouthful of ice cream.

"You really shouldn't talk with your mouth full," Kate said, gently.

Catherine swallowed the dessert.

"Sorry," she said.

"Oh, that's all right," Kate chuckled. "Sometimes I forget, too."

"You seem happy today," Catherine said as she scraped more ice cream out of the cup.

Kate and Catherine got together several times a week because Kate wanted to keep a close eye on the girl for whom she had assumed responsibility. They had grown very close. Their relationship had become less like mother-daughter, but more like sister-sister. Kate usually shared with Catherine her news, and her worries, about John and the war. Catherine was aware of how upset Kate had been over the past few weeks, and of her lingering sense that something bad had happened to the general. The change in Kate's demeanor today was obvious.

"I am happy, Catherine. And I feel much better today," Kate said.

"And that's because…," Catherine said, her voice trailing off.

"That's because," Kate said with a large smile, "I got another letter from General Reynolds yesterday. He is all right! He is safe!"

"Oh, that is so wonderful!" Catherine exclaimed as she put her spoon down, ignoring the last bit of ice cream beginning to melt in the cup. "Did something happen to him?"

"Well, he said he was captured."

"Captured?"

"Yes, can you believe that? He said he was held for about six weeks. That's why I didn't hear from him for so long. He was released in some sort of prisoner exchange. But he said he is fine and back with his old unit. I am so relieved!"

Catherine stayed silent for a few moments, stirring the melted ice cream in the cup with her spoon. She turned to look at Kate.

"But that means he is back in the war, doesn't it?" she asked.

Kate sighed.

"Yes, I am afraid it does. But I am hoping the war will be over soon. I mean, how much longer can it go on? I just have to keep praying for his safety, that's all."

Just then, the nun who had spoken to them moments before approached their table again. She had with her a nice-looking woman who looked to be in her thirties. Dressed handsomely, she was clearly a member of Philadelphia's upper class.

"Kate," the nun said. "Please forgive my interruption, but I wanted to introduce you to one of Eden Hall's strongest supporters."

The nun looked at the woman, then turned back to Kate, and smiled.

"And, she's not even Catholic!"

Kate stood and offered her hand to the woman.

"My goodness!" she said. "What a pleasure it is to meet you! My name is Catherine. Nearly everyone calls me Kate."

"The pleasure is all mine," the woman replied, shaking Catherine's hand. "My name is Eleanor."

"And this young woman," Kate said, "is Catherine Dunn, a very good friend of mine."

Catherine stood up from her chair and gave Eleanor a small curtsy.

"I am pleased to meet you, Miss Eleanor," she said.

"Likewise, I'm sure," said Eleanor. "You are a very polite young lady."

Catherine giggled and sat back down.

"Why don't we all sit," Kate said. "We have extra chairs here."

"I would love to stay and chat," the nun said to all of them, "but I have duties to perform. But, please, Eleanor, stay and enjoy the company. We are so pleased to have Kate here. She is doing so well with her conversion to Catholicism."

With a small wave of her hand, the nun turned and walked away. Eleanor pulled up an extra chair and sat down at the wrought-iron table.

"Conversion?" she said to Kate quizzically.

"Yes," Kate replied. "I was raised as a Protestant, a Baptist, actually. I come from a very strict Baptist family, and, well, let's just say that it was not a right fit for me. After I started teaching in a San Francisco Catholic school, which was where I met Catherine here, I became interested in the teachings of the Catholic Church. The Daughters of Charity were so kind to me. Their messages of love and faith touched me deeply. So, I decided to convert, and here I am."

"My goodness," Eleanor said. "That is quite a story. I am Protestant myself."

"Please forgive me. I mean no offense," Kate said. "But isn't it a bid odd for a non-Catholic to be so supportive of Eden Hall, a Catholic facility?"

"Yes, I suppose it is," Eleanor mused. "But I am opposed to all the anti-Catholic sentiment in this country. We are all one people, are we not? Are we not all Americans? Was not this country founded on a belief of religious freedom, to worship how we please? The work the nuns here are doing is excellent. The education and training of people, such as yourself, should be commended and supported. Oh, I do support my own church, too. Don't get me wrong. But I believe that as a community, especially here in Philadelphia where our nation was founded, we all have a responsibility to look after each other."

"I could not agree with you more, Eleanor," Kate said. "It warms my heart to hear you say those things. We are, indeed, all one people. That's why, for me, this awful war is so hard to understand. Americans fighting Americans? It's tragic, to be sure."

"Do you have family in the war. A father, perhaps? A brother?" Eleanor asked.

Kate hesitated a moment, then replied.

"No. Certainly not my father. I prefer not to get into that. Nor do I have any brothers in the war."

"I have two brothers who are both fighting for the North. One is in the Navy. The other is in the Army. I am very proud of them. William is an admiral in the Navy, and John is a general in the Army."

Kate froze. Catherine, listening quietly to the conversation, stared wide-eyed at Kate.

"A...a general, you say?" Kate stammered.

"Why, yes. Is there a problem?"

Kate forced herself to recover.

"Oh no," she said. "There's no problem. I am just impressed. A general. And an admiral in one family. That's, umm, remarkable."

"Yes, as I say, my other brothers and sisters and I, we are all very proud of them."

"What did you say your last name is?"

"Oh, I'm sorry. I guess I didn't. Reynolds. My name is Eleanor Reynolds. My brother William is the admiral, and my brother John is the general. Brigadier General John Fulton Reynolds."

Kate turned pale.

"Are you all right, my dear?" Eleanor asked with concern. "You look a little ill."

"Yes, yes, I'm fine. Really. I'm...I'm...fine. Perhaps I've had a little too much sun, that's all."

"But we are sitting in the sha—" Catherine started to interject.

"Never mind, Catherine," Kate interrupted. "I am feeling a little faint. I think we should go, Catherine."

Kate stood up. Catherine followed suit.

"I am so sorry, Eleanor," Kate said. "Please accept my apologies, but I fear I must go lay down for a while. I'll be all right, I'm sure. I hope so see you again. It has been a pleasure."

She took Catherine's hand, and they both quickly walked away. Eleanor stared with puzzlement at the retreating figures.

"Oh, my Lord!" Catherine said loudly as they hurried inside Eden Hall. "She is John's sister, isn't she?"

"Hush, Catherine! Come on!" Kate said, brusquely.

"Why didn't you say something?" Catherine whispered after they entered Kate's room. "Why didn't you tell her?"

"Tell her what?"

"That you are going to marry her bother, of course!"

Kate slumped down in a chair and let out a long sigh.

"I couldn't. I can't. It is a secret, remember? Oh, I wish I could tell her. I really wish I could. But I just can't."

John will be home soon, I am certain, she thought. *Then we can finally end this awful secrecy.*

CHAPTER TWENTY-FOUR

Manassas, Virginia
August 1862

When General Reynold caught up with General McDowell, the corps commander, he saw the pompous adjutant riding several yards behind him. He gave John a sour look as Reynolds pulled up to the column.

"General Reynolds," McDowell said by way of a greeting.

"General McDowell, sir," Reynolds replied.

John pulled his horse up beside McDowell's steed, and they moved along side by side at a steady pace.

"How are things back in the column, General?" McDowell asked.

There were so many Army of Virginia soldiers on the march that Reynolds's division was several miles to the rear.

"The Eighth Brigade lost a few men, dead and wounded, when the rebels back there opened fire on us with their artillery," John replied flatly.

They rode in silence for a few minutes. The only sound was the clip-cloping of the horses, the feet shuffling in the columns of men, the occasional squeak of wagon wheels, and the incessant "singing" of thousands of katydids in the trees on this hot August day.

Finally, McDowell turned slightly in his saddle to look at Reynolds.

"My adjutant tells me you are not happy with my orders to move on," McDowell said.

John said nothing for a moment, thinking how to best answer his commander without triggering a reprimand. He could feel the adjutant behind him, straining to hear what John had to say.

"Well, sir," John said finally. "Your orders have been carried out. But, speaking frankly, sir, I believe we have missed a good opportunity to cause the Confederates some trouble."

"How so?" McDowell asked.

"By taking out that unit of rebels, which, in my view, we could have done so without much of a problem, we would have established a strong defensive line ahead of Manassas Junction. In turn, that would have strengthened the Army's defense of Washington, which is the main goal, is it not, sir?"

McDowell said nothing for a long while. After several minutes, he spoke over the rhythmic clopping of the horses' hooves.

"General, you've just been attached to the Army of Virginia. I take it you don't know General Pope all that well."

"No, sir, not very well. That is correct."

"Well, Pope had great success against the Confederates over by the Mississippi River. That's why the president wanted him here. Pope is an excellent tactician. He knows how to read the enemy. So, when he wants this corps to advance to Manassas Junction, that's where we go. That's where he says the important enemy is, not along some ridge by the roadside."

Reynolds could feel his blood beginning to boil by that last remark. But he held his tongue.

"That's why you were ordered to disengage back there. Pope knows what he is doing. If he says the enemy is at Manassas Junction, that's where he is. I should hope you would understand that."

Behind them, the adjutant smiled oily at hearing the rebuke. Internally, John was seething, but his attention was diverted by the sight of two horsemen riding toward them at a high rate of speed. McDowell's aides, who were in the vanguard of the column, drew their weapons and pointed them at the approaching soldiers.

"Lower your weapons!" one of them shouted, almost out of breath as they drew close to the column. "We are messengers from General Pope!"

"Lower your weapons, boys," McDowell said to his aides. "What is your message?" he called out as the riders slowed their horses and stopped in front of the column.

"Let them pass, gentlemen," McDowell ordered his aides who maneuvered their horses aside so the messengers could approach the general.

"Sir," one of the riders said when he got close. "General Pope says he has intelligence which now says a main force of the enemy is at Centreville, not Manassas Junction. He wishes you to send two of your divisions in that direction."

McDowell turned to Reynolds.

"General, I want you to take your division and carry out those orders. You can divert your march and head toward Centreville along Sudly Springs Road."

"Yes, sir, General," John said without argument. He saluted and quickly reined his horse to turn and head back to his division. As he did, John heard McDowell issue further orders to the messengers.

"Ride back down the column and find General Franz Sigel. Tell him I wish that he takes his corps and join General Reynolds to advance on Centreville."

It was late afternoon, and as John rode at breakneck speed down one side of the column of men, he could see the messengers matching his stride down the other side. Thoughts raced through his mind as he spurred his horse to go faster. *Pope knows what he is doing, eh? Pope knows the enemy? I wonder.*

* * *

General Sigel's division formed up more quickly than John's Third Division, so Sigel led the way. They had gotten so far down the road on the way to Manassas that when McDowell changed their mission to Centreville, the two divisions had to backtrack several miles before turning north to their new destination.

They were still on the road when, as the sun was going down, Reynolds heard the thunder of heavy cannon fire in the distance. But it was not coming from Centreville. It was back in the direction toward Groveton, a little village off to his left. It was near the spot where Reynolds had encountered Southern artillery fire earlier in the day. John shook his head. *I knew it*, he thought. Those rebels were not a mere reconnaissance unit, nor were they just skirmishers. This was a major Confederate force from which he had been ordered by McDowell to disengage.

Reynolds turned to his aide-de-camp.

"Get these men on a quick march," he ordered. "We may have to alter our course. I am going to ride on ahead to Groveton to find out what the situation is."

"But, our orders…," the aide started to say.

"I know what our orders are, Colonel. My orders are to get these men up the road and prepared for a fight."

With that, Reynolds dug his heels into the sides of his horse, which sprang foreword and within two strides was at a full gallop across open country off to the left. It was well after dark by the time he had reached Groveton and the cannon fire had ceased. He caught up with battle-weary Union officers who told him the Confederates were part of General Stonewall Jackson's force.

John quickly figured out what had happened. General McDowell and, by extension, his commander, General Pope, had been duped by the Confederates. The enemy at Centreville was merely a single division of retreating Confederates on the way to join the massive Jackson force forming up just beyond Groveton.

"Can you at least hold this position until daylight?" Reynolds asked the other Union officers.

"We will try" was the answer.

"All right, I am going to get reinforcements," John said and rode off in the direction from which he had just come to rejoin his own unit.

Racing through the thick blackness of the night, he thought about what he was doing. *I have no orders to do this*, he told himself. *In fact, my orders run counter to this.* No matter, he decided. *I know where the enemy is. Once again Pope and McDowell have misjudged the Confederates. I know what has to be done.*

When John got back to his command, the August 29 dawn was about to break. He was worn out after his sleepless night but moved quickly to get his division ready to move, only to find General Sigel's division already on the march. His superiors had finally figured out what John already knew. Pope and McDowell had begun a counter-march to take Jackson on. Thus, Sigel had new orders and was acting on them.

But where were the orders for his Third Division, Reynolds wondered. It was the beginning of what would turn out to be a series of confusing, frustrating, maddening missteps of botched orders, misinterpreted commands, lack of coordination, and disregarded warnings.

It was finally decided that Reynolds's Third Division would join forces with General Sigel to confront the enemy. He was ordered to form his men to Sigel's left. It was an exhausted and hungry division of troops who Reynolds maneuvered into position. They had a grueling fight ahead them, he knew, and they would be fighting on empty stomachs.

"How are you holding out, soldier?" he asked one man who was digging an entrenchment.

"I could use something to eat, sir," the soldier said. "Otherwise, I'm good."

"When is the last time you were issued rations, son?"

"Well, lemme think, sir. I believe we were given two days' rations 'bout a week ago. Haven't gotten anything since. There's nothin' in the eating line. I'm tryin' to make it stretch."

John frowned. His concern for the health and welfare of his men was as strong as his sense of honor and determination to defeat the enemy.

"We'll see what we can do about that, soldier. Meantime, stay alert. The rebs are close."

"Yes, sir. Will do, sir," the soldier said as he resumed his digging.

It was touch-and-go for the Third Division throughout the day. Fresh Confederate troops arrived from distant locations and pushed against the line established by the Pennsylvania volunteers and a few other brigades. Reynolds had been promised reinforcements by Army of Virginia headquarters. By the time the sun went down, there was no sign of them. When night rolled around, Reynolds and his men had been pushed back about a mile with an enemy growing in numbers to the south and west of them.

* * *

As Saturday, August 30 dawned, it was oppressively hot and humid. Dull, heavy clouds hung over the battlefield. Both sides were poised for one more do-or-die, imperative engagement. Sixty-five thousand Union soldiers faced fifty thousand Confederate troops on a pair of four-mile-long fronts.[200]

As John rode out to inspect his units, the sight before him took his breath away.

"My God," he muttered to himself.

Descending into a shallow valley, he could see the slight hill opposite him was covered with the dead. They were all dressed in blue. All of them were Union bodies. One of his aides, astride his horse, came up beside him. They both surveyed the atrocious scene silently.

"The Confederates must have taken theirs away during the night," the aide said quietly after a moment.

So many bodies were strewn across the field, it was difficult for artillery batteries moving into position to avoid running over them. Soldiers moving on foot had to step carefully for the same reason.[201]

After a few moments, John turned away in disgust and sadness to make ready for the next fight. But, with the exception of a brief artillery duel, the battlefield remained tensely quiet for much of the day, which grew increasingly hotter as the clouds cleared away. Flies began to collect on the dead bodies. The distinct smell of death increased. Because of the intense heat, except for the insects, very little moved. It was still too risky to attempt any recovery of the bodies. Soldiers on both sides rested in the shades of trees the best they could, but remained alert, nevertheless.

"This silence is gettin' to me," one soldier from Pittsburgh said, as he obsessively polished his rifle.

"Yeah," said another. "It's…it's…what's the word? Ominous. Yeah, that's it. Ominous."

Suddenly, in midafternoon, the silence was broken by the sound of a cannon being fired. Seconds later, a shell crashed through the tree branches above the two soldiers, who dived for cover.

The stillness returned, more pronounced than before. The only sound was the faint buzzing of the flies. It seemed as though time had stopped. Then all hell broke loose. Thunderous cannon fire erupted from both sides of the line. Thousands of troops in blue and in gray grabbed their weapons. The battle had been launched. One of Reynolds's soldiers described it as "furious."

"A hundred guns on each side are at work," he said. "Whole batteries are discharging at once. Shell, round shot, grape-and-canister, case shot, railroad iron, and stones are being hurled at us. The rebels are bold. They are making their appearance from the woods in our front in heavy columns and firm, unbroken lines. As far as I can see toward the right are heavy bodies of our troops awaiting the approach of the rebels."[202]

"Fall in! Fall in!"

It was General Reynolds, pistol in hand atop his powerful horse, riding up and down his line of men.

"Forward! March!" he shouted.[203]

John rode over to join two of his brigade commanders who were observing the action from a nearby rise. One of the commanders was George Meade, the general whose career path was paralleling John's and with whom Reynolds had a long-standing friendly rivalry.

"How does it look to you, George?" John asked.

"Looks like a hell of a battle to me. But I think our volunteers are giving the rebs a fight. I just hope they can hold the line."

Just then a loud shout erupted from a group of Confederate soldiers closing in on a nearby battery. John drew his sword.

"Up, boys!" he shouted. "They are going to try to take this battery! Fix bayonets!"

Several dozen Union troops quickly attached bayonets to the barrels of their rifles. Several of them rubbed their eyes, which were burning from all the thick gun smoke drifting out over the battlefield.

"Boys, I know I can depend on the Pennsylvania Reserves!" Reynolds shouted very loudly.

"Yes, you can! Yes, you can!" The soldiers returned the shout.

"Forward, then! Charge!"

With John in the lead, his Union troops dashed forward with wild yells. Bullets flew like swarms of angry hornets.[204] The sounds of minié balls striking flesh and bone were lost in the cacophony of the chaos. So were the screams of the men they hit. The smoke became so thick, it was difficult for either side to see their enemy, even at close range hand-to-hand combat. Still, bayonets and swords glinted as the smoke swirled around them in the afternoon sun. Blood flowed, and men fell as the swords slashed and the bayonets sliced.

At one point, Reynolds himself became the target of enemy fire as he rode out to check on reports of a heavy concentration of rebels who were giving one of his brigades a very hard time at the other end of his long line.

"My God look at them all," he said to an orderly he had taken with him. From the top of a small hill, he was dismayed by the scene spread out before him. "It looks like a multicolored carpet off in the distance."

John was describing the long columns of Confederate cavalry in the gray uniforms, carrying red and blue Confederate battle flags, mounted on black, brown, and white horses moving as one toward them. Southern sharpshooters were clearing the way along a forward skirmish line. Reynolds knew that could mean only one thing; divisions of Southern infantry were masked behind the procession making ready for a major attack.[205] The orderly was clearly frightened.

"Holy Jesus, General," he blurted out. "I don't reckon I have ever seen—"

The orderly's head suddenly exploded. His body flew backward out of his saddle, rolled off the horse, and dropped heavily to the ground, blood pouring out of the open wound. His horse, spooked by the sudden violence, reared its front legs, let out a loud, distressed whinny, and galloped away, riderless. The orderly had taken a direct hit from a Confederate sharpshooter and was dead before he hit the ground.

Reynolds stared at the lifeless orderly's body, momentarily shocked by the obscenity. He quickly regained his wits as rifle rounds slammed into the trees around him, into the ground beneath him, and whizzed past his ears. He yanked hard on the reins and got his horse in motion, riding away as quickly as he could.

Jumping off his horse almost before it even stopped at McDowell's headquarters, Reynolds ran into the tent to report what he had seen. He was surprised to find the Army of Virginia's commander, General John Pope, standing there.

"You look like you have seen a ghost, General," Pope said to him.

"Not a ghost, sir. Confederates. Lots of them."

"Report what you have," Pope ordered.

"On my left flank, sir. Two, perhaps three divisions of Confederates, infantry, cavalry, and skirmishers. They are overpowering our forces on the left. I am not confident we can hold them back."

"Two or three divisions, you say?"

"Yes, sir. At least. Perhaps more."

Pope stood there a moment, looking down at the floor, hands clasped behind his back. Then he looked up at John.

"Oh, I guess not," he said.[206]

John blinked and took an involuntary step backward.

"I...ah...I'm sorry, sir? I don't understand."

"I said, I guess not," Pope said with just enough disdain. "What you tell me does not fit with the intelligence we have. Stonewall Jackson's force is not concentrated where you say it is. In fact, I'm told Jackson is in retreat. This just doesn't fit."

John was stunned. He could not believe what he was hearing.

"Begging your pardon, sir. I saw them with my own eyes. I have even lost an orderly to one of their sharpshooters. Sir, the man gave his life for this information!"

"Well, I am sorry to hear that, General. That is most unfortunate, of course. But I believe you may be overestimating the strength of what you saw. My intelligence officers are very good and usually very precise. They tell me nothing about a massive force in that area off to the left. As I said, they tell me the rebs are in retreat."

John could do nothing but stare. He was stupefied. But Pope seemed not to notice. He continued talking.

"I need you to return to your command and keep holding our left flank. General Porter, and his division have been ordered to attack from there. You will support him."

Pope then turned his attention to another matter, a clear, if unwelcome, indication that Reynolds was dismissed. John stood there, unmoving, for a few moments, not believing what had just happened. Although Pope's back was now turned toward him, John eventually rendered a salute, quietly said, "Yes, sir," did an about-face, and marched out of the tent.

When John returned to his command, he saw General Porter's men finally moving into position and trying to put up a stiff fight. But contrary to what Pope had claimed, the Confederates were not, by any means, in retreat. They were advancing so aggressively that Porter's division began to collapse. John was horrified to see Union soldiers running away from the battle, heading toward the rear.[207]

John rode quickly up and down the line of his own men, waving his pistol in the air.

"It looks like it is all up to us, boys!" he shouted. "Hold the line! Hold the line! Don't let rebs get through!"

This was the kind of fight for which Reynolds had been trained. He ordered his artillery to rain down cannon shells on the approaching enemy. Pieces of earth and pieces of bodies flew in every direction as the artillery found its mark. Reynolds moved men and units around to take better advantage of the terrain, hopefully to give his reserves the upper hand. He was making decisions and choices on the fly as bullets flew past him, the high-pitched sound of their friction against the air ringing in his ears. The noise of the battle was deafening. In the midst of the chaos, a messenger caught up with him.

"Sir! Sir!" the messenger shouted as he galloped up to the general. "I have orders for you from General McDowell!"

Now what, John thought, as he took the packet of papers from the messenger. He immediately became incensed by what he read. He had been ordered to withdraw immediately and move his division to the rear of the fleeing men of Porter's division so "the troops might be rallied."[208]

His adjutant was standing guard on his horse a few yards away. Reynolds turned to him with disgust.

"Now, they want us to a be a goddamn cheering section for those troops who are running away!"

The adjutant knew his boss was very angry because Reynolds rarely cursed like that.

"We are attacking! That is what we should do, not be wet nurses for boys who are too afraid to fight! This is an impossible mission! Look there, Colonel. Just where is the rear of Porter's division? There is no rear!"

Off in the distance, John saw mobs of Union soldiers running away as a disorganized rabble. The rough terrain, as well, made it difficult for any kind of coordinated retreat. It was a mess.

"This is a waste of manpower and resources," John complained to his adjutant, who nodded silently in assent.

Nevertheless, John knew, orders were orders. He sighed loudly.

"All right, Colonel," he said to the adjutant. "Have the bugler sound withdrawal. Let's get the men moving."

"Yes, sir," the adjutant said.

However, before he could follow through on John's order, one of General Pope's staff officers arrived, somehow managing to maneuver through the confusion.

"Orders, sir, from General Pope," the officer said, handing John a piece of paper.

After reading it, Reynolds turned to his aide.

"Keep the men in withdrawal, Colonel. But we have a new mission. We are to join a final defensive line on Henry House Hill."[209]

* * *

Reynolds had a better view of the entire battlefield from the top of Henry House Hill, less than a mile east of his Groveton position. It was a depressing sight. All up and down the Union line to the west, blue uniformed soldiers were retreating in the face of an overwhelming enemy. He knew, for this battle at any rate, this would be the Union Army's final stand.

Soldiers in Confederate gray were swarming toward the hill like colonies of ants. John did not like where he had been ordered to hold the line. He saw it beginning to fold. He knew that this was a defining moment. If the Union lost this battle, the Confederates would control a main artery eventually leading into Washington, DC. The very center of the nation's government would be in serious danger.

Looking around, John saw a glimmer of hope. Other Northern units were coalescing. He was grateful to see General George Sykes and his division known as Sykes's Regulars had arrived to join the fight. Reynolds dug his spurs into the sides of his horse, galloped ahead, shouting.

"Forward, Reserves! Forward!"[210]

Inspired by their commander's passion, the Pennsylvanians pressed ahead running into ferocious resistance. Reynolds saw the staff holding the flag of one his regiments lying in the grass, cut in half by enemy bullets. With no wasted motion, he jumped to the ground, picked up the flag, remounted his horse, and waved the colors over his head.

"On, my brave fellows! On!" he shouted over the din the battle.[211]

Again energized by the valor of their commander, the soldiers charged the rebel riflemen, eventually forcing them to pull back, but at a high cost to the boys in blue. "It was here," Reynolds wrote later," that the most severe loss of the division was sustained, both in men and material."[212]

When darkness fell, silence returned to the battlefield, except for the moaning of the wounded and dying. Both sides, completely spent from the hours of the arduous struggle, enacted sort of an ad hoc cease-fire. Battered and ripped to pieces, John's men were relieved by a division of fresh regular troops. Already angered by the earlier actions of General Pope, Reynolds put the blame for the severe loss squarely on the commander of the Army of Virginia.

"We found ourselves perfectly out of place," he said, "moved there by the direction of an officer of General Pope's staff."[213]

Although outnumbering the Confederates by more than fifteen thousand soldiers, General Pope had to admit he had been bested by General Robert E. Lee. Union soldiers began to retreat toward Centreville early in the evening. Reynolds's Pennsylvania volunteers were among the last to leave the field. It was not a retreat in the usual sense of the word. No one chased them. The Confederate side, though victorious in this battle, was too exhausted to continue its advance. The next morning, Reynolds even had the time to halt his men so, as he had promised, they could eat breakfast, their first meal in several days. It consisted of only hard bread and coffee, but to the famished and battle-weary men, it was a feast. One soldier called the rations "a perfect God-send."[214]

Reynolds was considered by his men and other officers an effective and thoughtful leader. But it was the end of the line, career wise, for Generals Pope and Porter. Pope was relieved of command and sent to the Indian frontier in Minnesota. The Army of Virginia was disbanded. A court-martial convicted Porter of a failure of command, specifically disobeying an order and misconduct in front of the enemy, all related to the rout of his men, leaving Reynolds and his volunteers to face the Confederates alone.

John, however, received praise, even from Pope himself, for his actions at Henry House Hill. He and General Sykes were given more credit years later when a review board overturned the court-martial conviction of General Porter. The board said that during the Battle on Henry House Hill, "Sykes with his disciplined brigades, and Reynolds, with his gallant Pennsylvania Reserves, seized the commanding ground in the rear and, like a rock, withstood the advance of the victorious enemy and saved the Union army from rout."[215]

New duties lie ahead for Brigadier General John Reynolds. So did another promotion.

CHAPTER TWENTY-FIVE

Ridgeville, Maryland
September 1862

"…having formed my division in the position indicated and opened with my rifled batteries to drive the enemy from the first ridge, the skirmishers advanced…"[216]

General Reynolds was in his tent, busily writing his after-action report from the battles at Groveton and Henry House Hill two weeks ago. His division had been given several days' rest, new uniforms, and fresh rations. They were on the march again, this time headed for Pennsylvania, home for most of the volunteers, to counter Robert E. Lee whose Confederates were now moving west and north toward that state.

John's Third Division was back once more as part of the Army of the Potomac. President Lincoln had ordered General McClellan to take command of all the Union soldiers in the east after Pope and Porter had been sent packing and the Army of Virginia dissolved.

McClellan had reorganized the Army. John's division of Pennsylvania volunteers was now part of the First Corps commanded by Major General John Hooker.

The division had stopped for the night at Ridgeville, Maryland. John was so focused on writing his report, he did not hear his adjutant enter the tent. The officer cleared his throat.

"Ahem. Excuse me, sir," the adjutant said.

Startled, John looked up with surprise, his hand holding a fountain pen hovering above the paper.

"Don't sneak up on me like that, Colonel. I might have shot you."

Seeing that his commander was joking, the adjutant grinned.

"Oh, I rather doubt that, sir. I'm too valuable to you."

John laughed, in spite of himself.

So, what excuse do you have for bothering me, Colonel?"

The colonel became serious.

"It is a message, sir. For you. You are wanted at headquarters."

"Hooker wants to see me?"

"No, sir."

"Who, then?"

"General McClellan, sir. The Army commander requests to speak to you."

"McClellan, you say? What do you think he wants?"

"I couldn't say, sir."

"Well, okay. I never will get this damn fool report finished," John muttered. He got up from his chair and reached for his jacket.

"Have my horse pulled up, Adjutant."

"Already have, sir. It's waiting outside."

Reynolds threw a sidelong glance at his aide.

"Is that what you are referring to when you say valuable, Colonel?"

"Precisely, sir."

They both laughed.

* * *

General George McClellan was relaxing in a chair, smoking a cigar, when John entered the Army headquarters tent.

"Good evening, General," John said, saluting his commander. "I understand you wanted to see me."

"Yes. Yes. Have a seat, John," McClellan said, getting up from his chair. "Would you like a drink. Whiskey, perhaps?"

"Yes, sir. That would be fine, thanks."

McClellan walked over to a little portable bar and poured a small amount of liquor into a glass. He handed it to John and resumed his seat.

"Thank you, sir," John said.

McClellan gave him a dour look.

"You may want more after you hear what I have to say."

"Sir?" was all John said.

"You are being relieved of command, General," McClellan said bluntly.

John nearly dropped his glass. He quickly regained his composure.

"Relieved, sir? What do you mean?"

"Let me say, I don't like it, John. It is not my idea. In fact, I have argued against it all the way up the line. Even spoke to Secretary of War Stanton about it. To no avail. General Hooker has argued against it as well."

McClellan rose from his chair again and walked over to a desk. He rummaged around some papers on the desktop until he found what he wanted.

"This is the message Hooker sent to Washington. I will read just part of it to you. Let's see," McClellan said, peering at the paper.

"Yes, here it is."

He began reading aloud.

"General Reynolds commands a division of Pennsylvania troops not of the best character, is well known to them, and I have no officer to fill his place."[217]

McClellan stared the paper for a moment, realizing what he had just read out loud. He looked at John.

"Umm, yes, well. I'm sure General Hooker meant that in the best possible way. Your volunteers do have a bit of a rowdy reputation. What Hooker means here is that you have done a stellar job training and commanding them."

John merely nodded. He cared not a whit about what Hooker had to say. He was losing his command, and that he did care about a lot.

"Could you explain, sir, why it is that I am being relieved?"

"It appears that you have friends…or should I say, enemies… in high places."

"Sir?"

"Do you know Andrew Curtin?"

"Of course, sir. He is the governor of Pennsylvania."

"Yes, well, Mr. Curtin has been all over the president to send him thousands more troops. Apparently, Curtin is concerned, very concerned, that his state is in serious danger from the Confederates. He thinks the whole rebel army is getting ready to invade, and he wanted your Pennsylvania volunteers back. The war department refused that request, saying the volunteers are too important to the Army of the Potomac, which, by the way, John, is testimony to your leadership."

McClellan smiled at Reynolds who sat very still and unsmiling, holding the glass of whiskey. He had not yet taken a drink. McClellan continued.

"So, as an alternative, it has been decided that a new unit will be formed for the governor, consisting of men only from Pennsylvania. You, my good general, have been anointed for the task."

McClellan dug around on his desktop and came up with another piece of paper.

"This is the message sent on behalf of Curtin to the secretary of war."

He started to read again.

"We want an active, energetic officer to command forces in the field, and one that could rally Pennsylvania around him. It is believed that General Reynolds would be the most useful."[218]

McClellan put the papers back down on the desk and turned to Reynolds.

"Your Governor Curtin must have some powerful pull in Washington," he said.

Finally, John downed a swallow of the whiskey. He needed it now. He sighed heavily.

"Yes. The governor has been very helpful, politically speaking, for President Lincoln," John said, thinking once again with disgust how often politics interferes with military affairs.

"I am aware of that," McClellan said, heavily. "Well, General, you are to depart immediately for Harrisburg to begin your new duties. I wish you Godspeed."

"May I ask who will take command of my division?"

"That will be General Meade," McClellan replied.

"Yes, sir. I shall depart for Harrisburg forthwith."

John finished his drink, set the class on a table, rose from his chair to salute McClellan, who returned the gesture. He left the headquarters tent with a heavy heart. This was not good news. His odds of being promoted any higher had just dropped dramatically, he believed. The quickest way to gain rank was through battle, and once again, he would be missing the real action. The only positive news was that his division would be commanded by his friend, George Meade.

* * *

Pennsylvania governor Curtin was so anxious to have John Reynolds begin his new duties that a special train was laid on to carry him and two aides to Harrisburg. On the way, John took time to write a letter to Kate, planning to mail it after he arrived at the state capital.

"My dearest Kate," he wrote. "I so hoped to find the opportunity to come visit you after our last confrontation with the rebels. But, alas, that is not to be. I have been ordered to Harrisburg to oversee the creation of a new military unit to protect the Commonwealth from the enemy. Thus, I have been relieved of my command of the Pennsylvania Reserve Division."

John stopped writing and stared out the window of the train as it chugged along, crossing the border between Maryland and Pennsylvania. He frowned, thinking of the unpleasant duty which lies ahead. He resumed writing.

"This is very much against my will, I must confess. Our Pennsylvania reserve volunteers have become fine soldiers. Their actions in our recent battles are to be highly commended. We have lost too many. The division will remain as part of the Army of the

Potomac, and my command has been taken over by General George Meade. I believe I have mentioned him to you. Meade is a fine fellow and a competent officer. However, I much prefer that it is I who would continue to lead our brave Pennsylvanians. My place, as I have said before, should be on the battlefield, not behind some desk. But orders are orders, and mine are to report to Governor Curtin without delay. How I miss you, my darling…"

John went on to profess, once again, his great love for Kate and how impatient he was to see her again. He said with optimism, unfounded as it was, that the war would be over soon and that, before long, they could begin their lives together as man and wife. He had no way of knowing, of course, that he had less than ten months to live.

CHAPTER TWENTY-SIX

Harrisburg, Pennsylvania
September 1862

Peering out the window of the train as it pulled into the Harrisburg station, John was taken aback by the scene. The station was jammed with men who had already arrived from all parts of the state, answering Governor Curtin's frantic calls to arms. A reporter on the scene called it "a glorious exhibition of patriotism." Citizens from all levels of society had gathered for the cause. "Men worth millions of dollars were in the ranks a private," the reporter said. "Members of Congress, professors of colleges with their classes, iron-masters with their workmen, ministers and the able-bodied men of their congregations were hastening to the rendezvous."[219]

They cheered with each new arrival, waved Pennsylvania state flags with gusto, and some even broke out in song. There was no lack of enthusiasm, but there was utterly no organization either. John grimaced at the sight. This was a rabble, he thought. Well intentioned, but a rabble, nevertheless. He turned to one of his aides.

"Get a message off to General-in-Chief Halleck as soon as you can," John said. "Tell him I think if the reserve corps could be spared from the army in front of Washington and dispatched here, it would be of great assistance in forming and organizing the new troops assembling at this point."

"Yes, sir," the aide said. "I believe that would be a wise move."

"Yes, well, I have no hope that this request will meet with favor, yet I cannot but think that it would prove a judicious move in the end."

John thought for a moment.

"Add to the message that if the reserves cannot be sent, there is one of its batteries recruiting in Washington which might be very well spared, and there is nothing here of that arm as yet,"[220] he said. "They, at least, might be helpful."

As John suspected, his request was flatly refused. His mission of creating a functioning military unit out of the ever-increasing number of passionate and zealous mobs of men quickly turned into a bureaucratic nightmare. Weapons and ammunition for thousands of men had to be acquired. Rations had to be found. Transportation, horses, and wagons had to be arranged. Leaders who could be officers had to be identified. What little training that could be scheduled was hardly sufficient to transform the massive throng into an effective fighting force.

Making matters worse, Reynolds was distracted by nearly constant demands from Washington for updates and for information about the enemy's movements over the border in Maryland. He had already informed headquarters that he was "fully impressed that the intention has been for some time entertained by them to invade this section of the State."[221]

Anticipating that Confederate general Robert E. Lee planned to attack and occupy Harrisburg, Reynolds began moving what troops he could of his new unit south to the state border. But that's as far as they would go. They intended to fight for Pennsylvania, but only for Pennsylvania. John wanted to go south as well so he could direct his untrained, untried forces firsthand. However, organizational demands upon his time kept him in Harrisburg. He was especially annoyed by the special favors he was being asked to grant.

"Look at this!" he fumed to aides. "Governor Curtin wants me to give one of his political supporters a special assignment! Of all the insolence! And here, look here! I'm being asked by the governor's office to give some private a staff job! Outrageous!"

Finally, he was able to get away from Harrisburg and head south to the state line. What he found there was highly discouraging. Confederate forces were amassing near Hagerstown, just a few miles inside Maryland. They were being fiercely challenged by the Army of the Potomac, but more help from Union troops was needed. John went to work building a support base at Hagerstown, setting up ammunition supply, extra rations, even getting help for the telegraph office. He also sent word back to his aide in Harrisburg, "Get the troops here."

A short time later, John was stunned to learn that most of the new Pennsylvania recruits refused to move beyond the state border. It was a situation about which a furious Reynolds informed Washington.

"I had at this place about 4,000 men, and directed the remainder to be forwarded today, expecting to bring on the field today about 14,000 men, but, much to my surprise, all the regiments refused to march. What will be done, or can be done, with the force here I cannot say, though I do not think much can be expected of them—not very much."[222] The force he did have was described as a "mob...that was fearfully demoralized."[223]

At one point, a unit of Confederate cavalry advanced on the relatively few, barely trained Pennsylvanians at Hagerstown. Reynolds had to personally intercede to get his men fighting.

"Open fire, you men!" he shouted from his horse. "Get up and meet the enemy! You there! Don't you even think about running! Forward, men, Forward!"

It was a quick skirmish. When it was over, an angry General Reynolds fired off a note to Pennsylvania governor Curtin.

"If I had not just happened to be on the spot," he wrote, "the men would have retired without firing a shot and might have stampeded the whole command. I really do not know what will be the result if the enemy should undertake to charge down the road tonight. I am afraid to leave the command for a moment after what I saw in front this evening."[224]

The Army of the Potomac eventually prevailed in this battle, and the "demoralized mob" was sent back to Harrisburg where the governor issued a general order discharging the militia. It was no longer needed, not that Reynolds thought they had contributed any-thing of real military value, anyway.

"I think if the Pennsylvania militia did not turn out to fight, they had better have remained at home," he wrote in a letter to his sis-ter Eleanor. He also told her that he, at last, was leaving Pennsylvania to rejoin the Army of the Potomac "having finally dispersed all the militia to their homes…," he continued in his bitter rant, "which they were so exceedingly anxious to defend, only they preferred to wait until the enemy actually reached their own doorsteps before they encountered him."[225]

After John fired off the verbal volleys of condemnation, his critics fired back. The relationship between the military and the American media had always been adversarial in nature, going back to before the War of Independence. Reynolds was reminded of that when he picked up issues of Pennsylvania newspapers.

"From all accounts," one paper complained, "General Reynolds did not elevate himself by his conduct towards the militia of Pennsylvania. We have the assurance of several gentlemen that his conduct was outrageous."

Another report took aim at the so-called military elite.

"General Reynolds—We hear much complaint of the manner in which this officer treated the militia. He is a 'regular,' and, we believe, a good fighter, but West Pointers will not accord with the opinions and education of a newly appointed militia. The distinction between them and regulars did not seem to have occurred to him, and his treatment of the former had been very severely commented upon."[226]

This war of words further infuriated John. He simply could not understand men who claimed to be soldiers but did not act like soldiers. The concept of not following orders was completely foreign to him. He believed, however, that he had the last word, several of them, in fact. They were contained in a letter to him from Andrew Curtin.

"I deem it proper," the Pennsylvania governor said, "to express my strong sense of the gratitude which Pennsylvania owes for the zeal, spirit and ability which you brought to her service when her home and safety were threatened."

So, armed with those words of praise, John rode off to join the next battle.

CHAPTER TWENTY-SEVEN

Sharpsburg, Pennsylvania
September–December 1862

"You two gentlemen have acquitted yourselves very well in the last few weeks," General George McClellan said. "You are to be commended."

The commander of the Army of the Potomac was speaking to both Brigadier Generals John Reynolds and George Meade. They were meeting in McClellan's headquarters near Sharpsburg following the costly Battle of Antietam, or what the Confederates called the Battle of Sharpsburg. Twenty-three thousand soldiers from both sides had been killed, wounded, or missing.

John, of course, had no real active role in that battle since he was busy trying to organize Pennsylvania citizens into an effective militia. He was still smarting from that barely manageable mission. His disgust with the citizen soldiers had not abated even a fraction.

"The militia," he said to Meade, "would not have stood five minutes if they had been attacked by one tenth their number."[227]

Meade, on the other hand, had been in the thick of it after he assumed command of John's Pennsylvania Reserves Division. Furthermore, Meade had been given temporary command of the entire First Corps when its commander was wounded during the battle. It was not lost on either men that the responsibility would have fallen to Reynolds had he not been otherwise occupied with a task he considered entirely useless.

"I am honored to have both you fine officers in my command. The men are better for your presence," McClellan continued. "George, I must return General Reynolds to a command position and have decided to make the First Corps his since he has seniority. John, from this moment, you are the commander of the First Corps. George, you will return to your division."

Inwardly, John breathed a sigh of relief. He had hoped, and even somewhat expected this would be the outcome, but he hadn't been sure. He also knew that Meade, although a friend, was as competitive as he was and expected he would argue that the command should go to him. He also knew that Meade, sometimes, had a temper. John, however, was surprised by Meade's reaction.

"Yes, sir, General," Meade said to McClellan. "I completely understand. I shall gracefully subside into a division commander."[228]

He turned to look at John.

"Congratulations, General. I look forward to a continued relationship with you."

"Thank you, George," Reynolds said. "That is most gracious of you. I know we make a good team, and I look forward to working with you as well. Together, we will teach those rebels a thing or two."

There were smiles all around. McClellan especially looked pleased. Too many of his ranking officers exhibited jealous behaviors regarding promotions and assignments. Too often political connections and expediency interfered with a worthier system of meritocracy. Reynolds and Meade both understood the value of advancing based on ability and performance, rather than on nepotism or favoritism. McClellan, a political animal himself who was negotiating his own partisan difficulties with Washington, nevertheless appreciated the straightforwardness of the two men before him.

"General Reynolds, General Meade," McClellan said formally. "You should be aware that I have put in for you both to be promoted to major general. You will be notified when that order has been issued."

Reynolds and Meade both snapped to attention, almost out of habit, and saluted their commander. McClellan returned the favor, then reached out to shake both their hands.

"Congratulation, gentlemen. Good luck and Godspeed."

"Thank you, sir," the two men said, nearly simultaneously.

As they left McClellan's tent to head back to their own commands, Reynolds and Meade chatted about the challenges that lie ahead for them.

"It appears we have our work cut out for us, George," Reynolds said.

"Truer words were never spoken," Meade replied.

At full strength, John's First Corps should have consisted of more than thirty-two thousand soldiers. In reality, only about fourteen thousand were present for duty. Thousands had been killed, wounded, or gone missing in the recent battles. Many more had deserted. Their priority was to bring the unit back up to full strength.

"So, what's first, do you think, George?" Reynolds asked his friend and, now, his subordinate.

"Well, supplies, I should think. Tents, blankets, field packs, clothing, you know, uniforms, and shoes, John. Especially boots and shoes. Many of the men have worn right through the ones they have, and winter is coming."

"Well, we will have support for that effort from Army headquarters. General McClellan, as you know, is working to refit and rebuild the entire Army."

"Yes," Meade said as they both returned the salutes of a company of men who marched past them. "And Little Mac is catching hell from the White House because of that, I hear."

John threw Meade a sidelong glance and grinned at his use of the nickname given to McClellan by some of the troops and which had been picked up by a few newspapers.

"Right, and though I hate political intrusion of military strategy, I have to admit the president is not entirely wrong," John said. "After Antietam, we may have the Confederates on the run. The best tactic now would be to keep the pressure on the enemy, keeping going after him."

"But with a weakened Army—" Meade started to say.

"You are right," John interrupted. "With a weakened Army, that strategy could backfire in the long run. The ranks are not just stripped of manpower, the men who remain are exhausted."

"That's what McClellan is trying to get the president, the secretary of war, and just about anyone in Washington who will listen to understand."

"Still, the president is already unhappy with McClellan," John said. "I believe that if Mr. Lincoln doesn't soon start seeing the results he expects, well, you know how the system works, George. General McClellan might find himself out of a job."

Meade nodded in agreement. Both men kept walking but remained silent as each thought about the ramifications of that happening. Both wondered privately who might be chosen to replace McClellan should he be dismissed as commander of the Army of the Potomac. Neither, of course, said anything about that out loud. They may eschew politics, but they were not fools, either.

"George, I must tell you," Reynolds finally said. "I am so pleased to have you as one of the First Corps' division commanders. I have complete trust and confidence in you. I couldn't ask for a better partner."

"That's kind of you to say, John, thank you. And likewise, if you lead this corps the way you have led your past brigade and division commands, we will be in fine shape."

Meade paused to look at John while they continued to walk.

"May I be frank, General Reynolds?"

"Of course, General Meade. Always."

"With all due respect, John, I…umm…do wish you had stayed away. I would like to have had a chance to command a corps in action.[229] Do not misunderstand. I harbor no resentment. You certainly deserve this command. Perhaps one day, I'll get my chance. I mean no insult."

John smiled.

"None taken," he said. "George, I appreciate your candor and honesty. Maintain that spirit when we meet the enemy, and I do not see how we can lose."

* * *

John went to work rebuilding his First Corps in support of McClellan's effort to reshape the entire Army. The Pennsylvania volunteers were still a rowdy bunch, and Reynolds was exasperated as ever by their behavior. He was still simmering, as well, over his unhappy experience with the Pennsylvania citizen militia he had tried to organize and with the criticism that he had been rude to them. He just couldn't let it go.

When Confederate cavalry troops, led by General J. E. B. Stuart, continued to pester Union positions around the Shenandoah Valley, darting in and out of Virginia, Maryland, and southern Pennsylvania, Reynolds was bitter in his criticism of the now disbanded Keystone State militia.

"I think it probably just as well for the south of the state that there were no militia in Chambersburg," he said to a few of his staff officers, "as I do not think, from what I saw of them, they would have been any use in preventing the raid of the rebel cavalry…"

He paused for a brief moment, then continued in what could have passed for sarcasm.

"Unless a courteous commander would have instilled a proportionate amount more of courage in them than I was able to elicit."[230]

It was a snide remark that was uncharacteristic of John Reynolds, who was known for his tact and dignified manner. But it was a measure of his anger. Except for that brief fit of pique, though, Reynolds was able to mostly contain his irritation. He labored throughout October to rebuild his corps with his usual strict discipline and calm demeanor. At one point, he punished six soldiers on maneuvers for stealing and killing a calf and dividing the meat.

"What shall we do with you?" John asked the offending soldiers who had been arrested and, along with the damming evidence, brought before him.

"Dunno, sir," one of them murmured.

"Well, you will report to your division commander for a proper court-martial. You are in General Meade's division, is that correct?"

"Yes, sir," another of the offenders muttered.

"For now, however, we must set an example."

Reynolds turned to a sergeant standing nearby.

"Sergeant, get some help and roll those six barrels over here."

"Yes, sir!" the sergeant said and hurried away, taking a few soldiers with him. Reynolds spoke to one if his aides.

"Major, please go into the headquarters tent and retrieve six pieces of blank paper and a marker."

"Right away, sir."

When the aide returned, Reynolds took the sheets of paper and began writing on each one of them.

When the barrels were in place, Reynolds handed the papers to the sergeant.

"Pin the six pieces of paper to the shirt back of each of those men."

The sergeant did as he was ordered. Everyone could now see what Reynolds had written on each sheet. It was the word "THIEF."

John looked at the confiscated calf's meat, which the six soldiers had already divided.

"Sergeant, however you can, place each of piece of meat on shoulders or backs of those men."

"Umm…yes, sir," the sergeant responded hesitantly.

When he finished the task, Reynolds approached the six condemned men.

"Each of you, up on the barrels, quickly," he ordered in a calm voice.

With help from the sergeant and other soldiers who had gathered to watch the spectacle, the six men awkwardly climbed on top of the barrels.

"You six," Reynolds said. "Stand at attention."

The men tried to stand straight and stiff but struggled to maintain their balance on the rickety barrels.

"Very good," John said. "Now, remain that way until you are dismissed. Sergeant, see that these men remain at attention for an hour."[231]

"Yes, sir!" the sergeant grinned.

Reynolds spun around and walked away without another word.

* * *

While John was laboring to bring his corps up to fighting condition, a larger struggle that would soon embroil him was taking place. Abraham Lincoln continued to be unhappy with General McClellan, who had similar feelings about his president. Lincoln signed the Emancipation Proclamation on September 22, and, for many, that act changed the whole nature of the war. It was no longer a conflict over states' rights. It was, for them, all about slavery. That was not the kind of war McClellan was ready to support with the enthusiasm the president expected.

After consistent urging from Washington, the Army of the Potomac finally began to move on November 1. But Lincoln had enough of McClellan's shilly-shallying. He relieved the general of his command a week later and appointed General Ambrose Burnside as the Army's new commander.

Reynolds was of two minds about the shake-up. On the one hand, he thought it "unwise, injudicious, as it was uncalled for."[232] He liked George McClellan and thought the general was an accomplished soldier. For John, this was yet another example of dangerous political interference in a war best left to the military. Without complete independence, he believed, generals could not conduct a proper or, for that matter, winning war.

On the other hand, while he hoped McClellan would eventually return, Reynolds believed the Army would generally accept the commander's ouster in obedience to the president. John also accepted Burnside's appointment, calling him "as noble a spirit as ever existed."[233]

However, John had no illusions about the magnitude of the job of running the entire Army and the difficulties it presented for anyone in that position. He also knew the political pressures on McClellan would be no less onerous for Burnside. Under those circumstances, he thought it nearly impossible for anyone to be an effective leader. As it turned out, just about every move Burnside made had to be approved by the White House.

It was clear that Lincoln wanted change, and Burnside accommodated him with a drastic realignment of the Army. He created three so-called grand divisions, which meant John would have to report to yet another commander. His First Corps, along with the Sixth Corps, was assigned to one of the grand divisions which was to be led by General William Franklin. In the chain of command, John's direct line to Burnside was, thus, eliminated. The plan may have given individual units more strength at the corps level, but some complained it made the command structure clumsy and barely manageable.

Reynolds, who had a reputation of efficiency and decision-making, was offended by the notion that three grand divisions, containing six separate corps, plus a reserve corps, meant that at least ten different generals would be involved in developing overall strategy to defeat the enemy. That didn't even take into account the president and the commander in chief of the military, General Halleck.

Burnside's grand strategy did not work out to anyone's satisfaction on the northern side of the war. He put the Army of the Potomac to work in mid-November. His war plan was to be ready by the beginning of December to cross the Rappahannock River and take on General Robert E. Lee and his Confederate Army in and around Fredericksburg.

But, his orders for pontoon bridges to cross the Rappahannock somehow got lost. The floating rafts didn't arrive until two weeks later, too late to be of any real use. They, also, were no longer a surprise because by then Confederate troops had retaken Fredericksburg across the river and had advantageous positions on the heights overlooking the river. Lee could see just about everything the Union Army was doing.

Confederate snipers made construction of the pontoon bridges slow going. Several engineers were hit by rifle fire from the ridge, their bodies suddenly stiffening when bullets slammed into them. With a grunt, they fell off the pontoons and plunged deep into the fast-flowing cold and dark river. Moments later their motionless and bleeding bodies popped to the surface and were carried away by the swift current.

The weather was also causing major problems. It had turned very cold, and by the end of the first week of December, four inches of snow had fallen. Two infantrymen froze to death.[234]

At the end of the second week, Reynolds, Sixth Corps commander William Smith, and grand division commander Franklin held an urgent discussion about their next strategic move.

"An all-out assault at first light tomorrow. That's what is called for here," Reynolds said.

"I agree," said General Smith. "We need to soften up the rebs with heavy sustained artillery aimed at the heights while our infantry units use the cover of the cannon fire to cross the river on the pontoon bridges."

General Franklin thought for a moment as the three of them huddled under the cold, gray winter sky. He nodded.

"That sounds right," he said. "General Burnside is coming down here to inspect our position this afternoon. We can lay out our plan to him then."

When Burnside arrived, Reynolds, Smith, and Franklin explained their strategy for him.

"It sounds as though you gentlemen have thought this through."

"Yes, sir," Franklin said. "We are all in agreement this is the best way to proceed. But we need your assent, sir, and begging your pardon, we need it as soon as possible."

"Yes, yes, I understand, General. Let me think upon this. I will send official approval to you inside of two or three hours."

"Sir," Reynolds spoke up, just a shade too harshly. "This advance on the enemy will be complicated, involving two corps of troops, infantry, and artillery units, not to mention the engineers who are still trying to construct the pontoon bridges. The snow and cold weather will naturally slow things down. The sooner we get approval, the better."

"I appreciate your concern, John," Burnside said. "You also need to appreciate there are many moving parts in this campaign. We must make sure whatever your grand division does works in concert with the other two grand divisions. I must go back to headquarters and piece all this together. I will send word to you as soon as I can. Thank you for your good work, gentlemen. That will be all."

Burnside mounted his horse and rode away, followed by a retinue of aides and orderlies. Reynolds stared at the retreating entourage and shook his head. But he held his tongue. There was nothing more to do than wait for the go-ahead from Burnside.

The three of them, Reynolds, Smith, and Franklin, waited for the remainder of the afternoon. They were still waiting when darkness fell. The hours wore on, and no word was forthcoming. They stayed awake late into the night, refining their plan of attack while waiting in vain for Burnside's approval to proceed. By three in the morning, Reynolds had enough.

"I know I have hard work ahead of me," he said to the other two officers. "I must get some sleep."[235]

He left the grand division headquarters and headed to his own tent, very worried about Burnside's leadership.

Finally, an impatient General Franklin sent orderlies to Army headquarters to retrieve the orders. But the messengers only got as far as Burnside's tent. They were told that the commanding general could not be disturbed until morning. He was asleep and had been from the time he reached headquarters after leaving Reynolds, Smith, and Franklin.[236]

Early next morning, the orders from Burnside finally arrived. But they were not what John and the others expected. Rather than a full assault on Confederate forces, they were to take the heights across the river with a division, "at least." The job went to Reynolds and his First Corps. He chose his best division, the Pennsylvania Reserves commanded by his old friend, George Meade, to lead the way in.

It was a very rough day for Reynolds and his troops. They gave the Confederates all they could muster, attacking the heights and, at first, gained some ground. But in doing so, four out of every ten

Union soldiers were either killed or wounded. The Confederate artillery on top of the heights was murderous. Reynolds called in more Union troops for support, but they weren't enough, and were slow to arrive. They failed to hold up against the overwhelming fire of Confederate cannons. Late in the day, Meade's division was forced to retreat. Not getting the amount of support he needed to counter the enemy, the general's temper let loose.

"My God, General Reynolds!" Meade exclaimed when he finally got his surviving troops away from the artillery bombardment. "Did they think my division could whip Lee's whole Army?"[237]

It was a catastrophe for the Army of the Potomac. By the end of the day, twelve thousand Union soldiers had fallen. The failure to contain Confederate forces in and around the town was made evident in numerous after-action reports and analysis.

Although Reynolds was disappointed in the performance of his own corps, he put the best spin on it in his official report.

"The gallantry and steadiness of the troops brought into action on the left is deserving of great praise, the new regiments viewing with the veterans in steadiness and coolness," he wrote. "That the brilliant attack made and the advanced position gained by them were not more successful in their results was due to the strong character of the enemy's defense."[238]

Privately, John was not so magnanimous.

"They didn't do as well as I expected, 'tho they advanced under artillery fire very well," he wrote to his sisters. "When it came to the attack of the wooded heights, they faltered and failed. We are fortunate that it is not worse…To have risked more than we did would probably have cost the loss of the whole Army in case of another repulse."[239]

Aware that he was treading on thin ice with that implied criticism of top-level commanders, John added a line to the letter.

"You must not show this to anyone."[240]

* * *

The finger-pointing after Burnside's defeat continued long after the battle was over. A few lower-level commanders were publicly criticized for not moving their troops fast enough to support Reynolds's men. Burnside was castigated for poor execution of a bad plan.

In his public comments, at least, Reynolds was more circumspect. At a congressional hearing three months after the battle, he was asked why were not more troops used against the enemy?

"I can hardly answer that question," John replied. "I can only give my opinion."

His opinion was that General Burnside apparently anticipated an attack by additional enemy forces and he wanted troops held in reserve for the potentiality. One of the senators noted that Reynolds had orders to attack a certain point, meaning the high ground at Fredericksburg.

"If that order contemplated that that point should be taken and held," the senator continued, "was it not the duty of the general commanding there to use his whole force to take that point?"

Reynolds was not about to throw Burnside under the carriage. He paused, took a deep breath, then answered.

"The commanding officer of the whole force there must judge for himself as to the manner in which he will carry out the orders he has received."[241]

John went on to suggest that aggressive punishing enemy action might have necessitated the need to keep a large force in reserve in case there was a breakthrough by the Confederates.

"In your judgment," the questioning persisted, "should there not have been other troops in a position to give prompt support to you?"

"Yes, sir. I think there should."

"Who is responsible for that not having been done?"

"I can hardly say who is responsible, for I am not acquainted with all the orders that were given."[242]

His carefully worded answers accomplished two things for the careful listener. If the Senate committee wanted to know why more troops weren't brought to bear on the enemy, he was saying, in effect, don't ask me. Ask the commanding general.

Whether it was his intent, or just his way of expression, by saying that orders regarding troop movements must be judged by the commander in charge, Reynolds was telling the committee to keep its nose out of military decisions. For a man who despised political intrusion, John had become adept at speaking a language politicians should understand.

Reynolds, himself, received hardly any criticism for his role in the battle. More to the point, he received accolades, even from the enemy. The most effective Union fire in the fateful battle came from Reynolds's artillery units. Although not in direct command of the big guns, John, as an experienced artilleryman, paid close attention to their placement. As a result, Confederate general Stonewall Jackson commented on the "heavy and rapids discharges of Union artillery" which were "warm and well-directed."[243]

Reynolds's guns were so well directed that Jackson was forced to abandon a plan of attack he had made.

"The artillery of the enemy was so judiciously posted as to make an advance of our troops across the plain very hazardous," Jackson said. "The first gun had hardly moved forward from the wood one hundred yards when the enemy's artillery reopened, and so completely swept our front as to satisfy me that the proposed movement should be abandoned."[244]

It was in the midst of all this that Reynolds received some more good news. His promotion had come through. He was now a major general, adding another star to his shoulder boards.

CHAPTER TWENTY-EIGHT

Philadelphia
Christmas 1862

After the debacle at Fredericksburg, John's First Corps went into winter quarters several miles north of the town. They were there to rest, refit, and lick their wounds. Major General John Reynolds took time off for the Christmas holiday, ostensibly, to visit family in Philadelphia. The person he really wanted to see, of course, was Kate.

Arriving aboard a self-driven carriage during a light snowfall on December 24, John went straight to the home of his sister Catherine and her husband, Harry Landis. His two other sisters, Eleanor and Harriet, lived there as well and were waiting for him. After their parents had passed away, the siblings had relocated from Lancaster and made Philadelphia their permanent residence. Since John had no place to live, other than in the military, they considered this his home, as well. Nevertheless, he planned to reunite with his family first and, after Christmas Day, make his excuses and spend the rest of his holiday leave privately with Kate.

"John! Oh, John!" Catherine squealed when she opened her front door to his knock. She wrapped her arms around him. "Oh, it is so good to see you! Please, come in!"

John stomped his feet and shook the snow off his coat as he entered the house. Eleanor and Harriet ran up to him, squealing his names as well. They all hugged and laughed. John finally disengaged himself from their loving sisterly arms.

"You two attack more aggressively than the rebels ever do!" he joked.

They all laughed again.

Harry Landis stood back a couple of steps, watching the scene with bemusement. When the women finally settled down, Harry gave John a formal military salute.

"Welcome home, General," he said with a smile.

Harry's real name was Henry Landis, but family and friends had always called him Harry. He was just four years younger than John, and the two had forged a close friendship since Harry's marriage to Catherine. He was tall, like John, ruggedly handsome, and, also like his brother-in-law, sported a dark full beard. The two men shared a sensibility of military matters. Landis was a captain in the Pennsylvania Reserves, commanding an artillery battery. That was one of the reasons John and Harry got along so well, with both being artillerymen. Harry learned a great deal about artillery tactics and strategy from his brother-in-law.

John returned the salute with a broad smile, his bright white teeth showing through his thick beard.

"Thank you, Captain," he said. "It's good to be home."

The two men dropped their salutes and hugged, each slapping the other on his back.

After getting settled in the guest room, John joined Harry in the parlor.

"Care for a cigar and a little brandy before dinner, John?" Harry asked.

"Yes, indeed," John answered. "That would be delightful."

While Harry poured drinks for both of them and opened a humidor to pull out a couple of cigars, John sat down in a large, very comfortable easy chair. Harry stepped over to him and handed John his drink and cigar. John leaned forward with the cigar in his mouth as Harry lit it for him. Dressed now in civilian clothes, John leaned back and let out with a long, satisfied sigh, blowing the first puff of blue-gray smoke high into the air.

"It's good to be away from the front for a while, isn't it, John?" Harry said.

"You have no idea," John replied, taking a sip of his brandy. Then he looked at Harry and changed his mind. "Well, I guess you do, as a matter of fact."

Harry chuckled, nodded, and took a swallow of his own drink. He had been in enough battles of his own to know what John meant.

"You have a much broader view of the war," Harry began, then grinned, "as a general, than I do…" He paused just briefly, timing his little joke. "As lowly captain."

"Oh, I assure you, lowly captain, we generals value your service to the cause. Without you, we would have fewer men to order around," John said over the rim of his glass as he took another drink. Both men laughed.

"Seriously, John, how is the war going? It is difficult to judge from inside the ranks."

John sighed again, but this time with frustration.

"To be candid, Harry, I am worried. The rebs are putting up a hell of a fight, I have to give them that. Lee, Jackson, Longstreet, Stuart…all good, smart commanders. West Point taught them well," John added, ruefully. "Furthermore, their men are tough and determined."

He took a long draw on his cigar before continuing.

"Don't get me wrong. We've had some good victories, and I was one who thought the war would be over by now. I see now, I was wrong. This, I am afraid, will drag on for much longer than most anyone anticipated."

Harry slowly sipped his brandy as he listened intently.

"Between you and me, Harry," John went on, "political meddling from Washington is hampering our ability to win. If they would just let generals be generals"—he nodded at Harry—"and let captains be captains, we would all be the better for it. Look, I will admit I haven't agreed with every strategic move General McClellan made, and, perhaps, I would have done some things differently, but he is a fine soldier and did not deserve the treatment he got from President Lincoln."

"Is all the intrusion coming from just the president?" Harry asked.

"Oh, well, others are involved to be sure. Secretary of War Stanton and various influential senators, for example. General-in-Chief Halleck never leaves his desk to see what's really happening in the field. But in my view, like a river, it all flows downhill from the top, the White House."

"Did you just say the Slop House?"

John looked at his brother-in-law with a frown.

"Now, now, Harry, let's not be disrespectful."

Then, John quickly lifted his glass to his mouth to hide his grin.

"What about General Burnside?" Landis continued. "Have things changed since he took over the Army of the Potomac?"

John slightly shook both his head and the liquor in his glass.

"At least McClellan tried to resist political interference in his war-making decisions. Burnside hardly makes a move without approval from Washington. The few decisions he made on his own have only gotten him into trouble. We got a licking at Fredericksburg. That should not have happened. My estimation is he won't last much longer in that job."

"What about you, John? Have you ever considered whether you'd want the job, be the Army commander?"

John sat quietly for several moments, sipping his brandy and puffing on his cigar, thinking about the question.

"To tell you the truth, Harry," he finally said. "I believe I could do the job and would consider taking it if asked. But I would insist on guarantees that my tactics and decisions on the battlefield are mine and not dictated from the White House, Congress, or any-where outside the military chain of command. When it comes to Army strategy, I would not abide political interference of any kind."

Just then Catherine appeared at the parlor door.

"Gentlemen, dinner is served. Because it is a late hour, we are having just a light supper tonight. We will plan a big family dinner for tomorrow, Christmas Day."

John and Harry snuffed out the cigars, put their glasses down, and rose from their chairs. John put his arm around his sister's waist as they headed for the dining room.

"Anything is better than Army rations," he said.

* * *

The next day, Christmas afternoon, all the Reynolds siblings, with the exception of William, gathered at the Landis home for the holiday meal. The house was lit with colorful candles and had the aroma of pine, with a tall gaily decorated Christmas tree in one corner of the living room. Other bright holiday decorations were on display throughout the house, giving it a pleasant, festive feeling. Warm fires crackled in the living and dining rooms as large intricate flakes of snow fell outside.

It was a military family that gathered in the house. Two of John's brothers, James, who was unmarried, along with Sam and his wife, had arrived. James was the quartermaster general for Pennsylvania and moved easily in the Commonwealth's political circles. The second oldest brother, William, now a commander in the US Navy, was the captain of his own ship at Port Royal in South Carolina and was unable to take leave. Two other sisters, Lydia and Mary Jane, had also arrived with their husbands.

So, it was a family of twelve that came together for this holiday setting, a rare treat, especially in this time of war.

"Attention! Attention, everyone!" Catherine called out to them in the parlor as the brothers, sisters, and in-laws chatted excitedly. It had been months since some had seen each other.

"Let's all gather in the dining room!" Catherine continued. "The meal is ready!"

"Oh, this is so lovely, Catherine," Jane gushed as they entered the room. "This is beautiful!"

The scene was elegant. The walls were painted a muted green, complemented by tasteful artwork and a handsome multicolored area rug under a large rectangular dining table. A delicate white linen tablecloth was draped over the table. Fine china and highly polished flatware were positioned just so at each table setting. Exquisite crystal glasses sparkled from the light of graceful candles placed strategically down the middle of the table. An intricate chandelier, also adorned with lighted candles, hung over it. Bottles of wine sat in buckets of ice on tall stands nearby.

"Jane, Harriet, and Eleanor, would you please sit there," Catherine said, indicting three chairs along one side of the table. "Jane, your husband can sit next to you. Sam, please sit between Harriet and Eleanor."

Catherine, appearing ever so much like a commanding officer examining troop movements, watched as her guests maneuvered their way around the table.

"Harry and I will sit at each end of the table," Catherine resumed. "John, you sit here next to me. Lydia, please sit up there next to Harry. Your husband can sit next to you, and, James, you and your wife should sit between him and John."

"Uh, I think I am here," James said to his wife.

"No, darling, I think Catherine said you are to sit in this seat, not that one."

"Oh, sorry."

They switched positions.

"Is this where I am supposed to be?"

"Yes, John," Catherine said. "Perfect."

"Am I here, or is my husband?" Jane asked from the other end of the table.

"You are, Jane." Catherine said, with just a hint of exasperation. "See? It's boy-girl, boy-girl."

Finally, after everyone found their seat, they sat down. The men waited until all the women were comfortably seated before they took their seats.

"Harry, will you please say the blessing?" Catherine asked.

"Please bow your heads, everyone."

Harry said a short prayer of thanks, making sure to ask that there be a short end to this already too-long war.

"Enjoy the meal and Merry Christmas, everyone!" Catherine said, raising a class of wine. "Here's to our men in blue!"

"Hear, hear!" they all said in union, raising their glasses in a collective toast. All twelve then dug into an assortment of fruits that already sat in front of them.

"How did you manage to find all these fruits, Catherine?" Jane asked. "I mean, there is a shortage because of the war, and it is winter, after all.'

"I did a lot of canning this fall," Catherine replied. "Just call me a canner planner."

Laughter erupted all around the table.

"So, John," Lydia said after a few bites. "Do we have the rebs on the run yet?"

Thus, the war talk commenced. The siblings wanted to know as much detail as John and the other men around the table could tell them. What happened at Richmond? What was it like being military governor of Fredericksburg? Are the Confederates really that tough? Tell us about the Pennsylvania volunteers? Isn't it strange to be fighting against old West Point friends? Is Philadelphia in danger? Are we in danger? Isn't this war just awful?

The animated conversation continued over salad, through the soup servings, and the main course, a large Christmas goose with all the trimmings prepared lovingly by Catherine, Eleanor, and Harriet. John Reynolds, being a man of few words, gave short, cursory answers. He was careful to describe only sanitized versions of the war-time horrors. He avoided telling them about the blown-apart bodies, the acres of bloody and bloated corpses scattered across battlefields, the wretched smell, or the agonized writhing of the wounded. These were not the subjects to discuss in polite company, he thought, let alone at a family feast.

Finally, as they were finishing their last forkfuls before dessert, Eleanor turned to John to change the subject.

"John, let me tell you about an odd thing that happened to me a few months back."

"Oh?" John said as he focused on cutting a piece of meat on his plate. "What's that?"

"Well, you know of Eden Hall, the Catholic boarding school for women run by the Daughters of Charity, right?"

John stopped cutting and looked up at his sister, wondering where she was headed with this.

"Yes, sure," he said.

"Well, late last summer I was invited to an ice cream social the nuns were having. They do great work, by the way. I am a big supporter of theirs. People have it wrong. Catholics aren't so bad."

Eleanor took a drink of her wine as the other siblings cast sidelong glances at one another, bemused by their sister's indelicate comment.

"Anyway," Eleanor continued, "one of the nuns introduced me to a woman who was there. A pretty thing, she was. A young girl sat with her. I believe the girl was the woman's ward, or something."

John slowly put down his knife and fork, now really wondering where this was going.

"They were both very pleasant," Eleanor went on. "I sat, and we talked for a while. Then a strange thing happened. We got to talking about the war, and I mentioned I had brothers in the military. I mentioned that Will is in the Navy and that you are a general in the Army. Suddenly, she turned very pale. She looked quite ill, I must say. She told me she felt faint and blamed it on the heat. Then she stood up, bid me farewell, and quickly walked away, the little girl close behind. It was so odd!"

"What was her name?" Jane asked.

"She said her name was…Kate, I believe. Yes. It was Kate."

Eleanor turned back to John, who had gotten very busy again with the piece of meat on his plate, avoiding Eleanor's gaze.

"Do you know anyone named Kate, John?" Eleanor asked. "She's someone who lives here in Philadelphia. I think maybe her reaction was not so much due to the heat, but for some reason a result of my mentioning your name. Are you familiar with her?"

John had stuffed the meat into his mouth, followed by a large piece of biscuit, so he only grunted with his mouth full.

An unintelligible "mmm-woom" was all he could muster. Eleanor cocked her head and gave John a suspicious look that was, nevertheless, full of mischief.

"Say, brother," she said, "do you, by any chance, have a secret love that you have not told the family about?"

John could feel the heat rising under his collar. He was slowly chewing his food, trying to figure out just what, exactly, to say. Before he could swallow, his brother-in-law Harry came to his rescue, speaking from the end of the table.

"I think, perhaps, we should let sleeping dogs lie," he said amiably. "Besides, it is time for dessert, isn't it, Catherine."

"Oh, yes," Catherine said, rising from her chair. "Harriett, would you please give me a hand clearing the table?"

As the two women went about their work, John glanced appreciatively at Harry, who sat in his chair with an innocent look on his face, pretending to be fascinated by the design on his napkin.

At the other end of the table, Eleanor was leaning back in her chair, arms crossed, staring at John, slightly nodding her head knowingly, a small amused smirk on her face.

* * *

By the next morning, the snow had stopped falling. The day was partly cloudy but pleasant. Bells jangled on the harness of a horse pulling a carriage through the snow-covered Pennsylvania countryside. Although it was chilly, the temperature was above freezing. The water of the brown Schuylkill River, flowing swiftly over and around rocks, sparkled with dabbled sunlight peeking through the clouds. John and Kate were snuggled together. A warm blue woolen blanket was stretched over their laps and covered their legs and feet. John held the reins loosely in his hands, letting the horse have its head as the big animal guided the carriage gracefully on a path along the banks of the river just beyond the city limits. Kate sighed with pleasure.

"I do so love these carriage rides, John," she said. "Especially when I am with you."

John smiled. He had one arm around Kate and pulled her closer.

"Being with you makes everything better," he said.

Kate grinned and kissed him on the cheek through his thick beard.

"So tell me, darling, how did you get away from your family? What did you tell them?"

John snickered a little.

"Well, I said I had an important meeting I must attend regarding the war. You know, strategy and all that. I gave my regrets and said I had to get back to Washington. That's true. I do have to be back in a few days. I have been called to testify in the court-martial of General Fitz John Porter."

He grinned again.

"I'm just taking the long way...to be with you first!"

"I am so very glad you are!" Kate said. "So, you didn't say anything to your family about us?"

"No, I didn't. But I should tell you, Kate, I think my sister Eleanor has her suspicions."

Kate sat straight up. She had a concerned look on her face.

"Why? Did she say something?"

"Well, apparently the two of you have met."

"Oh, Lord!" Kate exclaimed. Her hands flew to her cheeks, which were turning red. "The ice cream social last summer! At Eden Hall!"

"Yes. She said you became faint when you learned who she was."

"John, I was so embarrassed! I didn't know what to do! When she said you were her brother, I panicked. I was so afraid that she, somehow, had discovered our secret. That she knew about us!"

Kate tilted her head back, rested it on the back of the carriage seat, and closed her eyes.

"Oh dear, John! I was so rude! I just sort of, I don't know, blanked out, I guess. All I could think about was getting out of there! So, I got up and, I think, apologized and then hurried back to my room. I was mortified!"

"Catherine was there, right?"

"Yes, and she followed right behind me. I was so humiliated."

"Well, Eleanor is very bright, and I suspect she believes we are together. But she had the good manners not so say anything more about it."

Kate leaned over and put her head on John's shoulder, slipping one arm around his.

"I do wish we could stop all this secrecy," she said morosely. "It is not right, John. We love each other, and we should be able to tell it…no…shout it to the world."

"I know, my darling, I know," John said, trying to sound soothing. "We will, someday. It is just with the state of the country these days, the war, people are on edge, the nasty, harsh differences of opinion about race, slavery, politics, religion, taxes, tariffs. The country is falling apart. I don't want any of that to interfere with our love. So, I think it best that we keep our secret for a while longer."

Kate groaned softly.

"Oh, I know, John. I don't disagree. I just wish…well, you know."

Soon, they stopped for a long, leisurely late lunch at a tavern near Lansdowne, a few miles west of Philadelphia. By the time they finished eating, it was getting dark outside.

"I guess we had better get back to the city," Kate said, picking up a glass and drinking down the last bit of her water.

"Well, actually, I had a different idea," John said with a twinkle in his eyes.

"Oh? And what might that be, Major General John Reynolds?"

The tavern owner also had for rent a half dozen small cabins deep in the woods nearby. John had reserved one for the two of them. He reached across the table and took Kate's hands in his and looked longingly into her eyes.

"Would you care to spend the night with me, Miss Hewitt?"

She looked at him for a brief moment, then smiled and nodded her head.

"Yes. Yes, I would."

A half an hour later, they entered the snug one-room cabin. It had a little table with chairs for two in what passed as a kitchenette. Two easy chairs sat before a fireplace. A double bed was against one wall. Kate busied herself with lighting candles to ease the darkness in the quaint room while John built a fire. The cabin, already cozy, became more intimate.

They stood together, holding hands, in the middle of the room. Their shadows from the candles and the lit fireplace danced on the walls. They stood there for a long moment, saying nothing, but gazing into each other's eyes.

Then, Kate reached up and slowly began to unbutton John's military tunic.

CHAPTER TWENTY-NINE

Washington, DC
December 1862

When Reynolds arrived in Washington at the end of Christmas week, he was conflicted about the court-martial of General Fitz John Porter. On the one hand, John believed Porter was a good soldier and an accomplished commander. He also did not forget how supportive Porter had been through recent battles and how he had submitted glowing reports about John's performance during those engagements.

One the other hand, he remembered that day last August when, during that battle near Manassas, troops of Porter's corps had fled the battlefield in droves, leaving John's division to fight the enemy alone. But that alone, he thought, was not worthy of a court-martial.

He also recalled what Porter had told him confidentially. The Army of the Potomac, under General George McClellan, had been ordered by Washington to support the newly created Army of Virginia, under General John Pope. Porter had said that several corps commanders had urged McClellan to ignore those orders, believing the plan to confront the Confederates in and around the Shenandoah Valley was ill-fated and destined for disaster. A failure to follow orders, John agreed, was a court-martial offense.

McClellan, however, did what he was ordered, sending Porter and other unit commanders to join the newly appointed General Pope in the fight. For the next two days, Porter and Pope argued about strategy and tactics. On the last day of the battle, Porter's troops were cut to pieces by withering Confederate cannon and rifle fire. That is what John had witnessed when he saw Porter's men running away.

Adding to that was a personal animus Porter had toward Pope. He just didn't like the man. Several messages Porter had sent criticizing Pope had found their way up the chain of command, all the way to the president.

That, John thought to himself, *was a very bad move.* Lincoln, the secretary of war, and the general-in-chief, Henry Halleck, were among Pope's allies. In addition, Pope was a personal friend of the president. So, Porter's court-martial became as much about politics as about military discipline. John knew that going in, and he was not happy about being embroiled in the mess.

He was thinking deeply about all this when he entered headquarters where the court-martial was being held. Lost in thought, he did not see General Porter approach him outside the courtroom. He felt a light tap on his shoulder.

"Good morning, General Reynolds."

John turned to see Porter standing there.

"Good morning, General," John replied.

Porter looked around to see if anyone was listening. Then he leaned into John and spoke quietly.

"Are you with me, John?"

Reynolds didn't answer right away. He looked at Porter and let out with a small sigh

"I'll do what I can. I have a great deal of respect for you, Fitz, and I think you are getting a raw deal. But I will not lie."

"I appreciate that, and I would not expect anything but the truth from you. This is going to be a rough go. You know that Secretary of War Stanton handpicked the jury, don't you?"

"Are you saying the jury is stacked against you?"

Porter did not reply, but looked at John with raised eyebrows and bunched lips, as if to say, "What do you think?" John knew that, on one side, Stanton was an enemy of McClellan and, therefore, no friend of Porter. On the other side, Porter had retained an attorney who was well-known in Democratic circles and had been active in opposing Abraham Lincoln's election as president.[245] John could see that this court-martial was turning into a political circus. He would much rather face ten batteries of enemy artillery than enter the courtroom.

John said nothing in response to Porter's question but simply nodded and shook his hand.

"I'll see you inside," he said.

When John was called to the stand, he did as he had promised. He told the truth. But he told it in such a way as to not destroy Porter. He described what he saw in a straightforward, unemotional, and nonjudgmental manner. The closest thing said that could be considered criticism was when he was asked whether troops should have been ordered to advance on a night so black that visibility was reduced to near zero.

"It was a very dark night. I should not have considered it practicable to march that night. I should have considered it a very precarious undertaking"[246] was all he said.

Porter was found guilty and dismissed from the Army. His conviction, however, was overturned by a board of inquiry fifteen years later. After the court-martial, Reynolds quickly returned to the field, eager to escape the political quagmire.

CHAPTER THIRTY

Falmouth, Virginia
January 1863

While General Porter was losing his career, General Burnside was trying to save his. Once again, Reynolds was caught right in the middle of things. After his embarrassing defeat at Fredericksburg, Burnside was anxious to prove his worth as a commander. Thus, he planned another star-crossed assault that was quickly known among the troops as the Mud March.

After Porter's court-martial, John had settled down with his command at their winter quarters near Falmouth, Virginia. The weather was miserable. It was so cold, the Potomac River froze solid. Troops resorted to unique methods to stay warm. Some dug holes in the ground, covered them with three or more layers of tents, cut holes in the top for chimneys and built improvised fireplaces in their makeshift quarters. To get some relief from frigid boredom, Reynolds tried to keep his men busy with training drills.[247]

After a few weeks, Reynolds received orders from Burnside's headquarters to leave camp and head north and west along the Rappahannock River. The goal was to make a surprise crossing and hit the enemy before they knew what was happening. The problem was Burnside wanted to review the troops before they left. That meant a large and easily visible parade of soldiers passing in review.

Furthermore, to John's great frustration, Burnside prematurely issued, then withdrew, his marching orders before finally settling on January 20, 1863, as the day of departure. As a result, the troop movements were no longer secret. The Confederates, of course, had spies everywhere. They had ample time to report to General Lee's Southern Army what they had seen and heard.

When the units began their march, Reynolds could see that Burnside's planning was so disorganized that the road leading from camp quickly became clogged with supply trains, artillery wagons, called caissons, and thousands of troops. Little progress was made that afternoon. They had marched only about five miles by nightfall. There was no choice but to bivouac by the roadside.

To make matters worse, Mother Nature turned even meaner. Shortly after dark, the temperature was just above freezing, and rain began to fall. The troops had no tents to pitch and spent the night shivering in rain-soaked blankets or just the clothes on their backs, trying to get some warmth by large bonfires. Reynolds sympathized with the men and got angrier by the hour. This was hardly the mission of stealth that had been planned.

By morning, the road and pathways alongside it had turned into rivers of mud and slime. Horses, wagons, and men got bogged down in the muck. Caissons became unmovable. Teams of horses and mules had to be released from the carts to prevent them from being dragged down. Some were shot to avoid being strangled.

All the while, Confederate soldiers lined up on the opposite bank of the Rappahannock, watching the chaos with amusement. They shouted and whistled and taunted the Union troops struggling in the mud. Some of the rebels even held up makeshift signs written with such taunts as "Stuck in the Mud" or "This way to Richmond!"[248]

John was apoplectic.

"We are, indeed, stuck in the mud," he complained to an aide. "And Burnside goes to Washington to know what do!"

Apparently, General Burnside had returned to the capital for advice.

"If we do not get someone soon who can command an Army without consulting Stanton and Halleck at Washington," John continued his rant, "I do not know what will become of this Army!"

Reynolds spent the day up to his knees in mud, trying to help his officers and men escape the slop and mire. The more he worked, the more he got worked up.

"No general officer that I can find approved of this move, yet it was made," he said to another aide, out of earshot of the men who, literally, were in the muddy trenches. "I have been afraid all along the weather would fall on us in this way."

He reiterated a long-standing complaint that his men were suffering from orders by people who had never been in the field and had no military experience.

"No one who had not seen the roads in this country we have to move over could conceive of their wretched conditions," he groused.

Then he doubled down on his dislike for incompetent commanders, Burnside in particular, and meddling politicians.

"I do not know how it is that the general in command here is obliged to consult Washington every day, and yet there is no one there responsible for failure of operations here!"

Reynolds had faced determined Mexican enemy fighters, angry Indians, and ferocious Confederate artillery barrages. He had overseen the hauling of large supply trains across deserts and over mountains. Yet he called this predicament "about as difficult a problem to solve as ever fell to the lot of one man."[249] The mission was an abject failure. By the time the troops struggled and trudged their way back to camp a few days later, John was furious.

Washington was not happy either. Burnside was relieved of command two days later. For the second time in just a few months, Reynolds and the rest of the Army of the Potomac had a new commander, Major General Joseph Hooker.

* * *

During the early winter of 1863, Reynolds was dismayed and depressed over the failures of the war effort. So were his men. Morale in the Union Army was at an all-time low. So, John was encouraged to see the new commander trying to improve military life. That meant better meals for the men, improved health and sanitation standards, and a furlough schedule to give troops much-needed time off. When Hooker assumed command of the Army, three thousand officers and about eighty-two thousand enlisted men were listed as absent. The furlough program went a long way to cut down on desertions.

General Hooker was also a stickler for discipline, and he tightened up matters in that area. Reynolds, being a tough disciplinarian himself, was especially gratified by those actions. Following Hooker's example, John sent out a memo to his own officers reminding them about his strict admonition regarding enemy property.

"You will enforce the strictest discipline," he wrote to his subordinates, "and summarily punish any unauthorized plundering, it being understood that anything taken is for the government. Anything more than this is nothing more than robbery."[250] He simply did not tolerate looting of any kind. He never believed that civilians, as a group, were the enemy. What he did believe is that they should never be treated as such.

Hooker also got rid of the so-called grand divisions scheme and reorganized the corps system. That meant a bittersweet development for John. His old division of Pennsylvania Reserves was being detached from his corps and sent permanently to Washington. He was sorry to see them go. They had come a long way together, from being a rowdy bunch of untrained volunteers to a well-trained, effective, and disciplined fighting machine. But their reassignment meant the Pennsylvanians would, finally, be getting much-needed rest and relief from battle. John was happy for them.

As for the rest of his corps, large-scale operations were not practical because of the weather and the condition of the roads in their slippery, muddy, unnavigable state. So, Hooker had Reynolds and the other corps commanders to develop small operations keep the men sharp and attentive. Hooker also believed in holding regular reviews. President Lincoln even came out to review General Reynolds's First Corps in particular. John was proud of the display the men provided the president. He believed Lincoln was pleased with what he saw.

"As he ought to have been," John said. "If the troops only fight as well as they looked, no expectation, however great, need be disappointed."[251]

So, things were looking up, and John's confidence in Hooker was growing as he told his sisters in a letter.

"Our troops here," he wrote, "with proper management, which bids fair to be the case, will achieve success undoubtedly."[252]

* * *

The adjustments to furloughs that General Hooker established were a double-edged sword. The system was designed, mostly, to give the men in the ranks a break to boost their morale. It also meant, however, that time off for officers was less frequent. In late February, Reynolds was able to take ten days off. It was another opportunity to see Kate again, and he took it.

The couple enjoyed the better part of a week together in and around Philadelphia, always careful to meet in out-of-the-way places where they were not likely to run into any of John's family or anyone else they knew.

"I have to admit," John said one night over dinner in a quiet tavern, "this vow of secrecy we have is getting a bit tiresome."

"I couldn't agree more," Kate replied. "Do we really have to keep this up?"

"I'm afraid so, but, perhaps just for a little while longer," John said with resignation. "To go public now might make things quite awkward for us, as matters stand with the Army. I am gaining some dominance now in the chain of command, and if things continue as they have been, we could be very comfortable in our living situation, once the war is over. We don't want to do anything that might interfere with the order of things."

"I have been trying to keep up with what has been happening, not only with the war, but also with what appears to be political turmoil with the Army of the Potomac, at least if you believe the Philadelphia newspapers," Kate said.

"Reporters," John scoffed. "They do more harm than good and are not at all reliable. I have no use for them."[253]

"Be that as it may," Kate went on. "I worry about you. Yes, I worry about you being wounded or worse. But I also fret for your career when I read about all the problems in the higher command. General McClellan was fired. Then General Burnside was fired. Who is in charge now? General Joe…Joe…"

"Hooker," John said.

"Right. Hooker. Joe Hooker. How long will he last? And then there was that court-martial of another general—"

"Fitz John Porter," John interjected.

"Yes. Him. What an unusual name. I just worry that you might get caught up in all that. You are so close to the top now."

"Caught up in what?"

"The politics! That's what all this sounds like to me, at least from what I read. Nasty politics!"

"Well, I can't deny that, and I am fed up with all the political interference in military matters. The war must be fought by generals, not politicians. As the ancient Roman statesman Lucious Annaeus Seneca put it, 'Be wary of the man who urges an action in which he himself incurs no risk.' I try to keep my distance and do the best job I can on the battlefield, but I am wary, believe me."

"What of this General Hooker? I have not heard of him."

"He is a good soldier. The newspapermen have started calling him Fighting Joe Hooker. What cockamamie! But…"

John paused, staring off into the middle distance.

"But, what, my love?"

"I hesitate to say, but I am troubled about him."

"Troubled? Why is that?"

"I fear he may not use my corps to its fullest potential in the upcoming battles. He told me, on the one hand, that he does not undervalue the services of my men. But then he said something that sounded strange. He said that at the proper time full justice will be done and that it will be right at the proper time. Proper time? What is a proper time? What does he mean by that? I suppose I am concerned that he may sideline my corps or relegate to them a reserve or supporting role when they are needed most."

"Wouldn't that be safer for you? And your men?" Kate asked quietly.

John gave her a little smile.

"I understand what you mean, my darling, and I do appreciate your concern for my well-being. But, sweetheart, we are soldiers. We are meant to fight this war, not avoid it. The very future of our country is at stake. We take pride in battle to defend the American flag. It is the very essence of who we are."

He looked at her frankly.

"And, if I may wallow in a bit of self-indulgence, experience in battle is the fastest way to promotion. That's how generals build reputations, as long as they win, of course. I can't win if I can't fight. I just don't want to see another battle pass me by. I hope that doesn't sound too callous."

John picked up a cup of coffee in front of him and took a drink. Then he added one more thought.

"Perhaps my concerns are unnecessary. We shall see."

* * *

John and Kate's time together passed all too quickly. During the week, they spoke more of their plans to marry, how they would, at last, reveal their secret relationship, and they spoke of all those things people in love speak about.

They spent John's last night in Philadelphia together in the little cabin deep in the forest behind their favorite tavern. The next morning, after a romantic breakfast, John drove her in his carriage back to Eden Hall. She leaned over to kiss him goodbye.

"Please come back soon, my darling. As soon as you can. Even one day apart from you is too long."

"I promise, my love," John said earnestly. "I will be back as soon as I can. You can count on it."

CHAPTER THIRTY-ONE

Fredericksburg, Virginia
April–May 1863

From the time he had assumed command of the Army of the Potomac, General Hooker had been making detailed plans to, once and for all, defeat Robert E. Lee's Confederates. He was not a humble man.

"My plans are perfect," he said to a group of officers. "May God have mercy on General Lee, for I will have none."[254]

But it wasn't until late April that he was able to make a move. Mother Nature and the mud-clogged roads had seen to that. When Hooker put his plans into action, John, to his dismay, saw that his fears of being left out of the main fight were being realized.

Fredericksburg was, once again, the center of the strategy. Hooker planned to attack the enemy from the rear with most of his Army. He figured he could take the rebels by sending the main force north along the Rappahannock River to circle behind the Confederates. The commander needed a comparatively smaller force to head south and make a so-called demonstration so as to act as a decoy. Reynolds was disappointed to learn that was to be the mission for his First Corps, along with two other corps, the Third and the Sixth. "The object of this demonstration," the orders directed, "is to draw the enemy's force in that direction. While apparently endeavoring to conceal their train, they will let just enough be seen to betray the movement."[255] In other words, Reynolds was to let the enemy see his supply wagons and other movement of his troops, but not too much.

John did as he was ordered, but being left out of the main event once again put him in a foul mood. He was further annoyed because the three corps, with their combined mission, were under the command of yet another general, John Sedgwick. As a corps commander, Reynolds normally would report directly to the Army commander. Sedgwick's presence meant, yet again, an additional layer in the chain of command.

"Well, so much for my opportunity to act independently," John groused to himself.

Grumpy as he was, Reynolds lost patience with nearly everything and everyone. He was not prone to outbursts or profanity, but when his chief engineer fell behind in laying down pontoon bridges so the troops could cross the river, Reynolds let his irritability show. He had known the officer for a long time. They had fought in Mexico together. But, making a bad situation worse when the engineer stumbled up to him a few hours before midnight, the man was visibly drunk.

"Hurrah, Josh!" the engineer shouted, slurring his words and using John's West Point nickname. "Hurrah for here and Buena Vista!"[256]

"Goddamn it!" John spit out the words. "You are drunk, sir! What the hell do you think you are doing!"

Reynolds went on in that vein for several minutes, berating the engineer, stomping back and forth as he did, using language as blue as his aides had ever heard him say. He was so vocal about it, one of his nearby staff officers leaned over to speak quietly to another aide.

"The general swears pretty hard when things do not go to suit him," he whispered.

It didn't help John's mood when Confederate snipers across the river opened fire on his position. Reynolds had his troops hunker down and wait until morning to retaliate. His confrontation with the chief engineer resumed just after sunup. Now the engineer was in as foul a mood as John in the foggy morning.

"Where are the infantrymen, the riflemen, sharpshooters, or whatever?" he demanded. "I've needed them to protect my men laying the bridges! The rebs are taking potshots at them! They are sitting ducks out there!"

"I'm waiting for the fog to lift, General." Reynolds sat curtly. "Then I can determine how many of the enemy are out there, and I will respond in kind."

The engineer was not satisfied.

"Sir," he said angrily. "I reckon there are no more than fifty rebs over there. You have fifteen thousand men, for God's sake, General!"[257]

Moments later, the fog began to thin, and Reynolds could see where the gunfire was coming from. He ordered two regiments to cross the river on a completed bridge and attack, while the engineer paced impatiently nearby. The regimental troops moved quickly and efficiently. Dodging the Confederate snipers, they managed to chase the enemy out of their foxholes, capturing about ninety prisoners. Clearly, there were far more in place than the chief engineer had estimated. Sixty Union soldiers were lost in the skirmish. When it was over, Reynolds sent a message to Sedgwick. He was still angry at his engineer and let it show in what he wrote.

"The engineers say they will have the bridges in order in one hour, which means two."[258]

The engineer, splitting hairs in a later report, petulantly said five bridges were up in an hour and forty-five minutes, not two! Nevertheless, the ability to send fifty-five thousand men of the three corps across the Rappahannock came too late to be of any real use.

The element of deception was gone. As he carefully studied what little he could see of his enemy across the river, Reynolds began to suspect some grave trouble was developing. He fired off a telegraph message to General Hooker.

"The enemy's formation, as near as I can see, is in the hollow between the Bowling Green road and the range of heights... just opposite our bridges," he wrote. "Their position and formation threaten our bridgeheads. This is either bravado, in order to get up troops from Richmond, or they are really in force."

To John, the Confederates were behaving very suspiciously.

"They have never shown their troops in this way before. It may be that the artillery is simply horses arranged to look like teams."

Reynolds was getting very concerned, not for his troops, but for Hooker and the rest of the Army of the Potomac farther up the river, nearer to Fredericksburg. He sent another message to Hooker.

"I think that movements indicate that they are passing troops up to our right; that is, they are massing, and then moving the troops up the Valley beyond on the shortest line to Fredericksburg and above. The railroad seems to be busy to-day."

Almost immediately, Reynolds received a return message from Hooker's chief of staff, Daniel Butterfield.

"General Reynolds: What did the locomotives draw? Could it be transportation trains? Butterfield, Major General."

Reynolds answered.

"General Butterfield: The trains they ran were passenger and platform cars."[259]

Robert E. Lee had not at all been fooled by the feint maneuver and had left a relatively thin force to fight Reynolds and the other corps. The rest of Lee's troops, forty thousand strong, were sent to the main battle against Hooker.

* * *

The next morning John was still puzzled by what the Confederates were doing. He knew some of the rebel units were headed north, but he didn't know how many.

"Do you think it is a retreat, sir?" his aide-de-camp asked as they both gazed through heavy fog across the river, sipping coffee, just after dawn. The thick fog, drifting lazily off the Rappahannock, obscured most of the view of the other side of the river.

"No, I don't think so," Reynolds responded. "Damn it! We need better intelligence about what Lee is up to!"

In the fog, Reynolds felt he was literally groping in the dark. He had no idea about how many enemy troops were still facing him across the river. As he had indicated in his messages to General

Hooker last night, he suspected at least some Confederate units were pulling out to join the battle further up the river. Despite what he had reported, he guessed wrong and vastly underestimated the number that had left. He had the superior force now but did not know it.

"I think the proper view to take of affairs is this," he said to his aide. "If they have not detached more than one division from our front, then they are just keeping up appearances, trying to fool us into thinking they are moving out to delay Hooker, and, thereby, tempt us to make an attack on their fortified position. But, in reality, the Confederates may still be facing us in force."

"It is difficult to tell, sir. They are well hidden in this fog," the aide offered.

"Yes, they are, Colonel. But, captured deserters from the other side claim only a few units have departed. So, all that makes me think they hope to destroy us and strike over our supply depot over the bridges. I just wish we had a more definite sense of what is happening with General Hooker."[260]

Reynolds took a drink of his coffee and thought a moment.

"Colonel, send a message to headquarters asking them to inform us about what is happening on the front to our north."

"Yes, sir. Right away."

The colonel turned and disappeared into John's command tent to send the message.

Reynolds was not the only one frustrated by the lack of information regarding the enemy. All day long, messages flew back and forth by telegraph and by horse and rider among officers and troops at several levels trying to ascertain the strength and movement of Lee's Southern Army. Many of their observations were tentative at best.

> May 1, 1863. The enemy appear to remain in their position, and, as far as we can learn, have not changed...The fog is so thick that we can do little.

May 1, 1863. 10:10 a.m.—Wagon train moving up toward our right. There appears to be much artillery, many pieces with 8 horses.

May 1, 1863. 10:25 a.m.—A column of enemy's infantry, artillery, and wagons, extending whole length of ridge...The force is apparently heavy.

May 1, 1863. 11:00 a.m.—The enemy's direction is northwest...It is very hazy. We can only see the glittering of bayonets and wagon tops.

May 1, 1863. 12:30 p.m.—Enemy's battery on the crest of the hill in our front remains the same as yesterday...It is my belief that their infantry force is not as large as yesterday.

An unreliable telegraph and misunderstood messages added to the uncertainly and confusion.

May 1, 1863. 9:25 a.m. To General Gibbon—I have received a dispatch from the general, directing you to cross at Banks' Ford tomorrow at 9 am. This dispatch is dated May 1. I have strong reason to apprehend that it was intended that you should cross today at 9am. Very respectfully, Danl. Butterfield.

May 1, 1863. 4:00 pm. To Major-General Hooker: Sedgwick and Reynolds remain quiet. They consider that to attack before you have accomplished some success...might fail to dislodge the enemy...They are anxious to hear from you. I allow nothing to go to Washington and say nothing myself. Danl. Butterfield—Major General.

May 1, 1863. 8:45 pm. To Major-General Butterfield—You are mistaken in supposing I made an attack…I don't know what you mean by talking of going to Washington—Joseph Hooker, Major-General.

May 1, 1863. To Major General Sedgwick—Nothing had been said to General Hooker of anybody or anything going to Washington except telegrams. The dispatches have evidently been mutilated or misinterpreted.—Danl. Butterfield.

May 1, 1863. 8:45 p.m. To Major General Butterfield—The telegram for Sedgwick's demonstration reached him too late. Order it in immediately—Joseph Hooker.

May 1, 1863. 8:45 pm. To General Hooker. My dispatches do not seem to have been understood. The utmost vigilance has been ordered from the start. Danl. Butterfield, Major General.

The high command in Washington was anxiously watching the developments. The president, Secretary of War Stanton, and General-in-Chief Halleck were not happy about the slow pace and miscommunication. Stanton, especially, was angry about officers saying too much about their situations and fired off a verbal rocket to Hooker.

Washington, DC. May 2, 1863. 11 a.m. Major General Hooker—We cannot control intelligence in relation to your movements while your generals write letters giving details. A letter from General Van Alen to a person not connected with the War Department describes your position as intrenched at Chancellorsville. Can't you give his sword something to do, so that he will have less time for the pen? Edwin M. Stanton.[261]

Hooker was having big problems. The enemy was on the move, but he had no idea how many or where, exactly, they were going. Washington power brokers were mad at him. Many of his generals, including John Reynolds, we're losing confidence in him. At about eight forty that night, Reynolds received a message from General Sedgwick's adjutant, saying, "If you are not too tired, the general would be pleased to have you ride up here."[262]

Clearly, Sedgwick had some things on his mind that he wanted to share with John. But he wanted to do it privately and certainly not by a telegraph message that would be read by far too many people. So, John saddled his horse and rode the mile or so over to Sedgwick's headquarters.

When Reynolds walked into the general's tent, Sedgwick was waiting for him with a glass of brandy. He handed it to John.

"I think you probably will appreciate this, General," Sedgwick said, "especially after the day we've had."

John accepted the glass gratefully.

"Sir, this is exactly the elixir I need. I thank you for your courtesy and generosity," John said.

Sedgwick raised his own glass in a gesture of a toast.

"Here's to a better day tomorrow."

"Hear, hear," John said.

They both sat down on folding canvas chairs. They were alone. No aides or other officers were in the tent, so they felt they could talk freely.

"I have grave concerns, John," Sedgwick began. "Our intelligence network is all but nonexistent. The enemy is outwitting us at just about every turn. But what worries me most is the chaos and confusion at Army command level. I am loath to say it, but this campaign seems to be too much for General Hooker."

Sedgwick took a drink of his brandy. He was a gruff-looking officer with wavy dark hair and piercing eyes. Like so many of his Army colleagues, he had a thick, bushy mustache and a coarse growth of graying beard that hung down two inches below his chin. Also, like so many of his fellow generals, he looked very tired. Worn. Fatigued.

John remained silent as he sipped his brandy. Then he looked at Sedgwick.

"I have to agree with you, General. Our reconnaissance has simply failed us. I am forced to admit, I believe I was fooled today by Lee and his chaps. Clever fellows, they are, I must say."

Reynolds paused again, reluctant to talk ill of a fellow general and, especially, of his commander. He took a deep breath and plunged on.

"I fear, however, our biggest problem at this point is General Hooker. His orders are contradictory and confusing. He is holding back when he should be fighting, or he is fighting when he should be evading. I have come to the conclusion our demonstrations at this end of the river have deceived the rebels not in the least. Lee, I now believe, has moved most of his force away from here to overwhelm Hooker further upstream. Why has not the general ordered us to begin a march to reinforce him?"

John took another drink of his brandy, building up a head of steam.

"What are we doing here? It is nothing but a holding action. The real battle is not here. It is up there," he said, pointing in the general direction of north. "I don't have to tell you, General, it is difficult to keep men motivated if they do not believe they have any real role to play. None of this makes much sense."

"I've never questioned Hooker's courage," Sedgwick said. "But I don't understand why he hasn't been more aggressive in this campaign. He is being much too timid. I fear for his career."

* * *

Regardless of Sedgwick's brandy-laced toast, the next day was no better, except that morning fog had not returned. At least the sun was shining. But, at dawn, Hooker was virtually surrounded by an overwhelming number of Southern troops near Chancellorsville, about ten miles west of Fredericksburg. The place was little more than a crossroads named for the family that lived there. In the overnight hours, Hooker sent an urgent message to his chief of staff.

> Chancellorsville, VA. May 2, 1863. 1:55
> a.m. Major-General Butterfield: Direct all of the
> bridges to be taken up at Franklin's crossing and
> below before daylight, and for Reynolds' corps
> to march at once, with pack train, to report to
> headquarters. Joseph Hooker, Major-General,
> Commanding.[263]

He was finally calling Reynolds for help, or at least, for support. But the message got to Reynolds many hours later, which meant he no longer had the cover of darkness to move his troops, making them much more vulnerable to enemy artillery fire. In a fit of frustration over the delay, Chief of Staff Butterfield sent Reynolds what he apparently hoped would be a sympathetic and helpful message, suggesting the best route to take.

> May 2, 1863. Major-General Reynolds—
> Under present circumstances the shortest line
> would seem to be the one, but you must con-
> sider whether the fire your troops would receive
> from the enemy's artillery while passing along the
> River road…time is everything. It is one of the
> most unfortunate that has occurred that the gen-
> eral's orders, dated at 1:55 am, Chancellorsville,
> should not have reached here until 4:55.

Butterfield said the message had been delayed because its bearer had lost his way. That he was severely vexed was unmistakable in the chief of staff's last line. His respect for Reynolds was evident in his signature.

> If you were now with the general, I think
> there would be no doubt as to the result of the
> operations of today. Yours, truly and unoffi-
> cially, Danl. Butterfield, Major-General, Chief of
> Staff.[264]

Miscommunications, the faulty intelligence, and the weather all contributed to lack of effective warfare in this battle by Union troops. So did the so-called deserters from the rebel side. They turned out to be Confederate agents whose role was to deliver disinformation to the Union side. They had fooled John Reynolds. He wanted to even the score.

He ordered the units in his corps recover the bridges they had placed across the surface of the river and head north as soon as they did. Reynolds had his infantry and artillery units lay down a field of fire to cover the engineers dismantling the bridges. It was risky business because Confederates also kept firing down at them from the heights lining the river.

One of his divisions had been across the water, trying to find the enemy. Now they were hurrying back across a bridge not yet dismantled.

"Move it! Move it!" Reynolds shouted at them from the riverbank as the troops scrambled on the rocking, swaying pontoons. The vibrations of hundreds of running feet and the buffeting of the bridge by the swift flowing river made it difficult for the men to maintain their balance.

The noise of the gunfire from both sides was deafening. Confederate cannonballs crashed into the river all around the retreating Union soldiers, splashing them with heavy sprays of water. Rifle shot pinged off the pontoons and metal bridge supports. Several found their mark, and some of the blue-coated soldiers screamed as they plunged, bleeding, into the river, their cries of pain suddenly cut off as they sank beneath the water, which was turning a muddy red.

"Come on, men!" John shouted. "Let's go! Let's go!"

Suddenly he heard the distinctive boom of a large cannon hidden among the trees on the Confederate side. Instinctively, he turned toward the sound. What he saw was a rare sight. A solid black cannonball emerged from the tops of the trees and arched gracefully over the river toward the bridge. John was mesmerized by its flight. It was not often anyone could follow the trajectory of a shell shot from a cannon.

He quickly calculated where the cannonball would land and was horrified to see that it would smash down directly on top of a Pennsylvania regiment in the middle of the bridge.

"Look out!" he cried, too late, to the men.

The cannonball exploded into a great ball of flame as it slammed thunderously into the men. The force of the blast was overpowering. Bodies and parts of bodies flew everywhere. The shredded arm of a soldier landed at John's feet. Twenty men died instantly. Several others were severely wounded. The rest of the division turned around and ran back to the Confederate side of the river.

Reynolds was momentarily frozen in place, stunned by what he had seen. Gritting his teeth and with fire in his eyes, he jumped on his horse and rode quickly a few hundred yards upriver where he had earlier placed an artillery battery.

John hopped off the horse even before it had fully come to a stop.

"Captain!" he called to the young man in charge of the battery.

"Yes, sir!" the officer said, running up to Reynolds and saluting him.

"Did you see what the rebs just did?" John asked grimly.

"Yes, sir, I did. I sure did."

"Captain, I want you to put your battery into position and target that Confederate artillery unit and fire like you have never fired before! I want you to silence that gun! Can you do that for me, Captain?"

The officer did not hesitate a second.

"Yes, sir! I can do that, sir!"

The captain turned and sprinted over to his battery and began to shout out orders to the ten men in his artillery unit. In less than two minutes, they had the cannon turned, aimed, and loaded. John watched as the captain shouted his command.

"Ready! Fire!"

The cannon spit out a massive jet of orange-red flame and smoke. A cannonball flew through the middle of the inferno, raced over the river and into the grove of trees on the other side of the river.

It landed a few yards short of its intended target. Without breaking stride, the captain ordered an adjustment on the aim.

In just a couple of minutes, one of his men had cleaned out the barrel of the cannon, making sure any embers inside from the previous shot were extinguished. Another soldier loaded a cartridge, a burlap bag full of gunpowder. A third soldier picked up a forty-pound cannonball and stuffed it down the barrel. Yet another quickly set the friction primer into the small vent hole atop the cannon. Finally, one of the troops attached a lanyard to the primer. He held the loose end of the cord, took a few steps away from the cannon, and waited for the captain's order.

"Ready! Fire!"

The soldier yanked on the lanyard. Another thunderous explosion echoed through the trees as the second cannonball sailed across the river and found its target. A loud crash and a mighty boom came back across the water. A large cloud of dense smoke floated up through the trees. After that, silence. The enemy's battery had been knocked out.

"Good work, Captain," General Reynolds said. "Keep firing. Silence those other rebel guns!"

"Yes, sir!" The captain smiled, pleased with his unit's performance and even more pleased with the recognition by a major general.

No longer menaced by big Confederate guns, John got his beleaguered division back across the river and finally headed north to help Hooker and, perhaps, finally get into a real fight.

* * *

Relocating a full-size corps of troops, consisting of many thousands of men, was no easy matter. General Reynolds and his troops faced a twenty-three-mile march north and west in order to join General Hooker. The day was exceedingly warm by the time they reached Banks' Ford, a crossing on the Rappahannock that John hoped to use as a shortcut to Hooker's position.

"There is no bridge there, sorry to report, sir."

Reynolds had sent scouts ahead to reconnoiter the crossing. They had just returned with the bad news.

"Can we cross anyway?" Reynolds asked. "Is the river shallow enough there?"

"No, sir, 'fraid not. The water is quite deep, and the river is running very fast."

"Damn!" John cursed under his breath.

He and his adjutant got down off their horses to examine a map together. They found another crossing possibility at what was called the United States Ford, but it was at least six miles further upstream, northwest of Fredericksburg. His troops were already exhausted after the hot, dusty daylong march. *No matter*, John thought. *That's where we have to go.*

The leading column of the corps finally reached the bridge at United States Ford late in the afternoon. As his divisions and brigades crossed to the other side of the river and began to make camp, Reynolds rode off to report to General Hooker in person.

He barely had time to receive his orders when they heard a great hue and cry outside the headquarters tent. Looking to see what the commotion was all about, John saw troops from the Union Eleventh Corps fleeing in panic. They had been caught completely off guard by Stonewall Jackson's men.

The Confederate general had led twenty-six thousand of his men on a fourteen-mile march around and behind the Union lines. Units of the Eleventh Corps were resting and making coffee when Jackson's troops burst through the trees in what one Union soldier called a "perfect whirlwind of men." Even deer in the woods were startled and frantically bounded though the camp,[265] creating a confused, running mob of animals and men.

"General," John said urgently over his shoulder. "Those troops are disgracefully retreating in the direction of the United States Ford!"[266]

Hooker and his staff rushed outside and tried to stem the tide of fleeing men. The officers fired their guns in the air and physically attempted to stop the frightened rabble of men.

"Stop! Damn it! Stop!" they yelled. "Face the enemy! Don't be cowards!"

All their efforts were to no avail. One officer was slugged and knocked to the ground by a soldier he tried to prevent from running. One of the aides, later, could barely speak above a whisper. He had shouted and screamed so loudly at the deserting soldiers. Asked what had happened, he responded, "That damned Eleventh Corps ran away with my voice!"[267]

Hooker, greatly alarmed by the rout, turned to Reynolds.

"I need every man you have, General, to hold Jackson off. I need them now!"

Reynolds quickly rode back to his camp to rouse his units, which were just settling down after the long, difficult dawn-to-dusk march.

As the orders went out, thousands of weary Union soldiers, once again, picked up their rifles to form fighting lines. By now, the sun had set, and it was extremely difficult to see in the dark woods through which Stonewall's men were attacking. Reynolds's units also had trouble advancing on the roads because they were clogged with Eleventh Corps fugitives. One of John's brigades deployed across the road was forced to turn many of them back to the battle at gunpoint.[268] It was taking a great effort to keep the road clear so men of John's First Corps could move forward.

Reynolds waded into the frightened runaways from atop his big black stallion. He waved his sword, threatening the fleeing men.

"Get back, you cowards!" he shouted at them. "Turn around! You are not rabbits, Goddamn it! You are men! You are soldiers! Fight like men! Fight like soldiers! Turn and face the enemy, damn it! Turn!"

He saw one man had jumped into a ditch to slip past his security line and was making a break for the rear. Reynolds dug his heels into the side of his horse. The big animal sprang forward and thundered after the man. Closing on the fugitive from behind, John stuck out his foot and kicked him hard in the back. The man stumbled and fell violently onto the dusty, stony road. He rolled a couple of times and came to a stop, bleeding with cuts and scrapes from the fall. He looked up from his position on the ground to see John sitting in his saddle, towering over him. The general pointed a pistol at the soldier.

"You try to move, and I will shoot you right where you lay, soldier!" John growled. He turned to his adjutant who had just ridden up to see what was happening.

"Colonel, find the provost marshal," he ordered. "I want this coward arrested and court-martialed for desertion! Make an example of him!"

"Yes, sir," the adjutant replied.

"And find someone to keep watch over this man. I have to go be with the real men of this corps."

John gave the man a scowling, disgusted look and rode off. As he worked past the retreating soldiers, Reynolds was able to shore up the disintegrating Eleventh with his own Corps. By nine o'clock that night, the assault by Jackson's Southern troops petered out. Jackson, himself, rode ahead of his lines with a small group of men to get a sense of where Reynolds's units were located. As they returned from the woods in the darkness, Jackson was shot by his own men who had mistaken them for Union troops. General Stonewall Jackson died of his wounds about a week later.

* * *

Reynolds spent the next several days positioning his units supporting Hooker in fending off the advance by Jackson's troops, who remained relentless despite their commander being mortally wounded. It was a fierce fight. At one point, a Confederate shell crashed into a pillar on the porch of a house serving as Hooker's headquarters. Hooker, standing next to the pillar, was hurt when it split in two and slammed into his head and body.[269] He continued to command, but was in severe pain for several days.

The fight raged on through the morning. It was so furious, one soldier called it "the most terrible battle ever witnessed on earth."[270] Hooker's chief of staff, Daniel Butterfield, even found it necessary to inform the president with the following message.

Headquarters Army of the Potomac, May 3,
1863 1:30 p.m.

His Excellency Abraham Lincoln, President
of the United States—From all reports yet col-
lected, the battle has been most fierce and terrible. Loss heavy on both sides. General Hooker
slightly, but not severely, wounded. He has preferred thus far that nothing should be reported,
and does not know of this, but I cannot refrain
from saying this much to you. Daniel Butterfield,
Major General.[271]

As the battle developed, Hooker ordered Reynolds to place his
corps to the far right of the Union line facing the Confederates. To
his immediate left was his old friend, General George Meade, with
his Fifth Corps. Together their troops were spread over several miles
of the right side of the front in a very strong battle line. The problem, however, was that they were too far from the center of the front,
which was the crucial position to take the enemy on directly.

"At this rate, George, we are never going to get into the fight,
the real fight," Reynolds complained as the two met at the junction
where their corps joined together.

"It's the luck of the field, John." Meade observed.

"I think it is time to change that luck," John said.

"What do you mean?"

"I mean we should both go talk to Hooker and convince him to
let us join the battle."

Meade thought about that a minute, then nodded his head.

"Let's go," he said.

Both generals left their executive officers in charge of their
individual corps and rode their horses to Hooker's command
headquarters.

After exchanging pleasantries with Hooker and inquiring after
his health, Meade got down to the matter of things. With Reynolds
watching, Meade made his appeal.

"General, Reynolds and I believe we can be of great assistance in overcoming the rebel threat in the center of the front. John, here, has forty cannons ready but doing nothing. We know that J. E. B. Stuart's men are crossing near to our position. We can hit him easily. Let us go in, General."

Hooker shook his head and winced in pain.

"No, General. That is not my plan. I need both you and Reynolds to protect my right flank. I have other units that can take care of the enemy on in the center and on the left. Your request is denied."

He looked sternly at Meade.

"And one more thing, General. I do not approve your sending one of your brigades into battle without authorization."

The day before, Meade had sent a brigade to support another unit which was taking heavy fire from the Confederates. He did it on his own accord, without asking permission.

"Do not let that happen again," Hooker said bluntly as he plopped down in a chair, clearly in misery from his pain.

Meade and Reynolds looked at each other in exasperation.

"Begging your pardon, sir," Reynolds said, calmly. "Together, General Meade and I have thirty-seven thousand men we can bring to bear on the enemy's front. Most of them are sitting idle, doing nothing. We can end this thing fairly quickly, we believe."

"Gentlemen," Hooker said, "you have my decision. More importantly, you have my orders. Hold down my right flank. Thank you, gentlemen."

Reynolds and Meade knew they had been summarily dismissed. Both left headquarters shaking their heads. Both were in ugly moods.

"We are on the defensive, by God, when we should be attacking!" Reynolds exclaimed as they rode side by side back to their commands.

"Not only on the defensive," Meade observed. "Hooker is actually ordering some of the brigades to pull back from the center. That is a retreat! I can't imagine General-in-Chief Halleck, Secretary of War Stanton, or even the president will put up with this much longer."

* * *

The next day, John tried again to convince Hooker to include the First and Fifth Corps in the battle. Again, he was rebuffed. Furious at being left out of the main event, Reynolds devised a plan that automatically might draw his corps into the fight.

"Orderly," he said to one of the young messenger soldiers. "Go find Colonel Roy Stone and tell him I wish to speak with him."

Stone was a fiery brigade commander whom he knew well. A Pennsylvanian, like John, Stone never backed down from a fight.

"Reporting as ordered, sir," Stone said, entering Reynolds's tent and standing at attention, giving Reynolds a salute. The general saluted back.

"At ease, Colonel. I have a mission for you."

"Yes, sir," the colonel said eagerly.

"I want you to take your brigade out on a reconnaissance mission. J. E. B. Stuart is out there somewhere. I want you to find out what he is up to and what his cavalry is doing."

Reynolds paused, thinking. He had to choose his next words very carefully.

"Now, remember, Colonel. You must try not to engage in an open confrontation with the enemy. This is a reconnaissance mission, after all. But, by all means, protect yourself if attacked. Do you hear me? Protect yourself. And if you get into real trouble, send word, and the corps will come to your aide."

John looked at the colonel with an expression he hoped the officer would interpret correctly, that his words had an unspoken, but deeper meaning.

"Do you, umm, understand?" he asked, almost winking one eye.

"Yes, sir. Clearly, sir."

John wasn't so sure the colonel did understand. But it was the best he could do.

"Very well, then, Colonel Stone. Be on your way and be careful out there."

"Yes, sir."

Reynolds was betting that Stone's fiery and aggressive temperament would result in enough conflict with the enemy that the rest of the corps would have to ride to his rescue.

An hour or so later, John heard gunfire from the general direction where he believed Stuart's cavalry was located. The shooting continued for a long while. He sent an aide out to see what was happening. Stone, indeed, had run into Confederate snipers and while taking them on realized they masked a much larger force, which was now on the attack.

That was just the news John wanted to hear. As he was issuing orders to his other commanders, getting ready to ride to Stone's assistance, he was astonished to see the colonel and his troops arriving back at camp.

"What happened?" asked Reynolds incredulously.

"Well, sir," Colonel Stone replied. "We made contact with the rebs and, well, sir, we were ready to fight it out, especially when they revealed their reinforcements. We would have stood toe to toe with them and, in that case, of course, would have held them off while the rest of the corps came to join the fun. But, then, sir, I remembered your orders. You know, the orders not to unnecessarily engage the enemy. So I broke it off and we came back here, just like you wanted, sir."[272]

Reynolds stood there dumbfounded. The colonel hadn't caught the message after all. He missed the entire nuance of John's order. He took a deep breath.

"Good for you, Colonel," he said, covering his disappointment. "You did well. Please go report your intelligence gathering to my chief of staff."

"Yes, sir," the Colonel saluted and headed off.

When Reynolds returned to his headquarters tent, his adjutant looked at him slyly.

"You know, sir, Stone could have very easily gotten into a fight."

Reynolds nodded, dejectedly.

"I wish to God he had!"[273]

* * *

With the battle going badly, General Hooker wanted advice about what to do next. So, he called his corps commanders together for a conference. Five of them, including Reynolds, gathered for the council of war. Two others were unable to attend because they were engaged in firefights.

They held their meeting in a tent some distance from the Chancellor house that had been serving as Hooker's headquarters. The Army commander and his staff had been forced to abandon the house when Confederate troops advanced too closely. It now stood in the no-man's land between the two enemies and was furiously burning as a result of Confederate artillery. The woods directly behind the house were burning, as well. Wounded Union soldiers who had been placed among the trees for treatment were trapped. It was an awful sight. "Amid the crash of falling timber," one soldier recalled, "the roar of the billows of flame, and the lashing of the serpentlike tongues of the fiery element seizing upon its prey came the piteous groans of the wounded as they were being roasted in this furnace of fire. The wounded and the dying…were beyond the hope of rescue."[274]

In his temporary headquarters tent, Hooker was still suffering the effects of the wounds he had received earlier when the cannonball had smashed into the porch of the house. Through his pain, he addressed the five generals in front of him.

"Gentlemen, here is the situation," he said. "The enemy is putting up stiff resistance all along the front. I have ordered a limited withdrawal by some of the units."

Reynolds scowled. *Withdrawal, my ass*, he thought angrily. It's a retreat, if not a rout.

"Our right flank is holding firm," Hooker went on, "thanks to the First and Fifth Corps. General Reynolds, General Meade, you have my appreciation for that."

We are holding firm, Reynolds thought to himself, *because we don't have a damn thing to do*. He said nothing, but merely nodded, as did Meade. Neither man smiled.

"What I need from you officers," Hooker continued, "is your assessment of whether the Army should continue attempting to advance, or whether we should withdraw back across the Rappahannock. I am concerned by a number of matters, not the least of which is the steadiness of some of our troops as exhibited by uncalled for firing along some parts of the line."[275]

Reynolds was astonished, but not because Hooker was seeking advice from subordinates. An effective commander should take opinions of his command when considering courses of action. But here it appeared Hooker was attempting to place the blame for the lack of success on the troops and, by intimation, on the corps commanders when, Reynolds believed, it was Hooker's own faulty decision-making that had gotten them here.

All five general officers remained silent for several moments, each thinking carefully about what their response should be and precisely how to present it. Finally, General Meade spoke up.

"Sir," Meade said. "You are aware that several times I asked you for authorization to engage my troops, have them thrown forward, as it were, to confront the enemy, which was a scant eight hundred or so yards distant. Each time you declined my request. Sir, my troops are fully armed, certainly rested, and ready for action. Together, I believe with the other corps, especially General Reynolds's First Corps, we can gain the advantage over the rebels and turn the tide."

Hooker said nothing. He looked pale and appeared to be in significant pain from his wounds. He weakly stood up from his chair.

"General Meade," he said, "I appreciate your comments."

He looked at all of them.

"Gentlemen, I am going to excuse myself for a short while. I ask that you discuss this among yourselves and then take a vote. Advance? Or withdraw? I will await your decision."

With that, Hooker turned and headed out of the tent. All five generals quickly stood up and saluted their commander as he disappeared through the tent flap. When he was gone, the five officers sat down again and looked at each other. Reynolds was the first to speak.

"I agree with George's assessment," he said. "My belief is that we should advance rather than retreat…Excuse me, I mean withdraw. But, in as much as my corps has seen the least amount of action here at Chancellorsville, I will not press the issue. Whatever the group here decides is the best action, I will not argue."

John looked around the tent and spotted a couple of blankets on the floor in one corner.

"You gentlemen have heard my opinion. I have nothing more to say. As I have not slept in nearly two days, I ask that you please excuse me for a little rest."

He stood up, walked over to the blankets, covered himself with them as he lay down on the floor and closed his eyes. The other four officers stared at him for a few moments, then collectively shrugged and turned back to one another to continue the conversation.

In the end, the vote was three to two to advance and continue to engage the enemy. Reynolds, Meade, and one other corps commander wanted to go on fighting. The two who voted to withdraw commanded units that had been beaten up most by the Confederates. One of them observed that withdrawal would not be fatal for the country and that victory over the rebs at Chancellorsville was uncertain.[276]

After about an hour, Hooker returned to the tent. Hearing him enter, Reynolds awoke and returned to his seat.

"Well, gentlemen," Hooker said. "What is your opinion?"

"Sir," Meade replied. "Our vote is to advance, by three to two. We can take them, sir. The Confederates. We can take them."

Hooker said nothing for a very long time. He looked at each general individually, then sat looking down at the floor for several moments. The sounds of rifle and artillery fire could be heard in the distance outside the tent. No one spoke.

Finally, Hooker looked up. He had an unruly shock of dark hair, long sideburns, but unlike most of his colleagues, he had no long beard. He was clean-shaven. His eyes were red sockets in a pasty-looking face. His wounds were clearly taking their toll on him.

"Gentlemen," he said in a soft, quiet voice. "We shall withdraw. Please return to your commands and prepare for crossing back to the other side of the Rappahannock. I appreciate your input."

The five generals sat still, unmoving. Reynolds was stunned. Hooker had asked for their opinion but had overruled them! The men shook themselves from their stupor as they stood up and saluted Hooker. Reynolds was livid. On the way out, he said something to Meade that bordered on insubordination.

"What was the use of calling us together at this time of night when he intended to retreat anyhow?"[277]

Throughout the night in a driving rain and into the next day during, Reynolds, his First Corps, and the rest of the Army of the Potomac retreated back across the Rappahannock River. John was beside himself with anger. An officer who visited him in his head-quarters tent remarked that the general "was the picture of woe and disgust and said plainly that we had been badly out-generaled and whipped by half our number."[278]

John's ugly mood was reflected in bitter letters he wrote to his family and to Kate.

"We did not affect much more by our crossing," he said, "than to be slaughtered and to slaughter the rebels."[279]

He could not understand how a battle which had started out so brilliantly had ended with such a mortifying defeat. He was not the only one so confounded. Another soldier, a lowly private who had a talent for prose, said, "Thus ended the campaign which Hooker opened as with a thunderbolt from the hand of Mars and ended as impotently as an infant who has not learned to grasp its rattle."[280]

The Union suffered more than seventeen thousand casualties at Chancellorsville. The Confederates endured nearly thirteen thousand.[281]

CHAPTER THIRTY-TWO

Fredericksburg, Virginia
May 1863

Both armies, North and South, were so spent after Chancellorsville, no battle action of any real significance took place for the next month. But, idle hands, as it is said, are the devil's workshop, and the devil loves gossip. During the month of May 1863, rumors flew thick and heavy through the Union command as they rested near Fredericksburg. John was in the middle of most of it.

The most often repeated and titillating rumor was that Hooker was on his way out and Reynolds was on his way in. It was no surprise that such gossip would surface since so many of the senior officers, Reynolds included, were disgusted with Hooker's performance. Even President Lincoln was aware of the discord. He bluntly mentioned it in a message he sent to Hooker.

> Executive Mansion, Washington, DC, May 14, 1863—Major-General Hooker, Commanding: My Dear Sir: I must tell you that I have some painful intimations that some of your corps and division commanders are not giving you their entire confidence. This would be ruinous, if true, and you should therefore, first of

all ascertain the real facts beyond all possibility of doubt. Yours, truly, A. Lincoln.[282]

Hooker went on a tear, trying to find out who was spreading the rumors, blaming Reynolds and Meade for being behind them. He had heard from sources outside the military how unhappy the two generals were with him. No doubt he had been told of John's remark about being "out-generaled." Meade had written smoldering letters to his wife telling her such things as, "All I can say is that Hooker has disappointed the Army and myself in failing to show the nerve and coup d'oeil at the critical moment."[283]

In another, Meade unknowingly confirmed what President Lincoln had said to Hooker.

"I think these last operations have shaken the confidence of the Army in Hooker's judgment, particularly among the superior officers,"[284] he wrote.

Matters came to a head when Hooker summoned Meade to his headquarters, angry about a newspaper article reporting that corps commanders had opposed his decision to withdraw from Chancellorsville. It was a very tense conversation. When it was over, Meade stormed into Reynolds's quarters to tell him about it.

"General Hooker had the audacity," Meade said to John, "that you and I actually encouraged him to withdraw."

"That's a lie!" John exclaimed.

"That's what I told him. Well, not in so many words. I was stunned by what he said, and I told him he was twisting my words."

"How so?"

"Well, remember that night we all met when Hooker wanted our advice about advancing or withdrawing?"

"Of course."

"You will recall I told him it was impracticable to withdraw, meaning therefore I favored an advance. Somehow, John, somehow, he got it into his head that because he believed a withdrawal was indeed perfectly practicable, he did not consider my opinion to be in favor of an advance!"

"That makes no sense."

"Of course, it doesn't. I told him that was a very ingenious way of stating what I had said. I told him my opinion was clear and emphatic for an advance. So was yours, for that matter."

"How did he respond to that?" Reynolds asked.

"Well, he reiterated his opinion and said he would proclaim it. I tell you, John, that got my blood boiling! I told him I would deny it and would call on anyone who was there to testify as to whether he or I was right. Are you with me on that, John?"[285]

"You know I am, George. You were decidedly in favor of an advance in the direction of Fredericksburg at daylight the next morning. I simply said, as my corps was the only one which had not been engaged, I would not urge my opinion, but, remember, I agreed with you then.[286] I agree with you now. What Hooker is saying should not stand."

Meade nodded and took a deep breath. Then he looked up at John.

"I am sorry to tell you I am at open war with Hooker,"[287] he said.

* * *

Toward the end of the month, the two armies awoke from their slumber. Robert E. Lee's massive Confederate Army of Northern Virginia was beginning to move, like a great glacier, away from Chancellorsville and Fredericksburg to the north and west toward Pennsylvania. General John Reynolds received orders to get his corps ready to move, along with the entire Union Army of the Potomac. Reynolds, himself, however, received odd orders to report to Henry Halleck, the general-in-chief in Washington who had command over all the various Union armies. After sailing forty miles up the Potomac to Washington, Reynolds arrived at Halleck's headquarters.

"General Reynolds reporting as ordered to General Halleck," John said as he stood at attention in front of Halleck's adjutant.

"It is good to see you, General," the adjutant said, smiling. "General Halleck is expecting you."

The adjutant ushered John into Halleck's inner office where he found the general-in-chief sitting behind a large oak desk.

"Reporting as ordered, sir," John said, saluting his superior officer.

Halleck saluted back. At forty-eight years old, he was known as a scholarly lawyer and had been given the not always kind nickname of Old Brains. His strong points included military administration, logistics, and insider politics. He was less proficient at leading troops in the field. In other words, he was near perfect for the job in the heady world of Washington, DC. Halleck was clean-shaven, had thinning salt-and-pepper hair, a large forehead, smiled little, and had eyes that always seemed to be staring at something.

"At ease, General. Please sit down. Have a seat. Would you like coffee or, perhaps, tea?"

"Coffee would be fine, thank you, General."

"Adjutant," Halleck said to his aide, "will you please see that General Reynolds gets a cup of coffee? I'd like a cup of tea while you are at it, if you please."

"Yes, sir. Right away, sir," said the adjutant. He strode from the office, closing the door behind him.

"Well, John, it looks as though you had quite a go of it down there in Chancellorsville."

"Yes, sir, we did," John replied. "I would have wished for a better result, however."

Halleck cleared his throat.

"Yes, well, we all do. General Hooker seemed a little unsure of himself, wouldn't you agree?"

"That's really not for me to say," John replied diplomatically.

"Oh, sure it is, General. This is just between us chickens. Your reputation as a strategic thinker precedes you. Surely you have an opinion."

Just then there was a light knock on the door.

"Enter!" Halleck commanded.

A young orderly walked in carrying a tray supporting two pots, one filled with coffee, the other with tea. The tray also contained containers of sugar and cream. The orderly set the tray down on a side table and turned to Halleck.

"Will there be anything else, sir?"

"No, thank you, soldier. You may be dismissed."

"Yes, sir," the orderly said. He saluted the general and left the room, making sure to close the door as he did.

"Let's have something to drink, John," Halleck said.

They both stood and stepped to the side table. Each prepared his beverage, and they retook their seats.

"So, where were we?" Halleck asked, raising the cup to his lips. "Oh, yes, you were going to give me a critique of General Hooker."

"With all due respect, General, it is not my place to critique a commanding officer."

"But…," Halleck began.

"But," Reynolds continued, "I will say we could have been more aggressive in pursuing the enemy. I also believe my corps could have been put to better use."

Reynolds paused, taking a sip of his coffee. Halleck could see he was contemplating something else.

"Is there something else you'd like to say, John?"

"Permission to speak freely, sir?"

"Of course."

"You may have heard that General Hooker is claiming that General Meade and I encouraged him to withdraw from Chancellorsville. That is simply not the case, General. The night the corps commanders all met with him, Meade argued that the better alternative was to advance, and I agreed with him. So did one other corps commander. General Hooker's decision to withdraw was his alone and against the advice of the majority of his corps commanders."

Halleck looked at Reynolds with his wide staring eyes for a moment.

"Are you saying that Hooker is looking for a scapegoat?" he asked quietly.

"Those are your words, General, not mine. But I would not argue with you."

Halleck finished his tea with a loud slurp and set the teacup down in its saucer with a soft chink.

"Well, that's all very interesting, John. And that brings me to the reason I called you here."

"Yes, sir?"

"You have an appointment tomorrow morning at the White House. The president wants to see you."

* * *

The next morning. John was admitted to a waiting area outside President Lincoln's ornate office in the White House. He now knew, he believed, what this was all about. He was going to be offered, or ordered, to take the job of commanding the Army of the Potomac. This meant the rumors were true. Hooker was on his way out.

That wasn't so surprising to John. He knew, as did just about everyone in the chain of command, that the president was very displeased with Hooker. He was slightly surprised, however, that the president would want John Reynolds. After all, he was not the most senior general in the Army of the Potomac. Then, there were the politics.

Lincoln, of course, was a Republican. John's family had been lifelong Democrats. One of his father's closest friends had been former president James Buchanan who preceded Lincoln at the White House. It was Buchanan who had helped John get an appointment to West Point years ago. Buchanan, a Democrat, had been widely criticized for his ineffective presidency. His attitude toward the question of slavery, a critical issue for Lincoln, was summed up in Buchanan's inaugural address when he said it is "happily, a matter of but little practical importance."[288] Though he hated the mix of politics with the military, Reynolds was well aware of the political ramifications regarding what he believed what was about to happen.

But he knew this would be an enormous opportunity. He also realized it would be a major burden. He would have command over hundreds of thousands of soldiers. He would be responsible for waging an extraordinarily complex war that could decide the very fate of the nation. He wished Kate could have been there with him to share his thoughts.

However, at nearly forty-three years old, Reynolds was self-confident enough to know that he could do the job and, he believed, do it well. He had proven himself, he thought, time and again with the Indian Wars, the Mexican-American War, his stint as commandant of cadets at West Point and, so far, during this Civil War.

If he got the promotion, there would be no one in the Army higher in authority, other than General Halleck. There were Secretary of War Stanton and President Lincoln, of course. But John said to himself, *I will have to make it clear that as commander of the Army of the Potomac, I can broke no civilian interference. I will not tolerate any political pressure, that much is certain.*

John's train of thought was interrupted when a side door opened and out stepped a serious-looking man in a somber-looking black suit. He walked directly up to Reynolds.

"The president will see you now, General" was all the man said.

The man led John to the open door and stepped aside to let him enter the president's office. When John passed through, the man leaned over to grab the doorknob and quietly closed the door, leaving General Reynolds alone with the president of the United States.

* * *

"General Reynolds," President Lincoln said. "It is so good of you to take the time to come and see me."

"It is entirely my honor, Mr. President," John said. "Thank you for having me here."

The president was standing in front of his massive cherry wood desk, thus removing any physical or psychological barriers between two men. As John walked up to him, Lincoln stretched out his hand to give him a handshake. Reynolds was surprised by the firmness of the president's grip. It must be from all those years splitting rails for fences, John thought.

He was also surprised by the president's voice. It was high-pitched and reedy, not at all presidential sounding. But that was about the only thing about Lincoln that John thought was not presidential. Lincoln stood tall and straight. He spoke in a measured cadence, as if weighing every word. His beard had grown a little scraggily, stretching from one ear, down his face, across his chin, and up to the other ear. He had no mustache.

Looking closely at him, Reynolds realized the president looked very weary, as if weighed down by a ton of bricks. *But of course, he is,* John said to himself. This war would be a dreadful encumbrance for any president.

"Please, let's sit here on the sofa, General, so we can be comfortable."

John did as the president suggested, thinking this is going to be a long conversation.

The president began with some pleasantries, asking Reynolds about his family, his home, and other mundane details. Then he got down to business.

"General, let's be frank," Lincoln said. "I want your candid opinion about General Hooker. Please remember, this conversation is confidential, between you and me. But I very much need an honest assessment of the man. Without being overly dramatic, the success of the war depends upon it."

Reynolds sat still for a moment, thinking, *That's quite an opening salvo.* Then he took a deep breath and began.

"Mr. President, as you wish, I shall speak freely. I like Joe Hooker as man. And I am sure he has the best interests of the nation at heart. But, sir, I have lost confidence in him as a leader of men. I do not know what happened to him at Chancellorsville. His battle plan, at the beginning, was sound. But he seemed to lose his nerve, reluctant to put the soldiers he needed in the battle to win it. My own corps sat needlessly idle though most of that fight, despite my repeated overtures, along with General Meade, to send us in."

"Did you agree with his decision to withdraw?" the president asked.

"No, sir. Not at all, despite what General Hooker says now. He had polled five of his generals, including Meade and myself, about what we thought should be the most advantageous move, withdraw or advance. The vote was three to two to advance. As you know, sir, General Hooker ignored our advice. I truly believe had he been more aggressive, and had he better utilized his troops, especially my First Crops and Meade's Fifth Corps, we would have had a better than fighting chance in that battle."

Lincoln thought for a moment about John's response.

"Do you believe your loss of confidence, as you put it, in General Hooker is the feeling of other senior officers?"

"Yes, sir, I do. There has been a great deal of talk about that."

Lincoln remained quiet again for a few moments. Then he looked at Reynolds squarely in his eyes.

"Tell me, General. Do you think I should replace General Hooker?"

"Mr. President, sir, that is a decision I believe only you can decide. I have no place to say one way or the other."

The president sighed deeply.

"Well, General, I guess I am not disposed to throw away a gun because it misfired once. Rather, I would pick the lock and try it again."[289]

John smiled slightly at the president's homespun homily but said nothing further. The President put his hands on his thighs, stood up, crossed his arms, and strolled around the office, coming to a stop in front of his desk, half sitting on it. He looked at John.

"Despite what I just said, there is too much at stake here to risk any more hesitation. General, I know your reputation. I have seen your record and have spoken to others about it. I must say, I am greatly impressed by your abilities and your performance in the field over the years. I also know you have the respect and admiration of the troops, officers and enlisted alike. General Reynolds, I would like for you to be my Commander of the Army of the Potomac. Would you please give me the pleasure of accepting my offer?"

John stood up.

"Mr. President, words cannot express how honored I am that you have asked. May I just inquire, is this an offer or an order?"

"It is an offer, General. I do not want a man in this job that has to be ordered to do it."

Now it was John's turn to take a few steps around the office, thinking very deeply. He stopped and turned to face Lincoln.

"Sir, you asked me to speak candidly, so I will continue to do so. If you know my record, sir, then you must know how I feel about how to wage war."

"Yes, General, I do. That's why I am offering you the job."

"What I mean, sir, is that I firmly believe war must be fought by those who are or have been in the field. Strategy, tactics, and other military decisions must be made by military men, by the generals, and other superior officers who have tasted war, who know war. Speaking frankly, sir, it has been my experience than when civilians, especially civilians with political agendas, insert themselves into strategic decision-making, well, sir, that's when things go wrong. That's when battles are lost. Politics must not be allowed to interfere with the deadly serious business of waging war."

John paused for a moment. The president did not move a muscle.

"Sir, I am as loyal to the Union as anyone you will find. I understand that we are at a crossroads in this nation and that we must prevail. We must not, we cannot, lose this war. But, sir, I must ask, if I accept your offer, will you assure me that I will have complete independence about how to defeat the enemy? Can you assure me that I will have no interference from Congress, the secretary of war, and, if you beg my pardon, from you, yourself, sir?"

Lincoln stared at the general that for John seemed like a very long time. Finally, he shook his head slightly, but sadly.

"No, General. I cannot assure you of that. As I said, there is far too much at stake. While I respect what you say, there is much more to waging war than just what transpires on the battlefield. I am sure you understand this North-South conflict is extremely complicated with a multitude of difficult issues. It may sound strange to some, but diplomacy is part of waging war. Dealmaking is part of waging war. And whether you like it or not, political and economic wrangling are part of waging war. You are absolutely correct. We cannot afford to lose this war, but you cannot win it in a vacuum. We must all work together in this. You. Me. The secretary of war.

Members of Congress. All of us. So, no, General, I cannot give you those assurances."

Reynolds shook his head in understanding.

"That being the case, Mr. President, while I shall forever be honored that you have offered me this opportunity, without the independence I described, I believe I could not do the job to your satisfaction. Therefore, I must, respectfully, turn down your offer."

"I am truly very sorry to hear that, General, but I greatly respect your integrity. Ironically, that integrity is exactly what makes you the man for the job. But I hear you, and I will not order you to accept the position. As I said, I don't need a man that doesn't want it. May I ask, General, do you have advice about who might share your integrity, your experience, and abilities?"

"Yes, I do, sir," John said almost without hesitation.

"And who might that be?" President Lincoln asked.

"General Meade, sir. General George Meade."

CHAPTER THIRTY-THREE

Fredericksburg, Virginia
June 1863

When John returned to Fredericksburg, he said nothing to anyone about where he had been or that he had been offered the top position in the Army. While he did not, and would not, command the Army of the Potomac, he found that he was temporarily in charge of a good chunk of it. General Hooker had put him in overall command of the Army's right wing, which consisted of his own First Corps, General Meade's Fifth Corps, and the Eleventh Corps, the unit that broke and ran in panic during the Battle of Chancellorsville.

Robert E. Lee's juggernaut of a Confederate Army was still rumbling northwest toward Pennsylvania, John's home state. Reynolds had orders to track the rebels and try to determine exactly where they were headed. He received those orders from General Hooker's chief of staff. It was the chief's message, but Reynolds believed it was Hooker's language, and it set him on edge, given the accusations the commanding general had made about him and Meade.

"It is desired particularly to guard against their getting in advance of us...and getting in between this army and Washington."

One sentence was especially vexing for Reynolds.

"You will also realize the important duties entrusted to you."[290]

Given that John had just left a private audience with the president of the United States who had such high praise for him, Reynolds did not need condescending reminders of his duties.

Whatever the Confederate forces were up to, they already had a week's head start. That meant a forced march for Reynolds and the First Corps to catch up. He pushed his men and he pushed hard. Departing on June 12, his troops covered twenty very difficult heat-drenched miles the first day. They marched another fourteen dusty exhausting miles the next day. By the time they reached Centreville, Reynolds's contingent of three corps had endured a road march of sixty-four exceedingly tough miles. The heat in this month of June was unbearable. Water was scarce, even in the few puddles along the way. Many of the troops staggered and fell along the line of march.

"Close up, men, close up!"[291] Reynolds and his officers reported over and over again. As persistent as he was that the forced march continue, no matter the conditions, Reynolds empathized with his men and the discomfort they were feeling. Whenever a halt in the march was ordered, the troops would know how long the break would be.

"Tell your troops," he sometimes instructed his division and brigade commanders, "they will have time to make coffee, if they so desire."

That meant the halt in the march would be for more than just a brief rest. The men would have time to build campfires and boil coffee. Reynolds also made sure there would be no unnecessary frivolous moving of the troops around once they made camp after dark. He and his staff would ride ahead each day to locate a proper bivouac location and to make sure it would have plenty of food and water when the troops arrived.

His concern and care for his troops did not go unnoticed. One captain said, "There was no confusion, no waste of time...we soldiers of the First Corps were thankful that our General not only had common sense, but sufficient humanity in his heart to use it. We started calling him Old Common Sense."[292]

In return, Reynolds demanded discipline. His punishment for disobeying orders and other serious infractions was harsh and swift.

"No man is allowed to fall out of ranks under any pretext," he told his officers, "not without a pass from his company commander, approved by his regimental surgeon." A division commander even oversaw the execution of one soldier who deserted his brigade during the march.[293]

* * *

John's command over the right wing of the Army of the Potomac ended when Hooker arrived in Centreville.

"John, thanks for your service," Hooker said. "I appreciate it, but now I would rather communicate directly with my corps commanders. That includes you, of course."

"Of course," John said curtly.

He hated giving up command, especially to Hooker, although he knew it had been temporary from the beginning. It lasted only four days. However, Hooker's vacillating decision-making continued when, just nine days later, he ordered Reynolds to take command of the left wing of the Army, which consisted, again, of his Fifth Corps, the Eleventh Corps, and, this time, the Third Corps.

Hooker was still groping around, trying to ascertain Robert E. Lee's strategy. To be honest, John was equally mystified. In a letter to his sisters, he confessed his confusion, telling them, "It is impossible to say where the enemy is with any certainty."[294] He was leaning toward the possibility, however, that Lee intended to invade Pennsylvania. As the hours wore on, the more convinced John became that was going to be the case. He met one of his generals, Abner Doubleday, at a crossing on the Potomac River to talk about the problem.

"I believe it is necessary to attack the enemy at once," he told Doubleday, "to prevent his plundering the whole state."

"Attack him with the entire left wing?" Doubleday inquired.

John thought for a moment, then replied with his typical confidence.

"I think if we could meet the enemy with the First Corps, there would be no doubt of the result."[295]

Hooker, on the other hand, remained befuddled despite getting a warning from his own intelligence chief two weeks ago that Lee "was ready to start a major offensive." This was not going to be a simple raid in or near Washington. It would, he said, "be a campaign of long marches and hard fighting in a part of the country where they would have no railroad or transportation."[296] That would eliminate Washington as a target.

Hooker ignored the report, convinced the rebels wanted to take the capital. At least, he wanted to keep his Army between the Confederates and Washington until he found out where the rebels were really heading. They were moving up the Shenandoah Valley, but their intent was still unclear.

Hooker proposed a number of strategies, none of which the higher command, including President Lincoln, liked. The relationship between Hooker and the administration became so rancorous, Lincoln finally had to act. On June 28, he fired General Joe Hooker and, taking Reynolds's advice, appointed General George Meade as the new commander of the Army of the Potomac.

When Reynolds learned of the appointment, he dressed in his formal uniform and paid his old friend a visit.

"Well, I have been tried and condemned without a hearing," Meade said only half jokingly, when John congratulated him for the promotion. "I suppose I will have to go to execution."

"George, this command has finally gone to the right man," Reynolds assured him. "You have my promise, my guarantee, that I will support you all that I can. Rely on that."

"That's kind of you to say. But, to tell the truth, I wish the position had gone to you. I consider you a friend, a brother, really. You not only deserve the command. You can handle it."

"So can you, George, no doubt. We have been in competition for so many years. I know you. You know me. We are both now where we are supposed to be. There is no need to compete any longer. Let's work on a plan together to bring the rebs to a final battle."

For more than two hours, the pair of generals, Reynolds and Meade, poured over maps and situation reports, mapping out a strategy to confront General Lee's Army.

"We can beat the bastards, George," Reynolds finally said. "I know we can."

They shook hands, and John left Meade's tent to return to his unit.

Major General John Fulton Reynolds had fewer than three days to live.

CHAPTER THIRTY-FOUR

Philadelphia
June 1863

At the end of June 1863 Philadelphia newspapers screamed with headlines of war.

THE INVASION!

HARRISBURG TO BE ATTACKED ABOVE AND BELOW!

AN ADVANCE UPON THE CITY! THE TROOPS IN POSITION!

A BATTLE IMPENDING! SKIRMISHING IN PROGRESS!

The paper reported an emotional and frantic appeal by the mayor of Philadelphia.

"The foot of the rebel is already at the Capital, and unless you arouse to instant attention, it may in a few days hence cross your own threshold."[297]

Pennsylvania's governor had issued a proclamation warning that the state was in grave danger. Kate Hewitt sat reading the newspaper with great alarm. She feared not so much for the city, although the battle was coming much too close to home for comfort. But she feared greatly for her betrothed, John Reynolds. She knew that he would be in the middle of this fight. *I must go to him*, she thought, knowing even then how foolish it would be to even try.

The newspaper featured lengthy articles about various battles, the movement of troops, the names of towns and cities attacked. Much of the reporting was hysterical in nature and based largely on speculation. Some of it, however, was factual and based on quotes from high-ranking officers and government officials. Reading it all, Kate felt that uncomfortable sense return that something terrible was about to happen.

She came across one article that mentioned Union forces were taking up positions around Emmitsburg, Maryland. It also mentioned that three Army corps there were under the command of General John Reynolds.

Emmitsburg, Kate thought. That's just over the border from Pennsylvania. She knew the Daughters of Charity had a home and church in that town. *How can I get there?* she wondered. Then she had an idea. Kate quickly gathered her things and went outside to hail a horse-drawn hansom cab. When one arrived, she climbed aboard and said, "The train station, please."

* * *

By now, it was no longer a mystery. Robert E. Lee was, indeed, invading Pennsylvania with his entire Army. The forced march among Union soldiers had continued, trying to catch up with the Confederates who kept moving steadily north and west.

The heat was no longer such a big problem for weary troops of both armies. But the rain was. Heavy thunderstorms had rolled though the Shenandoah Valley, once again turning roads into slippery mudslides, making matters difficult for the men, no matter whether they were wearing blue or gray.

Riding ahead of the three corps now under his control, wing commander Reynolds arrived in Emmitsburg around midday on June 29. As his troops marched through little town with drums playing and flags flying, they were cheered by the residents.[298] When the soldiers passed a community run by an order of the Daughters of Charity, they saw nuns kneeling along the side of the road, praying for their safety.[299] The community would soon play a significant role in the life of Kate Hewitt who, at about the same time, was visiting the Philadelphia's Broad Street train station a little more than a hundred miles to the east.

* * *

"Would you tell me, please, sir, if there is a train from here to Emmitsburg, Maryland," Kate said to the bespectacled man behind the ticket window. The ticket agent peered over the top of his glasses at a train schedule on the desk in front of him.

"It appears there is one, madam, but it departs at four thirty in the morning, arriving in Emmitsburg around ten."

"May I purchase a ticket, please?"

"One-way or round-trip, miss?"

"Round-trip, please. When is the return, may I ask?"

"Well, let's see."

The agent ran his finger down the list of departures and arrivals.

"It says here that there is a train departing Emmitsburg at four o'clock tomorrow afternoon, arriving here in Philadelphia a little after nine in the evening."

"That will be fine," Kate said, digging into her purse to find the money to pay the man. He took her payment and gave her the tickets. *It's a long way to go for such a short visit*, she thought ruefully. *Well, no matter, it is more than worth the trip.*

"You should be careful, madam," the agent said. "There is a war going on out there, you know."

"Yes, sir. I know. Thank you."

That night, back in her room, Kate could hardly sleep because she was so excited at the prospect of seeing John again. She knew this was a risky trip. But she thought, *I am the woman who went all the way to California by myself. Certainly, I should be able to make a simple trip like this without trouble, war or no war.* She soon fell asleep, her joy at the prospect of seeing John again overcoming any fear she might have felt.

Kate awoke just a few hours later, at three in the morning to get ready to leave. She had arranged with the hansom cab driver yesterday to pick her up, promising him a generous tip if he did. The man and his patient horse attached to the cab were waiting for her when she emerged outside. The horse's hooves echoed through the silent dark streets as they made their way to the train station. She got there in plenty of time and, before long, sat comfortably in the nearly empty passenger car as the train began to chug its way out of the station.

* * *

As Kate's train made its way through the Pennsylvania countryside, blue-gray smoke pouring out its great smokestack, its steam whistle wailing at every crossroad, its wheels click-clacking along the rails, John was on the move, too.

He went north from Emmitsburg a few miles, across the Pennsylvania border to set up his headquarters in a tavern just six miles from Gettysburg. The tavern was a modest two-story building. It contained a dining room, family sitting room, and a kitchen on the first floor. A ballroom and five bedrooms were upstairs.

Setting up his office in the large kitchen area,[300] John quickly went to work, reading reports from scouts and talking to local citizens, learning that two of Lee's divisions were also near Gettysburg several miles to the west of him.[301] He was closer to the enemy than the rest of the Potomac Army and knew a fight was near.

He was also getting intelligence now from his talented and reliable cavalry commander, General John Buford, whose troops, on their fast and highly trained horses, were keeping close watch on enemy movements. John immediately passed those reports on to Army headquarters.

"Buford sends reliable information that the enemy occupies Chambersburg in force, and that they are moving down from Cashtown,"[302] one message read. Reynolds fired off dispatches to his old friend and new boss George Meade to let him know what he had learned. Meade also reissued the earlier order by his predecessor, General Hooker, that Reynolds was to maintain command of the left wing of the Army, consisting of the First, Third, and Eleventh Corps.[303]

John and his staff kept up an efficient system of sifting through the messages and reports trying to piece together a clear picture of the enemy's intentions. Officers, aides, orderlies, and local citizens came and went with information and requests. Throughout it all, he maintained an equilibrium that impressed an officer from General Meade's staff who stopped by in the middle of his busy day.

"General, would you like some tea and crackers?" Reynolds asked the officer, pushing aside maps, papers, and other reports on his desk.

"Why, yes, General, that would be nice," the officer replied. "A very frugal repast, considering the work we may have to do tomorrow."

John chuckled.

"Frugal indeed, General. Frugal indeed."

Returning to his own headquarters, the officer was highly complimentary about Reynolds.

"I shall never forget," he said, "his calm, yet quiet dignity and true soldierly appearance as he courteously arose to receive me and, offering me a chair, asked whether I was alone, and which way I was going."[304]

John's calm, dignified nature was disrupted somewhat, however, shortly after noon. An orderly knocked on his office door.

"Enter," John said.

"Sir," the orderly said as he approached John's desk, "you have a visitor."

"Another one?" John replied, without looking up from the report he was reading. "Okay. Send him in."

The orderly hesitated.

"Ahh…it's not a him, sir. It's a her."

"A her?" John asked, now looking up from his papers.

"Yes, sir. A woman. A female, sir. And begging your pardon, sir, she's right pretty."

John was very puzzled for a moment. Then, he thought, no, it couldn't be.

"Well, send her in, Corporal."

"Yes, sir."

The orderly disappeared through the door. A moment later, Kate walked through it, smiling brightly.

"Hello, John," she said.

"Kate! My God! How...wha...what are you doing here?" he stammered.

"Why, I am here to visit the man who is in charge of everything around here. That's you, isn't it?"

John sat still behind his desk, stunned by the sight of her. Then, remembering his place, he quickly stood up, walked over to the door, and closed it tight so they were alone. Then, he walked over to Kate. He looked at her for a moment and took her in his arms. They embraced and kissed, a long, lingering, loving kiss.

Then, giving her a warm hug, John took her hand.

"Let's sit over here on the sofa," he said.

After they sat down, John's expression turned stern.

"You should not be here, Kate," he said. "It is much too dangerous for you here."

"Oh, fiddledeedee," Kate said lightly. "I read you were near... well, sort of near...and I wanted to see you."

She looked around his office with mischievous eyes.

"Besides, I don't see any enemy around here, do you?" She laughed.

"Kate, this is no laughing matter," John lectured. "We are at war. Right here! I don't like seeing you here."

Kate looked hurt, sticking out her bottom lip.

"You don't like seeing me?" she said with feigned annoyance.

"I don't mean it like that, darling. You should know that. What I mean is the danger here is real and I don't want anything to happen to you! How...how in the world did you get here, anyway?"

"Well, I took the train from Philadelphia to Emmitsburg and went straight to the Daughters of Charity community when I arrived. They thought that you and your men had moved up the road to this tavern. Nice place, by the way. Anyway, the sisters found a driver and a carriage to bring me here. My, we passed thousands of soldiers on the road. Are they all your men?"

John sighed in exasperation, frustrated by the peril Kate had put herself in.

"Yes," he said without enthusiasm. "They are all my men. I now have command of three Army corps, nearly fifty thousand soldiers, give or take."

She looked at him lovingly

"I am not surprised, my darling. I knew you were destined for great things. Are you sorry you turned the president down?"

John had written Kate a letter, telling her all about his visit with President Lincoln.

"No, I am not," he said. "I am just not cut out for politics, and, unfortunately, politics is too much a part of the Army commander's job. I am happy where I am, out here in the field, with my men, fighting the rebels. I am also pleased my friend George got the job. He can handle the strategy, the pressure, and the politics just fine. He is the right choice."

Kate took his hands in hers.

"You worry about me. John, I worry about you!"

"I'll be fine."

"You say that…but…but…this…this war is terrible!"

She was close to tears.

"So much violence. So many men, good men, dying! John, my love, I don't want you to be one of them."

"I am careful, and, not to be immodest, I'm a good soldier."

"That's the problem, I'm afraid. You are too good. From what you have told me and from what I hear, you put yourself in great danger, going to the front lines in the battles, exposing yourself to all that gunfire. Isn't that a mistake, sweetheart? Aren't commanders supposed to…well…command from the rear, behind the lines, to have a clear understanding of the entire battle?"

John leaned over and pulled Kate close.

"My darling," he said quietly into her ear, "I believe men perform better, fight better, when they are led into battle, not pushed or directed into it. I must have and show courage for my men. When I do that, they become less afraid, they develop the courage they need to look death square in the face. That's how we win wars."

Kate kept her face buried in his neck, silently, fearfully weeping, tears slowly running down her cheeks. After a while, she sat up, pulled a small linen cloth from her purse, and wiped her eyes.

"So, tell me, Mr. Major General," she said, regaining her composure, "what is it like being in charge of fifty thousand men?"

They talked quietly for a couple of hours, interrupted now and again by his staff officers who had messages and reports that could not wait. It was very difficult for John. He wanted to give his full attention to Kate. He knew he had to give his full attention to battle matters. He tried to do both, only half succeeding with either. Finally, it was Kate who took the initiative.

"John, my darling, I think it is time for me to go. You have a war to fight. Besides, my train leaves Emmitsburg at four o'clock. If I leave now, I should have no trouble making it."

John pulled her close again.

"I hate to see you go," he said. "But you do need to go for your own safety."

He took hold of her shoulders and gently pushed so that they were face-to-face, just inches apart.

"Soon, my love, this war will be over. I am certain. Then we will be together, always and forever."

They kissed again for a very long time. Finally, they parted. John stood up and walked toward his closed office door.

"I'm going to arrange an escort for you going back to Emmitsburg. We are not going to take any chances."

He opened the door and addressed one of his staff in the outer office.

"Captain, will you please assign four infantrymen, a driver, and a carriage to take my guest back to the Emmitsburg train station? I want the men well armed to act as her bodyguards. She will be leaving within the next ten minutes."

"Yes, sir," the captain said, hurrying out of the office to do as he had been ordered.

John closed the door again to maintain their privacy and, he hoped, their secrecy.

"Please write to me as soon as you can, won't you, darling?" Kate asked.

"Of course, I will. Although it was a foolish thing to do, your visiting me here has been overwhelming. I cannot adequately express how much I do love you."

"I know, John. You are my life," she whispered into his ear. "You make me happier than I have ever been. I cannot wait until we are together every day, every hour."

They kissed again. Then John regained his military bearing, opening the door to usher Kate out as if she was just a visiting local citizen, trying to hide that they were lovers. Difficult as it was, they merely shook hands because soldiers were watching, while she climbed into the waiting carriage.

"On your way, driver," John commanded.

"Yes, sir," the driver responded. He slapped the horse with his reins, and the carriage began to move, escorted by four well-armed soldiers on horseback, two on each side.

As they pulled away, Kate turned back to wave at John, who stood tall and still watching them leave. He gave her a small wave back.

I will see you again soon, Kate, John said quietly to himself. *"I promise."*

It would be the last promise he would ever make to her, for it was the last time Kate Hewitt would see General John Fulton Reynolds alive.

CHAPTER THIRTY-FIVE

Gettysburg
July 1, 1863

Footsteps echoed across the floor of John's headquarters tavern. It was four o'clock in the morning. Reynolds slept fitfully on the wooden surface, dreaming of Kate, covered with a woolen blanket, even though the predawn July morning was already hot and uncomfortably muggy.

A lone figure stood over the general, silently watching him in the dim light of a nearby candle that barely pierced the darkness. He held something in his left hand. He leaned over and thrust his right hand forward. He shook the general to wake him.

"Huh? What? Who is that?" the general blurted, startled awake and instinctively reached for his gun lying next to him.

"Sir! It's only me. Major Riddle, sir!" the man said quickly, stepping back a foot or two and keeping an eye on the commander's gun hand.

"Riddle? Good God, man!" Reynolds exclaimed. "That's a right smart way to get yourself killed!"

"Yes, sir, I know. I'm sorry to wake you, sir," Riddle replied, "but we have orders to move out."

Major William Riddle was one of the general's senior aides. He had just returned from Taneytown, Maryland, about nine miles distant, where General Meade had set up temporary headquarters for the Army of the Potomac.[305]

"Orders?" Reynolds said, now fully awake.

"Yes, sir. I have them right here, from General Meade."

Riddle tried to hand the paper in his left hand to the general.

"No, Major. You read them. Stand closer to the candle. The light is too dim here."

The major took a few steps closer to the burning candle set atop a wooden chair.

"Meade wants the First and Eleventh Corps to move forthwith to Gettysburg," Riddle said, looking at the message.

Reynolds stayed quiet for a moment, still lying down, one arm under his head.

"Read that to me again, will you please, Riddle?"

"Yes, sir. The orders from General Meade are that the First and Eleventh Corps begin moving toward Gettysburg to be in position to support Brigadier General John Buford and his First Cavalry Division."[306]

From messages he had received the night before, Reynolds knew that Buford and his horse-mounted troops were making ready to confront and delay Confederate forces, which were moving to Gettysburg from the northwest. He got up from the floor and walked over to a desk piled with papers. He picked up one of them.

"Buford says here that Confederate troops are massing near Cashtown, about ten miles north and west of Gettysburg,"[307] John said out loud, as much to himself as to Major Riddle. He walked into an adjoining room and woke up the rest of his staff. Despite the late-night dispatches from Buford, he didn't sense the combat was imminent, however.

"I really don't expect a battle today," he said to other officers. "We will move forward only to be within supporting distance of Buford's cavalrymen."[308]

After Kate had left late yesterday afternoon, one of John's fellow corps commanders arrived at the tavern for a light supper. Afterward, they worked late into the night, developing battle strategy over piles of papers and maps. Reynolds had been depressed since Kate had left.[309] Whether it was Kate's departure or the uncertainty of the enemy's strength, position, and intention was difficult to know. But John's somber, severe countenance had returned, as if he intuited that a very bad day lay ahead, despite what he had just said.

* * *

Shortly before dawn, a local couple, Christian and Alice Shriver, arrived at the tavern to prepare breakfast for Reynolds and his staff. John had arranged for the couple to cook for them the day before.

"Good morning, sir. Madam," John said politely as the two entered the tavern.

"Good morning, General," Shriver said. "We trust you slept well."

"As well as can be expected in the times, I suppose," Reynolds said.

"Well, a hearty breakfast is just what you need," Alice Shriver said cheerfully. "How about some meat and eggs? I have fresh bread, too."

"That sounds perfect, madam. Thank you."

As the couple went about their business starting a cooking fire and preparing the meal, John returned to his desk to confer with aides.

The battlefield situation was changing rapidly. Now Buford's cavalry, to the northwest of the town, was struggling to hold the Confederates back. Reynolds needed to send support immediately. He quickly scratched out an order.

"Courier!" he called out to the next room. A young enlisted man quickly stepped to his desk. "Take this message to Division Commander Wadsworth. Tell him I desire him to move out immediately."

"Yes, sir," the young corporal said. He saluted and ran to his horse already saddled up outside.

Reynolds himself was eager to get moving. So, when breakfast was served, he ate quickly. He offered to give the Shrivers five dollars for their service.

"Oh, no, sir. We can't take that," Christian Shriver said. "We were honored to serve you."

"I insist that you take it," John replied. "I know this war is as hard on you folks as it is on the troops. I thank you for your kindness."[310] He shoved the five dollars into the man's hands.

Finally, at about eight o'clock, after receiving more messages about how the battle was shaping up, John climbed on his big black stallion, Fancy, and headed out. He caught up with the units already on the march and went ahead of them at a quick and steady pace.

A few miles up the road, Reynolds spotted a rider coming at him hard and fast, the horse kicking up clouds of dust as he galloped along. It was a messenger from General Buford.[311]

"Sir!" the soldier said, breathing heavily, almost out breath. "General Buford wants to inform you that the enemy is moving toward Gettysburg along the Chambersburg Pike."

"Are you not holding them back, soldier?" Reynolds asked.

"We are, sir. Or, I should say, we have been. But there are a hell of a lot...excuse me, sir...I mean a whole lot of them rebels. They just keep comin', sir!"

John immediately turned to one of his aides.

"Captain, ride quickly down the road and tell the commander of the First Corps back there to get a move on. Tell him I said to close the ranks and pick up the pace."

"Yes, sir," the younger officer said, turning his horse and galloping back the way they had just come.

John then put the spurs to Fancy. He raced toward Gettysburg with his staff close behind. He could hear the roar of cannon fire in the distance. Once inside the town limits, he paused only long enough to ask someone directions.

"Pardon me, sir," he called to a passerby. "How do I get to that battle over yonder? Where are the Union headquarters?"[312] Supplied with the answer, John ordered one of his staff to warn townspeople to stay in their homes. Many of them were outside, clustered in the streets, frightened by the sights and sounds of war. Then Reynolds dug his heels into Fancy's side again.

"Giddyap, boy," he called. "C'mon, let's go."

Fancy leaped forward, exploding into a full gallop. They approached the Lutheran seminary just behind what was called Seminary Ridge northwest of town. The sounds of the battle were much louder now. He could hear the shouts of men and see the smoke from their weapons just over the ridge. He found General Buford standing in the cupola of one of the buildings overlooking the battleground.

Reynolds reined in his horse and shouted up to Buford.

"What's the matter, John?"

Buford looked down and shouted back.

"The devil's to pay!"[313]

Buford climbed down from the cupola and jumped on his own horse. He and Reynolds rode out to the front to get a better view of the deteriorating situation.

Confederate units had kept up the pressure on Buford's cavalry since dawn. Large numbers of Southern infantrymen were now advancing slowly, but with determination through a wooded area close to the ridge. The gunfire was thick and murderous. Gun smoke billowed through the trees in great clouds of pale blue. Rebels yelled as they attacked. Yankees shouted as they returned fire. Men on both sides screamed when they were hit. The noise was deafening

John turned to Buford.

"Hold them back for as long as you can," he ordered.

Looking around, he found one of his aides.

"Captain Weld," Reynolds said urgently. "I want you to ride as fast as you can to find General Meade. Kill your horse if you have to. Tell Meade the situation here is serious. Tell him the enemy could very well seize the town if we don't get reinforcements here in time. Also, tell the general, if we are driven into town, we will fight step by step behind barricades until help arrives.[314] Now go! Go!"

Buford was worried about his commander and his habit of getting into the thick of battles.

"General, do not expose yourself so much,"[315] Buford warned.

Reynolds merely nodded, turned Fancy around and raced back toward Emmitsburg Road to find his First Corps and its 3,500 soldiers. Buford needed them, and he needed them now! He cut across an open field. On the way, he noticed wooden fences lining the road ahead. Without slowing down, he shouted out to his staff officers who were galloping along with him.

"Tear those fences down!" he ordered. "I want the infantry to cross this field to get to Seminary Ridge faster!"[316]

In his frantic effort to get more help to Buford, he ordered messengers to ride off and find the other two corps of his command, the Third and the Eleventh, and to hurry them up on their march to Gettysburg. A few miles down the road, he ran into the First Corps moving at a quick march forward. For Reynolds, it was not quick enough. He rode up to Brigadier General Lysander Cutler, the commander of the corps' Second Brigade, which was leading the large formation. Fancy hadn't even stopped moving when Reynolds called to Cutler.

"General, tell your men to take that shortcut across the field where the fences are down! Tell them to drop their packs and heavy gear and leave it all behind! They must get moving! Double quick. Move! Move! Move!"

Reynolds sat atop his black stallion watching the troop movements for several moments. The soldiers passing by saw a sad demeanor in their commander. He knew a defining moment was at hand. *I am sending many of these fine men to their deaths*, he thought with despair. *How many will not survive the morning?* he wondered. Too many, he knew. They must not die in vain![317]

As the First Corps band passed him, they were playing a song called "The Girl I Left Behind Me."[318] It was a chilling foreshadowing of what now lay only a few hours ahead.

Shaking himself out of his gloom, Reynolds wheeled Fancy around and urged the big horse forward at another full gallop across the field. He could hear his orders to the brigade being shouted back down the line from unit to unit. The infantry troops of the Second Brigade took off across the field as fast as their legs would carry them, some of the men loading their rifles as they ran. The trailing units of the First Corps followed suit. They included the already famed First Brigade, nicknamed the Iron Brigade for its fierce fighting in previous battles. The brigade consisted of regiments from Wisconsin, Indiana, and Michigan. Some folks called them the Black Hats because they proudly wore specially designed hats of that color.[319]

While Reynolds arrived back at Seminary Ridge ahead of the Second Brigade, what he saw was grim. The sun was rising in the morning sky and the day was getting hotter and hotter. The fighting had intensified. John quickly reviewed the numbers mentally. He wasn't sure how many men the Confederates had in this battle, but he guessed the number to be around fifteen thousand. Between Buford's cavalry and the First Corps, Union soldiers here would total less than eleven thousand, assuming the bulk of the corps would even arrive in time to be of any value.

The rebels have more manpower than we do, John thought, his military mind moving at light speed. *We just have to be smarter.* As the lead regiments of the First Corps began to appear on the ridge, scrambling to avoid the unrelenting Confederate gunfire, Reynolds hurriedly deployed them to strategic positions near and around the wooded area where the enemy was taking cover.

"You!" he barked as he rode past the units. "The 197th New York, and you, the 56th Pennsylvania, get over to other side of that road next to the trees and start laying down the heaviest fire you can!"

He moved quickly to the next unit just coming into the battle area.

"You troops!" he shouted. "Take positions over there on the left. Do not let the enemy advance past that wooded area!"

He rode back and forth across the ridge, issuing orders, shouting out commands, somehow dodging bullets and minié balls flying in all directions. He was stunned to see how close the Confederates were advancing through the trees. He spotted an ugly and dangerous gap in the left flank of the units he had so far deployed. *Men*, he thought. *I need more men!*

He turned to see some of his prayers being answered. Elements of the Iron Brigade had finally arrived and were moving up the ridge. He rode off to greet them and saw, as he got closer, it was the regiment of the Second Wisconsin. The Black Hats.

"Forward into the line double quick!" he shouted. The regiment seemed to move as one, forming a combat line and charging the crest of the ridge. They were hit with a vicious volley of enemy fire and fell back. Desperate now, Reynolds rode among the men, hollering at the top of his lungs.[320]

"Forward, forward, men! Drive those fellows out of the woods! Forward! For God's sake, forward!"[321]

Energized by their commander's zeal, the Black Hats pushed ahead once again. The Confederate response intensified even more. The fight was at its zenith now. It was all chaos and confusion, firing and yelling, smoke and flame, screaming and hollering.

Reynolds was in the thick of it, still distraught that he was so vastly outnumbered. He brought Fancy to a halt just yards from the tree line and turned in his saddle, frantically looking for other units to deploy.

Suddenly, time, somehow, stood still for him. He sensed, rather than felt, a sharp sting at the back of his head, like a severe insect bite. He thought he felt Fancy bolt uncontrollably, but he couldn't be sure. Kate was there for a fleeting moment. Then, there were no more thoughts. There was just nothingness.

* * *

"General! General Reynolds! Are you all right? General Reynolds!"

John's orderly, Sergeant Charles Veil, had seen Reynolds drop from his horse. The sergeant quickly leaped out of his own saddle and ran to his fallen commander. Reynolds lay on his side, unmoving. Veil leaned down and turned the general on his back. The orderly couldn't find a wound and saw no blood, so he was confused about what had happened to his commander. He didn't realize Reynolds had been shot.

Two other aides quickly joined Veil, the firefight continuing to rage around them. They had to get the unconscious Reynolds out of there and away from further danger. The rebel firing line was only a couple of hundred feet away behind a stretch of trees. Veil grabbed Reynolds by his arms, the two officers held his legs and the three of them struggled to carry him away from the line of fire. As they did, they heard a ragged sound emanate from deep in his throat. It was a death rattle, his body surrendering to the inevitable, giving up, confirming that John Reynolds was no longer among the living.

The three aides managed to get John's body behind the lines, away from the fury of gunfire. They found a surgeon from one of the infantry units who examined Reynolds more closely. The doctor discovered a small bullet hole behind his right ear, amazed that it had not produced more blood than it did. He officially pronounced the general dead and estimated he died almost immediately after being shot.

At about the same time, Captain Weld, the officer Reynolds had dispatched to inform General Meade about what was happening, reached the Army commander's headquarters. Weld told Meade what Reynolds had said, that he would fight step by step in the town, if that became necessary, until helped arrived.

"Good!" Meade said. "That is just like Reynolds. He will hold on to the bitter end!"[322]

Meade had no idea, of course, that for John the bitter end had arrived. It wasn't until about an hour and a half later that the shocking news of Reynolds's death reached headquarters. Meade was stunned beyond words. Meade's own son, a captain in the Union Army and one of this father's aides, said of Reynolds, "He was one of the most capable and trustworthy officers in the Army of the Potomac and… he had the full confidence of the commanding general."[323] The younger Meade also said, "Never, perhaps, has a general fallen in battle at a more momentous time."[324]

CHAPTER THIRTY-SIX

Philadelphia
July 2, 1863

Kate awoke the next morning in her modest boarding house room with that dreadful sense of foreboding pounding in her head. It was worse than ever. She felt as though the weight of a thousand boulders were bearing down on her.

She got out of bed, got dressed, and went outside to purchase a newspaper. Once again, the paper was filled with frantic headlines.

GETTYSBURG ATTACKED!

REBELS SWARM OVER UNION SOLDIERS!

CITIZENS FLEE!

As she read the accounts of the latest battles, Kate came across a sub-headline that took her breath away.

UNION GENERAL KILLED IN BATTLE!

She was afraid to read on but forced herself to do it.

It has been reported that a favorite son of our great state, Major General John Fulton Reynolds, has been struck down in a most grievous manner by the gray-coated enemy. Major General Reynolds, leading a courageous assault on enemy lines, was shot and killed yesterday by a cowardly rebel soldier hiding in a tree. Witness say the brave general was shot in the back of the neck and fell from his horse near the Lutheran seminary in Gettysburg. He died just fifty miles from Lancaster, Pennsylvania, where Reynolds was born and raised. He...

Kate couldn't read any more. She sat down heavily on a park bench, holding the newspaper limply in her lap. She sat there for a very long time, saying nothing, tears slowly rolling silently down her cheeks.

* * *

In Gettysburg, Reynolds's staff was also overcome with grief. They had taken the general's body to a house in town and tried to prepare it for travel the best they could. In a grotesque turn of their misery, they could not locate a coffin. The best they could find was a crate from a local stonemason. But it was too short for the better than the six-foot-long corpse. So, they were forced to knock one end out of the crate, which meant the general's feet were sticking out in a macabre way.[325] While handling his body, loosening his jacket, his aides were befuddled by what they discovered.

"Major Riddle," a captain said. "Take a look at this."

Riddle looked at two small silver chains around his general's neck. One of them had a medallion attached to it.

"That looks like a Catholic medallion of some sort, doesn't it?" The captain asked. "I didn't know General Reynolds was Catholic."

"He wasn't," the major said. "He was Protestant."

"I wonder why he was wearing that medallion, then?"

"Is there something written on that ring?" The major pointed to another chain from which a ring was suspended. The captain leaned over to gently lift the ring from Reynolds's body. He turned it over, peering closely at an inscription.

"It just says 'Dear Kate.'"

"Who is Kate?" another officer asked.

Everyone shook their heads, offering suggestions.

"A wife?"

"He wasn't married."

"A lady friend?"

"He never mentioned one."

"His mother?"

"No. His mother's name was Lydia."

"His sister?"

That last inquiry came from a young corporal sitting at a nearby desk doing paperwork. The major looked at him with disdain.

"Would you wear a ring with your dear sister's name around your neck, Corporal?"

"Umm, no. I guess not," the corporal mumbled and went back to his paperwork.

"Here is another thing," the captain said.

"What did you find," Major Riddle asked.

"It's more like what I don't find," the captain said. "Where is the general's West Point ring?"

They all looked at John's hands. The ring was missing.

"That's very odd," Riddle said. "West Point officers never remove their rings. Ever."

They all stood silently for a moment, pondering these questions and grieving over the loss of their beloved commander. Tears fell from Major Riddle's eyes.

Finally, they closed the crate with the general's feet sticking out of one end, loaded it into a carriage and traveled twenty-five miles to a rail station in Westminster, Maryland. Leaving Gettysburg was risky. The battle still raged. Despite John's death, his troops continued to fight valiantly to protect Gettysburg from the Confederates. Artillery fire rained down all around the sad ad hoc funeral cortege. Along the way, they were able to find a more suitable receptacle for the body, packing it in ice.[326]

The general's procession passed Union soldiers going the other way, still marching to engage the enemy. One of those soldiers recalled that the tortured faces of the escorts "told plainly enough what load the vehicle carried." The soldier said John's death "affected us much, for he was one of the soldier Generals of the army, a man whose soul was in his country's work, which he did with a soldier's high honor and fidelity."[327]

A train transported John's remains from Westminster to Baltimore. There, a mortician prepared his body, dressed it in his formal uniform, and transferred it to a proper coffin, which was adorned with the words:

> JOHN FULTON REYNOLDS
> U.S. ARMY
> JULY 1st, 1863[328]

John's sister Jane and her husband accompanied the remains with terrible sadness back to Philadelphia.

CHAPTER THIRTY-SEVEN

Philadelphia
July 3, 1863

John's body was brought to the home of his sister Catherine and her husband, Henry Landis, on Spruce Street in Philadelphia. They prepared it for viewing in the parlor. Friends of the family and colleagues of John came to pay their respects throughout the day on July 3. The Reynolds family was in shock. But, as shaken as his sisters and brothers were by his death, their mourning received another jolt with one particular knock at the door.

A funeral assistant came in the room carrying a note informing them that a Miss Hewitt "wishes to see the remains if agreeable."

It was Eleanor who asked the question.

"Is she Kate?"

Eleanor, of course, had met Kate at the Eden Hall ice cream social last year. She didn't know, for sure, if Kate and her brother John had a relationship. However, she had her suspicions, especially after the family gathering last Christmas. But those were thoughts that she had kept to herself.

Eleanor and her sister Harriet went to meet the woman at the door. Admitting her to their house, Eleanor said, "It is so good to see you again, Kate, even at this terribly sad time. You loved John a great deal, didn't you?"

Kate burst into tears, nodding yes and sobbing. Eleanor put her arms around the young woman and held her tight.

"Come in," she said quietly. "Come, say goodbye to him."

The three women walked toward the parlor slowly, Kate trying very hard to compose herself. When they got to the room, Eleanor motioned to the casket where John was laid out in what appeared to be a peaceful repose. His beard and mustache had been trimmed. His formal general's uniform looked fresh and regal, adorned with his medals and the three stars on each shoulder, indicating his rank.

"We shall leave you alone with him," Eleanor said gently. She and Harriet stepped away, joining some other guests, giving Kate some privacy.

Stepping to the coffin, Kate looked down at John, her eyes welling up with tears again. She reached out and gently touched his beard, the sadness in her heart so heavy, she could barely breathe. Here was the only real happiness she had ever had in her life, lying lifeless, all hope, all dreams gone. In death, he still looked so strong to her, so vital, so cardinal, as if in any moment he would open his eyes and rush to comfort her. *But he is not here*, she said to herself. *He will never be here, or anywhere on this earth. He will never feel my touch again. Nor I his.* Her sense of loss suddenly loomed larger and became darker than she could handle. Kate fell to her knees, her hands clutching the handles of the coffin, and she wept openly, sorrowfully.[329]

John's sisters and brothers sat at the other end of the room, silent in their grief, not only for themselves, but for Kate, as well. Catherine quietly reached into a small clutch purse, pulled out a delicate handkerchief, and wiped the moisture from her eyes.

Eleanor stood up and walked over to Kate and softly put her hands on the young woman's shoulders. Kate's sounds of sorrow slowly faded. Finally, she took a deep, shaky breath and sighed heavily. With red eyes, she looked up at Eleanor, gave her a sad smile, and shook her head, as if to say, "I am all right."

Kate slowly stood to her feet and turned to Eleanor. John's sister held out her arms and gave Kate a warm, long embrace. Releasing the embrace, Kate reached down a pulled and ring off a finger of her left hand. It was John's West Point ring.

"I made a promise when he put this ring on my finger," she said to Eleanor. "I would never take it off. But now I will give him up to his God."[330]

Kate kissed the ring and, ever so gently, placed it on the lid of his coffin.

"Come sit with us, Kate," Eleanor said softly. "We'd like to get to know you."

Eleanor walked Kate to the other end of the room and they sat with the rest of the Reynolds family.

"We are so sorry for your loss, Kate," Catherine said.

"It is your loss as well," Kate replied. "John loved you all so much. He was very proud to be your brother."

Harriet leaned forward in her chair.

"If you don't mind us asking," Harriet asked pleasantly. "How well did you know John?"

Kate was silent for a moment, looking down at the floor. Then she looked up at all of them.

"We were going to be married," she said.

Now it was the siblings' turn to be silent. Their expressions ranged from complete surprise to confusion. One of the sisters said the news hit them like a thunderclap.[331] They glanced at one another, then looked back at Kate.

"How long were you two together?" Henry Landis, John's brother-in-law, blurted out. He was immediately embarrassed. "Oh, I am so sorry, Kate. I didn't mean to be so abrupt."

"That's quite all right," Kate said." I know this must be very unsettling to you all, my appearing here like this and springing the news on you."

She had regained most of her composure now and was, at least, feeling relieved that she could reveal the secret she and John had harbored for long.

"John and I met almost three years ago," she said. "He gave me his West Point ring when he asked me to marry him. I gave him a ring on which he had my name inscribed. I also gave him the Catholic medallion that you saw."

"Three years ago?" Jane exclaimed. "And we never knew? How is that possible? Why did John, or you for that matter, not tell us?"

Catherine gave her sister a cross look.

"Oh, please forgive me, Kate," Jane quickly said. "I don't mean to be rude. It's just that…that, I guess, I don't understand. Our family never had secrets. Well, not really, anyway."

"That's quite all right," Kate said, again. "John and I wanted to tell you. We talked about it a lot. But, you see, I'm…I…umm…I'm obviously Catholic."

She hesitated, looking at each of the siblings.

"This is really quite embarrassing. With you all being Protestant, well, we weren't sure how you would receive our engagement."

John's brothers and sisters all frowned, again looking at one another.

"Oh, Kate," Lydia said, reaching out to grab her hands. "There were never any reasons to be concerned about that! Our family has no ill will toward Catholics, or toward anyone of any religion for that matter! All we care about is that our family is happy, and if you made John happy, that is all that really matters."

All the others vigorously shook their heads in agreement, speaking all at once.

"That's right,"

"That's so true."

"Lydia's correct."

Kate smiled sadly and closed her eyes.

"Oh, how I so wish we had told you. And now…and now…it is too late."

Tears fell from her eyes again.

Eleanor leaned over and handed Kate a tissue.

"You know, Kate," Eleanor said, trying to keep it light, speaking in a faux conspiratorial tone. "I had my suspicions about you two when we met at that ice cream social last year. Do you remember?"

Kate smiled through her tears.

"Yes, I do, indeed. I thought you might have guessed about us. I even mentioned it to John. I think I ran away from you, didn't I? I am so sorry about that. It was terribly rude of me."

"Don't give it a second thought," Eleanor said. "I never said anything about it. It was none of my business, and I figured if you two were a pair, well, someday you'd let us know. It is just so sad for you, and for us, that this is that day."

They all sat in silence, each thinking about moments missed and wasted worries.

Finally, it was Catherine who spoke.

"Kate, John wanted to make you part of our family. So, that's what you are. You are welcome here any time you wish. Please consider our home your home, too. You will remain here in Philadelphia, won't you?"

Kate gave Catherine a grateful look.

"That is so very kind of you," she said. "Thank you so much. I will always think of you all as my family now. But, no, I won't be staying in Philadelphia. You see, John and I made a promise about what I would do if…if…" She struggled to say the words. "If, umm, he did not make it through the war." Her voice got very quiet. "If he were killed."

"What was the promise?" Harriet asked.

"I vowed, and John agreed, that if he died…" Kate almost choked on the words. "I would continue my religious calling and join a community of religious service. That's what I will do. John was the only man in my life. The only other man I would ever want is Jesus Christ. So, my plan is to join the Daughters of Charity in Emmitsburg, Maryland, where I will devote my life to the Lord."

* * *

A week later, Kate did as she had promised. She packed up her few belongings and prepared to travel to Emmitsburg to join the same community where the sisters of the order had knelt in prayer by the side the road as General Reynolds and his troops had passed by on their way to Gettysburg. It was located only about ten miles from the spot where John had died.

Before she left Philadelphia, Kate met with Catherine Dunn, the young girl over whom she had been so protective since they both left California together three years ago. Catherine was now thirteen and doing very well in school.

"Catherine, I am so proud of you," Kate said. "You are becoming a very fine young woman."

"That is so very kind of you to say," Catherine replied. "And you are so kind to me, especially in this time of your grief. I feel so terribly sad about John. I know how much you loved him. I loved him, too. He was almost like the father I never had. I think it is very brave of you to keep the promise you made about joining the religious order."

"It's not brave, Catherine. It is my duty. More importantly, it is my desire. God had a plan for me. This is the plan. I believe that is true."

"Well, I shall miss you terribly," Catherine said. "You have been so good to me."

"Oh, we will still see each other. Emmitsburg is not really that far away. I will want to know everything you are doing. You must write to me often, and, when this war is over and it is easier and safer to travel, we must visit as often as we can."

"I would like that," Catherine said. "I love you, Kate."

"I love you, too, Catherine. I am confident that, under the guidance of the Daughters of Charity here in Philadelphia, you will do very well. They and God will protect you."

Kate and Catherine hugged for a long time. They finally said their goodbyes, and Kate set out for Emmitsburg and the rest of her life.

CHAPTER THIRTY-EIGHT

Over the years, Kate kept in regular touch with Catherine and the Reynolds family. John's brothers and sisters, as they had promised, treated her as a close member of their family, visiting her when they could at the Daughters of Charity. They regarded her, as John's sister Jane put it, "a very superior person."[332] Eleanor, who had surmised the affair, was perhaps the most generous of their feelings about Kate.

"Poor girl," Eleanor said. "She has been a heroic mourner and most worthy of our dear one." Referring again to John, Eleanor said of Kate, "From her I learned much of him, of his feelings, and inner life that I never knew before."

Eleanor was especially sanguine about their religious differences.

"She made no parade of her religion, nor in any way that was the least disagreeable," Eleanor wrote to her brother Will,[333] who was away at sea and unable to return home for John's funeral.

During one of the visits after the war, they mentioned to Kate that they had arranged to meet with one of John's aides in Gettysburg the next day. Sergeant Charles Veil had agreed to show them where John had fallen and where his final battle had taken place.

"Sergeant Veil?" Kate said. "I believe he was John's orderly. That is what I think it is called."

"Why, yes, he was," Eleanor replied. "John once told us Sergeant Veil was the most loyal, trustworthy, and faithful aide he ever had."

Kate nodded sadly.

"Would you please tell him I would like to see him? I, too, would like to learn more about what happened to John."

"Of course," Eleanor said. "We will be glad to do that."

"I have something I want to give him," Kate said, on the verge of tears.

* * *

The next day, three of John's sisters, Eleanor, Harriet, and Jane, met up with Sergeant Veil in Gettysburg. The four of them rode in a carriage about a mile northwest of town, taking the Chambersburg Pike to cross Seminary Ridge. At the top of the ridge they looked down upon Herbst Woods, a large outcropping of trees and thick shrubs where Major General Reynolds had frantically tried to rally his troops to attack the Confederates firing from within the forested area.

Descending a gentle slope toward the woods, the sisters were struck by the quiet peacefulness of the corn and wheat-covered fields of the small hills and shallow valleys surrounding this spot, once was the scene of unspeakable, terrible violence.

"This is the place," Veil said quietly when they arrived at the tree line.

"Please tell us what happened here," Eleanor said just as quietly.

Veil's mind went back to that horrible day, the first of July 1863, as he relived the battle that took the life of the commander he had so admired.

"It was all chaos and confusion," he said finally. "The rebs were aggressing through those trees."

Veil pointed into the thick woods just a few yards away.

"There were so many of them!" he said. "They kept firing and firing. Rifle rounds and shot were coming from everywhere! The noise was horrendous. Men yelling, screaming. Guns firing. The smoke got so thick, it was hard to see anything."

Veil paused and stared into the distance, as if trying to see into the past, through the smoke in his mind.

"Though it all, General Reynolds was there, on his beautiful big black stallion, riding up and down the firing line, rallying the troops, waving his sword, shouting at them to move forward. Attack, he yelled, drive the rebels out of the woods. I remember hearing him shout, 'Forward, for God's sake, forward.' He seemed oblivious to all the musket fire and minié balls flying around everywhere, flying around him. It was the bravest thing I ever saw."

Veil paused again. He closed his eyes as the tragic events unraveled in his memory.

"Suddenly, I saw the general fall from his saddle. When he hit the ground, his foot was caught in a stirrup. Fancy, his horse, was spooked and started to run, dragging the general a few yards. But then, his foot slipped out of the stirrup, and he lay on the ground, not moving."

Veil took a deep, ragged breath, trying very hard to keep his emotions in check.

"I was only about twenty or so yards away," he continued. "So, I jumped off my horse and ran over to the general to help him. At first, I couldn't figure out what had happened. I saw no blood or anything. It was only a little later that we discovered the bullet hole in the back of his head."

Veil looked at John's sisters with alarm, realizing he might have gotten too graphic with his description of how John had died. Eleanor picked up on his discomfort.

"It is all right, Sergeant," she said. "Please continue."

Veil took another deep breath.

"Two officers came to help, and the three of us got the general out of the line of fire."

Veil looked at the woman sadly.

"I am so sorry to say he was dead by then. He died quickly."

Veil paused yet again, finding it difficult to continue. Finally, he did.

"We got him, um, his body, back to Gettysburg. That's when we discovered he was wearing that Catholic medallion and the ring on chains around his neck."

Veil looked at Eleanor.

"Those were her medallions, weren't they? Kate, I mean, the name engraved on the ring? The woman John was supposed to marry?"

Eleanor nodded.

"Yes," she answered. "Kate gave them to John when they became engaged. As a matter of fact, Sergeant, she would like to see you."

"Me?"

"Yes. She would like to hear from you about John. She, too, wants to know about that day that he died. Apparently, she also has something to give you."

Veil frowned in puzzlement.

"But I don't even know where she is."

"We do," Jane responded. "She is right down the road in Emmitsburg. Kate has joined a convent there, the Daughters of Charity."

"Would you go?" Eleanor said. "Would you go talk to her? We could all meet there tomorrow, if that is convenient for you."

"Yes, of course, I would. It would be a great honor for me to meet the woman who had captured my commander's heart."

* * *

The next morning, Sergeant Charles Veil sat with his late commander's three sisters in a visiting room just inside the entrance of the main building where the Daughters of Charity worked and worshipped. Veil fidgeted, nervous at the prospect of meeting the woman who had obviously meant so much to the man he had admired.

When a side door to the room opened, Veil was stunned by the beauty of the woman who gracefully walked over the threshold. He quickly stood up, habitually standing at attention, his military training kicking in.

Kate, dressed in her nun's habit, smiled kindly at her visitors. She had taken the name of Sister Hildegardis,[334] and that is how Eleanor now greeted her.

"Good morning, Sister Hildegardis. It is my pleasure to introduce to you US Army Sergeant Charles Veil who, as you know, was John's, I mean, General Reynolds's orderly."

Kate walked straight toward Sergeant Veil, holding her hand out to shake his.

"Sergeant Veil," she said. "It is so kind of you to take the time to visit me. God bless you."

Veil blinked nervously two or three times while shaking her hand.

"Well, um, ma'am…er…umm…Sister…umm…"

"Hildegardis," Kate said gently, with a smile. "Sister Hildegardis."

"Yes, um, Sister Hildegardis. It is my honor, ma'am…er… Sister…to be meeting you. We…that is the men…we never knew that General Reynolds had…umm, well, a lady friend. Certainly not one so attractive as you."

Veil blushed beet red at the boldness of his own comment.

"Oh, jeez, sorry, ma'am, I mean, Sister. I meant no offense."

Kate and John's siblings all laughed lightly.

"None taken, Sergeant, I assure you. Please, let's sit down, and you can tell me all about General Reynolds."

For the next hour, Kate and Veil told each other what they knew about John with Veil learning about his commander's secret, private life and Kate learning about the admiration and respect the Army had for her lover. When it came to telling Kate what happened when John was shot, Veil hesitated.

"Please, Sergeant," Kate said. "Tell me everything. Do not hold back on my account."

So, carefully and quietly, Veil again recounted that July 1 battle, how Reynolds had led the troops, encouraged reinforcements, never giving an inch in the face of overwhelming enemy gunfire, and, finally, how he fell in death.

Kate listened to it all intently, hanging on Veil's every word. She looked very sad, but she did not cry. It was as if she had used up all her tears.

When Veil finished, everyone in the room sat very still for several long moments.

Then Kate reached into the folds of her habit and withdrew a little box, carefully wrapped and tied with a ribbon.

"Mr. Veil," she said, addressing the sergeant as if he were a civilian. "I have a little token here I had made for the general, some of it my own work. And I want to give it to you as a token of remembrance of both of us."

She handed the little box to Veil, who took it gingerly.

"Please, open it," she said.

Veil carefully untied the ribbon and took off the wrapping. Opening the box, he found a handkerchief, beautifully embroidered with the coat of arms of the United States. Now, tears did flow, but down the face of Sergeant Veil.

"Sister," he whispered. "This is wonderful. I have no words to adequately express my thanks. I will treasure this always. I will keep it safe. I promise. This will be a family heirloom."

Holding the handkerchief carefully in his hands, Veil stared at it for a long moment. Then, he just as carefully folded the cloth and gently put it back in the box. He pulled another cloth out of his own pocket and wiped away his tears.

He and Kate stood up to hug each other tightly, each sharing in the sorrow of losing the man they both had loved.

* * *

At the Daughters of Charity, Sister Hildegardis and the other nuns had worked tirelessly tending to the wounded soldiers on both sides of the war on the battlefields around Gettysburg. Their dedicated mission was particularly hard on Kate because it served as a constant reminder of John's love and tragic death.

After three years at Emmitsburg, she was transferred to Albany, New York, where she resumed her teaching experience at a Catholic school. While she was committed to devoting her life to Christ, Kate never really was at peace. She never got over losing the one true love she had ever had. Eleanor Reynolds visited her in upstate New York in the fall 1867, two years after the Civil War had ended.

"It is so good to see you again, Kate," Eleanor told her. "Are you not happy here?"[335]

It was not an idle question, because to Eleanor, Kate had a very sad air about her. She was also quite thin and pale.

"Oh," Kate sighed. "I am happier here than I would be out there, you know, in the world." She pointed listlessly to a window. "I do enjoy the children at the school though. They give me pleasure."

As perceptive as Eleanor had always been, she could also see, despite what Kate had said, she was not happy at all.

It became difficult for Sister Hildegardis to adhere to the strict rules of the order. Her early doubts about having what it takes to live the life of a nun were beginning to surface.

The Daughters of Charity in Albany were disappointed in her behavior and accused her of having a "violent temper." What they were witnessing, however, was Kate's bottomless sorrow over losing John. It clung to her like cobwebs cling to flies. It intruded on everything she did, every thought she had.

In 1868, the order rejected her petition to take the permanent vows of the Daughters of Charity. She was advised to "return home, from whence she came."[336]

Six years after John was killed, she finally did move back home to Stillwater, New York. For the next twenty-six years, she kept mainly to herself, even losing touch with the Reynolds family. She wallowed in her sorrow, grieving that the only real happiness she ever had in her life were the three years she had known and loved John Reynolds.

Eventually, her health declined dramatically. She developed a persistent cough that was so severe, it was debilitating. Finally in 1895, fifty-nine year old Catherine Mary "Kate" Hewitt died of pneumonia, alone and heartbroken.

EPILOGUE

Stillwater, New York
October 1896

A lone figure, dressed warmly against the rain and cold of an October morning, moved slowly though the cemetery. The visitor was looking for a particular gravestone. A bitter wind whipped through the trees, ripping leaves off branches and sending them flying, tumbling, scattering across the ground. The leaves had already turned the colors of fall, and it was their turn to die, the visitor thought, without amusement.

Finally, the visitor found what she was looking for. It was the grave marker for the woman who had nurtured and mentored her when she was just a young girl. She was a woman the visitor had loved only as a sister could love a sister, or as a daughter could love a mother. Catherine Dunn was a grown woman now, forty-six years old, happily married. She had come here to honor and pray for Kate Hewitt, who had been buried here in this modest, humble cemetery.

The grave marker, however, couldn't even be described as modest. It was just a small, simple octagonally shaped flat piece of concrete. Catherine knelt down to clear away the overgrown grass, weeds, and fallen leaves from around the marker. She thought again, as she always did here, about the beautiful love affair of Kate Hewitt and John Reynolds. She remembered how Kate's eyes had sparkled and the lilt in her voice whenever she spoke of John. She had such wondrous plans, Catherine remembered. She was so happy.

Those plans, Catherine reflected, were shattered in that brief instant a Confederate minié ball had smashed into the back of John's head. Kate had claimed she was prepared for such an event. That was a lie, Catherine thought. No one is ever prepared for something like that.

Catherine stood up and brushed the leaves and grass off her coat. She said a soft brief prayer over Kate's grave, then turned to depart. Kate may not have been as prepared for John's death as she might have thought, Catherine said to herself. But she did understand how her love fit in the life of the Civil War hero. Kate had once told her that for John, it is God first, his country second, and herself third.[337] As long as she had John, that had been good enough for her.

The End

ACKNOWLEDGMENTS

The story of General John Reynolds and Kate Hewitt is only one among countless tales about the loves, hardships, bravery, and courage endured by so many thousands of people during the Civil War. The narrative of that tragic and crucial period in American history is, at the same time, epic in scope and intensely personal.

The idea for this novel emerged from a privileged meeting the author had with Edwin C. Bearss at Fort Sumter in South Carolina. Bearss is the historian emeritus of the National Park Service and is considered one of the foremost experts on the Civil War. In his book *Fields of Honor: Pivotal Battles of the Civil War*, Bearss reserves a few lines for Kate Hewitt and how she met the Reynolds family. Bearss's brief but eloquent description foretold a fascinating and deeper story of two people in the midst of this country's bloodiest and most violent war.

My wholehearted thanks and appreciation to the National Park Rangers at Fort Sumter for sharing with me their knowledge of the Civil War and the interpretation of what it meant to the country and, in many ways, still does mean.

I am indebted to Bonnie Weatherly at the Daughters of Charity in Emmitsburg, Maryland, for providing details of Catherine Mary Hewitt when she was a sister in that community.

My thanks also to Mike Lear at the Shadek-Fackenthal Library at Franklin and Marshall College in Lancaster, Pennsylvania, for providing access to some of the early Reynolds family correspondence.

It is said in journalism that everyone needs an editor. I was privileged to have several for this novel. I am especially grateful for the ever watchful and discerning eyes of my brother-in-law Larry Clever, whose impressive editing skills helped me keep the fiction created in the twenty-first century in line with the facts of the nineteenth.

My warm appreciation goes out also to Marge Sander and Ryan Zacharczyk, whose input was priceless. My never-ending thanks, also, goes to my son, Blair, a Hollywood screenwriter, for his valuable suggestions. My sister, Joan Krause, was also indispensable in this process.

I am grateful to Page Publishing and, especially, to publication coordinator Jenna Amy who shepherded me all along the path of getting this work off my computer and onto bookshelves.

My appreciation also goes out to Jason Bidgood, Ben Fitch, Crof Mackin, Bobby Mawyer, Joe Ort, Rick Reinhart, John Stine and Rich Viega, my Thursday morning coffee buddies, for their support and friendship.

Most of all, I profess my love and everlasting admiration for my wife, Marcia Sue Clever, without whose encouragement and faith this book would never have been written.

References

1. Major Frederick L. Hitchcock, War from the Inside: The Story of the 132nd Regiment, Pennsylvania Volunteer Infantry in the War for the Suppression of the Rebellion, chapter VIII, 1982–1863, Press of J.B. Lippincott Company, 1904.

2. Edwin C. Bearss, Fields of Honor, page 154, National Geographic Society, 2006.

3. Edward J. Nichols, Towards Gettysburg: A Biography of John F. Reynolds, Pickle Partners Publishing, 2015.
    Michael A. Riley, For God's Sake, Forward! as part of Lawrence Knorr, General John Fulton Reynolds, pages 41–42, Sunbury Press, 2013.

4. Ibid.

5. Ibid.

6. Ibid.

7. Veil, Charles Henry, Viola, Herman J, The Memoirs of Charles Henry Veil, A Soldier's Recollection of the Civil War and the Arizona Territory, page 96, Thorndike, Press, 1996.

8. Nichols, Towards Gettysburg.

9. Ibid.

10. Ibid.

11. Ibid.

12. Ibid.

13. Ibid.

14. Ibid.

15. Alonzo F. Hill, "Virginia" in Reynold's Reserves in the Civil War, Big Byte Books, 2016.

16. Meade, Captain George, The Life and Letters of George Gordon Meade, Major-General United States Army, Page 346, Charles Scribner's Sons, 1913.

17. Nichols, Towards Gettysburg.
18. An Act for the Gradual Abolition of Slavery, Supreme Executive Council of Pennsylvania, March 1, 1780, Pennsylvania State Archives.
19. Library of Congress, Exhibitions, Thomas Jefferson to John Holmes.
20. Ibid.
21. Marian Latimer, Is She Kate? The Woman Major General John Fulton Reynolds Left Behind, page 11, Farnsworth Military Impressions, 2005.
22. Ibid.
23. Ibid.
24. Nichols, Towards Gettysburg.
25. Ibid.
26. Ibid.
27. Ibid.
28. Ibid.
29. The Papers of Thomas Jefferson, Princeton University, www.jeffersonpapers. princeton.edu/selected-documents/jefferson's-draft.
30. Shadel-Fackenthal Library, Franklin and Marshall College, Letter: Jennie Reynolds Gildersleeve to William Reynolds, July 5, 1863.
31. Riley, For God's Sake, Forward! in Knorr, General John Fulton Reynolds.
32. Nichols, Towards Gettysburg.
33. Ibid.
34. Ibid.
35. Ibid.
36. Riley, For God's Sake, Forward! in Knorr, General John Fulton Reynolds.
37. Ibid.
38. Nichols, Towards Gettysburg.
39. Ibid.
40. Ibid.
41. U.S. History, Pre-Columbian to the New Millennium, www.ushistory.org.
42. Fort Sumter Exhibit, 2019.
43. Riley, For God's Sake, Forward! in Knorr, General John Fulton Reynolds, page 21.
44. Nichols, Towards Gettysburg.
45. Ibid.
46. Ibid.
47. American Battlefield Trust, www.battlefields.org/learn/biographies/ braxton-bragg.
48. Riley, For God's Sake, Forward! in Knorr, General John Fulton Reynolds, page12.
49. Ibid.
50. Ibid.
51. William T. Sherman, Memoirs of William T. Sherman, Digireads.com Publishing, 2015.

52. Nichols, Towards Gettysburg.
53. Riley, For God's Sake, Forward! in Knorr, General John Fulton Reynolds, page 14.
54. T. B. Thorpe, Our Army on the Rio Grande, Carey and Hart, 1846.
55. Nichols, Towards Gettysburg.
56. Ibid.
57. Meade, The Life and Letters of George Gordon Meade, vol. I, page 91.
58. Ibid.
59. Nichols, Towards Gettysburg.
60. Ibid.
61. Ibid.
62. Riley, For God's Sake, Forward! in Knorr, General John Fulton Reynolds, page 15.
63. Rosengarten, Joseph G. Reynolds Memorial Address, Philadelphia, J.B. Lippincott & Co, 1880.
64. Riley, For God's Sake, Forward! in Knorr, General John Fulton Reynolds, page 15.
65. Ibid.
66. Nichols, Towards Gettysburg.
67. Riley, For God's Sake, Forward! in Knorr, General John Fulton Reynolds, page 15.
68. Nichols, Towards Gettysburg.
69. Ibid.
70. Ibid.
71. Ibid.
72. Klingenberg, Mitchell G., "The Curious Case of Catherine Mary Hewitt and US Major General of Volunteers John Fulton Reynolds: Bodies, Mourning the Dead, Religion in the Era of the US Civil War," American Nineteenth Century History, volume 19, issue 3, 2018.
73. Ibid.
74. Justin Harvey Smith, The War with Mexico, Page 389, The MacMillan Company, 1919.
75. Nichols, Towards Gettysburg.
76. Ibid.
77. Riley, For God's Sake, Forward! in Knorr, Major General John Fulton Reynolds, page 16.
78. Ibid.
79. Captain James Henry Carleton, The Battle of Buena Vista, With the Operations of the Army of the Occupation for One Month, pages 95–96, Harper and Brothers, 1848.
80. Ibid.
81. Ibid.
82. Ibid.

83. Nichols, Towards Gettysburg.

84. Ibid.

85. Ibid.

86. Cullum, Major General George W., Biological Register of the Officers and Graduates of the West Point Military Academy, 1802–1890, vol. I, page 93, Houghton, Mifflin and Company, 1891.

87. Wool, Brigadier John to Major W. W. S. Bliss, Assistant Adj. Gen., Niles National Register, no. 15., vol. XXII, May 1847.

88. May, Brevet Lt. Col. C. A, 2nd Dragoons, Commanding to Major W. W. S. Bliss, Assistant Adj. Gen. Army of Occupation, Niles National Register, no. 13, vol. XXII, June 1857.

89. Nichols, Towards Gettysburg.

90. Ibid.

91. Latimer, Is She Kate?, page 20.

92. Riley, For God's Sake, Forward! in Knorr, General John Fulton Reynolds, pages 17–18.

93. Nichols, Towards Gettysburg.

94. Lafayette Cemetery Research Project, New Orleans, Online, https://sites.google.com/site/lcrpnola/.

95. Nichols, Towards Gettysburg.

96. Riley, For God's Sake, Forward! in Knorr, General John Fulton Reynolds, page 18.

97. Ibid.

98. Ibid.

99. Ibid.

100. Riley, For God's Sake, Forward! in Knorr, General John Fulton Reynolds, page 20.
Nichols, Towards Gettysburg.

101. Ibid.

102. Ibid.

103. Ibid.

104. Riley, For God's Sake, Forward! in Knorr, General John Fulton Reynolds, pages 20–21.

105. Nichols, Towards Gettysburg.

106. The Civil War in the East, http://civilwarintheeast.com/west-point-officers-in-the-civil-war/class-of-june-1861/.

107. West Point Military Academy, https://www.westpointaog.org/netcommunity/document.doc?id=621.

108. Bruce G. Kauffman, "The United States Military Academy at West Point," www.historylessons.net/the-united-states-military-academy-at-west-point.

109. Duane Schultz, "West Point's Worst Cadet—George Armstrong Custer," www.historynet.com/west-points-worst-cadet-george-armstrong-custer.htm.

110. National Park Service, www.nps.gov/inde/learn/historyculture/stories-libertybell.htm.
111. Nichols, Towards Gettysburg.
112. Bostick, Douglas W., Fort Sumter National Monument: Where the Civil War Began, page 39, Charleston Postcard Company, 2016.
113. Riley, For God's Sake, Forward! in Knorr, General John Fulton Reynolds, page 21.
114. "West Point's Worst Cadet: George Armstrong Custer," www.historynet.com/west-points-worst-cadet-george-armstrong-custer.htm.
115. Riley, For God's Sake, Forward! in Knorr, General John Fulton Reynolds, page 21.
116. Sypher, J. R., History of the Pennsylvania Reserve Corps, Page 25, Elias Barr & Company, 1865.
117. Nichols, Towards Gettysburg.
118. Ibid.
119. Ibid.
120. Klingenburg, "The Curious Case of Catherine Mary Hewitt."
121. Ibid.
122. Ibid.
123. Nichols, Towards Gettysburg.
Riley, For God's Sake, Forward! in Knorr, General John Fulton Reynolds, page 22.
124. Ibid.
125. Nichols, Towards Gettysburg.
126. Ibid.
127. Ibid.
128. Ibid.
129. Riley, For God's Sake Forward! in Knorr, General John Fulton Reynolds, page 22.
130. Nichols, Towards Gettysburg.
131. Ibid.
132. Riley, For God's Sake Forward! in Knorr, General John Fulton Reynolds, page 22.
133. "War of the Rebellion: Official Records of the Civil War," Serial 5, page 480, Department of History, Ohio State University.
134. Nichols, Towards Gettysburg.
135. Ibid.
136. Ibid.
137. Ibid.
138. Ibid.
139. American Battlefield Trust, www.battlefields.org/learn/biographies/irvin-mcdowell.
140. Nichols, Towards Gettysburg.

141. Ibid.

142. Sypher, History of the Pennsylvania Reserve Corps.

143. Nichols, Towards Gettysburg.

144. Fletcher, Henry Charles, History of the American War, Volume II, Second Year of the War, 1862–63, page 73, Richard Bentley, New Burlington Street, London, Publisher in Ordinary to Her Majesty, 1865.

145. "War of the Rebellion: Official Records of the Civil War," Serial 12, page 1028.

146. Ibid.

147. Powell, William H., Lt. Colonel, The Fifth Army Corps (Army of the Potomac): A Record of Operations During the Civil War In the United States of America, 1861–1864, page 82, G. P. Putnam's Sons, 1896.

148. "War of the Rebellion," Serial 14, page 238.

149. Wittenburg, Eric J., We Have It Damned Hard Out Here: The Civil War Letters of Sergeant Thomas W. Smith, 6th Pennsylvania Cavalry, page 46, the Kent State University Press, 1999.

150. Howell, The Fifth Army Corps, page 83.

151. Nichols, Towards Gettysburg.

152. Ibid.

153. "Report on the Comprehensive Survey of the Water Resources of the Delaware River Basin," The US Army Corps of Engineers, Philadelphia District, 1960.

154. Powell, The Fifth Army Corps, page 86.

155. Riley, For God's Sake, Forward! in Knorr, General John Fulton Reynolds, page 25.
Nichols, Towards Gettysburg.

156. Powell, The Fifth Army Corps, page 85.

157. Riley, For God's Sake, Forward! in Knorr, General John Fulton Reynolds, page 25.

158. Ibid.

159. Nichols, Towards Gettysburg.

160. Powell, The Fifth Army Corps, page 87.

161. "The War of the Rebellion: A Compilation of the Official Records of the Union and Confederate Armies," Ser.1, v.11, pt. 2, Reports, Major General F. J. Porter, The Peninsular Campaign, VA, Government Printing Office, 1884.

162. Nichols, Towards Gettysburg.

163. McClellan, General George B., "Peninsular Campaign: Seven Days Battle Report," 1862.

164. Powell, The Fifth Army Corps, page 81.

165. Nichols, Towards Gettysburg.

166. Powell, The Fifth Army Corps, page 86.

167. Nichols, Towards Gettysburg.

168. Ibid.
169. Powell, The Fifth Army Corps, page 87.
170. Ibid.
171. "The War of the Rebellion," Serial 12, page 271.
172. Nichols, Towards Gettysburg.
173. "The War of the Rebellion," Serial 12, page 56.
174. Nichols, Towards Gettysburg.
175. Ibid.
176. "American Civil War: Major General John F Reynolds," https://www.thoughtco.com/major-general-john-f-reynolds-2360431.
177. Nichols, Towards Gettysburg.
178. The Seven Days Contest, Pennsylvania Reserves, General McCall's Report, Office of the Rebellion Record, New York, 1864, page 668.
179. Ibid.
180. Ibid. Page 669.
181. Zombek, Angela M., "Libby Prison," Encyclopedia Virginia, Library of Virginia, 2014, www.encyclopediavirginia.org/libby_prison#start_entry.
182. Ibid.
183. Ibid.
184. Ibid.
185. Nichols, Towards Gettysburg
186. Nichols, Towards Gettysburg
187. "The War of the Rebellion: Official Records of the Civil War," Cornell University, series II, vol. IV, page 809, Government Printing Office, 1899.
188. Riley, For God's Sake, Forward! in Knorr, General John Fulton Reynolds, page 26.
189. Woodward, E. M. History of the Third Pennsylvania Reserve, page 137, MacCrellish & Quigley, 1883.
190. Powell, The Fifth Army Corps, page 239.
191. Hill, A. F., Our Boys: The Personal Experiences of a Soldier in the Army of the Potomac, page 312, John E. Potter, 1864.
192. Riley, For God's Sake, Forward! in Knorr, General John Fulton Reynolds, page 27.
193. Powell, The Fifth Army Corps, page 234.
194. Nichols, Towards Gettysburg.
195. Riley, For God's Sake, Forward! in Knorr, General John Fulton Reynolds, page 27.
196. Papers of the Military Historical Society of Massachusetts, Vol. II, "The Virginia Campaign of 1862 Under General Pope," page 132, Ticknor and Company, 1886.
197. Hill, Our Boys, page 371.
198. Ibid.

199. Regional Oral History Office, The Bancroft Library, http://bancroft.berkeley.edu/ROHO/projects/dreyers/timeline.html, The Regents of the University of California, 2013.

200. Nichols, Towards Gettysburg.

201. Hill, Our Boys, page 380.

202. Ibid. Page 382.

203. Ibid. Page 384.

204. Ibid. Page 384.

205. Nichols, Towards Gettysburg.

206. Riley, For God's Sake, Forward! in Knorr, "General John Fulton Reynolds," page 28.

207. Ibid.

208. "War of the Rebellion," serial 16, page 394.

209. Nichols, Towards Gettysburg.

210. Thomson, O. R. Howard and Rauch, William H., The History of the Bucktails, Electric Printing Company, 1906, page 192.

211. Hill, Our Boys, page 384.

212. "War of the Rebellion," serial 16, page 395.

213. Ibid.

214. Nichols, Towards Gettysburg.

215. "War of the Rebellion," serial 16, page 532.

216. Ibid. Report of General John Reynolds, page 394.

217. Ibid. Hooker Message, serial 28, pages 273–274.

218. Ibid, Message to Stanton, serial 28, page 250.

219. Coffin, Charles, Four Years of Fighting, page 113, Ticknor and Fields, 1866.

220. "War of the Rebellion," serial 28, page 288.

221. Ibid. Page 288.

222. "War of the Rebellion," serial 28, page 332.

223. McClure, Alexander K., Old Time Notes of Pennsylvania, vol. 1, The John C. Winston Company 1905, page 570.

224. Nichols, Towards Gettysburg.

225. Ibid.

226. Ibid.

227. The Life and Letters of George Gordon Meade, vol. I, page 314.

228. Ibid.

229. Ibid. Page 315.

230. Nichols, Towards Gettysburg.

231. McCalmont, Alfred B., Extract of Letters from the Front During the War of the Rebellion, page 22, Private Circulation, Robert McCalmont, 1908.

232. Nichols, Towards Gettysburg.

233. Ibid.

234. Powell, The Fifth Army Corps, page 432.

235. Riley, For God's Sake, Forward! In Knorr, General John Fulton Reynolds, page 32.
236. Powell, The Fifth Army Corps, page 440.
237. Nichols, Towards Gettysburg.
238. "War of the Rebellion," serial 31, page 455.
239. Nichols, Towards Gettysburg.
240. Ibid.
241. "Report of the Joint Committee of the Conduct of the War," Part I, The Army of the Potomac, page 699, Government Printing Office, 1863.
242. Ibid.
243. "War of the Rebellion," serial 31, page 632.
244. Ibid. Page 634.
245. The Civil War: Articles Exploring the American Civil War, "The Court Martial of General Fitz John Porter," http://www.thecivilwaromnibus.com/articles/74/.
246. Speech of Honorable Joseph Wheeler of Alabama in the House of Representatives, "Fitz John Porter: Fiat Justitia," February 1883.
247. Powell, The Fifth Army Corps, page 470.
248. Ibid. Page 473.
249. Nichols, Towards Gettysburg.
250. Ibid.
251. Ibid.
252. Riley, For God's Sake, Forward! in Knorr, General John Fulton Reynolds, page 33.
253. Nichols, Towards Gettysburg.
254. Gallagher, Gary, "Civil War Series, The Battle of Chancellorsville," National Park Service, Eastern National, 2007.
255. "War of the Rebellion," Serial 40, page 234.
256. Riley, For God's Sake, Forward! in Knorr, General John Fulton Reynolds, page 35.
257. Nichols, Towards Gettysburg.
258. "War of the Rebellion," serial 40, page 288.
259. Ibid. Page 313.
260. Ibid. Page 337.
261. Ibid. Pages 336–351.
262. Ibid. Page 341.
263. Ibid. Page 351.
264. Ibid. Pages 368–369.
265. Burns, Ken, The Civil War, page 204, Alfred A. Knopf, 1990.
266. "War of the Rebellion," serial 399, page 255.
267. Goss, Warren Lee, Recollections of a Private: A Story of the Army of the Potomac, page 163, T. Y. Crowell & Co. 1890.

268. Bigelow, John, The Campaign of Chancellorsville: A Strategic and Tactical Study, page 306, Yale University Press, 1910.

269. Nichols, Towards Gettysburg.

270. "War of the Rebellion," series 40, page 377.

271. Ibid. page 378.

272. Nichols, Towards Gettysburg.
Riley, God's Sake, Forward! in Knorr, General John Fulton Reynolds.

273. Nichols, Towards Gettysburg
Riley, God's Sake, Forward! in Knorr, General John Fulton Reynolds.

274. The Fifth Army Corps, page 548.

275. Ibid. Page 559.

276. Ibid. Page 560.

277. Battles and Leaders of the Civil War, Vol 3, Page 171, The Century War Series, The Century Company, 1887–1888.

278. Riley, For God's Sake, Forward! in Knorr, General John Fulton Reynolds, page 35.

279. Ibid. Page 35.

280. Goss, Recollections of a Private, page 163.

281. The Campaign of Chancellorsville, pages 473, 475.

282. "The War of the Rebellion," serial 40, page 479.

283. The Life and Letters of George Gordon Meade, vol. I, page 374.

284. Ibid. Page 373.

285. Ibid. Page 377.

286. "The War of the Rebellion," serial 39, page 510.

287. The Life and Letters of George Gordon Meade, vol. I, page 377.

288. James Buchanan Inaugural Speech, March 4, 1857, UVA Miller Center, https://millercenter.org/the-presidency/presidential-speeches/march-4-1857-inaugural-address.

289. The Life and Letters of George Gordon Meade, vol. I, page 385.

290. "The War of the Rebellion," serial 45, pages 86–87.

291. Pearson, Henry Greenleaf, James S. Wadsworth of Geneseo: Brevet Major General of the United States Volunteers, page 195, John Murray/London 1913.

292. Beecham, R. K., Gettysburg: Pivotal Battle of the Civil War, pages 120–122, A.C. McClurgh & Co, 1911.

293. James S. Wadsworth, page 195.

294. John Reynolds Letter to His Sisters, From Guilford Station, VA, June 1863.

295. Riley, For God's Sake, Forward! In Knorr, General John Fulton Reynolds.

296. Coddington, Edwin B., The Gettysburg Campaign: A Study in Command, page 49, Simon & Schuster, 1968.

297. "The Press," Philadelphia, June 29, 1863.

298. Pfanz, Harry W., Gettysburg: The First Day, page 33, The University of North Carolina Press, 2001, Page 33.

299. Casey, Sister Eleanor, DC, "The Daughters of Charity & The Battle of Gettysburg," www.emmitsburg.net/archive_list/articles/history/civil_war/doc_civil_war.htm.

300. Watson, Diane E., Reynolds: The Last Six Miles in Knorr, General John Fulton Reynolds, page 54.

301. "War of the Rebellion," serial 45, page 397.

302. "War of the Rebellion," serial 45, page 422.

303. Pfanz, Gettysburg: The First Day, page 45.

304. Nichols, Towards Gettysburg.

305. Watson, The Last Six Miles in Knorr, General John Fulton Reynolds, page 55.

306. Nichols, Towards Gettysburg.

307. Riley, For God's Sake, Forward! in Knorr, General John Fulton Reynolds, page 38.

308. Pfanz, Gettysburg: The First Day, page 70.

309. Watson, The Last Six Miles, in Knorr, General John Fulton Reynolds, pages 55–56.

310. Watson, The Last Six Miles, page 58.

311. Pfanz, Gettysburg: The First Day, page 73.

312. Ibid.

313. Riley, For God's Sake, Forward! in Knorr, General John Fulton Reynolds, page 40.

314. Coddington, The Gettysburg Campaign, page 267.

315. Watson, The Last Six Miles, in Knorr, General John Fulton Reynolds, page 61.

316. Coddington, The Gettysburg Campaign, page 267.

317. Watson, The Last Six Miles, in Knorr, General John Fulton Reynolds, page 62.

318. Ibid.

319. Coddington, The Gettysburg Campaign, page 262.

320. Pfanz, The First Day, page 77.
     Riley, For God's Sake, Forward!, pages 41–42.

321. Coddington, The Gettysburg Campaign, page 269.
     Pfanz, The First Day, page 77.

322. Life and Letters of General Meade, page 36.

323. Ibid. Page 33.

324. Ibid. Page 46.

325. Pfanz, The First Day, pages 78–79.

326. Ibid. Page 79.

327. Haskell, Frank A, The Battle of Gettysburg, Page 14, Wisconsin History Commission, 1908.

328. Pfanz, The First Day, page 79.

329. Letter, Eleanor Reynolds to William Reynolds, July 5, 1863.

330. Ibid.
331. The Memoirs of Charles Henry Veil, page 19.
332. Nichols, Towards Gettysburg.
333. Ibid.
334. Daughters of Charity Provincial Archives, www.dcarchives.wordpress.com/2013/06/14/kate-hewitt-and-john-reynolds/.
335. Maloney, Mary R., "General Reynolds and Dear Kate," American Heritage Magazine, volume 15, issue 1, December 1963.
336. Latimer, Is She Kate?, page 25.
337. Ibid. Page 22.

ABOUT THE AUTHOR

J. Paul "Jim" Hickey is a former correspondent for ABC News. He spent nearly a half century covering news events around the world. Upon retiring from broadcast journalism, Jim turned to the printed word. This is his second novel. The first, *Naked Ambition*, a shipboard murder mystery, was published in 2018. He also writes an online blog, "The Cutting Edge." This book of historical fiction was sparked by his work as a docent with the National Park Service at Fort Sumter. Jim lives with his wife, Marcia Sue Clever, in South Carolina.

CPSIA information can be obtained
at www.ICGtesting.com
Printed in the USA
LVHW051019040720
659731LV00001B/69